DATE DUE

FEB 2 2 2005		
MAR 0 3 2006		

TWI

The Collected St

STED

ies of Jeffery Deaver

Jeffery Deaver

SIMON & SCHUSTER
New York • London • Toronto • Sydney

SIMON & SCHUSTER
Rockefeller Center
1230 Avenue of the Americas
New York, NY 10020

"All the World's a Stage" previously appeared in *Much Ado About Murder* (Berkley Prime Crime).
"Beautiful" previously appeared in *Ellery Queen Mystery Magazine* and *The World's Finest Mystery and Crime Stories: Third Annual Collection: Vol. 3* (Forge).
"The Blank Card" previously appeared in *Ellery Queen Mystery Magazine*.
"Eye to Eye" previously appeared in *Irreconcilable Differences* (HarperCollins).
"The Fall Guy" previously appeared in *Ellery Queen Mystery Magazine* and *The Year's 25 Finest Crime and Mystery Stories,* 7th Edition (Carroll and Graf).
"For Services Rendered" previously appeared in *Ellery Queen Mystery Magazine* and *The World's Finest Crime and Mystery Stories,* 1st Edition (Berkley).
"Gone Fishing" previously appeared in *Ellery Queen Mystery Magazine*.
"The Kneeling Soldier" previously appeared in *Ellery Queen Mystery Magazine* and *The Year's 25 Best Crime,* 7th Edition (Carroll and Graf).
"Lesser Included Offense" previously appeared in *Ellery Queen Mystery Magazine*.
"Nocturne" previously appeared in *Ellery Queen Mystery Magazine* and *Blue Lightning* (Slow Dancer).
"Together" previously appeared in *Ellery Queen Mystery Magazine, Crimes of the Heart* (Berkley) and *Opening Shots,* Vol. 2 (Cumberland House).
"Triangle" previously appeared in *Ellery Queen Mystery Magazine*
"The Weekender" previously appeared in *Alfred Hitchcock Mystery Magazine* and *A Century of Great Suspense Stories* (Berkley) and *Best American Mysteries #1* (Houghton Mifflin).
"The Widow of Pine Creek" previously appeared in *A Confederacy of Crime* (Signet) and *The World's Finest Mystery and Crime Stories: Second Annual Collection: Vol. 2* (Forge).
"Without Jonathan" previously appeared in *Ellery Queen Mystery Magazine*.

SIMON & SCHUSTER and colophon are registered trademarks of Simon & Schuster, Inc.

For information regarding special discounts for bulk purchases, please contact Simon & Schuster Special Sales:
1-800-456-6798 or business@simonandschuster.com

Designed by Joel Avirom and Jason Snyder

Manufactured in the United States of America

10 9 8 7 6 5 4 3 2 1

Library of Congress Cataloging-in-Publication Data is available.

ISBN 0-7432-6095-3

To my sister and fellow writer, Julie Reece Deaver

CONTENTS

TWISTED

INTRODUCTION

My experience with the short story form goes back to the distant past.

I was a clumsy, chubby, socially awkward boy with no aptitude for sports whatsoever and, as befit someone like that, I was drawn to reading and writing, particularly the works of short story writers like Poe, O. Henry, A. Conan Doyle and Ray Bradbury, not to mention one of the greatest forums for short surprise-ending drama in the past fifty years: *The Twilight Zone.* (I defy any fans of the show to tell me they don't get a chill recalling the famous social services manual, *To Serve Man.*)

When I was given a writing assignment in junior high school, I'd invariably try my hand at a short story. I didn't, however, write detective or science fiction stories, but, with youthful hubris, created my own subgenre of fiction: These tales usually involved clumsy, chubby, socially awkward boys rescuing cheerleaders and pompom girls from catastrophes that were both spectacular and highly improbable, such as my heroes' daring mountaineering exploits (embarrassingly set just outside of Chicago, where I lived, and where mountains were conspicuously absent).

The stories were met with just the exasperation you'd expect from teachers who'd spent hours offering us the entire pantheon of literary superstars as models. ("Let's *push* ourselves, Jeffery"— the 1960s' equivalent of today's jargon, "Think outside the box.")

Fortunately for their sanity, and my career as a scribe, I abandoned this vein of angst-ridden outpourings rather quickly and grew more diligent in my efforts to become a writer, a path that led me to poetry, songwriting, journalism and, eventually, novels.

Although I continued to read and enjoy short fiction—in *Ellery Queen, Alfred Hitchcock, Playboy* (a publication that I'm told also featured photography), *The New Yorker* and anthologies—I just didn't seem to have the time to write any myself. But a few years after I quit my day job to be a full-time novelist, a fellow author, compiling an anthology of original short stories, asked if I'd consider contributing one to the volume.

Why not? I asked myself and plowed ahead.

I found, to my surprise, that the experience was absolutely delightful—and for a reason I hadn't expected. In my novels, I adhere to strict conventions; though I love to make evil appear to be good (and vice versa) and to dangle the potential for disaster before my readers, nonetheless, in the end, good is good and bad is bad, and good more or less prevails. Authors have a contract with their readers and I think too much of mine to have them invest their time, money and emotion in a full-length novel, only to leave them disappointed by a grim, cynical ending.

With a thirty-page short story, however, all bets are off.

Readers don't have the same emotional investment as in a novel. The payoff in the case of short stories isn't a roller coaster of plot reversals involving characters they've spent time learning about and loving or hating, set in places with atmosphere carefully described. Short stories are like a sniper's bullet. Fast and shocking. In a story, I can make good bad and bad badder and, most fun of all, really good really bad.

I found too that as a craftsman, I like the discipline required by short stories. As I tell writing students, it's far easier to write long than it is to write short, but of course this business isn't about what's easy for the *author;* it's about what's best for the reader, and short fiction doesn't let us get away with slacking off.

Finally, a word of thanks to those who've encouraged me to write these stories, particularly Janet Hutchings and her inestimable *Ellery Queen Mystery Magazine,* its sister publication *Alfred Hitchcock,* Marty Greenberg and the crew at Teknobooks, Otto Penzler and Evan Hunter.

The stories that follow are quite varied, with characters ranging from William Shakespeare to brilliant attorneys to savvy lowlifes to despicable killers to families that can, at the most generous, be called dysfunctional. I've written an original Lincoln Rhyme and Amelia Sachs story, "The Christmas Present," just for this volume, and see if you can spot the revenge-of-the-nerd tale included here, a—dare I say—twisted throw-back to my days as an adolescent writer. Unfortunately, as with most of my writing, I can't say much more for fear I'll drop hints that spoil the twists. Perhaps it's best to say simply: Read, enjoy . . . and remember that not all is what it seems to be.

—J.W.D.

WITHOUT JONATHAN

Marissa Cooper turned her car onto Route 232, which would take her from Portsmouth to Green Harbor, twenty miles away.

Thinking: This was the same road that she and Jonathan had taken to and from the mall a thousand times, carting back necessities, silly luxuries and occasional treasures.

The road near which they'd found their dream house when they'd moved to Maine seven years ago.

The road they'd taken to go to their anniversary celebration last May.

Tonight, though, all those memories led to one place: her life without Jonathan.

The setting sun behind her, she steered through the lazy turns, hoping to lose those difficult—but tenacious—thoughts.

Don't think about it!

Look around you, she ordered herself. Look at the rugged scenery: the slabs of purple clouds hanging over the maple and oak leaves—some gold, some red as a heart.

Look at the sunlight, a glowing ribbon draped along the dark pelt of hemlock and pine. At the absurd line of cows, walking single file in their spontaneous day-end commute back to the barn.

At the stately white spires of a small village, tucked five miles off the highway.

And look at you: a thirty-four-year-old woman in a sprightly silver Toyota, driving fast, toward a new life.

A life without Jonathan.

Twenty minutes later she came to Dannerville and braked for the first of the town's two stoplights. As her car idled, clutch in, she glanced to her right. Her heart did a little thud at what she saw.

It was a store that sold boating and fishing gear. She'd noticed in the window an ad for some kind of marine engine treatment. In this part of coastal Maine you couldn't avoid boats. They were in tourist paintings and photos, on mugs, T-shirts and key chains. And, of course, there were thousands of the real things everywhere: vessels in the water, on trailers, in dry docks, sitting in front yards—the New England version of pickup trucks on blocks in the rural South.

But what had struck her hard was that the boat pictured in the ad she was now looking at was a Chris-Craft. A big one, maybe thirty-six or thirty-eight feet.

Just like Jonathan's boat. Nearly identical, in fact: the same colors, the same configuration.

He'd bought his five years ago, and though Marissa thought his interest in it would flag (like that of any boy with a new toy) he'd proved her wrong and spent nearly every weekend on the vessel, cruising up and down the coast, fishing like an old cod deckhand. Her husband would bring home the best of his catch, which she would clean and cook up.

Ah, Jonathan . . .

She swallowed hard and inhaled slowly to calm her pounding heart. She—

A honk behind her. The stoplight had changed to green. She drove on, trying desperately to keep her mind from speculating about his death: The Chris-Craft rocking unsteadily in the turbulent gray Atlantic. Jonathan overboard. His arms perhaps flailing madly, his panicked voice perhaps crying for help.

Oh, Jonathan . . .

Marissa cruised through Dannerville's second light and continued toward the coast. In front of her she could see, in the last of the sunlight, the skirt of the Atlantic, all that cold, deadly water.

The water responsible for life without Jonathan.

Then she told herself: No. Think about Dale instead.

Dale O'Banion, the man she was about to have dinner with in Green Harbor, the first time she'd been out with a man in a long while.

She'd met him through an ad in a magazine. They'd spoken on the phone a few times and, after considerable waltzing around on both their parts, she'd felt comfortable enough to suggest meeting in person. They'd settled on the Fishery, a popular restaurant on the wharf.

Dale had mentioned the Oceanside Café, which had better food, yes, but that was Jonathan's favorite place; she just couldn't meet Dale there.

So the Fishery it was.

She thought back to their phone conversation last night. Dale had said to her, "I'm tall and pretty well built, little balding on top."

"Okay, well," she'd replied nervously, "I'm five-five, blonde, and I'll be wearing a purple dress."

Thinking about those words now, thinking how that simple exchange typified single life, meeting people you'd met only over the phone.

She had no problem with dating. In fact she was looking forward to it, in a way. She'd met her husband when he was just graduating from medical school and she was twenty-one. They'd gotten engaged almost immediately; that'd been the end of her social life as a single woman. But now she'd have some fun. She'd meet interesting men, she'd begin to enjoy sex again.

Even if it was work at first, she'd try to just relax. She'd try not to be bitter, try not to be too much of a widow.

But even as she was thinking this her thoughts went somewhere else: Would she ever actually fall in *love* again?

The way she'd once been so completely in love with Jonathan?

And would anybody love *her* completely?

At another red light Marissa reached up and twisted the mirror toward her, glanced into it. The sun was now below the horizon and the light was dim but she believed she passed the rearview-mirror test with flying colors: full lips, a wrinkleless face reminiscent of Michelle Pfeiffer's (in a poorly lit Toyota accessory, at least), a petite nose.

Then, too, her bod was slim and pretty firm, and, though she knew her boobs wouldn't land her on the cover of the latest Victoria's Secret catalog, she had a feeling that, in a pair of nice, tight jeans, her butt'd draw some serious attention.

At least in Portsmouth, Maine.

Hell, yes, she told herself, she'd find a man who was right for her.

Somebody who could appreciate the cowgirl within her, the girl whose Texan grandfather had taught her to ride and shoot.

Or maybe she'd find somebody who'd love her academic side—her writing and poetry and her love of teaching, which had been her job just after college.

Or somebody who could laugh with her—at movies, at sights on the sidewalk, at funny jokes and dumb ones. How she loved laughing (and how little of it she'd done lately).

Then Marissa Cooper thought: No, wait, wait . . . She'd find a man who loved *everything* about her.

But then the tears started and she pulled off the road quickly, surrendering to the sobs.

"No, no, no . . ."

She forced the images of her husband out of her mind.

The cold water, the gray water . . .

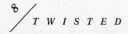

Five minutes later she'd calmed down. Wiped her eyes dry, reapplied makeup and lipstick.

She drove into downtown Green Harbor and parked in a lot near the shops and restaurants, a half block from the wharf.

A glance at the clock. It was just six-thirty. Dale O'Banion had told her that he'd be working until about seven and would meet her at seven-thirty.

She'd come to town early to do some shopping—a little retail therapy. After that she'd go to the restaurant to wait for Dale O'Banion. But then she wondered uneasily if it would be all right if she sat in the bar by herself and had a glass of wine.

Then she said to herself sternly, What the hell're you thinking? Of *course* it'd be all right. She could do anything she wanted. This was *her* night.

Go on, girl, get out there. Get started on your new life.

■

Unlike upscale Green Harbor, fifteen miles south, Yarmouth, Maine, is largely a fishing and packing town and, as such, is studded with shacks and bungalows whose occupants prefer transport like F-150s and Japanese half-tons. SUVs too, of course.

But just outside of town is a cluster of nice houses set in the woods on a hillside overlooking the bay. The cars in *these* driveways are Lexuses and Acuras mostly and the SUVs here sport leather interiors and GPS systems and not, unlike their downtown neighbors, rude bumper stickers or Jesus fish.

The neighborhood even has a name: Cedar Estates.

In his tan coveralls Joseph Bingham now walked up the driveway of one of these houses, glancing at his watch. He double-checked the address to make sure he had the right house then rang the bell. A moment later a pretty woman in her late thirties opened the door. She was thin, her hair a little frizzy, and even through the screen door she smelled of alcohol. She wore skintight jeans and a white sweater.

"Yeah?"

"I'm with the cable company." He showed her the ID. "I have to reset your converter boxes."

She blinked. "The TV?"

"That's right."

"They were working yesterday." She turned to look hazily at the gray glossy rectangle of the large set in her living room. "Wait, I was watching CNN earlier. It was fine."

"You're only getting half the channels you're supposed to. The whole neighborhood is. We have to reset them manually. Or I can reschedule if—"

"Naw, it's okay. Don't wanta miss *COPS*. Come on in."

Joseph walked inside, felt her eyes on him. He got this a lot. His career wasn't the best in the world and he wasn't classically good-looking but he was in great shape—he worked out every day—and he'd been told he "exuded" some kind of masculine energy. He didn't know about that. He liked to think he just had a lot of self-confidence.

"You want a drink?" she asked.

"Can't on the job."

"Sure?"

"Yep."

Joseph in fact wouldn't have minded a drink. But this wasn't the place for it. Besides, he was looking forward to a nice glass of spicy Pinot Noir after he finished here. It often surprised people that somebody in his line of work liked—and knew about—wines.

"I'm Barbara."

"Hi, Barbara."

She led him through the house to each of the cable boxes, sipping her drink as she went. She was drinking straight bourbon, it seemed.

"You have kids," Joseph said, nodding at the picture of two young children on a table in the den. "They're great, aren't they?"

"If you like pests," she muttered.

He clicked buttons on the cable box and stood up. "Any others?"

"Last box's in the bedroom. Upstairs. I'll show you. Wait . . ." She went off and refilled her glass. Then joined him again. Barbara led him up the stairs and paused at the top of the landing. Again, she looked him over.

"Where are your kids tonight?" he asked.

"The pests're at the bastard's," she said, laughing sourly at her own joke. "We're doing the joint custody thing, my ex and me."

"So you're all alone here in this big house?"

"Yeah. Pity, huh?"

Joseph didn't know if it was or not. She definitely didn't seem pitiful.

"So," he said, "which room's the box in?" They'd stalled in the hallway.

"Yeah. Sure. Follow me," she said, her voice low and seductive.

In the bedroom she sat on the unmade bed and sipped the drink. He found the cable box and pushed the "on" button of the set.

It crackled to life. CNN was on.

"Could you try the remote?" he said, looking around the room.

"Sure," Barbara said groggily. She turned away and, as soon as she did, Joseph came up behind her with the rope that he'd just taken from his pocket. He slipped it around her neck and twisted it tight, using a pencil for leverage. A brief scream was stifled as her throat closed up and she tried desperately to escape, to turn, to scratch him with her nails. The liquor soaked the bedspread as the glass fell to the carpet and rolled against the wall.

In a few minutes she was dead.

Joseph sat beside the body, catching his breath. Barbara had fought surprisingly hard. It had taken all his strength to keep her pinned down and let the garrote do its job.

He pulled on latex gloves and wiped away whatever prints he'd left in the room. Then he dragged Barbara's body off the bed and into the center of the room. He pulled her sweater off, undid the button of her jeans.

But then he paused. Wait. What was his name supposed to be?

Frowning, he thought back to his conversation last night.

What'd he call himself?

Then he nodded. That's right. He'd told Marissa Cooper his name was Dale O'Banion. A glance at the clock. Not even seven P.M. Plenty of time to finish up here and get to Green Harbor, where she was waiting and the bar had a decent Pinot Noir by the glass.

He unzipped Barbara's jeans then started tugging them down to her ankles.

■

Marissa Cooper sat on a bench in a small, deserted park, huddled against the cold wind that swept over the Green Harbor wharf. Through the evergreens swaying in the breeze she was watching the couple lounging in the enclosed stern of the large boat tied up to the dock nearby.

Like so many boat names this one was a pun: *Maine Street*.

She'd finished her shopping, buying some fun lingerie (wondering, a little discouraged, if anyone else would ever see her wearing it), and had been on her way to the restaurant when the lights of the harbor—and the gently rocking motion of this elegant boat—caught her attention.

Through the plastic windows on the rear deck of the *Maine Street*, she saw the couple sipping champagne and sitting close together, a handsome pair—he was tall and in very good shape, plenty of salt-and-pepper hair, and she, blonde and pretty. They were laughing and talking. Flirting like crazy. Then, finishing their champagne, they disappeared down into the cabin. The teak door slammed shut.

Thinking about the lingerie in the bag she carried, thinking about resuming dating, Marissa again pictured Dale O'Banion. Wondered how this evening would go. A chill hit her and she rose and went on to the restaurant.

Sipping a glass of fine Chardonnay (sitting boldly at the bar by herself—way to go, girl!), Marissa let her thoughts shift to what she might do for work. She wasn't in a huge hurry. There was the insurance money. The savings accounts too. The house was nearly paid for. But it wasn't that she needed to work. It was that she wanted to. Teaching. Or writing. Maybe she could get a job for one of the local newspapers.

Or she might even go to medical school. She remembered the times Jonathan would tell her about some of the things he was doing at the hospital and she'd understood them perfectly. Marissa had a very logical mind and had been a brilliant student. If she'd gone on to graduate school years ago, she could've gotten a full scholarship for her master's degree.

More wine.

Feeling sad then feeling exhilarated. Her moods bobbed like orange buoys marking the lobster traps sitting on the floor of the gray ocean.

The deadly ocean.

She thought again about the man she was waiting for in this romantic, candlelit restaurant.

A moment of panic. Should she call Dale and tell him that she just wasn't ready for this yet?

Go home, have another wine, put on some Mozart, light a fire. Be content with your own company.

She began to lift her hand to signal the bartender for the check.

But suddenly a memory came to her. A memory from life *before* Jonathan. She remembered being a little girl, riding a pony beside her grandfather, who sat on his tall Appaloosa. She recalled watching the lean old man calmly draw a revolver and sight down on a rattlesnake that was coiled to strike at Marissa's Shetland. The sudden shot blew the snake into a bloody mess on the sand.

He'd worried that the girl would be upset, having witnessed the death. Up the trail they'd dismounted. He'd crouched beside her and told her not to feel bad—that he'd *had* to shoot the snake. "But it's all right, honey. His soul's on its way to heaven."

She'd frowned.

"What's the matter?" her grandfather had asked.

"That's too bad. I want him to go to hell."

Marissa missed that tough little girl. And she knew that if she called Dale to cancel, she would have failed at something important. It would be like letting the snake bite her pony.

No, Dale was the first step, an absolutely necessary step, to getting on with her life without Jonathan.

And then there he was—a good-looking, balding man. Great body too, she observed, in a dark suit. Beneath it he wore a black T-shirt, not a white polyester shirt and stodgy tie you saw so often in this area.

She waved and he responded with a charming smile.

He walked up to her. "Marissa? I'm Dale."

A firm grip. She gave him back one equally firm.

He sat next to her at the bar and ordered a glass of Pinot Noir. Sniffed it with pleasure then clinked his glass to hers.

They sipped.

"I wasn't sure if you'd be late," she said. "Sometimes it's hard to get off work when you want to."

Another sniff of wine. "I pretty much control my own hours," he said.

They chatted for a few minutes and then went to the hostess's stand. The woman showed them to the table he'd reserved. A moment later they were seated next to the window. Spotlights on the outside of the restaurant shone down into the gray water; the sight troubled her at first, thinking about Jonathan in the deadly ocean, but she forced her thoughts away and concentrated on Dale.

They made small talk. He was divorced and had no children, though he'd always wanted them. She and Jonathan hadn't had children either, she explained. Talking about the weather in Maine, about politics.

"Been shopping?" he asked, smiling. Nodding at the pink-and-white-striped bag she'd set beside her chair.

"Long underwear," she joked. "It's supposed to be a cold winter."

They talked some more, finishing a bottle of wine, then had one more glass each, though it seemed to her that she drank more than he did.

She was getting tipsy. Watch out here, girl. Keep your wits about you.

But then she thought about Jonathan and drank down the glass.

Near ten P.M. he looked around the emptying restaurant. He fixed her with his eyes and said, "How about we go outside?"

Marissa hesitated. Okay, this is it, she thought to herself. You can leave, or you can go out there with him.

She thought of her resolution, she thought of Jonathan.

She said, "Yes. Let's go."

Outside, they walked side by side back to the deserted park she'd sat in earlier.

They came to the same bench and she nodded at it and they sat down, Dale close beside her. She felt his presence—the nearness of a strong man, which she hadn't felt for some time now. It was thrilling, comforting and unsettling all at the same time.

They looked at the boat, the *Maine Street*, just visible through the trees.

They sat in silence for a few minutes, huddling against the cold.

Dale stretched. His arm went along the back of the bench, not quite around her shoulders, but she felt his muscles.

How strong he was, she reflected.

It was then that she glanced down and saw a twisted length of white rope protruding from his pocket, about to fall out.

She nodded at it. "You're going to lose something."

He glanced down. Picked it up, flexed the rope in his fingers. Unwound it. "Tool of the trade," he said, looking at her querying frown.

Then he slipped it back into his pocket.

Dale looked back to the *Maine Street*, just visible through the trees, at the couple now out of the bedroom and sipping champagne again on the rear deck.

"That's him in there, the handsome guy?" he asked.

"Yes," Marissa said, "that's my husband. That's Jonathan." She shivered again from the cold—and the disgust—as she watched him kiss the petite blonde.

She started to ask Dale if he was going to do it tonight—to murder her husband—but then decided that he, probably like most professional killers, would prefer to speak in euphemisms. She asked simply, "When's it going to happen?"

■

They were now walking slowly away from the wharf; he'd seen what he needed to.

"When?" Dale asked. "Depends. That woman in there with him? Who's she?"

"One of his little slut nurses. I don't know. Karen, maybe."

"She's spending the night?"

"No. I've been spying on him for a month. He'll kick her out about midnight. He can't stand clinging mistresses. There'll be another one tomorrow. But not before noon."

Dale nodded. "Then I'll do it tonight. After she leaves." He glanced at Marissa. "I'll handle it like I was telling you—after he's asleep I'll get on board, tie him up and take the boat out a few miles. Then I'll make it look like he got tangled in the anchor line and went overboard. Has he been drinking much?"

"Is there water in the ocean?" she asked wryly.

"Good, that'll help. Then I'll drive the boat close to Huntington and take a raft back in. Just let her drift." Nodding at the *Maine Street*.

"You always make it look like an accident?" Marissa asked, wondering if a question like this was breaking some kind of hit-man protocol.

"As often as I can. That job I did tonight I mentioned? It was taking care of a woman in Yarmouth. She'd been abusing her own kids. I mean, beating them. 'Pests,' she called them. Disgusting. She wouldn't stop but the husband couldn't get the children to say anything to the police. They didn't want to get her in trouble."

"God, how terrible."

Dale nodded. "I'll say. So the husband hired me. I made it look like that rapist from Upper Falls broke in and killed her."

Marissa considered this. Then she asked, "Did you . . . ? I mean, you were pretending to be a rapist. . . ."

"Oh, God, no," Dale said, frowning. "I'd never do that. I just made it *look* like I did. Believe me, it was pretty gross finding a used condom from behind that massage parlor on Knightsbridge Street."

So hit men have standards, she reflected. At least some of them do.

She looked him over. "Aren't you worried I'm a policewoman or anything? Trying to set you up? I mean, I just got your name out of that magazine, *Worldwide Soldier*."

"You do this long enough, you get a feel for who're real customers and who aren't. Anyway, I spent the last week checking you out. You're legitimate."

If a woman paying someone twenty-five thousand dollars to kill her husband can be called legitimate.

Speaking of which . . .

She took a thick envelope out of her pocket. Handed it to Dale. It disappeared into the pocket with the white rope.

"Dale . . . wait, your name's not really Dale, is it?"

"No, but it's the one I'm using for this job."

"Okay, well, Dale, he won't feel anything?" she asked. "No pain?"

"Not a thing. Even if he were conscious that water's so cold he'll probably pass out and die of shock before he drowns."

They'd reached the end of the park. Dale asked, "You're sure about doing this?"

And Marissa asked herself, Am I sure about wanting Jonathan dead?

Jonathan—the man who tells me he goes fishing with the boys every weekend but in truth takes his nurses out on the boat for his little trysts. Who spends our savings on them. Who announced a few years after getting married that he'd had a vasectomy and didn't want the children he'd promised we'd have. Who speaks to me like a ten-year-old about his job or current events, never even hearing me say, "I understand, honey. I'm a smart woman." Who nagged me into quitting a job I loved. Who flies into a rage every time I want to go back to work. Who complains whenever I wear sexy clothes in public but who stopped sleeping with me years ago. Who gets violent whenever I bring up divorce because a doctor at a teaching hospital needs a wife to get ahead . . . and because he's a sick control freak.

Marissa Cooper suddenly pictured the shattered corpse of a rattlesnake lying bloody on a hot patch of yellow Texas sand so many years ago.

That's too bad. I want him to go to hell. . . .

"I'm sure," she said.

Dale shook her hand and said, "I'll take care of things from here. Go home. You should practice playing the grieving widow."

"I can handle that," Marissa said. "I've been a grieving wife for years."

Pulling her coat collar up high, she returned to the parking lot, not looking back at either her husband or at the man who was about to kill him. She climbed into her Toyota and fired up the engine, found some rock and roll on the radio, turned the volume up high and left Green Harbor.

Marissa cranked the windows down, filling the car with sharp autumn air, rich with the scent of wood smoke and old leaves, and drove fast through the night, thinking about her future, about her life without Jonathan.

THE WEEKENDER

The night went bad fast.

I looked in the rearview mirror and didn't see any lights but I knew they were after us and it was only a matter of time till I'd see the flashers.

Toth started to talk but I told him to shut up and got the Buick up to eighty. The road was empty, nothing but pine trees for miles around.

"Oh, brother," Toth muttered. I felt his eyes on me but I didn't even want to look at him, I was so mad.

They were never easy, drugstores.

Because, just watch sometime, when cops make their rounds they cruise drugstores more often than anyplace else. Because of the perco and Valium and the other drugs. You know.

You'd think they'd stake out convenience stores. But those're a joke and with the closed-circuit TV you're going to get your picture took, you just are. So nobody who knows the business, I mean really *knows* it, hits them. And banks, forget banks. Even ATMs. I mean, how much can you clear? Three, four hundred tops? And around here the "Fast Cash" button gives you twenty only. Which tells you something. So why even bother?

No. We wanted cash and that meant a drugstore, even though they can be tricky. Ardmore Drugs. Which is a big store in a little town. Liggett Falls. Sixty miles from Albany and a hundred or so from where Toth and me lived, farther west into the mountains. Liggett Falls's a poor place. You'd think it wouldn't make sense to hit a store there. But that's exactly why—because like everywhere else, people there need medicine and hair spray and makeup, only they don't have credit cards. Except maybe a Sears or Penney's. So they pay cash.

"Oh, brother," Toth whispered again. "Look."

And he made me even madder, him saying that. I wanted to shout look at what, you son of a bitch? But then I could see what he was talking about and I didn't say anything. Up ahead. It was like just before dawn, light on the horizon. Only this was red and the light wasn't steady. It was like it was pulsing and I knew that they'd got the roadblock up already. This was the only road to the interstate from Liggett Falls. So I should've guessed.

"I got an idea," Toth said. Which I didn't want to hear but I also wasn't going to go through another shootout. Surely not at a roadblock, where they was ready for us.

"What?" I snapped.

"There's a town over there. See those lights? I know a road'll take us there."

Toth's a big guy and he looks calm. Only he isn't really. He gets shook easy and he now kept turning around, skittish, looking in the backseat. I wanted to slap him and tell him to chill.

"Where's it?" I asked. "This town?"

"About four, five miles. The turnoff, it ain't marked. But I know it."

This was that lousy upstate area where everything's green. But dirty green, you know. And all the buildings're gray. These gross little shacks, pickups on blocks. Little towns without even a 7-Eleven. And full of hills they call mountains but aren't.

Toth cranked down the window and let this cold air in and looked up at the sky. "They can find us with those, you know, satellite things."

"What're you talking about?"

"You know, they can see you from miles up. I saw it in a movie."

"You think the state cops do that? Are you nuts?"

This guy, I don't know why I work with him. And after what happened at the drugstore, I won't again.

He pointed out where to turn and I did. He said the town was at the base of the Lookout. Well, I remembered passing that on the way to Liggett Falls this afternoon. It was this huge rock a couple hundred feet high. Which if you looked at it right looked like a man's head, like a profile, squinting. It'd been some kind of big deal to the Indians around here. Blah, blah, blah. He told me but I didn't pay no attention. It was spooky, that weird face, and I looked once and kept on driving. I didn't like it. I'm not really superstitious but sometimes I am.

"Winchester," he said now, meaning what the name of the town was. Five, six thousand people. We could find an empty house, stash the car in a garage and just wait out the search. Wait till tomorrow afternoon—Sunday—when all the weekenders were driving back to Boston and New York and we'd be lost in the crowd.

I could see the Lookout up ahead, not really a shape, mostly this blackness where the stars weren't. And then the guy on the floor in the back started to moan all of a sudden and just about give me a heart attack.

"You. Shut up back there." I slapped the seat and the guy in the back went quiet.

What a night. . . .

We'd got to the drugstore fifteen minutes before it closed. Like you ought to do. 'Cause mosta the customers're gone and a lot've the clerks've left and people're tired and when you push a Glock or Smitty into their faces they'll do just about anything you ask.

Except tonight.

We had our masks down and walked in slow, Toth getting the manager out of his little office, a fat guy who started crying and that made me mad, a grown man doing that. Toth kept a gun on the customers and the clerks and I was telling the cashier, this kid, to open the tills and, Jesus, he had an attitude. Like he'd seen all of those Steven Segal movies or something. A little kiss on the cheek with the Smitty and he changed his mind and started moving. Cussing me out but he was moving. I was counting the bucks as we were going along from one till to the next and sure enough we were up to about three thousand when I heard this noise and turned around and, what it was, Toth was knocking over a rack of chips. I mean, Jesus. He's getting Doritos!

I look away from the kid for just a second and what's he do? He pitches this bottle. Only not at me. Out the window. Bang, it breaks. There's no alarm I can hear but half of them are silent anyway and I'm really pissed. I could've killed him. Right there.

Only I didn't. Toth did.

He shoots the kid, bang, bang . . . Shit. And everybody else is scattering and he turns around and shoots another one of the clerks and a customer, just blam, not thinking or nothing. Just for no reason. Hit this girl clerk in the leg but this guy, this customer, well, he was dead. You could see. And I'm going, "What're you doing, what're you doing?" And he's going, "Shut up, shut up, shut up. . . ." And we're like we're swearing at each other when we figured out we hadta get outa there.

So we left. Only what happens is, there's a cop outside. That's why the kid threw the bottle, to get his attention. And he's outa his car. So we grab another customer, this guy by the door, and we use him like a shield and get outside. And there's the cop, he's holding his gun up, looking at the customer we've got, and the cop, he's saying, It's okay, it's okay, just take it easy.

And I couldn't believe it, Toth shot him too. I don't know

whether he killed him but there was blood so he wasn't wearing a vest, it didn't look like, and I could've killed Toth there on the spot. Because why'd he do that? He didn't have to.

We threw the guy, the customer, into the backseat and tied him up with tape. I kicked out the taillights and burned rubber outa there. We made it out of Liggett Falls.

That was all just a half hour ago but it seemed like weeks.

And now we were driving down this highway through a million pine trees. Heading right for the Lookout.

■

Winchester was dark.

I don't get why weekenders come to places like this. I mean, my old man took me hunting a long time ago. A couple times and I liked it. But coming to places like this just to look at leaves and buy furniture they call antiques but's really just busted-up crap . . . I don't know.

We found a house a block off Main Street with a bunch of newspapers in front and I pulled into the drive and put the Buick behind the place just in time. Two state police cars went shooting by. They'd been behind us not more than a half mile, without the lightbars going. Only they hadn't seen us 'causa the broke taillights and they went by in a flash and were gone, going to downtown.

Toth got into the house and he wasn't very clean about it, breaking a window in the back. It was a vacation place, pretty empty, and the refrigerator was shut off and the phone too, which was a good sign—there wasn't anybody coming back soon. Also, it smelled pretty musty and had stacks of old books and magazines from the summer.

We brought the guy inside and Toth started to take the hood off this guy's head and I said, "What the hell're you doing?"

"He hasn't said anything. Maybe he can't breathe."

This was a man talking who'd just laid a cap on three people back there and he was worried about this guy *breathing*? Man. I just laughed. Disgusted laughing, I mean. "Like maybe we don't want him to *see* us?" I said. "You think of that?" See, we weren't wearing our ski masks anymore.

It's scary when you have to remind people of stuff like that. I was thinking Toth knew better. But you never know.

I went to the window and saw another squad car go past. They were going slower now. They do that. After like the first shock, after the rush, they get smart and start cruising slow, really looking for what's funny—what's *different,* you know? That's why I didn't take the papers up from the front yard. Which would've been different than how the yard looked that morning. Cops really do that Colombo stuff. I could write a book about cops.

"Why'd you do it?"

It was the guy we took.

"Why?" he whispered again.

The customer. He had a low voice and it sounded pretty calm, I mean considering. I'll tell you, the first time I was in a shootout I was totally freaked for a day afterwards. And I had a gun.

I looked him over. He was wearing a plaid shirt and jeans. But he wasn't a local. I could tell because of the shoes. They were rich-boy shoes, the kind you see all the Yuppies wear. I couldn't see his face because of the mask but I pretty much remembered it. He wasn't young. Maybe in his forties. Kind of wrinkled skin. And he was skinny too. Skinnier'n me and I'm one of those people can eat what I want and I don't get fat. I don't know why. It just works that way.

"Quiet," I said. There was another car going by.

He laughed. Soft. Like he was saying, What? You think they can hear me all the way outside?

Kind of laughing *at* me, you know? I didn't like that at all.

And, sure, I guess you *couldn't* hear anything out there but I didn't like him giving me any crap so I said, "Just shut up. I don't want to hear your voice."

He did for a minute and just sat back in the chair where Toth put him. But then he said again, "Why'd you shoot them? You didn't have to."

"Quiet!"

"Just tell me why."

I took out my knife and snapped that sucker open then threw it down so it stuck in a tabletop. Sort of a *thunk* sound. "You hear that? That was a eight-inch Buck knife. Carbon-tempered. With a locking blade. It'd cut clean through a metal bolt. So you be quiet. Or I'll use it on you."

And he gave this laugh again. Maybe. Or it was just a snort of air. But I was thinking it was a laugh. I wanted to ask him what he meant by it but I didn't.

"You got any money on you?" Toth asked and pulled the wallet out of the guy's back pocket. "Lookit." He pulled out what must've been five or six hundred. Man.

Another squad car went past, moving slow. It had a spotlight and the cop turned it on the driveway but he just kept going. I heard a siren across town. And another one too. It was a weird feeling, knowing those people were out there looking for us.

I took the wallet from Toth and looked through it.

Randall C. Weller, Jr. He lived in Connecticut. A weekender. Just like I thought. He had a bunch of business cards that said he was vice president of this big computer company. One that was in the news, trying to take over IBM or something. All of a sudden I had this thought. We could hold him for ransom. I mean, why not? Make a half million. Maybe more.

"My wife and kids'll be sick, worrying," Weller said. It spooked me, hearing that. 'Cause there I was, looking right at a picture in his wallet. And what was it of? His wife and kids.

"I ain't letting you go. Now, just shut up. I may need you."

"Like a hostage, you mean? That's only in the movies. They'll shoot you when you walk out and they'll shoot me too if they have to. That's the way the cops do it in real life. Just give yourself up. At least you'll save your life."

"Shut up!" I shouted.

"Let me go and I'll tell them you treated me fine. That the shooting was a mistake. It wasn't your fault."

I leaned forward and pushed the knife against his throat, not the blade 'cause that's real sharp but the blunt edge, and I told him to be quiet.

Another car went past, no light this time but it was going slower, and all of a sudden I got to thinking what if they do a door-to-door search?

"Why did he do it? Why'd he kill them?"

And funny, the way he said *he* made me feel a little better 'cause it was like he didn't blame me for it. I mean, it *was* Toth's fault. Not mine.

Weller kept going. "I don't get it. That man by the counter? The tall one. He was just standing there. He didn't do anything. He just shot him down."

But neither of us said nothing. Probably Toth, because he didn't know why he'd shot them. And me, because I didn't owe this guy any answers. I had him in my hand. Completely, and I had to let him know that. I didn't *have* to talk to him.

But the guy, Weller, he didn't say anything else. And I got this weird feeling. Like this pressure building up. You know, because nobody was answering his damn, stupid question. I felt this urge to say something. Anything. And that was the last thing I wanted to do. So I said, "I'm gonna move the car into the garage." And I went outside to do it.

I looked around the garage to see if there was anything worth taking and there wasn't except a Snapper lawn mower but how do you fence one of those? So I drove the Buick inside and closed the door. And went back into the house.

And then I couldn't believe what happened. I mean, Jesus. When I walked into the living room the first thing I heard was Toth saying, "No way, man. I'm not snitching on Jack Prescot."

I just stood there. And you should've seen the look on his face. He knew he'd blown it big.

Now this Weller guy knew my name.

I didn't say anything. I didn't have to. Toth started talking real fast and nervous. "He said he'd pay me some big bucks to let him go." Trying to turn it around, make it Weller's fault. "I mean I wasn't going to. I wasn't even thinking 'bout it, man. I told him forget it."

"But what's with tellin' him my name?"

"I don't know, man. He confused me. I wasn't thinking."

I'll say he wasn't. He hadn't been thinking all night.

I sighed to let him know I wasn't happy but I just clapped him on the shoulder. "Okay," I said. "S'been a long night. These things happen."

"I'm sorry, man. Really."

"Yeah. Maybe you better go spend the night in the garage or something. Or upstairs. I don't want to see you around for a while."

"Sure."

And the funny thing was, just then, Weller gave this little snicker or something. Like he knew what was coming. How'd he know that? I wondered.

Toth went to pick up a couple magazines and the knapsack with his gun in it and extra rounds.

Normally, killing somebody with a knife is a hard thing to do. I say *normally* even though I've only done it one other time. But I remember it and it was messy and hard work. But tonight, I don't know, I was all filled up with this . . . *feeling* from the drugstore. Mad. I mean, really. Crazy too a little. And as soon as Toth turned his back I got him around the neck and went to work and it wasn't three minutes later it was over. I drug his body behind the couch and then—why not—pulled Weller's hood off. He already knew my name. He might as well see my face.

He was a dead man. We both knew it.

■

"You were thinking of holding me for ransom, right?"

I stood at the window and looked out. Another cop car went past and there were more flashing lights bouncing off the low clouds and off the face of the Lookout, right over our heads.

Weller had a thin face and short hair, cut real neat. He looked like every ass-kissing businessman I ever met. His eyes were dark and calm like his voice and it made me even madder he wasn't shook up looking at that big bloodstain on the rug and floor.

"No," I told him.

He looked at the pile of all the stuff I'd taken from his wallet and kept going like I hadn't said anything. "It won't work. A kidnapping. I don't have a lot of money and if you saw my business card and're thinking I'm an executive at the company, they have about five hundred vice presidents. They won't pay diddly for me. And you see those kids in the picture? It was taken twelve years ago. They're both in college now. I'm paying major tuition."

"Where," I asked, sneering. "Harvard?"

"One's at Harvard," he said, like he was snapping at me. "And one's at Northwestern. So the house's mortgaged to the hilt. Besides, kidnapping somebody by yourself? No, you couldn't bring that off."

He saw the way I looked at him and he said, "I don't mean

you personally, Jack. I mean somebody by himself. You'd need partners."

And I figured he was right.

That silence again. Nobody saying nothing and it was like the room was filling up with cold water. I walked to the window and the floors creaked under my feet and that only made things worse. I remember one time my dad said that a house had a voice of its own and some houses were laughing houses and some were forlorn. Well, this was a forlorn house. Yeah, it was modern and clean and the *National Geographics* were all in order but it was still forlorn.

Just when I felt like shouting because of the tension Weller said, "I don't want you to kill me."

"Who said I was going to kill you?"

He gave me his funny little smile. "I've been a salesman for twenty-five years. I've sold pets and Cadillacs and typesetters and lately I've been selling mainframe computers. I know when I'm being handed a line. You're going to kill me. It was the first thing you thought of when you heard him"—nodding toward Toth—"say your name."

I just laughed at him. "Well, that's a damn handy thing to be, sorta a walking lie detector," I said and I was being sarcastic.

But he just said, "Damn handy," like he was agreeing with me.

"I don't want to kill you."

"Oh, I know you don't *want* to. You didn't want your friend to kill anybody back there at the drugstore either. I could see that. But people *got* killed and that ups the stakes. Right?"

And those eyes of his, they just dug into me and I couldn't say anything.

"But," he said, "I'm going to talk you out of it."

He sounded real certain and that made me feel better. 'Cause

I'd rather kill a cocky son of a bitch than a pathetic one. And so I laughed. "Talk me out of it?"

"I'm going to try."

"Yeah? How you gonna do that?"

Weller cleared his throat a little. "First, let's get everything on the table. I've seen your face and I know your name. Jack Prescot. Right? You're, what? About five-nine, a hundred fifty pounds, black hair. So you've got to assume I can identify you. I'm not going to play any games and say I didn't see you clearly or hear who you were. Or anything like that. We all squared away on that, Jack?"

I nodded, rolling my eyes like this was all a load of crap. But I gotta admit I was kinda curious what he had to say.

"My promise," he said, "is that I won't turn you in. Not under any circumstances. The police'll never learn your name from me. Or your description. I'll never testify against you."

Sounding honest as a priest. Real slick delivery. Well, he *was* a salesman and I wasn't going to buy it. But he didn't know I was on to him. Let him give me his pitch, let him think I was going along. When it came down to it, after we'd got away and were somewhere in the woods upstate, I'd want him relaxed. No screaming, no hassles. Just a couple fast cuts or shots and that'd be it.

"You understand what I'm saying?"

I tried to look serious and said, "Sure. You're thinking you can talk me out of killing you. You've got reasons why I shouldn't?"

"Oh, I've got reasons, you bet. One in particular. One that you can't argue with."

"Yeah? What's that?"

"I'll get to it in a minute. Let me tell you some of the practical reasons you should let me go. First, you think you've got to kill me because I know who you are, right? Well, how long you think your

identity's going to be a secret? Your buddy shot a cop back there. I don't know police stuff except what I see in the movies. But they're going to be looking at tire tracks and witnesses who saw plates and makes of cars and gas stations you might've stopped at on the way here."

He was just blowing smoke. The Buick was stolen. I mean, I'm not stupid.

But he went on, looking at me real coy. "Even if your car was stolen they're going to check down every lead. Every shoe print around where you or your friend stole it, talk to everybody in the area around the time it vanished."

I kept smiling like it was nuts what he was saying. But this was true, the shooting-the-cop part. You do that and you're in big trouble. Trouble that sticks with you. They don't stop looking till they find you.

"And when they identify your buddy," he nodded toward the couch where Toth's body was lying, "they're going to make some connection to you."

"I don't know him that good. We just hung around together the past few months."

Weller jumped on this. "Where? A bar? A restaurant? Anybody *ever* see you in public?"

I got mad and I shouted, "So? What're you saying? They gonna bust me anyway then I'll just take you out with me. How's *that* for an argument?"

Calm as could be he said, "I'm simply telling you that one of the reasons you want to kill me doesn't make sense. And think about this—the shooting at the drugstore? It wasn't premeditated. It was, what do they call it? Heat of passion. But you kill me, that'll be first-degree. You'll get the death penalty when they find you."

When they find you. Right, I laughed to myself. Oh, what he said made sense but the fact is, killing isn't a making-sense kind of thing. Hell, it *never* makes sense but sometimes you just have to do it. But I was kind of having fun now. I wanted to argue back. "Yeah, well, I killed Toth. That wasn't heat of passion. I'm going to get the needle anyway for that."

"But nobody gives a damn about him," he came right back. "They don't care if he killed *himself* or got hit by a car. You can take that piece of garbage out of the equation altogether. They care if you kill *me*. I'm the 'Innocent Bystander' in the headlines. I'm the 'Father of Two.' You kill me you're as good as dead."

I started to say something but he kept going.

"Now here's another reason I'm not going to say anything about you. Because you know my name and you know where I live. You know I have a family and you know how important they are to me. If I turn you in you could come after us. I'd never jeopardize my family that way. Now, let me ask you something. What's the worst thing that could happen to you?"

"Keep listening to you spout on and on."

Weller laughed at that. I could see he was surprised I had a sense of humor. After a minute he said, "Seriously. The worst thing."

"I don't know. I never thought about it."

"Lose a leg? Go deaf? Lose all your money? Go blind? . . . Hey, that looked like it hit a nerve. Going blind?"

"Yeah, I guess. That'd be the worst thing I could think of."

That *was* a pretty damn scary thing and I'd thought on it before. 'Cause that was what happened to my old man. And it wasn't not seeing anymore that got to me. No, it was that I'd have to depend on somebody else for . . . Christ, for everything, I guess.

"Okay, think about this," he said. "The way you feel about going blind's the way my family'd feel if they lost me. It'd be that bad for them. You don't want to cause them that kind of pain, do you?"

I didn't want to, no. But I knew I *had* to. I didn't want to think

about it anymore. I asked him, "So what's this last reason you're telling me about?"

"The last reason," he said, kind of whispering. But he didn't go on. He looked around the room, you know, like his mind was someplace else.

"Yeah?" I asked. I was pretty curious. "Tell me."

But he just asked, "You think these people, they have a bar?"

And I'd just been thinking I could use a drink too. I went into the kitchen and of course they didn't have any beer in the fridge on account of the house being all closed up and the power off. But they did have scotch and that'd be my first choice anyway.

I got a couple glasses and took the bottle back to the living room. Thinking this was a good idea. When it came time to do it it'd be easier for him and for me both if we were kinda tanked. I shoved my Smitty into his neck and cut the tape his hands were tied with then taped them in front of him. I sat back and kept my knife near, ready to go, in case he tried something. But it didn't look like he was going to do anything. He read over the scotch bottle, kind of disappointed it was cheap. And I agreed with him there. One thing I learned a long time ago, you going to rob, rob rich.

I sat back where I could keep an eye on him.

"The last reason. Okay, I'll tell you. I'm going to *prove* to you that you should let me go."

"You are?"

"All those other reasons—the practical ones, the humanitarian ones . . . I'll concede you don't care much about those—you don't look very convinced. All right? Then let's look at the one reason you should let me go."

I figured this was going to be more crap. But what he said was something I never would've expected.

"You should let me go for your own sake."

"For me? What're you talking about?"

"See, Jack, I don't think you're lost."

"Whatta you mean, lost?"

"I don't think your soul's beyond redemption."

I laughed at this, laughed out loud, because I just *had* to. I expected a hell of a lot better from a hotshot vice-president salesman like him. "Soul? You think I got a soul?"

"Well, everybody has a soul," he said, and what was crazy was he said it like he was surprised that I didn't think so. It was like I'd said wait a minute, you mean the earth ain't flat? Or something.

"Well, if I got a soul it's taken the fast lane to hell." Which was this line I heard in this movie and I tried to laugh but it sounded flat. Like Weller was saying something deep and I was just kidding around. It made me feel cheap. I stopped smiling and looked down at Toth, lying there in the corner, those dead eyes of his just staring, staring, and I wanted to stab him again I was so mad.

"We're talking about your soul."

I snickered and sipped the liquor. "Oh, yeah, I'll bet you're the sort that reads those angel books they got all over the place now."

"I go to church but, no, I'm not talking about all that silly crap. I don't mean magic. I mean your conscience. What Jack Prescot's all about."

I could tell him about social workers and youth counselors and all those guys who don't know nothing about the way life works. They think they do. But it's the words they use. You can tell they don't know a thing. Some counselors or somebody'll talk to me and they say, Oh, you're maladjusted, you're denying your anger, things like that. When I hear that, I know they don't know nothing about souls or spirits.

"Not the afterlife," Weller was going on. "Not morality. I'm talking about life here on earth that's important. Oh, sure, you look skeptical. But listen to me. I really believe if you have a connection with somebody, if you trust them, if you have faith in them, then there's hope for you."

"Hope? What's that mean? Hope for what?"

"That you'll become a real human being. Lead a real life."

Real . . . I didn't know what he meant but he said it like what he was saying was so clear that I'd have to be an idiot to miss it. So I didn't say nothing.

He kept going. "Oh, there're reasons to steal and there're reasons to kill. But on the whole, don't you really think it's better not to? Just think about it: Why do we put people in jail if it's all right for them to murder? Not just us but all societies."

"So, what? Ooooo, I'm gonna give up my evil ways?"

And he just lifted his eyebrow and said, "Maybe. Tell me, Jack, how'd you feel when your buddy—what's his name?"

"Joe Roy Toth."

"Toth. When he shot that customer by the counter? How'd you feel?"

"I don't know."

"He just turned around and shot him. For no reason. You knew that wasn't right, didn't you?" And I started to say something. But he said, "No, don't answer me. You'd be inclined to lie. And that's all right. It's an instinct in your line of work. But I don't want you *believing* any lies you tell me. Okay? I want you to look into your heart and tell me if you didn't think something was real wrong about what Toth did. Think about that, Jack. You knew something wasn't right."

All right, I did. But who wouldn't? Toth screwed everything up. Everything went sour. And it was all his fault.

"It dug at you, right, Jack? You wished he hadn't done it."

I didn't say nothing but just drank some more scotch and

looked out the window and watched the flashing lights around the town. Sometimes they seemed close and sometimes they seemed far away.

"If I let you go you'll tell 'em about me."

Like everybody else. They all betrayed me. My father—even after he went blind, the son of a bitch turned me in. My first PO, the judges. Sandra. My boss, the one I knifed.

"No, I won't," Weller said. "We're talking about an agreement. I don't break deals. I promised I won't tell a soul about you, Jack. Not even my wife." He leaned forward, cupping the booze between his hands. "You let me go, it'll mean all the difference in the world to *you*. It'll mean that you're not hopeless. I guarantee your life'll be different. That one act—letting me go—it'll change you forever. Oh, maybe not this year. Or for five years. But you'll come around. You'll give up all this, everything that happened back there in Liggett Falls. All the crime, the killing. You'll come around. I know you will."

"You just expect me to believe you won't tell anybody?"

"Ah," Weller said and lifted his bound-up hands to drink more scotch. "Now we get down to the big issue."

Again, that silence and finally I said, "And what's that?"

"Faith."

There was this burst of siren outside, real near, and I told him to shut up and pushed the gun against his head. His hands were shaking but he didn't do anything stupid and a few minutes later, after I sat back, he started talking again. "Faith. That's what I'm talking about. A man who has faith is somebody who can be saved."

"Well, I don't have any goddamn faith," I told him.

But he kept right on talking. "If you believe in another human being you have faith."

"Why the hell do you care whether I'm saved or not?"

"Because life's hard and people're cruel. I told you I'm a

churchgoer. A lot of the Bible's crazy. But some of it I believe. And one of the things I believe is that sometimes we're put in these situations to make a difference. I think that's what happened tonight. That's why you and I both happened to be at the drugstore at the same time. You've felt that, haven't you? Like an omen? Like something happens and is telling you you ought to do this or shouldn't do that."

Which was weird 'cause the whole time we were driving up to Liggett Falls, I kept thinking something funny's going on. I don't know what it is but this job's gonna be different.

"What if," he said, "everything tonight happened for a purpose? My wife had a cold so I went to buy NyQuil. I went to that drugstore instead of 7-Eleven to save a buck or two. You happened to hit that store at just that time. You happened to have your buddy"—he nodded toward Toth's body "with you. The cop car just happened by at that particular moment. And the clerk behind the counter just happened to see him. That's a lot of coincidences. Don't you think?"

And then—this sent a damn chill right down my spine—he said, "Here we are in the shadow of that big rock, that face."

Which is one hundred percent what I was thinking. *Exactly the same*—about the Lookout, I mean. I don't know why I was. But I happened to be looking out the window and thinking about it at that exact same instant. I tossed back the scotch and had another and, oh, man, I was pretty freaked out.

"Like he's looking at us, waiting for you to make a decision. Oh, don't think it was just you, though. Maybe the purpose was to affect everybody's life there. That customer at the counter your friend shot? Maybe it was just his time to go—fast, you know, before he got cancer or had a stroke. Maybe that girl, the clerk, had to get shot in the leg so she'd get her life together, maybe get off drugs or give up drinking."

"And you? What about you?"

"Well, I'll tell you about me. Maybe you're the good deed in *my* life. I've spent years thinking only about making money. Take a look at my wallet. There. In the back."

I pulled it open. There were a half dozen of these little cards, like certificates. *Randall Weller—Salesman of the Year. Exceeded Target Two Years Straight. Best Salesman of 1992.*

Weller kept going. "There are plenty of others back in my office. And trophies too. And in order for me to win those I've had to neglect people. My family and friends. People who could maybe use my help. And that's not right. Maybe you kidnapping me, it's one of those signs to make me turn my life around."

The funny thing was, this made sense. Oh, it was hard to imagine not doing heists. And I couldn't see myself, if it came down to a fight, not going for my Buck or my Smitty to take the other guy out. That turning the other cheek stuff, that's only for losers. But maybe I *could* see a day when my life'd be just straight time. Living with some woman, maybe a wife, and not treating her the way I'd treated Sandra, living in a house. Doing what my father and mother, whatever she was like, never did.

"If I was to let you go," I said, "you'd have to tell 'em something."

He shrugged. "I'll say you locked me in the trunk and then tossed me out somewhere near here. I wandered around, looking for a house or something, and got lost. It could take me a day to find somebody. That's believable."

"Or you could flag down a car in an hour."

"I could. But I won't."

"You keep saying that. But how do I *know*?"

"That's the faith part. You don't know. No guarantees."

"Well, I guess I don't have any faith."

"Then *I'm* dead. And *your* life's never gonna change. End of story." He sat back and shrugged.

That silence again but it was like it was really this roar all around us. "You just want . . . What do you want?"

He drank more scotch. "Here's a proposal. Let me walk outside."

"Oh, right. Just let you stroll out for some fresh air or something?"

"Let me walk outside and I promise you I'll walk right back in again."

"Like a test?"

He thought about this for a second. "Yeah. A test."

"Where's this faith you're talking about? You walk outside, you try to run and I'd shoot you in the back."

"No, what you do is you put the gun someplace in the house. The kitchen or someplace. Somewhere you couldn't get it if I ran. You stand at the window, where we can see each other. And I'll tell you up front I can run like the wind. I was lettered track and field in college and I still jog every day of the year."

"You know if you run and bring the cops back it's all gonna get bloody. I'll kill the first five troopers come through that door. Nothing'll stop me and that blood'll be on your hands."

"Of course I know that," he said. "But if this's going to work you can't think that way. You've got to assume the worst is going to happen. That if I run I'll tell the cops everything. Where you are and that there're no hostages here and that you've only got one or two guns. And they're going to come in and blow you to hell. And you're not going to take a single one down with you. You're going to die and die painfully 'cause of a few lousy bucks. But, but, but . . ." He held up his hands and stopped me from saying anything. "You gotta understand, faith means risk."

"That's stupid."

"I think it's just the opposite. It'd be the smartest thing you'd ever do in your life."

I tossed back another scotch and had to think about this.

Weller said, "I can see it there already. Some of that faith. It's there. Not a lot. But some."

And yeah, maybe there was a little. 'Cause I was thinking about how mad I got at Toth and the way he ruined everything. I didn't want anybody to get killed tonight. I *was* sick of it. Sick of the way my life had gone. Sometimes it was good, being alone and all. Not answering to anybody. But sometimes it was real bad. And this guy Weller, it was like he was showing me something different.

"So," I said. "You just want me to put the gun down?"

He looked around. "Put it in the kitchen. You stand in the doorway or window. All I'm gonna do is walk down to the street and walk back."

I looked out the window. It was maybe fifty feet down the driveway. There were these bushes on either side of it. He could just take off and I'd never find him.

All through the sky I could see police-car lights flickering.

"Naw, I ain't gonna. You're nuts."

I expected begging or something. Or him getting pissed off more likely—which is what happens to me when people don't do what I tell them. Or don't do it fast enough. But, naw, he just nodded. "Okay, Jack. You thought about it. That's a good thing. You're not ready yet. I respect that." He sipped a little more scotch, looking at the glass. And that was the end of it.

Then all of a sudden these searchlights started up. They was some ways away but I still got spooked and backed away from the window. Pulled my gun out. Only then I saw that it wasn't nothing to do with the robbery. It was just a couple big spotlights shining on the Lookout. They must've gone on every night, this time.

I looked up at it. From here it didn't look like a face at all. It was just a rock. Gray and brown and these funny pine trees growing sideways out of cracks.

Watching it for a minute or two. Looking out over the town. And something that guy was saying went into my head. Not the words, really. Just the *thought*. And I was thinking about everybody in that town. Leading normal lives. There was a church steeple and the roofs of small houses. A lot of little yellow lights in town. You could just make out the hills in the distance. And I wished for a minute I was in one of them houses. Sitting there. Watching TV with a wife next to me.

I turned back from the window and I said, "You'd just walk down to the road and back? That's it?"

"That's all. I won't run off, you don't go get your gun. We trust each other. What could be simpler?"

Listening to the wind. Not strong but a steady hiss that was comforting in a funny way even though any other time I'da thought it sounded cold and raw. It was like I heard a voice. I don't know. Something in me said I oughta do this.

I didn't say nothing else 'cause I was right on the edge and I was afraid he'd say something that'd make me change my mind. I just took the Smith & Wesson and looked at it for a minute then went and put it on the kitchen table. I came back with the Buck and cut his feet free. Then I figured if I was going to do it I oughta go all the way. So I cut his hands free too. Weller seemed surprised I did that. But he smiled like he knew I was playing the game. I pulled him to his feet and held the blade to his neck and took him to the door.

"You're doing a good thing," he said.

I was thinking: Oh, man. I can't believe this. It's crazy. Part of me said, Cut him now, cut his throat. Do it!

But I didn't. I opened the door and smelled cold fall air and wood smoke and pine and I heard the wind in the rocks and trees above our head.

"Go on," I told him.

Weller started off and he didn't look back to check on me, see if I went to get the gun . . . faith, I guess. He kept walking real slow down toward the road.

I felt funny, I'll tell you, and a couple times when he went past some real shadowy places in the driveway and could disappear I was like, Oh, man, this is all messed up. I'm crazy.

I almost panicked a few times and bolted for the Smitty but I didn't. When Weller got down near the sidewalk I was actually holding my breath. I expected him to go, I really did. I was looking for that moment—when people tense up, when they're gonna swing or draw down on you or bolt. It's like their bodies're shouting what they're going to be doing before they do it. Only Weller wasn't doing none of that. He walked down to the sidewalk real casual. And he turned and looked up at the face of the Lookout, like he was just another weekender.

Then he turned around. He nodded at me.

Which is when the cop car came by.

It was a state trooper. Those're the dark ones and he didn't have the light bar going. So he was almost here before I knew it. I guess I was looking at Weller so hard I didn't see nothing else.

There it was, two doors away, and Weller saw it the same time I did.

And I thought: That's it. Oh, hell.

But when I was turning to get the gun I saw this motion down by the road. And I stopped cold.

Could you believe it? Weller'd dropped onto the ground and rolled underneath a tree. I closed the door real fast and watched from the window. The trooper stopped and turned his light on the driveway. The beam—it was real bright—it moved up and down and hit all the bushes and the front of the house then back to the road. But it was like Weller was digging down into the pine needles to keep from being seen. I mean, he was *hiding* from those sons of bitches. Doing whatever he could to stay out of the way of the light.

Then the car moved on and I saw the lights checking out the house next door and then it was gone. I kept my eyes on Weller the whole time and he didn't do nothing stupid. I seen him climb out from under the trees and dust himself off. Then he came walking back to the house. Easy, like he was walking to a bar to meet some buddies.

He came inside. Gave this little sigh, like relief. And laughed. Then he held his hands out. I didn't even ask him to. I taped 'em up again and he sat down in the chair, picked up his scotch and sipped it.

And, damn, I'll tell you something. The God's truth. I felt good. Naw, naw, it wasn't like I'd seen the light or anything like that crap. But I was thinking that of all the people in my life—my dad or my ex or Toth or anybody else, I never did really trust them. I'd never let myself go all the way. And here, tonight, I did. With a stranger and somebody who had the power to do me some harm. It was a pretty scary feeling but it was also a good feeling.

A little thing, real little. But maybe that's where stuff like this starts. I realized then that I'd been wrong. I could let him go. Oh, I'd keep him tied up here. Gagged. It'd be a day or so before he'd get out. But he'd agree to that. I knew he would. And I'd write his name and address down, let him know I knew where him and his family lived. But that was only part of why I'd let him go. I wasn't sure what the rest of it was. But it was something about what'd just happened, something between me and him.

"How you feel?" he asked.

I wasn't going to give too much away. No, sir. But I couldn't help saying, "That car coming by? I thought I was gone then. But you did right by me."

"And you did right too, Jack." And then he said, "Pour us another round."

I filled the glasses to the top. We tapped 'em.

"Here's to you, Jack. And to faith."

"To faith."

I tossed back the whisky and when I lowered my head, sniffing air through my nose to clear my head, well, that was when he got me. Right in the face.

He was good, that son of a bitch. Tossed the glass low so that even when I ducked, which of course I did, the booze caught me in the eyes, and, man, that stung like nobody's business. I couldn't believe it. I was howling in pain and going for the knife. But it was too late. He had it all planned out, exactly what I was going to do. How I was gonna move. He brought his knee up into my chin and knocked a couple teeth out and I went over onto my back before I could get the knife outa my pocket. Then he dropped down on my belly with his knee—I remembered I'd never bothered to tape his feet up again—and he knocked the wind out, and I was lying there like I was paralyzed, trying to breathe and all. Only I couldn't. And the pain was incredible but what was worse was the feeling that he didn't trust me.

I was whispering, "No, no, no! I was going to do it, man. You don't understand! I was going to let you go."

I couldn't see nothing and couldn't really hear nothing either, my ears were roaring so much. I was gasping, "You don't understand, you don't understand."

Man, the pain was so bad. So bad . . .

Weller must've got the tape off his hands, chewed through it, I guess, 'cause he was rolling me over. I felt him tape my hands together then grab me and drag me over to a chair, tape my feet to the legs. He got some water and threw it in my face to wash the whisky out of my eyes.

He sat down in a chair in front of me. And he just stared at me for a long time while I caught my breath. He picked up his glass, poured more scotch. I shied away, thinking he was going to throw it in my face again but he just sat there, sipping it and staring at me.

"You . . . I was going to let you go. I *was*."

"I know," he said. Still calm.

"You know?"

"I could see it in your face. I've been a salesman for years, re- member? I know when I've closed a deal."

I'm a pretty strong guy, 'specially when I'm mad, and I tried real hard to break through that tape but there was no doing it. "Goddamn you!" I shouted. "You said you weren't going to turn me in. You, all your goddamn talk about faith—"

"Shhhh," Weller whispered. And he sat back, crossed his legs. Easy as could be. Looking me up and down. "That fellow your friend shot and killed back at the drugstore? The customer at the counter?"

I nodded slowly.

"He was my friend. It's his place my wife and I're staying at this weekend. With all our kids."

I just stared at him. His friend? What was he saying? "I didn't—"

"Be quiet," he said, real soft. "I've known him for years. Gerry was one of my best friends."

"I didn't want nobody to die. I—"

"But somebody *did* die. And it was your fault."

"Toth. . . ."

He whispered, "It was your fault."

"All right, you tricked me. Call the cops. Get it over with, you goddamn liar."

"You really don't understand, do you?" Weller shook his head. Why was he so calm? His hands weren't shaking. He wasn't looking around, nervous and all. Nothing like that. He said, "If I'd wanted to turn you in I would just've flagged down that squad car a few minutes ago. But I said I wouldn't do that. And I won't. I gave you my word I wouldn't tell the cops a thing about you. And I won't. Turning you in is the last thing I want to do."

"Then what *do* you want?" I shouted. "Tell me!" Trying to bust through that tape. And as he unfolded my Buck knife with a click, I was thinking of something I told him.

Oh, man, no . . . Oh, no.

Yeah, being blind, I guess. That'd be the worst thing I could think of.

"What're you going to do?" I whispered.

"What'm I going to do, Jack?" Weller said, feeling the blade of the Buck with his thumb and looking me in the eye. "Well, I'll tell you. I spent a good deal of time tonight proving to you that you shouldn't kill me. And now . . ."

"What, man? *What?*"

"Now I'm going to spend a good deal of time proving to you that you should've."

Then, real slow, Weller finished his scotch and stood up. And he walked toward me, that weird little smile on his face.

FOR SERVICES RENDERED

"At first I thought it was me . . . but now I know for sure: My husband's trying to drive me crazy."

Dr. Harry Bernstein nodded and, after a moment's pause, dutifully noted his patient's words on the steno pad resting on his lap.

"I don't mean he's *irritating* me, driving me crazy that way— I mean he's making me question my sanity. And he's doing it on purpose."

Patsy Randolph, facing away from Harry on his leather couch, turned to look at her psychiatrist. Even though he kept his Park Avenue office quite dark during his sessions he could see that there were tears in her eyes.

"You're very upset," he said in a kind tone.

"Sure, I'm upset," she said. "And I'm scared."

This woman, in her late forties, had been his patient for two months. She'd been close to tears several times during their sessions but had never actually cried. Tears are important barometers of emotional weather. Some patients go for years without crying in front of their doctors and when the eyes begin to water any competent therapist sits up and takes notice.

Harry studied Patsy closely as she turned away again and picked at a button on the cushion beside her thigh.

"Go on," he encouraged. "Tell me about it."

She snagged a Kleenex from the box beside the couch.

Dabbed at her eyes but she did so carefully; as always, she wore impeccable makeup.

"Please," Harry said in a soft voice.

"It's happened a couple of times now," she began reluctantly. "Last night was the worst. I was lying in bed and I heard this voice. I couldn't really hear it clearly at first. Then it said . . ." She hesitated. "It said it was my father's ghost."

Motifs in therapy didn't get any better than this, and Harry paid close attention.

"You weren't dreaming?"

"No, I was awake. I couldn't sleep and I'd gotten up for a glass of water. Then I started walking around the apartment. Just pacing. I felt frantic. I lay back in bed. And the voice—I mean, *Pete's* voice—said that it was my father's ghost."

"What did he say?"

"He just rambled on and on. Telling me about all kinds of things from my past. Incidents from when I was a girl. I'm not sure. It was hard to hear."

"And these were things your husband knew?"

"Not all of them." Her voice cracked. "But he could've found them out. Looking through my letters and my yearbooks." Things like that.

"You're sure he was the one talking?"

"The voice sounded sort of like Peter's. Anyway, who else would it be?" She laughed, her voice nearly a cackle. "I mean, it could hardly be my father's ghost, now, could it?"

"Maybe he was just talking in his sleep."

She didn't respond for a minute. "See, that's the thing . . . He wasn't in bed. He was in the den, playing some video game."

Harry continued to take his notes.

"And you heard him from the den?"

"He must have been at the door . . . Oh, Doctor, it sounds

ridiculous. I know it does. But I think he was kneeling at the door—it's right next to the bedroom—and was whispering."

"Did you go into the den? Ask him about it?"

"I walked to the door real fast but by the time I opened it he was back at the desk." She looked at her hands and found she'd shredded the Kleenex. She glanced at Harry to see if he'd noticed the compulsive behavior, which of course he had, and then stuffed the tissue into the pocket of her expensive beige slacks.

"And then?"

"I asked him if he'd heard anything, any voices. And he looked at me like I was nuts and went back to his game."

"And that night you didn't hear any more voices?"

"No."

Harry studied his patient. She'd been a pretty girl in her youth, he supposed, because she was a pretty woman now (therapists *always* saw the child within the adult). Her face was sleek and she had the slightly upturned nose of a Connecticut socialite who debates long and hard about having rhinoplasty but never does. He recalled that Patsy'd told him her weight was never a problem: she'd hire a personal trainer whenever she gained five pounds. She'd said—with irritation masking secret pride—that men often tried to pick her up in bars and coffee shops.

He asked, "You say this's happened before? Hearing the voice?"

Another hesitation. "Maybe two or three times. All within the past couple of weeks."

"But why would Peter want to drive you crazy?"

Patsy, who'd come to Harry presenting with the classic symptoms of a routine midlife crisis, hadn't discussed her husband much yet. Harry knew he was good-looking, a few years younger than Patsy, not particularly ambitious. They'd been married for three years—second marriages for both of them—and they didn't seem to have many interests in common. But of course that was just Patsy's version. The "facts" that are revealed in a therapist's office can be very fishy. Harry Bernstein worked hard to become a human lie detector and his impression of the marriage was that there was much unspoken conflict between husband and wife.

Patsy considered his question. "I don't know. I was talking to Sally. . . ." Harry remembered her mentioning Sally, her best friend. She was another Upper East Side matron—one of the ladies who lunch—and was married to the president of one of the biggest banks in New York. "She said that maybe Peter's jealous of me. I mean, look at us—I'm the one with the social life, I have the friends, I have the money. . . ." He noticed a manic edge to her voice. She did too and controlled it. "I just don't know why he's doing it. But he is."

"Have you talked to him about this?"

"I tried. But naturally he denies everything." She shook her head and tears swelled in her eyes again. "And then . . . the birds."

"Birds?"

Another Kleenex was snagged, used and shredded. She didn't hide the evidence this time. "I have this collection of ceramic birds. Made by Boehm. Do you know about the company?"

"No."

"They're very expensive. They're German. Beautifully made. They were my parents'. When our father died Steve and I split the inheritance but he got most of the personal family heirlooms. That really hurt me. But I did get the birds."

Harry knew that her mother had died ten years ago and her father about three years ago. The man had been very stern and had favored Patsy's older brother, Stephen. He had been patronizing to her all her life.

"I have four of them. There used to be five but when I was twelve I broke one. I ran inside—I was very excited about something and I wanted to tell my father about it—and I bumped into the table and knocked one off. The sparrow. It broke. My father spanked me with a willow switch and sent me to bed without dinner."

Ah, an Important Event. Harry made a note but decided not to pursue the incident any further at that moment.

"And?"

"The morning after I heard my father's ghost for the first time . . ." Her voice grew harsh. "I mean, the morning after *Peter* started whispering to me . . . I found one of the birds broken. It was lying on the living room floor. I asked Peter why he'd done it—he knows how important they were to me—and he denied it. He said I must have been sleepwalking and did it myself. But I know I didn't. Peter had to've been the one." She'd slipped into her raw, irrational voice again.

Harry glanced at the clock. He hated the legacy of the psychoanalyst: the perfectly timed fifty-minute hour. There was so much more he wanted to delve into. But patients need consistency and, according to the old school, discipline. He said, "I'm sorry but I see our time's up."

Dutifully Patsy rose. Harry observed how disheveled she looked. Yes, her makeup had been carefully applied but the buttons on her blouse weren't done properly. Either she'd dressed in a hurry or hadn't paid attention. And one of the straps on her expensive, tan shoes wasn't hooked.

She rose. "Thank you, Doctor . . . It's good just to be able to tell someone about this."

"We'll get everything worked out. I'll see you next week."

After Patsy had left the office Harry Bernstein sat down at his desk. He spun slowly in his chair, gazing at his books—the *DSM-IV, The Psychopathology of Everyday Life*, the APA *Handbook of Neuroses*, volumes by Freud, Adler, Jung, Karen Horney, hundreds of others. Then looking out the window again, watching the late-afternoon sunlight fall on the cars and taxis speeding north on Park Avenue.

A bird flew past.

He thought about the shattered ceramic sparrow from Patsy's childhood.

And Harry thought: What a significant session this has been. Not only for his patient. But for him too.

Patsy Randolph—who had until today been just another mildly discontented middle-aged patient—represented a watershed event for Dr. Harold David Bernstein. He was in a position to change her life completely.

And in doing so maybe he could redeem his own.

Harry laughed out loud, spun again in the chair, like a child on a playground. Once, twice, three times.

A figure appeared in the doorway. "Doctor?" Miriam, his secretary, cocked her head, which was covered with fussy white hair. "Are you all right?"

"I'm fine. Why're you asking?"

"Well, it's just . . . I don't think I've heard you laugh for a long time. I don't think I've *ever* heard you laugh in your office."

Which was another reason to laugh. And he did.

She frowned, concern in her eyes.

Harry stopped smiling. He looked at her gravely. "Listen, I want you to take the rest of the day off."

She looked mystified. "But . . . it's quitting time, Doctor."

"Joke," he explained. "It was a joke. See you tomorrow."

Miriam eyed him cautiously, unable, it seemed, to shake the quizzical expression from her face. "You're sure you're all right?"

"I'm fine. Good night."

" 'Night, Doctor."

A moment later he heard the front door to the office click shut.

He spun around in his chair once more, reflecting: Patsy Randolph . . . I can save you and you can save me.

And Dr. Harry Bernstein was a man badly in need of saving.

Because he hated what he did for a living.

Not the business of helping patients with their mental and emotional problems—oh, he was a natural-born therapist. None better. What he hated was practicing Upper East Side psychiatry. It had been the last thing he'd ever wanted to do. But in his second year of Columbia Medical School the tall, handsome student met the tall, beautiful assistant development director of the Museum of Modern Art. Harry and Linda were married before he started his internship. He moved out of his fifth-floor walk-up near Harlem and into her town house on East Eighty-first. Within weeks she'd begun changing his life. Linda was a woman who had high aspirations for her man (very similar to Patsy, in whose offhand comment several weeks ago about her husband's lack of ambition Harry had seen reams of anger). Linda wanted money, she wanted to be on the regulars list for benefits at the Met, she wanted to be pampered at four-star restaurants in Eze and Monaco and Paris.

A studious, easygoing man from a modest suburb of New York, Harry knew that by listening to Linda he was headed in the wrong direction. But he was in love with her so he continued to listen. They bought a co-op in a high-rise on Madison Avenue and he hung up his shingle (well, a heavy, brass plaque) outside this three-thousand-dollar-a-month office on Park and Seventy-eighth.

At first Harry had worried about the astronomical bills they were amassing. But soon the money was flowing in. He had no trouble getting business; there's no lack of neuroses among the rich, and the insured, on the isle of Manhattan. He was also very good at what he did. His patients came and they liked him and so they returned weekly.

"Nobody understands me sure we've got money but money isn't everything and the other day my housekeeper looks at me like I'm from outer space and it's not my fault and I get so angry when my mother wants to go shopping on my one day off and I think Samuel's seeing someone and I think my son's gay and I just cannot lose these fifteen pounds . . ."

Their troubles may have been plebeian, even laughably minor at times, but his oath, as well as his character, wouldn't let Harry minimize them. He worked hard to help his patients.

And all the while he neglected what he really wanted to do. Which was to treat severe mental cases. People who were paranoid schizophrenics, people with bipolar depression and borderline personalities—people who led sorrowful lives and couldn't hide from that sorrow with the money that Harry's patients had.

From time to time he had volunteered at various clinics—particularly a small one in Brooklyn that treated homeless men and women—but with his Park Avenue caseload and his wife's regimen of social obligations, there had been no way he could devote much time to the clinic. He'd wrestled with the thought of just chucking his Park Avenue practice. Of course, if he'd done that, his income would have dropped by ninety percent. He and Linda had had two children a couple of years after they'd gotten married—two sweet daughters Harry loved very much—and their needs, very *expensive* needs, private school sorts of needs, had taken priority over his personal contentment. Besides, as idealistic as he was in many ways, Harry had known that Linda would leave him in a flash if he'd started working full-time in Brooklyn.

But the irony was that even after Linda *did* leave him—for someone she'd met at one of the society benefits that Harry couldn't bear to attend—he hadn't been able to spend any more time at the clinic than he had when he'd been married. The debts

Linda had run up while they were married were excruciating. His oldest daughter was in an expensive college and his younger was on her way to Vassar next year.

Yet, out of the dozens of patients who whined about minor dissatisfactions, here came Patsy Randolph, a truly desperate patient: a woman telling him about ghosts, about her husband trying to drive her insane, a woman clearly on the brink.

A patient, at last, who would give Harry a chance to redeem his life.

That night he didn't bother with dinner. He came home and went straight into his den, where sat stacked in high piles a year's worth of the professional journals that he'd never bothered to read since they dealt with serious psychiatric issues and didn't much affect the patients in his practice. He kicked his shoes off and began sifting through them, taking notes. He found Internet sites devoted to psychotic behavior and he spent hours online, downloading articles that could help him with Patsy's situation.

Harry was rereading an obscure article in the *Journal of Psychoses*, which he'd been thrilled to find—it was the key to dealing with her case—when he sat up, hearing a shrill whistle. He'd been so preoccupied . . . had he forgotten he'd put on the tea kettle for coffee? But then he glanced out the window and realized that it wasn't the kettle at all. The sound was from a bird sitting on a branch nearby, singing. The hour was well past dawn.

■

At her next session Patsy looked worse than she had the week before. Her clothes weren't pressed. Her hair was matted and hadn't been shampooed for days, it seemed. Her white blouse was streaked with dirt and the collar was torn, as was her skirt. There were runs in her stockings. Only her makeup was carefully done.

"Hello, Doctor," she said in a soft voice. She sounded timid.

"Hi, Patsy, come on in. . . . No, not the couch today. Sit across from me."

She hesitated. "Why?"

"I think we'll postpone our usual work and deal with this crisis. About the voices. I'd like to see you face-to-face."

"Crisis," she repeated the word warily as she sat in the comfortable armchair across from his desk. She crossed her arms, looked out the window—these were all body-language messages that Harry recognized well. They meant she was nervous and defensive.

"Now, what's been happening since I saw you last?" he asked.

She told him. There'd been more voices—her husband kept pretending to be the ghost of her father, whispering terrible things to her. What, Harry asked, had the ghost said? She answered: what a bad daughter she'd been, what a terrible wife she was now, what a shallow friend. Why didn't she just kill herself and quit bringing pain to everyone's life?

Harry jotted a note. "Did it sound like your father's voice? The tone, I mean?"

"Not my *father*," she said, her voice cracking with anger. "It was my *husband*, pretending to be my father. I told you that."

"I know. But the sound? The timbre?"

She thought. "Maybe. But my husband had met him. And there are videos of dad. Peter must've heard them and impersonated him."

"Where was Peter when you heard him?"

She studied a bookshelf. "He wasn't exactly home."

"He wasn't?"

"No. He went out for cigarettes. But I figured out how he did it. He must've rigged up some kind of a speaker and tape recorder. Or maybe one of those walkie-talkie things." Her voice faded.

"Peter's also a good mimic. You know, doing impersonations. So he could do *all* the voices."

"*All* of them?"

She cleared her throat. "There were more ghosts this time." Her voice rising again, manically. "My grandfather. My mother. Others. I don't even know who." Patsy stared at him for a moment then looked down. She clicked her purse latch compulsively, then looked inside, took out her compact and lipstick. She stared at the makeup, put it away. Her hands were shaking.

Harry waited a long moment. "Patsy . . . I want to ask you something."

"You can ask me anything, Doctor."

"Just assume—for the sake of argument—that Peter wasn't pretending to be the ghosts. Where else could they be coming from?"

She snapped, "You don't believe a word of this, do you?"

The most difficult part of being a therapist is making sure your patients know you're on their side, while you continue pursuing the truth. He said evenly, "It's certainly possible—what you're saying about your husband. But let's put that aside and consider that there's another reason for the voices."

"Which is?"

"That you did hear something—maybe your husband on the phone, maybe the TV, maybe the radio but whatever it was had nothing to do with ghosts. You projected your own thoughts onto what you heard."

"You're saying it's all in my head."

"I'm saying that maybe the words themselves are originating in your subconscious. What do you think about that?"

She considered this for a moment. "I don't know. . . . It could be. I suppose that makes some sense."

Harry smiled. "That's good, Patsy. That's a good first step, admitting that."

She seemed pleased, a student who'd been given a gold star by a teacher.

Then the psychiatrist grew serious. "Now, one thing: When the voices talk about your hurting yourself . . . you're not going to listen to them, are you?"

"No, I won't." She offered a brave smile. "Of course not."

"Good." He glanced at the clock. "I see our time's just about up, Patsy. I want you to do something. I want you to keep a diary of what the voices say to you."

"A diary? All right."

"Write down everything they say and we'll go through it together."

She rose. Turned to him. "Maybe I should just ask one of the ghosts to come along to a session . . . but then you'd have to charge me double, wouldn't you?"

He laughed. "See you next week."

■

At three A.M. the next morning Harry was wakened by a phone call.

"Dr. Bernstein?"

"Yes?"

"I'm Officer Kavanaugh with the police department."

Sitting up, trying to shake off his drowsiness, he thought immediately of Herb, a patient at the clinic in Brooklyn. The poor man, a mild schizophrenic who was completely harmless, was forever getting beat up because of his gruff, threatening manner.

But that wasn't the reason for the call.

"You're Mrs. Patricia Randolph's psychiatrist. Is that correct?"

His heart thudded hard. "Yes, I am. Is she all right?"

"We've had a call. . . . We found her on the street outside her apartment. No one's hurt but she's a bit hysterical."

"I'll be right there."

■

When he arrived at the Randolphs' apartment building, ten blocks away, Harry found Patsy and her husband in the front lobby. A uniformed policeman stood next to them.

Harry knew that the Randolphs were wealthy but the building was much nicer than he'd expected. It was one of the luxurious high-rises that Donald Trump had built in the eighties. There were penthouse triplexes selling for $20 million, Harry had read in the *Times*.

"Doctor," Patsy cried when she saw Harry. She ran to him. Harry was careful about physical contact with his patients. He knew all about transference and countertransference—the perfectly normal attraction between patients and their therapists— but contact had to be handled carefully. Harry took Patsy by the shoulders so that she couldn't hug him and led her back to the lobby couch.

"Mr. Randolph?" Harry asked, turning to her husband.

"That's right."

"I'm Harry Bernstein."

The men shook hands. Peter Randolph was very much what Harry was expecting. He was a trim, athletic man of about forty. Handsome. His eyes were angry and bewildered and looked victimized. He reminded Harry of a patient he'd treated briefly—a man whose sole complaint was that he was having trouble maintaining a life with a wife and two mistresses. Peter wore a burgundy silk bathrobe and supple leather slippers.

"Would you mind if I spoke to Patsy alone?" Harry asked him.

"No. I'll be upstairs if you need me." He said this to both Harry and the police officer.

Harry too glanced at the cop, who also stepped away and let the doctor talk to his patient.

"What happened?" Harry asked Patsy.

"The bird," she said, choking back tears.

"One of the ceramic birds?"

"Yes," she whispered. "He broke it."

Harry studied her carefully. She was in bad shape tonight. Hair stringy, robe filthy, fingernails unclean. As in her session the other day, only her makeup was normal.

"Tell me about what happened."

"I was asleep and then I heard this voice say, 'Run! You have to get out. They're almost here. They're going to hurt you.' And I jumped out of bed and ran into the living room and there—there was a Boehm bird. The robin. It was shattered and scattered all over the floor. I started screaming—because I knew they were after me." Her voice rose. "The ghosts . . . They . . . I mean, *Peter* was after me. I just threw on my robe and es-caped."

"And what did Peter do?"

"He ran after me."

"But he didn't hurt you?"

She hesitated. "No." She looked around the cold, marble lobby with paranoid eyes. "Well, what he did was he called the po-lice. . . . But don't you see? Peter didn't have any choice. He *had* to call the police. Isn't that what somebody would normally do if their wife ran out of the apartment, screaming? *Not* calling them would have been suspicious. . . ." Her voice faded.

Harry looked for signs of overmedication or drinking. He could see none. She looked around the lobby once more.

"Are you feeling better now?"

She nodded. "I'm sorry," she said. "Making you come all the way over here tonight."

"That's what I'm here for. . . . Tell me: You don't hear any voices now, do you?"

"No."

"And the bird? Could it have been an accident?"

She thought about this for a moment. "Well, Peter *was* asleep. . . . Maybe I was looking at it earlier and left it on the edge of the table." She sounded perfectly reasonable. "Maybe the housekeeper did. I *might've* bumped it."

The policeman looked at his watch and then ambled over. He asked, "Can I talk to you, Doctor?"

They stepped into a corner of the lobby.

"I'm thinking I oughta take her downtown," the cop said in a Queens drawl. "She was pretty outta control before. But it's your call. You think she's ED?"

Emotionally disturbed—the trigger diagnosis for involuntary commitment. If he said, yes, Patsy would be taken off and hospitalized.

This was the critical moment. Harry debated.

I can help you and you can help me. . . .

He said to the cop, "Give me a minute."

He returned to Patsy, sat down next to her. "We have a problem. The police want to take you to a hospital. And if you claim that Peter's trying to drive you crazy or hurt you, the fact is the judge just isn't going to believe you."

"Me? *I'm* not doing anything! It's the voices! It's them . . . I mean, it's Peter."

"But they're not going to believe you. That's just the way it is. Now, you can go back upstairs and carry on with your life or they can take you downtown to the city hospital. And you don't want that. Believe me. Can you stay in control?"

She lowered her head to her hands. Finally she said, "Yes, Doctor, I can."

"Good . . . Patsy, I want to ask you something else. I want to see your husband alone. Can I call him, have him come in?"

"Why?" she asked, her face dark with suspicion.

"Because I'm your doctor and I want to get to the bottom of what's bothering you."

She glanced at the cop. Gave him a dark look. Then she said to Harry, "Sure."

"Good."

After Patsy'd disappeared into the elevator car the cop said, "I don't know, Doctor. She seems like a nut case to me. Things like this . . . they can get real ugly. I've seen it a million times."

"She's got some problems but she's not dangerous."

"You're willing to take that chance?"

After a moment he said, "Yes, I'm willing to take that chance."

■

"How was she last night, after I left?" Harry asked Peter Randolph the next morning. The two men sat in Harry's office.

"She seemed all right. Calmer." Peter sipped the coffee that Miriam had brought him. "What exactly is going on with her?"

"I'm sorry," Harry said. "I can't discuss the specifics of your wife's condition with you. Confidentiality."

Peter's eyes flared angrily for a moment. "Then why did you ask me here?"

"Because I need you to help me treat her. You do want her to get better, don't you?"

"Of course I do. I love her very much." He sat forward in the chair. "But I don't understand what's going on. She was fine until a couple of months ago—when she started seeing *you,* if you have to know the truth. Then things started to go bad."

"When people see therapists they sometimes confront issues they've never had to deal with. I think that was Patsy's situation. She's getting close to some important issues. And that can be very disorienting."

"She claims I'm pretending to be a ghost," Peter said sarcastically. "That seems a little worse than just disoriented."

"She's in a downward spiral. I can pull her out of it . . . but it'll be hard. And I'll need your help."

Peter shrugged. "What can I do?"

Harry explained, "First of all, you can be honest with me."

"Of course."

"For some reason she's come to associate you with her father. She has a lot of resentment toward him and she's projecting that onto you. Do you know why she's mad at you?"

There was silence for a moment.

"Go on, tell me. Anything you say here is confidential—just between you and me."

"She might have this stupid idea that I've cheated on her."

"Have you?"

"Where the hell do you get off, asking a question like that?"

Harry said reasonably, "I'm just trying to get to the truth."

Randolph calmed down. "No, I haven't cheated on her. She's paranoid."

"And you haven't said or done anything that might trouble her deeply or affect her sense of reality?"

"No," Peter said.

"How much is she worth?" Harry asked bluntly.

Peter blinked. "You mean, her portfolio?"

"Net worth."

"I don't know exactly. About eleven million."

Harry nodded. "And the money's all hers, isn't it?"

A frown crossed Peter Randolph's face. "What're you asking?"

"I'm asking, if Patsy were to go insane or to kill herself would you get her money?"

"Go to hell!" Randolph shouted, standing up quickly. For a moment Harry thought the man was going to hit him. But he pulled his wallet from his hip pocket and took out a card. Tossed it onto Harry's desk. "That's our lawyer. Call him and ask him about the prenuptial agreement. If Patricia's declared insane or if she were to die the money goes into a trust. I don't get a penny."

Harry pushed the card back. "That won't be necessary. . . . I'm sorry if I hurt your feelings," he said. "My patient's care comes before everything else. I had to know there's no motive for harming her."

Randolph adjusted his cuffs and buttoned his jacket. "Accepted."

Harry nodded and looked Peter Randolph over carefully. A prerequisite for being a therapist is the ability to judge character quickly. He now sized up this man and came to a decision. "I want to try something radical with Patsy and I want you to help me."

"Radical? You mean commit her?"

"No, that'd be the worst thing for her. When patients are going through times like this you can't coddle them. You have to be tough. And force *them* to be tough."

"Meaning?"

"Don't be antagonistic but force her to stay involved in life. She's going to want to withdraw—to be pampered. But don't spoil her. If she says she's too upset to go shopping or go out to dinner, don't let her get away with it. Insist that she does what she's supposed to do."

"You're sure that's best?"

Sure? Harry asked himself. No, he wasn't the least bit sure.

But he'd made his decision. He had to push Patsy hard. He told Peter, "We don't have any choice."

But after the man left the office Harry happened to recall an expression one of his medical school professors had used frequently. He'd said you have to attack disease head-on. *"You have to kill or cure."*

Harry hadn't thought of that expression in years. He wished he hadn't today.

■

The next day Patsy walked into his office without an appointment.

In Brooklyn, at the clinic, this was standard procedure and nobody thought anything of it. But in a Park Avenue shrink's office impromptu sessions were taboo. Still, Harry could see from her face that she was very upset and he didn't make an issue of her unexpected appearance.

She collapsed on the couch and hugged herself closely as he rose and closed the door.

"Patsy, what's the matter?" he asked.

He noticed that her clothes were more disheveled than he'd ever seen. They were stained and torn. Hair bedraggled. Fingernails dirty.

"Everything was going so well," she sobbed, "then I was sitting in the den early this morning and I heard my father's ghost again. He said, 'They're almost here. You don't have much time left. . . . ' And I asked, 'What do you mean?' And he said, 'Look in the living room.' And I did and there was another one of my birds! It was shattered!" She opened her purse and showed Harry the broken pieces of ceramic. "Now, there's only one left! I'm going to die when it breaks. I know I am. Peter's going to break it tonight! And then he'll kill me."

"He's not going to kill you, Patsy," Harry said calmly, patiently ignoring her hysteria.

"I think I should go to the hospital for a while, Doctor."

Harry got up and sat on the couch next to her. He took her hand. "No."

"What?"

"It would be a mistake," Harry said.

"Why?" she cried.

"Because you can't hide from these issues. You have to confront them."

"I'd feel safer in a hospital. Nobody'd try to kill me in the hospital."

"Nobody's going to kill you, Patsy. You have to believe me."

"No! Peter—"

"But Peter's never tried to hurt you, has he?"

A pause. "No."

"Okay, here's what I want you to do. Listen to me. Are you listening?"

"Yes."

"You know that whether Peter was pretending to say those words to you or you were imagining them *they weren't real.* Repeat that."

"I—"

"Repeat it!"

"They weren't real."

"Now say, 'There was no ghost. My father's dead.' "

"There was no ghost. My father's dead."

"Good!" Harry laughed. "Again."

She repeated this mantra several times, calming each time. Finally a faint smile crossed her lips. Then she frowned. "But the bird . . ." She again opened her purse and took out the shattered ceramic, cradling the pieces in her trembling hand.

"Whatever happened to the bird doesn't matter. It's only a piece of porcelain."

"But . . ." She looked down at the broken shards.

Harry leaned forward. "Listen to me, Patsy. Listen carefully." Passionately the doctor said, "I want you to go home, take that last bird and smash the hell out of it."

"You want me to . . ."

"Take a hammer and crush it."

She started to protest but then she smiled. "Can I do that?"

"You bet you can. Just give yourself permission to. Go home, have a nice glass of wine, find a hammer and smash it." He reached under his desk and picked up the wastebasket. He held it out for her. "They're just pieces of china, Patsy."

After a moment she tossed the pieces of the statue into the container.

"Good, Patsy." And—thinking, the hell with transference—the doctor gave his patient a huge hug.

■

That evening Patsy Randolph returned home and found Peter sitting in front of the television.

"You're late," he said. "Where've you been?"

"Out shopping. I got a bottle of wine."

"We're supposed to go to Jack and Louise's tonight. Don't tell me you forgot."

"I don't feel like it," she said. "I don't feel well. I—"

"No. We're going. You're not getting out of it." He spoke in that same weird, abrupt tone he'd been using for the past week.

"Well, can I at least take care of a few things first?"

"Sure. But I don't want to be late."

Patsy walked into the kitchen, opened a bottle of the expen-

sive Merlot and poured a large glass just like Dr. Bernstein had
told her. She sipped it. She felt good. Very good. "Where's the
hammer?" she called.

"Hammer? What do you need the hammer for?"

"I have to fix something."

"I think it's in the drawer beside the refrigerator."

She found it. Carried it into the living room. She glanced at
the last Boehm bird, an owl.

Peter looked at the tool then back to the TV. "What do you
have to fix?"

"You," she answered and brought the blunt end down on the
top of his head with all her strength.

It took another dozen blows to kill him and when she'd finished she stood back and gazed at the remarkable patterns the
blood made on the carpet and couch. Then she went into the bedroom and picked up her diary from the bedside table—the one Dr.
Bernstein had suggested she keep. Back in the living room Patsy
sat down beside her husband's corpse and she wrote a rambling
passage in the booklet about how, at last, she'd gotten the ghosts
to stop speaking to her. She was finally at peace. She didn't add as
much as she wanted to; it was very time-consuming to write using
your finger for a pen and blood for ink.

When Patsy'd finished she picked up the hammer and
smashed the Boehm ceramic owl into dust. Then she began
screaming as loudly as she could, "The ghosts are dead, the
ghosts are dead, the ghosts are dead!"

Long before she was hoarse the police and medics arrived.
When they took her away she was wearing a straitjacket.

∎

A week later Harry Bernstein sat in the prison hospital waiting
room. He knew he was a sight—he hadn't shaved in several days

and was wearing wrinkled clothes—which in fact he'd slept in last night. He stared at the filthy floor.

"You all right?" This question came from a tall, thin man with a perfect beard. He wore a gorgeous suit and Armani-framed glasses. He was Patsy's lead defense lawyer.

"I never thought she'd do it," Harry said to him. "I *knew* there was risk. I *knew* something was wrong. But I thought I had everything under control."

The lawyer looked at him sympathetically. "I heard you've been having some trouble too. Your patients . . ."

Harry laughed bitterly. "Are quitting in droves. Well, wouldn't you? Park Avenue shrinks are a dime a dozen. Why should they risk seeing me? I might get them killed or committed."

The jailor opened the door. "Dr. Bernstein, you can see the prisoner now."

He stood slowly, supporting himself on the door frame.

The lawyer looked him over and said, "You and I can meet in the next couple days to decide how to handle the case. The insanity defense is tough in New York but with you on board I can make it work. We'll keep her out of jail. . . . Say, Doctor, you going to be okay?"

Harry gave a shallow nod.

The lawyer said kindly, "I can arrange for a little cash for you. A couple thousand—for an expert witness fee."

"Thanks," Harry said. But he instantly forgot about the money. His mind was already on his patient.

■

The room was as bleak as he'd expected.

Face white, eyes shrunken, Patsy lay in bed, looking out the window. She glanced at Harry, didn't seem to recognize him.

"How are you feeling?" he asked.

"Who are you?" She frowned.

He didn't answer her question either. "You're not looking too bad, Patsy."

"I think I know you. Yes, you're . . . Wait, are you a ghost?"

"No, I'm not a ghost." Harry set his attaché case on the table. Her eyes slipped to the case as he opened it.

"I can't stay long, Patsy. I'm closing my practice. There's a lot to take care of. But I wanted to bring you a few things."

"Things?" she asked, sounding like a child. "For me? Like Christmas. Like my birthday."

"Uh-hum." Harry rummaged in the case. "Here's the first thing." He took out a photocopy. "It's an article in the *Journal of Psychoses*. I found it the night after the session when you first told me about the ghosts. You should read it."

"I can't read," she said. "I don't know how." She gave a crazy laugh. "I'm afraid of the food here. I think there are spies around. They're going to put things in the food. Disgusting things. And poison. Or broken glass." Another cackle.

Harry set the article on the bed next to her. He walked to the window. No trees here. No birds. Just gray, downtown Manhattan.

He said, glancing back at her, "It's all about ghosts. The article."

Her eyes narrowed and then fear consumed her face. "Ghosts," she whispered. "Are there ghosts here?"

Harry laughed hard. "See, Patsy, ghosts were the first clue. After you mentioned them in that session—claiming that your husband was driving you crazy—I thought something didn't sound quite right. So I went home and started to research your case."

She gazed at him silently.

"That article's about the importance of diagnosis in mental health cases. See, sometimes it works to somebody's advantage to *appear* to be mentally unstable—so they can avoid responsibility. Say, soldiers who don't want to fight. People faking insurance claims. People who've committed crimes." He turned back. "Or who're *about* to commit a crime."

"I'm afraid of ghosts," Patsy said, her voice rising. "I'm afraid of ghosts. I don't want any ghosts here! I'm afraid of—"

Harry continued like a lecturing professor. "And ghosts are one of the classic hallucinations that sane people use to try to convince other people that they're insane."

Patsy closed her mouth.

"Fascinating article," Harry continued, nodding toward it. "See, ghosts and spirits *seem* like the products of delusional minds. But in fact they're complex metaphysical concepts that someone who's really insane wouldn't understand at all. No, true psychotics believe that the actual *person* is there speaking to them. They think that Napoleon or Hitler or Marilyn Monroe is really in the room with them. You wouldn't have claimed to've heard your father's *ghost.* You would actually have heard *him.*"

Harry enjoyed the utterly shocked expression on his patient's face. He said, "Then a few weeks ago you admitted that maybe the voices were in your head. A true psychotic would never admit that. They'd swear they were completely sane." He paced slowly. "There were some other things too. You must've read somewhere that sloppy physical appearance is a sign of mental illness. Your clothes were torn and dirty, you'd forget to do straps . . . but your makeup was always perfect—even on the night the police called me over to your apartment. In genuine mental health cases makeup is the first thing to go. Patients just smear their faces with it. Has to do with issues of masking their identity—if you're interested.

"Oh, and remember? You asked if a ghost could come to one of our sessions? That was very funny. But the psychiatric literature defines humor as ironic juxtaposition of concepts based on common experience. Of course that's contrary to the mental processes of psychotics."

"What the hell does that mean?" Patsy spat out.

"That crazy people don't make jokes," he summarized. "That cinched it for me that you were sane as could be." Harry looked through the attaché case once more. "Next . . ." He looked up, smiling. "After I read that article and decided you were faking your diagnosis—and listening to what your subconscious was telling me about your marriage—I figured you were using me for some reason having to do with your husband. So I hired a private eye."

"Jesus Christ, you did what?"

"Here's his report." He dropped the folder on the bed. "It says basically that your husband *was* having an affair and was forging checks on your main investment account. You knew about his mistress and the money and you'd talked to a lawyer about divorcing him. But Peter knew that *you* were having an affair too—with your friend Sally's husband. Peter used that to blackmail you into not divorcing him."

Patsy stared at him, frozen.

He nodded at the report. "Oh, you may as well look at it. Pretending you can't read? Doesn't fly. Reading has nothing to do with psychotic behavior: it's a developmental and IQ issue."

She opened the report, read through it then tossed it aside disgustedly. "Son of a bitch."

Harry said, "You wanted to kill Peter and you wanted me to establish that you were insane—for your defense. You'd go into a private hospital. There'd be a mandatory rehearing in a year and, bang, you'd pass the tests and be released."

She shook her head. "But you knew my goal was to kill Peter—and you let me do it! Hell, you *encouraged* me to do it."

"And when I saw Peter I encouraged *him* to antagonize you. . . . It was time to move things along. I was getting tired of our sessions." Then Harry's face darkened with genuine regret. "I never thought you'd actually kill him, just assault him. But, hey, what can I say? Psychiatry's an inexact science."

"But why didn't you go to the police?" she said, whispering, close to panic.

"Ah, that has to do with the third thing I brought for you."

I can help you and you can help me. . . .

He lifted an envelope out of his briefcase. He handed it to her.

"What is this?"

"My bill."

She opened it. Took out the sheet of paper.

At the top was written *For Services Rendered*. And below that: *$10 million.*

"Are you crazy?" Patsy gasped.

Given the present location and context of their conversation, Harry had to laugh at her choice of words. "Peter was nice enough to tell me exactly what you were worth. I'm leaving you a million . . . which you'll probably need to pay that slick lawyer of yours. He looks expensive. Now, I'll need cash or a certified check before I testify at your trial. Otherwise I'll have to share with the court my honest diagnosis about your condition."

"You're blackmailing me!"

"I guess I am."

"Why?"

"Because with this money I can afford to do some good. And help people who really need helping." He nodded at the bill. "I'd write that check pretty soon—they have the death penalty in New

York now. Oh, and by the way, I'd lose that bit about the food being poisoned. Around here, you make a stink about meals, they'll just put you on a tube." He picked up his attaché case.

"Wait," she begged. "Don't leave! Let's talk about this!"

"Sorry." Harry nodded at a wall clock. "I see our time is up."

H e'd found her already.

Oh, no, she thought. Lord, no . . .

Eyes filling with tears of despair, wracked with nausea, the young woman sagged against the window frame as she stared through a crack in the blinds.

The battered Ford pickup—as gray as the turbulent Atlantic Ocean a few hundred yards up the road—eased to a stop in front of her house in this pretty neighborhood of Crowell, Massachusetts, north of Boston. This was the very truck she'd come to dread, the truck that regularly careened through her dreams, sometimes with its tires on fire, sometimes shooting blood from its tailpipe, sometimes piloted by an invisible driver bent on tearing her heart from her chest.

Oh, no . . .

The engine shut off and tapped as it cooled. The dusk light was failing and the interior of the pickup was dark but she knew the occupant was staring at her. In her mind she could see his features as clearly as if he were standing ten feet away in broad August sunlight. Kari Swanson knew he'd have that faint smile of impatience on his face, that he'd be tugging an earlobe marred with two piercings long ago infected and closed up, leaving an ugly scar. She knew his breathing would be labored.

Her own breath in panicked gasps, hands trembling, Kari drew back from the window. Crawling to the front hallway, she tore open the drawer of a small table and took out the pistol. She looked outside again.

The driver didn't approach the house. He simply played his all-too familiar game: sitting in the front seat of his old junker and staring at her.

He'd found her already. Just one week after she'd moved here! He'd followed her over two thousand miles. All the efforts to cover her tracks had been futile.

The brief peace she'd enjoyed was gone.

David Dale had found her.

■

Kari—born Catherine Kelley Swanson—was a sensible, pleasant-mannered twenty-eight-year-old, who'd been raised in the Midwest by a loving family. She was a natural-born student with a cum laude degree to her name and plans for a Ph.D. Her career until the move here—fashion modeling—had provided her with both a large investment account and a chance to work regularly in such pampering locales as Paris, Cape Town, London, Rio, Bali and Bermuda. She drove a nice car, had always bought herself modest but comfortable houses and had provided her parents with a plump annuity.

A seemingly enviable life . . . and yet Kari Swanson had been forever plagued by a debilitating problem.

She was utterly beautiful.

She'd hit her full height—six feet—at seventeen and her weight hadn't varied more than a pound or so off its present mark of 121. Her hair was a shimmery, natural golden (yes, yes, you could see it flying in slow motion on many a shampoo commercial) and her skin had a flawless translucent eggshell tone that often left makeup artists with little to do at photo shoots but dab on the currently in-vogue lipstick and eye shadow.

People, Details, W, Rolling Stone, Paris Match, the London *Times* and *Entertainment Weekly* had all described Kari Swanson as the "most beautiful woman in the world" or some version of that title. And virtually *every* publication in the industrialized world had run a picture of her at one time or another, many of those photos appearing on the magazines' covers.

That her spellbinding beauty could be a liability was a lesson she learned early. Young Cathy—she didn't become "Kari" the supermodel until age twenty—longed for a normal teenhood but her appearance kept derailing that. She was drawn to the scholastic and artistic crowds in high school but they rejected her point-blank, assuming either that she was a flighty airhead or was mocking the gawky students in those circles.

On the other hand, she was fiercely courted by the cliqueish in-crowd of cheerleaders and athletes, few of whom she could stand. To her embarrassment she was regularly elected queen of various school pageants and dances, even when she refused to compete for the titles.

The dating situation was even more impossible. Most of the nice, interesting boys froze like rabbits in front of her and didn't have the courage to ask her out, assuming they'd be rejected. The jocks and studs relentlessly pursued her—though their motive, of course, was simply to be seen in public with the most beautiful girl in school or to bed her as a trophy lay (naturally none succeeded, but stinging rumors abounded; it seemed that the more adamant the rejection, the more the spurned boy bragged about his conquest).

Her four years at Stanford were virtually the same—modeling, schoolwork and hours of loneliness, interrupted by rare evenings and weekends with the few friends who didn't care what she looked like (tellingly, her first lover—a man she was still friendly with—was blind).

After graduation she'd hoped that life would be different,

that the spell of her beauty wouldn't be as potent with those who were older and busy making their way in the world. How wrong that was . . . Men remained true to their dubious mission and, ignoring Kari the person, pursued her as greedily and thoughtlessly as ever. Women grew even more resentful of her than in school, as their figures changed, thanks to children and age and sedentary lives.

Kari threw herself into her modeling, easily getting assignments with Ford, Elite and the other top agencies. But her successful career created a curious irony. She was desperately lonely and yet she had no privacy. Simply because she was beautiful, complete strangers considered themselves intimate friends and constantly approached her in public or sent her long letters describing their intimate secrets, begging for advice and offering her their own opinions on what she should do with her life.

She grew to hate the simple activities that she'd enjoyed as a child—Christmas shopping, playing softball, fishing, jogging. A trip to the grocery store was often a horror; men would speed into line behind her at the checkout stand and flirt mercilessly. More than once she fled, leaving behind a full cart.

But she never felt any real terror until David Dale, the man in the gray pickup truck.

Kari had first noticed him in a crowd of onlookers when she was on a job for *Vogue* two years ago.

People always watched photo shoots, of course. They were fascinated with physiques they would never have, with designer clothes that cost their monthly salary, with the gorgeous faces they'd seen gazing at them from newsstands around the country. But something had seemed different about this man. Something troubling.

Not just his massive size—well over six feet tall with huge legs and heavy thighs, long, dangling arms. What had bothered

her was the way he'd looked at her through his chunky, out-of-fashion glasses—his expression had been one of familiarity.

As if he knew a great deal about her.

And with a chill Kari had realized that *he* was familiar to *her* too—she'd seen him at other shoots.

Hell, she'd thought, I've got a stalker.

At first David Dale would simply appear at shoots like the one in Pacific Grove, California, parking his pickup truck nearby and standing silently just outside the ring of activity. Then she began to see him around the modeling agencies that repped her.

He began to write her long letters about himself: his lonely, troubled childhood, his parents' deaths, his former girlfriends (the stories sounded made-up), his current job as an environmental engineer (Kari read "janitor"), his struggle with his weight, his love of Dungeons & Dragons games, television shows he watched. He also knew a frightening amount of information about her—where she'd grown up, what she'd studied at Stanford, her likes and dislikes. He'd clearly read all of the interviews she'd ever given. He took to sending her presents, usually innocuous things like slippers, Day-Timers, picture frames, pen-and-pencil sets. Disturbingly, he'd sometimes send her lingerie: tasteful Victoria's Secret items, in her exact size, with a gift receipt courteously enclosed. She threw everything out.

Kari generally ignored Dale but the first time he'd parked his gray pickup in front of her house in Santa Monica, California, she'd stormed up to and confronted him. Tugging at his damaged ear, breathing in an asthmatic, eerie way, he ignored her rage and simply stared at her with an adoring gaze as he studied her face, muttering, "Beautiful, beautiful." Upset, she returned to her house. Dale, however, happily pulled out a thermos and began sipping coffee. He remained parked on the street until midnight—a practice that would soon become a daily ritual.

Dale would dog her on the street. He'd sit in restaurants where she was eating and occasionally have a bottle of cheap wine sent to her table. She kept her phone number unlisted and had her mail sent to her agent's office but he still managed to get notes delivered to her. Kari was one of the few people in America without e-mail on her computer; she was sure that Dale would find her address and inundate her with messages.

She went to the police, of course, and they did what they could but it wasn't much. On the cops' first visit to Dale's ramshackle condo in a low-rent neighborhood, they found a copy of the state's antistalking statute sitting prominently on his coffee table. Sections were underlined; David Dale knew exactly how far he could go. Still, Kari convinced a magistrate to issue a restraining order. Since Dale had never done anything exactly illegal, though, the order was limited to preventing him from setting foot on her property itself. Which he'd never done anyway.

The incident that finally pushed her over the edge occurred last month. Dale had made a practice of following the few men whom Kari had the effrontery to date. In this case it'd been a young TV producer. One day Dale had walked into the man's health club in Century City and had a brief conversation with him. The producer had broken their date that night, leaving the harsh message that he would've appreciated it if she'd told him she was engaged. He never returned Kari's calls.

That incident had warranted another visit from the police but the cops found Dale's condo empty and the pickup gone when they'd arrived.

But Kari knew he'd be back. And so she'd decided it was time to end the problem once and for all. She'd never intended to be a model for more than a few years and she'd figured that this was a good time to quit. Telling only her parents and a few close friends, she'd instructed a real estate company to lease her house and moved to Crowell, Massachusetts, a town she'd been to several years before on a photo shoot. She'd spent a few days here after the assignment and had fallen in love with the clean air and dramatic coastline—and with the citizens of the town too. They were friendly but refreshingly reserved toward her; a beautiful face didn't place very high on the scale of austere New England values.

She'd left L.A. at two A.M. on a Sunday morning, taking mostly back streets, doubling back and pausing often until she was sure she'd evaded Dale. As she'd driven across the country, elated at the prospect of a new life, she'd occupied much of her time with a fantasy about Dale's committing suicide.

But now she knew that the son of a bitch was very much alive. And somehow had found out where she'd moved.

Tonight, huddled in the living room of her new house, she heard his pickup's engine start. It idled roughly, the exhaust bubbling from the rusty pipe—sounds she'd grown oh-too-familiar with over the past few years. Slowly the vehicle drove away.

Crying quietly now, Kari rested her head on the carpet. She closed her eyes. Nine hours later she awoke and found herself on her side, knees drawn up, clutching the thirty-eight-caliber pistol to her chest, the same way that, as a little girl, she'd wake up every morning, curled into a ball and cuddling a stuffed bear she'd named Bonnie.

■

Later that morning an embittered Kari Swanson was sitting in the office of Detective Brad Loesser, head of the Felonies Division of the Crowell, Massachusetts, Police Department.

A solid, balding man with sun-baked freckles across the bridge of his nose, Loesser listened to her story with sympathy. He shook his head then asked, "How'd he find out you were here?"

She shrugged. "Hired a private eye, for all I know." David

Dale was exactly as resourceful as he needed to be when it came to Kari Swanson.

"Sid!" the detective shouted to a plainclothes officer in a cubicle nearby.

The trim young man appeared. Loesser introduced Kari to Sid Harper. Loesser briefed his assistant and said, "Check this guy out and get me the records from . . ." He glanced at Kari. "What police department'd have his file?"

She said angrily, "That'd be departments, Detective. Plural. I'd start with Santa Monica, Los Angeles and the California State Police. Then you might want to talk to Burbank, Beverly Hills, Glendale and Orange County. I moved around a bit to get away from him."

"Brother," Loesser said, shaking his head.

Sid Harper returned a few minutes later.

"L.A.'s overnighting us their file. Santa Monica's is coming in two days. And I ran the Mass real estate records round here." He glanced at a slip of paper. "David Dale bought a condo in Park View two days ago. That's about a quarter mile from Ms. Swanson's place."

"*Bought?*" Loesser asked, surprised.

"He says it makes him feel closer to me if he owns a house in the same town," Kari explained, shaking her head.

"We'll talk to him, Miss Swanson. And we'll keep an eye on your house. If he does anything overt you can get a restraining order."

"That won't stop him," she scoffed. "You know that."

"Our hands're pretty much tied."

She slapped her leg hard. "I've been hearing that for years. It's time to *do* something." Kari's eyes strayed to a rack of shotguns on the wall nearby. When she looked back she found the detective was studying her closely.

Loesser sent Sid Harper back to his cubicle and then said, "Hey, got something to show you, Ms. Swanson." Loesser reached forward and lifted a picture frame off his desk and handed it to her. "The snapshot on the left there. Whatta you think?"

A picture of a grinning, freckled teenage boy was on the right. On the left side was a shot of a young woman in a gradua- tion gown and mortarboard.

" 'S'my daughter. Elaine."

"She's pretty. You going to ask me if she's got a future in modeling?"

"No, ma'am, I wasn't. See, my girl's twenty-five, almost the same age as you. You know something—she's got her whole life ahead of her. Tons and tons of good things waiting. Husband, kids, traveling, jobs."

Kari looked up from the picture into the detective's placid face. He continued, "You got the same things to look forward to, Miss Swanson. I know this's been hell for you and it may be hell for a while to come. But if you go taking matters into your own hands, which I have a feeling you've been thinking about, well, that's gonna be the end of your life right there."

She shrugged off the advice and asked, "What's the law on self-defense here?"

"Why're you asking me a question like that?" Loesser asked in a whisper.

"What's the answer?"

The detective hesitated then said, "The commonwealth's real strict about it. Outside of your own house, even on your front porch, it's practically impossible to shoot somebody who's un- armed and get away with a self-defense claim. And, I'll tell you, we look right away to see if the body was dragged in after and maybe a knife got put into the corpse's hand." The detective paused then added, "And, I'm gonna have to be frank, Ms. Swanson, a jury's going to look at you and say, 'Well, of *course* men're going to be following her around. Moth to the flame. She ought've had a thicker skin.' "

"I better go," Kari said.

Loesser studied her for a moment then said in a heartfelt tone, "Don't go throwing your life away over some piece of trash like this crazy man."

She snapped, "I don't *have* a life. That's the problem. I thought I could get one back by moving to Crowell. That didn't work."

"We all go through rough spots from time to time. God helps us through 'em."

"I don't believe in God," Kari said, pulling on her raincoat. "He wouldn't do this to anybody."

"God didn't send David Dale after you," Loesser said.

"I don't mean that," she replied angrily. She lifted a trembling, splayed hand toward her face. "I mean, if He existed, He wouldn't be cruel enough to make me beautiful."

■

At eight P.M. a car door slammed outside of Kari Swanson's house.

It was Dale's pickup. She recognized the sound.

With shaking hands Kari set down her wine and shut off the TV, which she always watched with the sound muted so she'd have some warning if Dale decided to approach the house. She ran to the hallway table and pulled out her gun.

Outside of your own house, even on your front porch, it's practically impossible to shoot somebody who's unarmed and get away with a self-defense claim. . . .

Gripping the pistol, Kari peeked through the front-door curtain. David Dale walked slowly toward her yard, clutching a huge bouquet of flowers. He knew enough not to set foot on her property and so, still standing in the street, he bowed from the waist, the way people do when meeting royalty, and set the bouquet on the grass of the parking strip, resting an envelope next to it. He arranged the flowers carefully, as if they were sitting on a grave, then stood up and admired them. He returned to the truck and drove into the windy night.

Barefoot, Kari walked out into the cold drizzle, seized the flowers and tossed them into the trash. Returning to the front porch, she paused under the lantern and tore open the envelope, hoping that maybe Detective Loesser had spoken with Dale and frightened him into leaving. Maybe this was a good-bye message.

But, of course, this wasn't the case.

To my most Beautiful Lover—

This was a wonderful idea you had, I mean, moving to the east Coast. There were too many people in California vieing (or whatever . . . ha, you know I'm a bad speller!!!) for your love and attention and it means a lot to me that you wanted them out of your life. And quitting your modeling job so I don't have to share you with the world any more . . . You did that ALL for me!!!!

I know we'll be happy here.

I love you always and forever.

—David

P.S. Guess what? I FINALLY found that old New York Scene magazine where you modeled those lether skirts. Yes, the one I've been looking for for years! Can you believe it!!!! I was so happy! I cut you out and taped you up (so to speak, ha!!!). I have a "Kari" room in my new condo, just like the one in my old place in Glendale (which you never came to visit—boo hoo!!!) but I decided to put these pictures in my bedroom. I

got this nice light, it's very low like candle light and I leave it
on all night long. Now I even look forward to having bad
dreams so I can wake up and see you.

Walking inside, she slammed the door and clicked the three deadbolts. Sinking to her knees, she sobbed in fury until she was exhausted and her chest ached. Finally she calmed, caught her breath and wiped her face with her sleeve.

Kari stared at the pistol for a long moment then put it back in the drawer. She walked into the den and, sitting in a straight-back chair, stared into her windswept backyard. Understanding at last that the only way this nightmare would end was with David Dale's death or her own.

She turned to her desk and began rummaging through a large stack of papers.

■

The bar on West Forty-second Street was dim and stank of Lysol.

Even though Kari was dressed down—in sweats, sunglasses and a baseball cap—three of the four patrons and the bartender stared at her in astonishment, one bleary-eyed man offering her a flirty smile that revealed more gum than teeth. The fourth customer snored sloppily at the end of the bar. Everyone, except the snoozer, smoked.

She ordered a model's cocktail—Diet Coke with lemon—and sat at a table in the rear of the shabby place.

Ten minutes later a tall man with ebony skin, a massive chest and huge hands entered the bar. He squinted through the cigarette smoke and made his way to Kari's table.

He nodded at her and sat, looking around with distaste at the decrepit bar. He appeared exactly like she'd remembered him from their first meeting. That had been a year ago in the Domini-

can Republic when she'd been on a photo assignment for *Elle* and he'd been taking a day off from a project he'd been working on in nearby Haiti. When, after a few drinks, he'd told her his line of work and wondered if she might need anyone with his particular skills, she'd laughed at the absurd thought. Still, David Dale came to mind and she'd taken his phone number.

"Why didn't you want to meet at my place?" he now asked her.

"Because of him," she said, lowering her voice, as if uttering the pronoun alone could magically summon David Dale like a demon. "He follows me everywhere. I don't think he knows I came to New York. But I can't take any chances that he'd find out about you."

"Yo," the bartender's raspy voice called, "you want something? I mean, we don't got table service."

The man turned to the bartender, who fell silent under his sharp gaze and returned to inventorying the bottles of cheap, well liquor.

The man across from Kari cleared his throat. With a grave voice he said, "You told me what you wanted but there's something I have to say. First—"

Kari held up a hand to stop him. She whispered, "You're going to tell me it's risky, you're going to tell me that it could ruin my life forever, you're going to tell me to go home and let the police deal with him."

"Yeah, that's pretty much it." He looked into her flinty eyes and when she said nothing more he asked her, "You're sure you want to handle it this way?"

Kari pulled a thick white envelope out of her purse and slid it toward him. "There's the hundred thousand dollars. That's my answer."

The man hesitated then picked up the envelope and put it in his pocket.

■

Nearly a month after his meeting with Kari Swanson, Detective Brad Loesser sat in his office and gazed absently at the rain streaming down his windows. He heard a breathless voice from his doorway.

"We got a problem, Detective," Sid Harper said.

"Which is?" Loesser spun around. Problems on a night like this . . . that's just great. Whatever it was, he bet he'd have to go outside to deal with it.

Harper said, "We got a hit on the wiretap."

After Kari Swanson had met with him Loesser had had several talks with David Dale, urging—virtually threatening—him to stop harassing the woman. The man had been infuriating. He'd appeared to listen reasonably to the detective but apparently hadn't paid any attention to the lecture and, with psychotic persistence, explained how he and Kari loved each other and that it was merely a matter of time until they'd be getting married. On their last meeting Dale had looked Loesser up and down coldly and then began cross-examining *him,* apparently convinced that the cop himself had a crush on her.

That incident had so unnerved the detective that he'd convinced a commonwealth magistrate to allow a wiretap on Dale's phone.

"What happened?" Loesser now asked his assistant.

"*She* called him. Kari Swanson called Dale. About a half hour ago. She was nice as could be. Asked to see him."

"*What?*"

"She's gotta be setting him up," Harper offered.

Loesser shook his head in disgust. He'd been concerned about this very thing happening. From the moment in his office when he'd seen her eyeing the department's shotguns he'd known that she was determined to end Dale's stalking one way or another. Loesser had kept a close eye on the situation, calling Kari at home frequently over the past weeks. He'd been troubled by her demeanor. She'd seemed detached, almost cheerful, even when Dale had been parked in his usual spot, right in front of her house. Loesser could only conclude that she'd finally decided to stop him and was waiting for an opportune time.

Which was, it seemed, tonight.

"Where's she going to meet him? At her house?"

"No. At the old pier off Charles Street."

Oh, hell, Loesser thought. The pier was a perfect site for a murder—there were no houses nearby and it was virtually invisible from the main roads in town. And there were stairs nearby, leading down to a small floating dock, where Kari, or someone she'd hired, could easily take the body out to sea to dispose of it.

But she didn't know about the wiretap—or that they now had a clue as to what her plans were. If she killed Dale she'd get caught. She'd get life in prison for a lying-in-wait murder.

Loesser grabbed his coat and sprinted toward the door.

■

The squad car skidded to a stop at the chain-link fence on Charles Street. Loesser leapt out. He gazed toward the pier, a hundred yards away.

Through the fog and rain the detective could vaguely make out David Dale in a raincoat, clutching a bouquet of roses, walking slowly toward Kari Swanson. The tall woman stood with her back to Dale, hands on the rotting railing, gazing out over the turbulent gray Atlantic.

The detective shouted for Dale to stop. The sound of the wind and waves, though, was deafening—neither the stalker nor his prey could hear.

"Boost me up," Loesser cried to his assistant.

"You want—?"

The detective himself formed Harper's fingers into a cradle, planted his right foot firmly in the man's hands and then vaulted over the top of the chain link. He landed off balance and tumbled painfully onto the rocky ground.

By the time the officer climbed to his feet and oriented himself, Dale was only twenty feet from Kari.

"Call for backup and an ambulance," he shouted to Harper and then took off down the muddy slope to the pier, unholstering his weapon as he ran. "Don't move! Police!"

But he saw he was too late.

Kari suddenly turned and stepped toward Dale. Loesser couldn't hear a gunshot over the roaring waves or see clearly through the misty rain but there was no doubt that David Dale had been shot. His hands flew to his chest and, dropping the flowers, he stumbled backward and sprawled on the pier.

"No!" Loesser muttered hopelessly, realizing that he himself was going to be the eyewitness who put Kari Swanson in jail. Why hadn't she listened to him? But Loesser was a seasoned professional and he kept his emotions in check as he followed procedure to the letter. He lifted his gun toward the model and shouted, "On the ground, Kari! Now!"

She was startled by the cop's sudden appearance but she immediately did as she was told and lay face forward on the wet wood of the pier.

"Hands behind your back," Loesser ordered, running to her. He quickly cuffed her and then turned to David Dale, who was struggling to his knees amid the crushed roses, writhing and howling in agony. At least he wasn't dead yet. Loesser rolled Dale onto his back and ripped open his shirt, looking for the entry wound. "Stay calm. Don't move!"

But he couldn't find a bullethole.

"Where're you hit?" the detective shouted. "Talk to me. Talk to me!"

But the big man continued to sob and shake hysterically and didn't respond.

Sid Harper ran up, panting. He dropped to his knees beside Dale. "Ambulance'll be here in five minutes. Where's he hit?"

The detective said, "I don't know. I can't find the wound."

The young cop too examined the stalker. "There's no blood."

Still, Dale kept moaning as if he were in unbearable pain. "Oh, God, no . . . No . . ."

Finally Loesser heard Kari Swanson call out, "He's fine. I didn't hurt him."

"Get her up," the detective said to Harper as he continued to examine Dale. "I don't understand it. He—"

"Jesus Christ," Sid Harper's stunned voice whispered.

Loesser glanced at his assistant, who was staring at Kari with his mouth open.

The detective himself turned to look at her. He blinked in astonishment.

"I really didn't shoot him," Kari insisted.

Except . . . *Was* this Kari Swanson? The woman was the same height and had the same figure and hair. And the voice was the same. But in place of the extraordinary beauty that had burned itself into Loesser's memory on their first meeting, this woman's face was very different: she had a bumpy, unfortunate nose, thin, uneven lips, a fleshy chin, wrinkles in her forehead and around her eyes.

"Are you . . . Who are you?" Loesser stammered.

She gave a faint smile. "It's me, Kari."

"But . . . I don't understand."

She gave a contemptuous glance at Dale, still lying on the pier, and said to Loesser, "When he followed me to Crowell I finally realized what had to happen: One of us had to die . . . and I picked me."

"You?"

She nodded. "I killed the person he was obsessed with: Kari the supermodel." Looking out to sea, breathing deeply, she continued. "Last year, down in the Caribbean, I met this plastic surgeon. His office was in Manhattan but he also ran a free clinic in Haiti, where he was born. He'd rebuild the faces of locals injured in accidents." She laughed. "He was trying to pick me up, of course, joking that if I ever needed a plastic surgeon, give him a call. But he wasn't obnoxious and I liked the volunteer work he did. We hit it off. When I decided last month I had to do something about Dale I called him. I figured if he could make really deformed people look normal, he could make a beautiful person look normal too. I met with him in New York. He didn't want to do the operation at first but I gave him a hundred thousand for his clinic. That changed his mind."

Loesser studied her closely. She wasn't ugly. She simply looked average—like any of ten million women you'd meet on the street and not glance at twice.

David Dale's terrible moaning rose up over the sound of the wind, not from physical pain but from horror—that the beauty that had obsessed him was now gone. "No, no, no . . ."

Kari asked Loesser, "Can you take these things off me?" Holding up the cuffs.

Harper unhooked them.

As Kari pulled her coat tighter around her a mad voice suddenly filled the air, rising above the sound of the waves. "How could you?" Dale cried, rising to his knees. "How could you do this to me?"

Kari crouched in front of him. "To *you*?" she raged. "What I look like, who I am, the life I lead . . . those don't have a goddamn

thing to do with you and they never did!" She gripped his head in both hands and tried to turn it toward her. "Look at me."

"No." He struggled to keep his face averted.

"Look at me!"

Finally he did.

"Do you love me now, David?" she asked with a cold smile on her new face.

He scrabbled away in revulsion and began to run back toward the street. He stumbled then picked himself up and continued to sprint away from the pier.

Kari Swanson rose and shouted after him, "Do you love me, David? Do you love me now? Do you? Do you?"

■

"Hey, Cath," the man said, surveying the grocery cart she was pushing.

"What?" she asked. The plastic surgery had officially laid "Kari" to rest and she was now accepting only variations on Catherine.

"I think we're missing something," Carl replied with exaggerated gravity.

"What?"

"Junk food," he answered.

"Oh, no." She too frowned in mock alarm as she examined the cart. Then she suggested, "Nachos'd solve the problem."

"Ah. Good choice. Back in a minute." Carl—a man with an easy temperament and an endless supply of bulky fisherman's sweaters—ambled off down the snack food aisle. He was a late bloomer, a second-career lawyer who was exactly five years older and two inches taller than Cathy. He'd picked her up in the annual Crowell St. Patrick's Day festival ten days ago and they'd spent a half dozen delightful afternoons and evenings together, doing absolutely nothing.

Was there a future between them? Cathy had no idea. They certainly enjoyed each other's company but Carl had yet to spend the night. And he still hadn't given her the skinny on his ex-wife.

Both of which were, of course, vital benchmarks in the life of a relationship.

But there was no hurry. Catherine Swanson wasn't looking for a man. Her life was a comfortable mélange of teaching high school history, jogging along the rocky Massachusetts shore, working on her master's at BU and spending time with a marvelous therapist, who was helping her forget David Dale—she hadn't heard anything from the stalker in the past six months.

She moved forward in the checkout line, trying to remember if she had charcoal for the grill. She thought—

"Say, miss, excuse me," mumbled a man's low voice behind her. She recognized his intonation immediately—the edgy, intimate sound of obsession.

Gasping, Cathy spun around to see a young man in a trench coat and a stocking cap. Instantly she thought of the hundreds of strangers who had relentlessly pursued her on the street, in restaurants and in checkout lines just like this one. Her palms began to sweat. Her heart started pounding fiercely, jaw trembling. Her mouth opened but she couldn't speak.

But then Cathy saw that the man wasn't looking at her at all. His eyes were fixed on the magazine rack next to the cash register. He muttered, "That *Entertainment Weekly* there? Could you hand it to me?"

She passed him the magazine. Without thanking her, he flipped quickly to an article inside. Cathy couldn't tell what the story was about, only that it featured three or four cheesecakey pictures of some young, brunette woman, which he stared at intently.

Cathy slowly forced herself to be calm. Then, suddenly, her shaking hands rose to her mouth and she began laughing out loud. The man looked up once from the pictures of his dream girl then returned to his magazine, not the least curious about this tall, plain woman and what she found so funny. Cathy wiped the tears of laughter from her eyes, turned back to the cart and began loading her groceries onto the belt.

THE FALL GUY

The headlights lit the sensuous sweep of the road ahead of her.

Cruising through the dark pines, swaying left right, left right. A damp evening, a cold spring. Her Lexus strayed slightly over the centerline of the wet asphalt and she wondered whether she'd had two martinis with Don or three.

Only two, she decided, and sped up.

She drove this same road, from her job in New Hampshire to her home just over the Massachusetts border, every weekday night—and every night she thought the same thing on this stretch of Route 28: sensuous curves.

Like the cliché of a sign two miles back: *Soft Shoulder.*

A lot of nights—slightly drunk, listening to Michael Bolton on the radio—she'd laugh at those words on the yellow diamond. Tonight she was somber.

Twelve miles from home.

Carolyn eased her stockinged foot off the gas. Her white Ferragamo spike heels rested on the seat next to her (she often drove barefoot, less for control than to avoid scuffing). Then she piloted the car through the final set of, yes, sensuous curves that led to the minuscule town of Dunning.

The gas station, the general store, a propane company, an old motel, a liquor store and an antique shop in which she'd never—in the five years of commuting to and from the hospital—seen anyone buy a single thing.

She slowed to thirty at the rusted harvester, which is where the avid young cops of Dunning caught their speeders and tormented anybody driving a vehicle nicer than a Buick. She stopped here every night on the way home from work—buying gas and a large coffee—but the service station attendants never seemed to notice that she was a regular.

As she climbed out of the car she saw another customer, a man with a rough face and a five o'clock shadow, leaning against his car, talking on a cell phone. He nodded unhappily; whoever was speaking on the other end of the line was delivering bad news.

Carolyn slipped the nozzle into her gas tank and set the catch on the handle. She stood up, felt a chill. She was wearing her beige Evan Picone suit, low cut, no blouse, and a short skirt. With some satisfaction she noticed the customer's eyes lift from the asphalt and scan her body. Even though there was something crude about him—the craggy face, the meaty hands—he was dressed well. A smooth gray suit and a dark trench coat with lots of flaps. His car was a Lincoln, golden brown. It cost, she figured, about the same as hers. She approved of men in expensive cars.

The nozzle snapped off and she went inside to pay.

A cup of black coffee, a roll of Lifesavers. Pep-O-Mint. Without a hint of recognition, the young clerk looked up from his portable TV only long enough to glance at her chest while he gave her the change; maybe it was just her face he didn't recognize.

She stepped back outside, glancing at the man with the Lincoln as he tossed his phone on the seat of the car and reached into his pocket, fishing for money. He glanced toward her again.

Then he froze. His eyes went wide, focusing just past her.

And she felt an arm snake around her waist, felt cold metal at her ear.

"Oh, God . . ."

"Shut up, lady," a young man's voice stuttered in her ear. He was nervous and smelled of whisky. "We're gonna get in your car and drive. You scream, you're dead."

Carolyn had never been mugged. She'd lived in Chicago and New York City and briefly in Paris but the only time she'd ever been physically threatened, the perpetrator hadn't been a crook but the wife of the man who lived across the hall from her on the Left Bank. She was now paralyzed with fear.

As the mugger dragged her toward her car she stammered, "Please, just take the keys."

"No way, babe. I want you's much as I want your wheels."

"Please, no!" she moaned. "I'll give you a lot of money. I'll—"

"Shut up. You're coming with me."

"No, she's not." Lincoln Man had walked up to the passenger side of her Lexus. He was standing between them and the car. His eyes were steady. He didn't seem afraid. The skinny kid, on the other hand, seemed terrified. He shoved the gun forward. "Get the hell outa the way, mister. Nobody'll get hurt, you do what I say."

The man said calmly, "You want the car, take the car. Take *my* car. It's new. Got twelve thousand miles on it." He held up the keys.

"I'm taking her and her car and you're getting outa my way. I don't want to shoot you." The gun wavered. He was a scrawny young guy, backwoods, with dishwater-brown hair in a snaky ponytail.

Lincoln Man smiled and continued to talk calmly. "Look, friend. Carjacking's no big deal. But a kidnapping or rape count? Forget about it. You'll go away forever."

"Get the hell out of my way!" his voice crackled. He moved forward a few feet, forcing Carolyn along with him. She was whimpering. Hated herself for it but she had no control.

Lincoln Man stood his ground and the kid shoved the gun directly into his face.

What happened next happened fast.

She saw:

Lincoln Man turning his palms toward the mugger in a gesture of surrender, stepping back slightly.

The passenger door swinging open and the kid shoving her inside. (Carolyn, thinking crazily: I've never been in the passenger seat of my car before, the seat's too far forward, I'll tear my panty hose. . . .)

The mugger walking around the front of the car to the driver's side of the Lexus, forcing Lincoln Man—hands still raised—out of the way.

Carolyn glanced hopelessly into the gas station window. The young attendant was still behind the counter, still eating potato chips, still watching *Roseanne* on the tiny TV.

The mugger started to climb into the car, then paused, looking back, realizing the nozzle was still in the gas tank of the car.

Then Lincoln Man was lunging, grabbing the mugger's gun hand. He gasped in surprise and fought fiercely to free his hand.

But Lincoln Man was stronger. Carolyn pushed open her door and sprang out as the two men tumbled onto the hood of the Lexus and grappled for the gun. Lincoln Man banged his opponent's wrist onto the windshield several times and the black pistol flew from his grasp. Carolyn squinted as it landed at her feet. The gun didn't go off.

She'd never held a gun in her life, not a pistol anyway, and she now crouched down and lifted it, felt its heavy weight, felt its heat. She shoved the muzzle into the face of the mugger. He went limp as cloth.

Lincoln Man—a good foot taller than the kid—rolled off the hood and took him by the collar.

The mugger looked at Carolyn's uneasy eyes and must've

concluded that she wasn't going to be shooting anybody. He pushed Lincoln Man away with surprising strength and took off at a gallop into the brush beside the gas station.

Carolyn thrust the gun generally in his direction.

Lincoln Man said urgently, "Just shoot for his legs, not his back. You'll be in trouble, you kill him."

But her hands began to tremble and by the time she forced herself to steady it, he was gone.

In the distance a car started, a car with a rattling tailpipe. Then a screech of tires.

"Oh, God, oh, God . . ." Carolyn closed her eyes and leaned against her car.

Lincoln Man came up to her. "You all right?"

She nodded. "Yes. No. I don't know. . . . What can I say? Thank you."

"Uhm . . . " He nodded toward the gun, which she was carelessly pointing at his belly.

"Oh, sorry." She offered it to him. But he glanced down and said, "You better hold on to it until the cops get here. I'm not supposed to have too much to do with guns."

Carolyn didn't understand this. For a moment she thought that he was in recovery and touching a gun would be like somebody in AA taking a drink. Maybe people got addicted to guns the way other people—her husband, for instance—got hooked on gambling or women or coke.

"What?"

"I have a record." He said this without shame or pride but in a tone that suggested he was used to mentioning it early in a conversation, getting the fact out of the way, and seeing what the reaction was. Carolyn had none, and he continued, "Somebody finds me with a pistol . . . well, it'd be a problem."

"Oh," she said, as if he were a Safeway clerk explaining

about an expired spaghetti sauce coupon. His eyes dipped again to her beige suit. Well, more accurately: to the part of her body where her suit was not.

He glanced inside the station, where the clerk continued obliviously to watch his TV program, then he said, "We better call the cops. *He's* sure not going to do it."

"Wait," she said. "Can I ask a question?"

"Sure."

"What'd you do time for?"

He hesitated. "Well," he said slowly. And then must've decided that Carolyn, with her beautiful suit, her tight skirt, her black lacy stockings from Victoria's Secret, this wonderful, fragrant package (Opium, $49 an ounce) would never be his and so he had nothing to lose. He said, "Assault with a deadly weapon. Five counts. Guilty on all of them. Oh, and conspiracy to commit assault. So, should we call those cops?"

"No," she answered, slipping the gun into the glove compartment of her car. "I think we should have a drink."

And nodded toward the lounge of the motel across the road.

■

They awoke three hours later.

He looked like a smoker but he wasn't. He looked like a drinker too and drink he did but he'd had only one beer to her three from the six-pack they bought at the party store beside the motel, after one martini each in the bar.

They stared at the cracked ceiling.

"You have someplace you have to be?" she asked.

"Doesn't everybody?"

"I mean now. Tonight."

"No. I'm just in the area for the day. Going back home tomorrow."

Home, he'd explained over the martini, was Boston. He was staying the night at the Courtyard Inn in Klammath.

His name was Lawrence—emphatically not Larry. After prison he'd gone straight and given up his job of collecting debts for some men he described vaguely as "local businessmen."

"I collected the vig, they call it," he'd explained. "The interest on loan shark loans. You gotta pay the vig."

"Like Rocky."

"Yeah, sorta," Lawrence said.

When she asked his last name his eyes went cloudy and though he said, "Anderson," he might as well have answered "Smith."

He said, "None of the above," to her inquiry about a wife and family and she was inclined to believe him.

The one thing she knew about him for certain was that he was an incredible lover.

Sensuous road, sensuous curves . . .

Nothing soft about his shoulders.

For nearly two hours, they'd kissed, touched, tasted, pressed together. There was nothing kinky about him, nothing odd. He was simply, well, overwhelming. That was the only way she could describe it. His strong arms around her, his large body atop hers . . .

As they lay now in the warm, cheap bed, she watched his chest rising and falling. There was a nasty scar on it, clearly visible beneath the black, curly hair. She wanted to ask him about it but couldn't bring herself to.

"Lawrence?"

He glanced at her cautiously. This was the revered moment after coupling. A risky time. Certain conventions had to be followed. Honesty was dangerous but sincerity a must. Synonyms for *commitment* and *love* and *the future*—if not those words themselves—had ruined many rosy evenings.

But Carolyn's mind wasn't on any of those matters. She was picturing the black gun in her glove compartment and the high, frantic voice of the man who'd nearly kidnapped her.

"What do you do for a living now?" she asked him.

A pause.

"I used to sell auto parts. Well, manage a store. I'm between things right now."

"Got fired?"

"Yeah, got fired." He stretched, a bone popped. "You have a record, they'll fire you if some kid in the mailroom takes a box of staples home. You're always the number-one suspect. I came up for a job interview in Hammond today. Didn't work out."

She remembered his sullen face during the conversation on his cell phone:

"Can I ask *you* a question?" he asked.

"Sure. I'm married, no children. I love sex and I drink too much. Anything else?"

"Why didn't you want to call the cops?"

But instead of answering she asked, "Why didn't you get shook back there?"

He shrugged those great shoulders again. "I've had guns pointed at me before. I can tell when somebody's going to use a piece and when he's not. Oh, that kid'd been a pro, I'd've said so long, lady, and hoped the state troopers got to you before it was too late."

"Have you ever killed anybody?"

The hesitation was his answer.

"No more questions from you till you answer mine," he said. "Why no cops?"

"Because I have a business proposition for you."

"What, you need some auto parts?"

"No, I want you to murder my husband."

■

"Divorce him," Lawrence said. "That's what they make lawyers for."

"He's worth a lot of money."

"If he's cheating, you'll get half. Maybe more."

"Well . . ."

"Oh. He's not the only guilty party." Lawrence laughed and gestured toward the bed they were lying in. "Guess not. Who cheated first?"

"He did." Then she added, "Well, he got caught first."

"Tough luck. But I'm not a hit man. I never was."

"What can I say to convince you?"

"Nothing. Not. A. Thing."

"What can I *do* to convince you?" She moved her hands along his body, pinched his thigh playfully.

He laughed.

He stopped smiling when she asked, "Fifty thousand?"

But after a moment: "I've done my time. I didn't like it."

"A hundred?"

The hesitation was probably only a millisecond but to Carolyn it was plenty long enough.

Lawrence said, "I don't think so."

"*I don't think*—that's not the same as *no*."

"It's not easy killing somebody. Well, matter of fact, that part *is* easy. But getting away's tricky. That's the almost-impossible part."

As she often did in the meetings she ran at the hospital—when the people who worked for her would come up with excuses for not having their reports or proposals in on time—Carolyn said, "I'm hearing *almost*. I'm hearing *tricky*. But all that tells me is it's doable."

"You ever threatened him?"

She shrugged. "I found him with his girlfriend once at the mall. I lost it. I said I'd kill them both. . . . No, I think I said they'd wish they were dead by the time I got through with them."

"Ouch."

"I don't think anybody heard me."

"Well," he said slowly, like a doctor formulating an opinion. "You've got a reason to kill him. That's a problem. It means you've got to find a fall guy. You've got to make it look like it's more likely somebody else committed the crime than you, even if you have a motive. We need—"

"Another suspect?"

"Yeah."

She smiled and eased her breasts against him. "Like a carjacker. Or a mugger?"

"Sure." His eyes swung toward the gas station. He nodded. "That kid, we've got his gun . . ."

Stan had several guns. Carolyn remembered the forms he'd had to fill out to buy them; she knew gun shops kept good records of ownership. She mentioned this now.

"Might be stolen, might not be his," Lawrence said.

"It'd have his fingerprints on it."

"We'd have to wipe it—you touched it, remember?" But then he laughed.

"What?"

"Well, even if we wiped the gun, the bullets'd still have *his* prints on them."

She nuzzled against his neck.

"But," Lawrence added, "he's just a carjacker. You really want to bring him down on a murder charge?"

"He was going to rape me," she pointed out. "Maybe kill me. Look at it like this: We'll be doing a good deed, getting him put away before he hurts someone."

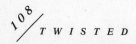

"A hundred thousand?" Lawrence gazed up at the ceiling. "You know, those social workers and counselors . . . in prison, I mean? They'd ask about all sorts of crazy stuff. What appealed to me about antisocial behavior? What was I angry about? Was my childhood *conflicted?*" He laughed. "They didn't like my answers. I told 'em I could make five thousand a day just to break some poor schmuck's arm. Who the hell *wouldn't* want a job like that?"

"Well, here's a chance for your nest egg." She kissed his ear and whispered the words that always thrilled her, "Tax free."

He thought for a moment. "We'd have to set it up carefully. Maybe we find the motel where he's meeting his girlfriend—"

"I know it. They always go to the same place."

"How does it work?" He laughed. "I was married for ten years and I never had an affair. Would she leave the place first? Or him?"

"She'd leave first. He'd wait, pay for the room."

"Okay, after he pays he gets in the car. I'm there waiting for him."

"And you shoot him?"

Lawrence laughed. "In a motel parking lot? With people around? I don't think so. No, I'll force him to drive me someplace deserted. Do it there. Make it look like we fought and I shot him. Then I panicked and jumped out of the car and ran. I'll drop the gun on the way. You follow and pick me up. . . . When should we do it? Sooner's better. I need the money bad. I owe big-time on that Lincoln."

"Stan usually goes to see her on Tuesday and Thursday nights."

"Today's Tuesday," he said.

She nodded. "That's where he is now."

"Well, day after tomorrow. Sure. It's a good setup. We've got a murder weapon that can't be traced to us, a good motive. And a fall guy."

Carolyn rolled atop Lawrence once more, straddled him, feeling his interest in her Pamela Anderson body rapidly reviving. And she thought: We sure *do* have a fall guy, Lawrence. You. An ex-con out of work, a man with a great motive to rob Stan—and kill him in the process.

"I think it'll work," he said.

"I think it will too," Carolyn said. And started to chew on his lower lip.

■

Sensuous curves . . .

The car gently rocking back and forth.

It was Thursday, another overcast spring evening, and Carolyn was wearing a long-sleeved navy blouse and a pleated skirt that ended halfway between knee and ankle. A couple of the assistants in the hospital office had looked at her with surprise. No cleavage today, no thigh, no straining buttons. The AquaNet had remained capped and her hair was pulled back in a plain ponytail. She'd decided that after she made the anonymous call to the police reporting one man shooting another in a green Cadillac, she'd have to speed back home and prepare to be the demure, innocent widow. A costume change might be hard to manage in time.

She found herself in an odd state: nearly aroused. The sashaying of the car, the cool air on her skin. And, she had to admit, the thought of Stan dying turned her on.

So did getting her hands on his money. He was such a miser. He wouldn't even *buy* her the damn Lexus. It had to be a lease.

Thinking about Lawrence too.

Such a great lover.

But a better fall guy.

Too bad, Larry.

It wouldn't be easy, though. She couldn't call the cops from the car phone, of course; there'd be a record of the call. So she decided to pick the place for the hit herself. This would make sense to Larry—she was the native; he wouldn't know the area. She'd suggest that he drive Stan to Cardiff Falls. There, the county road stretched through a steep valley. A mile up the road was a convenience store with two telephones outside.

She'd follow them and after Larry'd killed Stan and gone to meet her she'd slip out of her car and flatten the rear tire of Stan's Cadillac with the kitchen knife she had in her purse (she'd let the air out of the spare tire that morning). Then she'd leave Lawrence there and speed to the store, make the call to the cops and race home. Lawrence'd be trapped in the valley. It would take him forty minutes to get out on foot; the cops would be there in minutes.

Perfect.

Her thoughts segued again to the Heritage Hotel, where her husband was right at the moment.

She pictured them in bed together.

Pictured his girlfriend: Loretta Samples . . . Lorrie . . . an unremarkable woman. Blonde, boringly pretty. When Carolyn had stalked them to the mall, Lorrie was wearing a ludicrous black floppy hat and was walking close to Stan with his elbow seated hard against her chest. They'd braked to a fast stop in front of the banshee wife. Oh, had Carolyn enjoyed *that* little scene.

Lor-rie . . .

What were they doing at this minute? Carolyn wondered, gripping the Lexus's steering wheel so hard her fingers cramped. Drinking wine? Was he kissing her feet? Lying on top of her and hooking his longish brown hair behind his ears?

Then Lawrence's motel loomed and she braked hard. She

pulled past it, like they'd agreed, and he stepped out from behind a row of bushes and climbed into the car before it stopped moving.

"Go," he said.

She sped back onto the road.

She'd expected that he'd be dressed in, well, killer clothes. Like a commando, maybe. At least a black sweater and jeans, or something. But he was just wearing one of his business suits under the elaborate trench coat. His tie was printed with tiny yellow fish. Ugly, tasteless. For some reason this made her feel better about turning him in.

"You're sure he's at the hotel?"

"He called and said he was going to be late for dinner. He had a meeting with Bill Mathiesson."

"And he doesn't?"

"Not unless it's in London, which is where Bill is this week. According to his office."

Lawrence gave a bitter laugh. "You gonna lie, lie smart." He looked at his watch. "What do you know about his girlfriend?"

Another heat flash of jealousy coursed through her. "She's got small boobs and needs a nose job."

"She married too?"

"Yeah. She's just like Stan. Rich bitch. Inherited daddy's money and thinks she can get away with anything. They deserve each other."

"Well, let's hope she leaves the room first. Witnesses're no good." He pulled on tight-fitting cotton work gloves.

"Don't you wear rubber gloves?"

"No," he said. "Cloth is better. No fingerprints inside. To trace you to the gloves."

"Oh." She supposed that Lawrence Anderson Smith, aka the Lincoln Man, aka the Lovemaker, had been very good at collecting debts.

He opened the glove compartment and took out the pistol.

Carolyn glanced at it. They all looked alike to her. Black, dangerous.

He clicked it open. She saw there were six bullets in the six chambers. Lawrence asked, "Did you wipe it?"

"No," she said. "I don't know how."

He laughed. "You just . . . wipe it." He pulled a Kleenex from the box on her dashboard and carefully wiped the metal.

"There," she said. "There it is."

Ahead of them was the hotel. The red *Vacancy* light pulsed unappealingly. It was a seedy place. (Carolyn insisted that *her* lovers take her to bed-and-breakfasts. Or at least the Hyatt.)

She parked on the street, with a view of the parking lot. There was Stan's Cadillac. She wondered which car was Lorrie's.

"Oh, there's a good place I know to do it," she said, as if she'd just thought of the idea. "Cardiff Falls, Route Fifty-eight. It's about five miles from here. It's real deserted. Just keep going on Maple Branch about a mile to the Mobil station then turn left. That'll be Route Fifty-eight."

"Good." He nodded then said, "You stay right here. I'm going to hide in the bushes. I'll get him in the Caddie and drive there, find a place by the side of the road. You follow us."

Carolyn took a deep breath. "Okay."

"Afterwards, you drop me at my hotel and go home. When he doesn't show up tonight, call the cops. Remember, don't over-act when you find out what happened. It's better to look stunned than hysterical. Sort of zoned out."

"Stunned not hysterical." Carolyn nodded.

Then he leaned forward and gripped her neck hard, pulled her lips to his. She kissed back, just as hard. She enjoyed a kinky little shiver, feeling the gloves on her neck. Maybe she'd have to play dress-up sometime with Don. Or some other lover. Maybe leather would be fun. . . .

He released her and she looked into his eyes. "Good luck," she said.

He climbed out, crouched beside the car, looked around. The street was deserted. Still hunched over, he ran through a wedge of shadow beside the hotel and disappeared behind a row of boxwood.

Carolyn laid her head against the leather rest and clicked on Lite FM.

Now, finally, the nervousness descended like a spray of cold rain. The horror of the evening unfurled within her and her hands began to quiver.

What'm I doing? she wondered.

The answer came to her: what I should've done a long time ago. Suddenly her uneasiness turned to rage. I hate these damn clothes, I want to be dressed up, I want to be going out for nice wine and martinis, I want that idiot Stan out of my life, I want to get the whole thing over. I want—

Two sharp cracks from the hotel.

Sitting forward, staring into the parking lot at Stan's Cadillac.

Two more bangs. They sounded like gunshots.

Lights went on in some of the hotel windows.

Carolyn felt the fear inside her like a cold stone.

No, no. They were just backfires. That's all. She scanned the parking lot. More lights came on. Doors opened. Several people stepped onto balconies, looking around.

Then there was motion to her right. She glanced toward it.

Lawrence stood in the shadows. His eyes were wide; on his face, a look of terror. Was he holding his stomach? Had he been shot? She couldn't tell.

"What?" Carolyn screamed.

He looked around, in panic, then gestured her frantically to

leave. Mouthing, "Go . . . go. Get home fast." He disappeared back into the bushes.

Had a guard or off-duty cop seen him with the gun? Did *Stan* have a gun with him?

Two people stepped from the hotel manager's office, a fat woman in a turquoise jumpsuit and a skinny man wearing a short-sleeved white shirt. They looked around the U-shaped building, said something to each other, then listened to some of the people on the balconies and the sidewalk in front of the ground-floor rooms. Carolyn couldn't tell what they were saying.

She looked back toward where Lawrence had whispered his warning. No sign of him.

Time to go, she thought. This is trouble.

She floored the accelerator.

But as the car sped forward she heard a soft pop and the *whup whup whup* of a tire going flat.

No! Not now! Please . . .

She kept going. The hotel guests and the couple from the manager's office were staring at the Lexus as it swerved down the street. Then the rubber fell off the rim of the flat rear tire and the car jolted to a stop against the curb.

"Damn! Damn, damn!" she screamed, slamming her fist on the steering wheel.

In the rearview mirror, flashing lights—a police car was speeding toward the hotel.

No, no . . .

The young officers glanced at her car but passed it by and parked up the street. They trotted to the crowd of guests by the manager's office. Several of them pointed to a room on the first floor and the cops hurried to it.

Two other squad cars showed up and then a boxy ambulance.

Run or stay?

Hell, they can trace my car. It'd seem more suspicious if she ran.

I'll come up with a story. My husband called me and asked for a ride.

My husband wanted me to meet him here. . . .

I happened to see my husband's car . . .

The cops knocked on the door to room 103 and, when there was no answer, the skinny man in the white shirt unlocked the door. He stood back as the cops, their guns drawn, pushed inside.

One stepped back outside and spoke to the ambulance attendants. They walked inside slowly. If it was Stan's room, and if Stan was inside, Carolyn guessed he was dead.

But what had happened? What—

A rapping on her car window. She screamed and turned around. A large cop was standing beside her. She stared at him, her mouth open.

"Miss, could you move your car?" asked the beefy crew-cut cop politely.

"I— The tire. It's flat."

"Is something wrong, ma'am?"

"No. Nothing's wrong. I just . . . It's just that I had a flat tire."

"Could I see your license and registration, please?"

"Why?"

"Please? Your license and registration."

"Well, sure," she said, staring at him, his badge, his walkie-talkie. She didn't move.

A moment passed. "Now."

"I—"

"Ma'am, you're acting kind of strange. I'd like to ask you to step out of your vehicle."

"Well, now, Officer . . ." She smiled and leaned toward him,

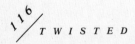

easing her arms together. Only after a glance at his perplexed face did she realize that the attention-getting valley between her breasts was hidden by her conservative blue blouse.

She climbed out of the car, handed him the documents.

"You been drinking?"

"No, Officer. Well, I had one beer a couple of hours ago. Well, two."

"I see."

Then she glanced at the rear wheel, frowning. It looked as if somebody had put a trap under the tire—a piece of wood with a couple of nails hammered through it.

The cop noticed her gaze. "Damn kids. They do that sometimes for pranks. Throw 'em in the road. Think it's funny. This your current address?" Nodding at her license.

"Yes," she said absently. Eyes on the hotel room. More police cars had arrived; there were a dozen now, their lights flashing in alarming red and blue. Two men in suits and badges around their necks—one with bushy hair, one balding—arrived and stepped into room 103.

The cop walked to the rear of the Lexus to check the license plate. He seemed calm and reasonable. Carolyn was relaxing. He'd let her go. Sure he would. It'll be okay. Just stay calm and they'll never put anything together.

Then the crew-cut cop's walkie-talkie crackled. "We have a multiple homicide at the Heritage Hotel. Victims are a Loretta Samples, female cauc, thirty-two and a Stanley Ciarelli, male cauc, thirty-nine."

"What?" blurted the cop, looking up from the driver's license he held.

"Oh, Jesus," said Carolyn Ciarelli.

"Detective!" the traffic cop shouted to the bald man with the badge around his neck. "Think you better come over here."

 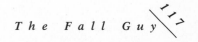

Five minutes later she was sitting in the back of the patrol car—no handcuffs, at least—where she'd been asked to remain until everything got sorted out.

A young patrolman came running up to the detectives. He held a large plastic bag containing the pistol Lawrence had apparently dropped as he fled.

"What've we got here?" one detective asked.

"Probable murder weapon," the young officer said a little too eagerly. He drew snickers from the seasoned detectives, Mutt and Jeff.

"Let's see it," the balding detective said. "Hey, Charlie, any latents?"

An officer wearing latex gloves walked over to them. He was carrying a box with a wand attached, like a small neon tube. He shone a greenish light on the gun, examining it carefully.

"Nup, not a whorl or ridge."

Thank God, Lawrence had wiped the prints off.

"But," Charlie added, pulling on an eye loupe, "we got something here. Looks like a bit of blue tissue caught in the cylinder release catch." He examined it closely. "Yep, pretty sure it's Kleenex."

Oh, my God, no . . .

She glanced behind her to see the crew-cut cop walk to the Lexus, retrieve something and return. "Look what I found here, sir."

He pointed to the wad of blue Kleenex that Lawrence had dropped on the floor after he'd wiped the gun.

Well, so what? There were hundreds of thousands of boxes of Kleenex around the country. How could they prove—

Charlie unwadded the Kleenex carefully. There was a triangular tear in the center. Where the scrap on the gun would fit like the last piece in a jigsaw puzzle.

Another officer came up to the detectives holding the cloth

gloves Lawrence had worn. The bushy-haired detective, now wearing latex gloves himself, lifted them. Smelled the palm. "Women's perfume."

Carolyn could smell the scent too. Opium. She started to hyperventilate.

"Sir," another cop called, "ran the registration on that weapon. It's the victim's. Stanley Ciarelli."

No, impossible! It was the same gun the mugger'd had! She was sure. Had he stolen it from Stan's den? But how could he?

Carolyn realized all the cops were staring at her.

"Mrs. Ciarelli?" the bushy-headed detective asked, pulling his handcuffs from the back of his belt. "Could you stand up and turn around, please?"

"No, no, you don't understand," she cried.

After he read her the Miranda rights and put her back in the rear seat of the patrol car she heard a faint squealing of tires in the distance. She stared at the approaching car but her mind was elsewhere.

All right, let's figure it out, she thought. Let's say Lawrence and the mugger are in this together. Maybe the mugger's a friend of his. They steal Stan's gun. I stop in Dunning for coffee and gas. They could've followed me and found out I stop there every night. They make it look like it's a mugging, I sleep with Lawrence. . . .

But why?

What's he up to? Who *is* he?

Just then the car that had been speeding toward the hotel skidded to a stop nearby. It was a golden-brown Lincoln.

Lawrence leapt out, leaving the door open, and ran in panic toward the doorway of room 103.

"No, no! My wife . . ."

A cop restrained him and pulled him back from the door. He was sobbing. "I came as soon as you called! I can't believe it! No, no, no . . ."

The cop's arm slipped around the shoulders of the fancy, navy blue trench coat and he led the sobbing man back to the detectives, who gazed at him with sympathy. The bald one asked softly, "Your name's Samples?"

"That's right," he said, struggling to control his sorrow. "Lawrence Samples." Breathlessly, he asked, "You mean . . . she was cheating on me? My wife was cheating on me? And somebody's killed her?"

You've got to make it look like it's more likely somebody else committed the crime than you, even if you have a motive. . . .

And for an instant, unseen by the officers, Lawrence cast a glance toward Carolyn, a look that could only be described as amused. Then, as she began screaming at him in fury, slamming her shackled wrists against the window, his eyes went dull again and he covered them with shaking hands. "Oh, Lorrie . . . Lorrie . . . I just don't believe it! No, no, no . . ."

EYE TO EYE

"**I**'d help you if I could," the boy said. "But I can't."

"Can't, hmm?" Boz asked, standing over him. Peering down at the top of the brown cowlick. *"Can't? Or don't wanta?"*

His partner, Ed, said, "Yup, he knows something."

"Don't doubt it," Boz added, hooking his thumb around his $79.99 police baton, genuine imported and gleaming black.

"No, Boz. I don't. Really. Come on."

An engine-block-hot dusk. It was August in the Shenandoah Valley and the broad river rolling by outside the window of the sheriff's department interview room didn't do anything to take the edge off the temperature. Other towns, the heat had the locals cutting up and cutting loose. But Caldon, Virginia, about ten miles from Luray—yeah, that's the one, home of *the* cave— was a small place, population 8,400. Heat this bad usually sent most of the bikers, trash and teens home to their bungalows and trailers, where they stared, groggy from joints or Bud, at HBO or ESPN (satellite dishes being significant anticrime measures out here).

But tonight was different. The deputies had been yanked from their own stupors by the town's first armed robbery/shooting in four years—an honest-to-God armored-car stickup, no less. Sheriff Elm Tappin was grudgingly en route back from a fishing trip in North Carolina and FBI agents from D.C. were due later tonight as well.

Which wasn't going to stop these two from wrapping up the case themselves. They had a suspect in the lockup and, here in front of them, an eyewitness. Reluctant though he was.

Ed sat down across from Nate Spoda. They called him *boy* behind his back, but he wasn't a boy at all. He was in his mid-twenties and only three years younger than the deputies themselves. They'd all been at Nathaniel Hawthorne High together for a year, Nate a freshman, the other two seniors. Nate was still skinny as a post, had eyes darty and sunken as any serial killer's and was known throughout town for being as ooky now as he was in high school.

"Now, Nate," Ed said kindly, "we know you saw *something*."

"Come on," the boy said in a whiny voice, fingers drumming uneasily on his bony knee. "I didn't. Really."

Boz, the fat cop, the breathless cop, the sweaty cop, took over when his partner glanced at him. "Nate, that just don't jibe with what we know. You sit on your front porch and you spend hours and hours and hours not doing diddly. Just sitting there, watching the river." He paused, wiped his forehead. "Why d'you do that?" he asked curiously.

"I don't know."

Though everybody in town knew the answer. Which was that when Nate was in junior high, his parents had drowned in a boating accident on the very river the boy would gaze out at all day long while he read books and magazines (Frances at the post office said he subscribed to some "excruciatingly" odd mags, about which she couldn't say more, being a federal employee and all) and listened to some sick music, which he played too loud. After his parents' deaths an uncle had come to stay with the boy—a slimy old guy from West Virginia no less (well, the whole town had an opinion on *that* living arrangement). He'd seen the boy through high school and when Nate hit eighteen, off the kid went

to college. Four years later Ed and Boz had served their stint in the service, becoming all they could be, and were back home. And who showed up that June, surprising them and the rest of the town? Yep, Nate. He booted his uncle back west and took to living by himself in that dark, spooky house overlooking the river, surviving, they guessed, on his folks' savings account (nobody in Caldon ever amassed anything that lived up to the word *inheritance*).

The deputies hadn't liked Nate in high school. Not the way he dressed or the way he walked or the way he didn't comb his hair (which was too damn long, scary long). They didn't like the way he talked to the other kids, in a sick whisper. Didn't like the way he talked to girls, not healthy ways, not joking or gossiping, but just *talking* soft, in that weird way that kind of hypnotized them. He'd been in French Club. He'd been in Computer Club. Chess Club, for Christ's sake. Of course he didn't go out for a single sport, and just think about all those times in class when nobody could answer Mrs. Hard-On's question and Nate—the school'd advanced the nerd bone-whacker a couple years—would sashay up to the board to write the right answer in his fag handwriting, getting chalk dust all over himself. Then just turn back to the class and everybody'd stop snickering, 'cause of his scary eyes. Got picked on some, sure. Got his Keds boloed over the high-tension wires. But who didn't? Besides, he asked for it. Sitting on his porch, reading books (probably porn) and listening to this eerie music (probably satanic, another deputy had suggested) . . . Well, sir, he was simply unnatural.

And speaking of natural: Every time a report of a sex crime came in, Boz and Ed thought of Nate. They'd never been able to pin anything on him but he'd disappear for long periods of time and the deputies were pretty sure he'd vanish into the woods and fields around Luray to peer through girls' bedroom windows (or more likely boys'). They knew Nate was a voyeur; he had a telescope on his porch, next to the rocker he always sat in—his mother's chair (and, yep, the whole town had an opinion about *that* too). Unnatural. Yep, that was the word.

So the Caldon Sheriff's Department deputies—Ed and Boz at least—never missed a chance to do their part to, well, set Nate straight. Just like they'd done in high school. They'd see him buying groceries and they'd smile and say, "Need a hand?" Meaning: Why don'tcha get married, homo?

Or he'd be bicycling up Rayburn Hill and they'd come up behind him in their cruiser and hit the siren and shout over the loudspeaker, "On your left!" Which'd once scared him clean into some blackberry bushes.

But he never took the hints. He just kept doing what he was doing, wearing a dark trench coat most of the time, living his shameful life and walking out of Ed's and Boz's way when he ran into them on Main Street. Just like in the halls of Hawthorne High.

So it felt pretty good, Ed had to admit, having him trapped in the interview room. Scared and twitchy and damp in the summer heat.

"He had to've walked right by you," Boz continued in his grumbling voice. "You must've seen him."

"Uhm. I didn't."

Him was Lester Botts, presently sitting unshaven and stinking in the nearby lockup. The scruffy thirty-five-year-old loser had been a sore spot to the Caldon Sheriff's Department for years. He'd never been convicted of anything but the deputies knew he was behind a lot of the petty crimes around the country. He was white trash, gave the nasty eyeball to the good girls in town and wasn't even a lip-service Christian.

Lester was currently the number-one suspect in this evening's robbery. He had no alibi for five to six P.M.—the time of the heist. And though the armored car's driver and his partner

hadn't seen his face, what with the ski mask, the robber'd carried a nickel-plated Colt revolver—exactly the type of gun that Lester had drunkenly brandished at Irv's Roadside not long ago. And there'd been a report last week that somebody with Lester's build had stolen a half pound of Tovex from Amundson Construction. Which was the same explosive used to blow the door off the Armored Courier truck. At six-thirty tonight they'd picked him up—he was sweating a storm and acting plenty guilty—hitching home along Route 334, even though he had a perfectly good Chevy pickup at home, which fired up the first time Ed turned the key, just to test out if Lester's claim that it "wasn't runnin'" was true. He'd also been carrying a long hunting knife and fumbled the answer when they'd asked him why ("Well, I just, you know, *am*.").

The sheriff's department *Procedure Manual* had explained all about motive, means and opportunity in investigating felonies. Boz and Ed had scoped all that out in this case. It was sweet and simple. No, there was no doubt in their minds that Lester had done the job. And because Nate's property was on a direct line from the heist to where they picked up Lester, there was also no doubt that Nate could place him near the scene of the crime.

Boz sighed. "Just tell us you saw him."

"But I didn't. That wouldn't be the truth."

Nerd then, nerd now. Christ . . .

"Look, Nate," Boz continued, as if speaking to a five-year-old. "Maybe you don't get how serious this is. Lester whacked the driver of that armored car over the head with a wrench while he was peeing in the men's room at the Texaco on Route Four. Then he went out to the truck, shot the driver's partner in the side—"

"Oh, no. Is he okay?"

"Nobody's *okay*, they get shot in the side," Boz spat out. "Lemme finish."

"Sorry."

"Then drives the truck to Morton Woods Road, blows the back door off. He loads the money into another car and takes off, heading west—directly toward your place. We pick Lester up on the *other* side of your property a hour ago. He had to go past your house to get to where we found him. What d'you think about that?"

"I think it . . . Well, it seems like it makes sense. But I didn't see him. I'm sorry."

Boz reflected for a minute. "Nate, look," he finally said, "we just don't see eye to eye here."

"Eye to eye?" Nate asked uncertainly.

"You're in a different world from us," the deputy continued, exasperated. "We know the kinda man Lester is. We live in that sewer every day."

"Sewer?"

"You're thinking you'll just clam up and everything'll be okay," Ed filled in. "But that's not how it'll work. We know Lester. We know what he's capable of."

"What's that?" Nate asked. Trying to sound brave. But his hands were clenched, trembling, in his lap.

"Using his damn knife on you, what d'you *think*?" Boz shouted. "Jesus. You really *don't* get it, do you?"

They were doing the good- and bad-cop thing. The *Procedure Manual* had a whole section on it.

"Say you don't finger him now," Ed offered gently. "He gets off. How long you think it'll take for him to find you?"

" 'Cause he thinks I'm a witness, you mean?"

"Find you and gut you," Boz snapped. "Why, it'll be no time at all. And I'm beginning not to care."

"Come on," Ed said to his partner. "Let's go easy on the poor kid." Then looked at Nate's frightened face. "But if we get him for armed robbery and attempted murder . . . He'll go away for thirty years. You'll be safe."

"I want to do the right thing," Nate said. "But . . ." His voice trailed off.

"Boz, he wants to help. I know he does."

"I do," Nate said earnestly. And scrunched his eyes closed, thinking hard. "But I can't lie. I *can't*. My dad . . . You remember my dad. He taught me never to lie."

His dad was a nobody who couldn't swim worth shit. That's all they knew about his dad. Boz plucked his shirt away from his fat chest and examined the black patches of sweat under his arms. He walked in a slow circle around the boy, sighing.

Nate cringed faintly, as if he were afraid of losing his gym shoes again.

Finally Ed said in an easy voice, "Nate, you know we've had our disputes."

"Well, you guys used to pick on me a lot in school."

"Hell, that? That was just joshing," Ed said earnestly. "We only did it with the kids we liked."

"Yeah?" Nate asked.

"But sometimes," Ed continued, "I guess it got a little out of hand. You know how it is? You're fooling around, you get pumped up."

Neither of them thought this little salamander had *ever* been pumped up (for Christ's sake, a man does at least *one* sport).

"Look, Nate, will you let bygones be bygones?" Ed held out his hand. "I'll apologize for all of that stuff we done."

Nate stared at Ed's meaty hand.

Burning bushes, Ed thought, he's gonna cry. He glanced at Boz, who said, "I'll second that, Nate." The *Procedure Manual* said that after the subject has been worn down, the bad cop comes around and starts to act like a good cop. "I'm sorry for what we done."

Ed said, "Come on, Nate. What d'you say? Let's put our differences behind us."

Nate's spooky face looked from one deputy to the other. He took Ed's hand, shook it cautiously. Ed wanted to wipe it after they released the grip. But he just smiled and said, "Now, man to man, what can you tell us?"

"Okay. I did see someone. But I couldn't swear it was Lester."

Ed and Boz exchanged cool glances.

Nate continued fast. "Wait. Let me tell you what I saw."

Boz—who of the two had worse handwriting but could spell better—opened a notebook and began to write.

"I was sitting on my porch reading."

Porn, probably.

"And listening to music."

"I love you, Satan. Take me, take me, take me . . ."

Ed kept an encouraging smile on his face. "Go ahead."

"Okay. I heard a car on Barlow Road. I remember it because Barlow Road isn't real close but the car was making a ton of noise so I figured it had a bad muffler or something."

"And then?"

"Okay . . ." Nate's voice cracked. "Then I saw somebody running through the grass, heading down to the river across from my place. And maybe he was carrying some big white bags."

Bingo!

Boz: "That's near the caves, right?"

Not as sexy as Luray's maybe, but plenty big enough to hide a half million dollars. Ed glanced at him and nodded. "And he went into one of 'em?" he asked Nate.

"I guess. I didn't see exactly 'cause of that old black willow."

"You can't give us *any* description?" Boz asked, smiling but wishing oh so badly that he could be a bad cop again.

"I'm sorry, guys," Nate whined. "I'd help you if I could. All that grass, the tree. I just couldn't see."

Pussy faggot . . .

But at least he'd pointed them in the right direction. They'd find some physical evidence that would lead to Lester.

"Okay, Nate," Ed said, "that's a big help. We're going to check out a few things. Think we better keep you here till we get back. For your own protection."

"I can't leave?" He was brushing at the cowlick. "I really wanta get home. I got a lot of stuff to do."

Involving *Playboy* and your right hand? Boz asked silently.

"Naw, better you stay here. We won't be long."

"Wait," Nate said uneasily. "Can Lester get out?"

Boz looked at Ed. "Oh, hey, be practically impossible for him to get outa that lockup." Ed nodded.

"Practically?" the boy asked.

"Naw, it's okay."

"Sure, it's okay."

"Wait—"

Outside, they walked to the squad car. Boz won the toss and got in the driver's seat.

"Oooo-eee." Ed said, "that boy's gonna sweat up a storm every time Lester rubs his butt on his chair."

"Good," said Boz and sped out onto the road.

■

They were surprised.

They'd been talking in the car and decided that Nate had made up most of what he was telling them just so he could get home. But, no, as soon as they started down Barlow Road, they spotted fresh tire tracks, even in the failing evening light.

"Well, lookie that."

They followed the trail into the grove of low hemlock and juniper and, weapons drawn, as the *Procedure Manual* dictated, they came up on either side of the low-riding Pontiac.

"Ain't been here long," Boz said, reaching through the grill and touching the radiator.

"Keys're inside. Fire it up, see if it's what the boy heard."

Boz cranked the engine and from the tailpipe came the sound of a small plane.

"Stupid for a getaway car," he shouted. "That Lester's got wood for brains."

"Back her out. Let's take a look."

Boz eased the old car into a clearing, where the light was better. He shut off the engine.

They didn't find any physical evidence in the front or back seats.

"Damn," Boz muttered, poking through the glove compartment.

"Well, well, well." Ed called. He was peering into the trunk.

He lifted out a large Armored Courier cash bag, plump and heavy. He opened it up and pulled out thick packets of hundred-dollar bills.

"Phew." Ed counted it. "I make it nineteen thousand bucks."

"Damn, my salary without overtime. Just sitting there. Lookit that."

"Where's the rest of it, I wonder."

"Which way's the river?"

"There. Over there."

On foot, they started through the grass and sedge and cat-tails that bordered the Shenandoah. They searched for footprints in the tall grass but couldn't find any. "We can look for 'em in the morning. Let's get to the caves, have a look-see there."

Ed and Boz walked down to the water's edge. They could clearly see Nate's house overlooking the bluff. Nearby were several cave entrances.

"Those caves right there. Must be the ones."

They continued along the riverbank to the spindly black willow Nate had mentioned.

This time Boz lost the toss and dropped to his hands and knees. Breathing heavily in the hot, murky air, he disappeared into the largest of the caves.

Five minutes later Ed bent down and called, "You okay?"

And had to dodge another canvas bag, as it came flying out of the mouth of the cave.

"Lordy, whatta we got here?"

Eighty thousand dollars, it turned out.

"S'the only one in there," Boz said, climbing out, panting. "Lester must've planted the bags in different caves."

"Why?" Ed wondered. "We find one around here, we'd just keep searching till we found the rest."

"Wood for brains is why."

They poked through a few other caves, feeling hot and itchy-sweaty and sickened by the stink of a dead catfish, but didn't find any more money.

They looked down at the bag. Neither said a word. Ed glanced up at the sky through a notch in the Massanuttens, at the nearly full moon, glowing with brilliance and promise. Standing on either side of the bag the two men rocked on their heels like nervous boys at a junior high dance. The shoal beneath their feet was smooth and black and soft, just like a thousand other banks along the Shenandoah, banks where these two had spent so many hours fishing and drinking beer and—in their daydreams—making love with roadhouse waitresses and cheerleaders.

Ed said, "This's a lot of money."

"Yeah," Boz said, stretching a lot of syllables out of the word. "What're you saying, Edward?"

"I'm—"

"Don't beat around the bush."

"I'm thinking, there's only two people know about it, 'side from us."

Nate and Lester. "Keep going."

"So what would happen . . . I'm just thinking out loud here. What would happen if they got together—accidental, of course—in a room back at the station? If, say, Lester had his knife back."

"Accidental."

"Sure."

"Well, he'd gut Nate and leave him like that catfish over there."

" 'Course, if that happened," Ed continued, "we'd have to shoot Lester, right?"

"Have to. Prisoner gets loose, has a weapon . . ."

"Be a sad thing to have happen."

"But necessary," Boz offered. Then: "That Nate, he's dangerous."

"Never liked him."

"He's the sort'd go postal in a year or two. Climb up to the South Bank Baptist Church tower and let loose with an AR-15."

"Don't doubt it."

"Where's that knife of Lester's?"

"Evidence locker. But it could find its way back upstairs."

"We sure we want to do this?"

Ed opened the canvas bag. Looked inside. So did Boz. Stared for a time.

"Let's get a beer," Boz said.

"Okay, let's."

Even though alcohol on duty was clearly prohibited by the *Procedure Manual.*

An hour later they snuck in the back door of the station.

Boz went down to the evidence room and found Lester's knife. He padded back upstairs, made sure that Sheriff Tappin hadn't returned yet and slipped into the main interview room. He left the knife on the table—under a folder, hidden but not too hidden—and stepped innocently back into the corridor.

Ed brought Lester Botts up to the door, hands cuffed in front of him, which was definitely contrary to procedure, and escorted him inside.

"I don't see why the hell you're holding me," the tendony man said. His thinning hair was greasy and stuck out in all directions. His clothes were muddy and hadn't been washed in months, it looked like.

"Sit down, shut up," Boz barked. "We're holding you 'cause Nate Spoda ID'd you as the one stashing Armored Courier bags down by the river tonight."

"That son of a bitch!" Lester roared and started to rise.

Boz shoved him back in his seat. "Yep, ID'd you right down to that tattoo of yours, which is the ugliest-looking woman I have *ever* seen, by the way. Say, that your mother?"

"That Nate," Lester muttered, looking at the door, "he's meat. Oh, that boy's gonna pay."

"Enough of that talk," Ed said. Then: "We're going downstairs for five minutes, see the Commonwealth's Attorney. He's gonna wanta talk to you. So you just cool your heels in here and don't cause a ruckus."

They stepped outside and locked the door. Boz cocked his head and heard the shuffle of chains moving toward the table. He gave Ed a thumbs-up.

At the end of the corridor, thick with August heat and moisture, they found Nate Spoda by the vending machines, sitting at a broken Formica table, sipping Pepsi and eating a Twinkie.

"Come on down here, Nate, just got a few more questions."

"After you, sir," Ed said, gesturing with his hand.

Nate took another bite of Twinkie and preceded them down the hall toward the interview room. Ed whispered to Boz, "He'll scream. But we gotta give Lester time to finish it before we go in."

"Okay, sure. Hey, Ed?"

"What?"

"You know I never shot anybody before."

"It ain't *anybody*. It's Lester Botts. Anyway, we'll shoot together. At the same time. How's that? Make you feel better?"

"Okay."

"And if Nate's still alive, shoot him too, and we'll say it was—"

"—accidental."

"Right."

Outside the door, Nate turned to them, washed down the Twinkie with the soda. There was Twinkie cream on his chin. Disgusting.

"Oh, one thing—" the kid began.

"Nate, this won't take long. We'll have you home in no time." Ed unlocked the door. "Go on inside. We'll be in, in a minute."

"Sure. But there's something—"

"Just go on in."

Nate hesitated uncertainly. He started to open the door.

"Nate," a man's voice called.

Boz and Ed spun around to see three men walking up the hall. They were in suits. And if they weren't federal agents, Boz thought, I'm Elvis's ghost. Shit.

"Hi, Agent Bigelow," Nate said cheerfully.

He *knows* them? Ed's heart began to race. They interviewed

him while we were gone? . . . Okay, think, goddamnit. What'd he tell 'em? Whatta we do?

But he couldn't think.

Wood for brains . . .

The agent was a tall, somber man, balding, his short blond hair in a monk's fringe just above narrow ears. He and the others flashed IDs—yep, FBI—and asked, "You're deputy Bosworth Peller and you're deputy Edward Rankin?"

"Yessir," they offered.

Boz was thinking: Lord, failure to secure a prisoner is a suspendable offense.

Ed, thinking pretty much the same, turned to Nate and said, "Tell you what, Nate, let's us go back to the canteen. Get another soda?"

"Or Twinkie. Those're good, ain't they?"

"It's cooler in here," Nate said and pushed inside the room where Lester and his well-honed knife awaited.

"No!" Boz shouted.

"What's the matter, Deputy?" one of the FBI agents asked.

"Well, nothing," Boz said quickly.

Both Boz and Ed found themselves staring at the door, behind which Nate was probably being stabbed to death at this moment. They forced their attention back to the federal law officers.

Wondering how they could salvage it. Well, sure . . . if Lester came out in a rush, all bloody, holding the knife, they could still nail him. The agents might even join in.

Damn, it was quiet in there. Maybe Lester had slit Nate's throat real sudden and was trying to get out through the window.

"Let's go inside," Bigelow suggested, nodding toward the door. "We should talk about the case."

"Well, I don't know if we want to do that."

"Why not?" another agent said. "Nate said it was cooler."

"After you," Bigelow said and motioned to the two deputies.

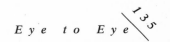

Who looked at each other and kept their hands near their service revolvers as they stepped through the door.

Lester was sitting in a chair, legs crossed, cuffed hands in his lap. Sitting across the table from him was Nate Spoda, flipping through a battered copy of the sheriff's department *Procedure Manual.* The knife was just where Boz'd left it.

Thank you, Lord in heaven . . .

Boz looked at Ed. Silence. Ed recovered first. "I suppose you're wondering why this suspect's here, Agent Bigelow. I guess there was a mix-up, don't you think, Boz? Wasn't the Commonwealth's Attorney supposed to be here?"

"That's what I thought. Sure. A mix-up."

"What suspect?" Bigelow asked.

"Uhm, well, Lester here."

"You better charge me or release me pretty damn soon," the man barked.

Bigelow asked, "Who's *he*? What's he doing here?"

"Well, we arrested him for the robbery tonight," Boz said. His tone asked, Am I missing something?

"You did?" the agent grumbled. "Why?"

"Uhm" was all that Boz could muster. Had they jeopardized the case with sloppy forensics?

A fourth FBI agent came into the room and handed a file to Bigelow. He read carefully, nodding. Then he looked up. "Okay. We've got probable cause."

Boz shivered with relief and turned a slick smile on Lester. "Thought you were off the hook, huh? Well—"

Bigelow nodded his shiny head and in a flash the other agents had relieved Boz and Ed of their weapons and belts, including the overpriced, made-in-Taiwan billy club Boz was so proud of.

"Officers, you have the right to remain silent . . ."

The rest of the *Miranda* warning trickled from his somber lips and when it was through they were cuffed.

"What's this all about?" Boz shouted.

Bigelow tapped the folder he'd received. "We just had an evidence response team go through the getaway car. Both your fingerprints were all over it. And we found dozens of footprints that seem to be police-issue shoes—like both of yours—leading down to the water near Mr. Spoda's house."

"I backed the car out to search it," Boz protested. "That's all."

"Without gloves? Without a crime scene unit present?"

"Well, it was an open-and-shut case . . ."

"We also happened to find over ninety thousand dollars in the back of your personal car, Officer Rankin."

"We just didn't have a chance to log it in. What with all—"

"The excitement," Boz said. "You know."

Ed said, "Check out those bags. They'll have Lester's prints all over them."

"Actually," Bigelow said as calm as a McDonald's clerk, "they don't. Only the two of yours. And there's a chrome-plated thirty-eight in your glove compartment. Tentative ballistics match the gun used in the robbery. Oh, and a ski mask too. Matches fibers found in the armored truck."

"Wait . . . it's a setup. You ain't got a case here. It's all circumstantial!"

"Afraid not. We have an eyewitness."

"Who?" Boz glanced toward the corridor.

"Nate, *are* these the men you saw walking by the river near your house just after the robbery this afternoon?"

Nate looked from Boz to Ed. "Yessir. This's them."

"You liar!" Ed cried.

"And they were in uniform?"

"Just like now."

"What the hell is going on here?" Boz snapped.

Ed choked faintly then turned a cold eye toward Nate. "You little—"

Bigelow said, "Gentlemen, we're transferring you to the federal lockup in Arlington. You can call attorneys from there."

"He's lying," Boz shouted. "He told us he didn't see who was in the bushes."

Finally Bigelow cracked a smile. "Well, he's hardly going to tell *you* that you're the ones he saw, is he? Two bullies with guns and nightsticks standing over him? He was terrified enough telling *us* the truth."

"No, listen to me," Ed pleaded. "You don't understand. He's just out to get us because we picked on him in high school."

The agent beside Bigelow snickered. "Pathetic."

"Take 'em to the van."

The men disappeared. Bigelow ordered the cuffs taken off Lester Botts. "You can go now."

The scrawny man glanced contemptuously around the room and stalked outside.

"Can I go too?" Nate asked.

"Sure can, sir." Bigelow shook his hand. "Bet it's been a long day."

■

Nate Spoda put on a CD. Hit the "play" button.

Mostly, late at night, he listened to Debussy or Ravel—something soothing. But tonight he was playing a Sergey Prokofiev piece. It was boisterous and rousing. As was Nate's mood.

He listened to classical music all day long, piped out onto the front porch through $1,000 speakers. Nate often laughed to himself, recalling the time he'd overheard somebody in town mention the "satanic" music he listened to. He wasn't sure what

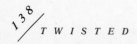

the particular hail-the-devil piece was but the timing of the comment suggested that what the grain salesman had overheard was Rachmaninoff.

Sorry it ain't Garth, fellas. . . .

He walked through the house, shutting out lights, though he left on the picture lights illuminating the Miró and the Jackson Pollock—his mood, again. He had to get to Paris soon. A dealer friend of his had acquired two small Picassos and had promised Nate first pick. He also missed Jeanette; he hadn't seen her in a month.

He wandered out onto his porch.

It was nearly midnight. He sat down in his mother's JFK rocker and gazed upward. This time of year the sky above the Shenandoah Valley was usually too hazy to see the heavens clearly—the local joke was that Caldon should've been named Caldron. But tonight, where the black of the trees became the black of the heavens, a brilliant dusting of stars spread out in a hemisphere above him. He sat this way for some minutes, taking pleasure in the constellations and moon.

He heard the footsteps long before he saw the figure moving up the path.

"Hey," he called.

"Hey," Lester Botts called back. He climbed the stairs, panting, and dropped four heavy canvas bags on the gray-painted porch. He sat, as he always did, not in one of the chairs but on the deck itself, his back against a post.

"You left over *ninety* thousand?" Nate asked.

"Sorry," Lester said, cringing, ever deferential to his boss. "I counted wrong."

Nate laughed. "Probably was a good idea." He'd thought Boz and Ed would fall for the scam if they'd seeded as little as thirty or forty thousand in the cave and getaway car. You wave double a man's annual salary, tax free, in front of his face and nine times out of ten you've bought him. But a job this big, it was probably a good idea to have a little extra bait.

Nate and Lester would still net nearly $400,000.

"We've gotta sit on it for a while, even if it's cash?" Lester asked.

"Better be real careful with this one," Nate said. As a rule they never operated in Virginia. Usually they traveled to New York, California or Florida for their heists. But when Nate learned from an associate in D.C. that the local Armored Courier branch was moving a cash shipment up to a new bank in Luray, he couldn't resist. Nate knew the guards would be lightweights and had probably never handled anything but check-cashing runs on paydays at the local plants. The money was appealing, of course. But what tipped the scale was that Nate figured that in order to make the scam work they needed two unwitting participants, preferably law enforcers. He didn't have any doubt whom to pick; adolescent grudges last as long as those of spurned lovers.

"You *have* to shoot him?" Nate asked. Meaning the guard. One of his rules was no gunplay unless absolutely necessary.

"He was a kid. Looking like he was going to go for that Glock on his hip. I was careful, only tapped a rib 'r two."

Nate nodded, eyes on the sky. Hoping for a shooting star. Didn't see one.

"You feel sorry for them?" Lester asked, after a moment.

"Who, the guards?"

"Naw, Ed and Boz."

Nate considered this for a moment. The music and the fragrant late-summer air and the rhythmic symphony of insects and frogs had turned Nate philosophical. "I'm thinking about something that Boz said. About how I didn't see eye to eye with him and Ed. He was talking about the heist but what he was really talking about was my life and theirs—whether he knew it or not."

"Most likely didn't."

"But it makes sense," he reflected. "Sums things up pretty well. The difference between us. . . . I could've lived with it if those boys'd just gone their own way, in school and afterwards. But they didn't. Nope. They made an issue out of it every chance they could. Too bad. But that was their choice."

"Well, good for us y'all *didn't* see eye to eye," said Lester, introspective himself. "Here's to differences."

"Here's to differences."

The men clinked beer cans together and drank.

Nate leaned forward and began to divvy up the cash into two equal piles.

TRIANGLE

"Maybe I'll go to Baltimore."

"You mean . . ." She looked over at him.

"Next weekend. When you're having the shower for Christie."

"To see . . ."

"Doug," he answered.

"Really?" Mo Anderson looked carefully at her fingernails, which she was painting bright red. He didn't like the color but he didn't say anything about it. She continued. "A bunch of women round here—boring. You'd enjoy yourself in Maryland. It'll be fun," she said.

"I think so too," Pete Anderson said. He sat across from Mo on the front porch of their split-level house in suburban Westchester County. The month was June and the air was thick with the smell of the jasmine that Mo had planted earlier in the spring. Pete used to like that smell. Now, though, it made him sick to his stomach.

Mo inspected her nails for streaks and pretended to be bored with the idea of him going to see Doug, who was her boss, an "important" guy who covered the whole East Coast territory. He'd invited both Mo and Pete to his country place but she'd planned a wedding shower for her niece. Doug had said to Pete, "Well, why don't you come on down solo?" Pete had said he'd think about it.

Oh, sure, she *seemed* bored with the idea of him going by himself. But she was a lousy actress; Pete could tell she was really excited at the thought and he knew why. But he just watched the lightning bugs and kept quiet. Played dumb. Unlike Mo, he *could* act.

They were silent and sipped their drinks, the ice clunking dully in the plastic glasses. It was the first day of summer and there must've been a thousand lightning bugs in their front yard.

"I know I kinda said I'd clean up the garage," he said, wincing a little. "But—"

"No, that can keep. I think it's a great idea, going down there."

I *know* you think it'd be a *great* idea, Pete thought. But he didn't say this to her. Lately he'd been thinking a lot of things and not saying them.

Pete was sweating—more from excitement than from the heat—and he wiped the moisture off his face and his short-cut blond hair with a napkin.

The phone rang and Mo went to answer it.

She came back and said, "It's your *father*," in that sour voice of hers. She sat down and didn't say anything else, just picked up her drink and examined her nails again.

Pete got up and went into the kitchen. His father lived in Wisconsin, not far from Lake Michigan. He loved the man and wished they lived closer together. Mo, though, didn't like him one bit and always raised a stink when Pete wanted to go visit. Pete was never exactly sure what the problem was between Mo and the man. But it made him mad that she treated him badly and would never talk to Pete about it.

And he was mad too that Mo seemed to put Pete in the middle of things. Sometimes Pete even felt guilty he *had* a father.

He enjoyed talking but hung up after only five minutes because he felt Mo didn't want him to be on the phone.

Pete walked out onto the porch. "Saturday. I'll go visit Doug then."

Mo said, "I think Saturday'd be fine."

Fine . . .

They went inside and watched TV for a while. Then, at eleven, Mo looked at her watch and stretched and said, "It's getting late. Time for bed."

And when Mo said it was time for bed, it was definitely time for bed.

■

Later that night, when she was asleep, Pete walked downstairs into the office. He reached behind a row of books resting on the built-in bookshelves and pulled out a large, sealed envelope.

He carried it down to his workshop in the basement. He opened the envelope and took out a book. It was called *Triangle* and Pete had found it in the true-crime section of a local used-book shop after flipping through nearly twenty books about real-life murders. Pete had never stolen anything in his life but that day he'd looked around the store and slipped the book inside his windbreaker then strolled casually out of the store. He'd *had* to steal it; he was afraid that—if everything went as he'd planned— the clerk might remember him buying the book and the police would use it as evidence.

Triangle was the true story of a couple in Colorado Springs. The wife was married to a man named Roy. But she was also seeing another man—Hank, a local carpenter and a friend of the family. Roy found out and waited until Hank was out hiking on a mountain path, then he snuck up and pushed him over a cliff. Hank grabbed on to a tree root but he lost his grip—or Roy smashed his hands; it wasn't clear—and Hank fell a hundred feet to his death on the rocks in the valley. Roy went back home and had a drink with his wife just to watch her reaction when the call came that Hank was dead.

 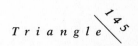

Pete didn't know squat about crimes. All he knew was what he'd seen on TV and in the movies. None of the criminals in those shows seemed very smart and they were always getting caught by the good guys, even though *they* didn't really seem much smarter than the bad guys. But that crime in Colorado was a smart crime. Because there were no murder weapons and very few clues. The only reason Roy got caught was that he'd forgotten to look for witnesses.

If the killer had only taken the time to look around him, he would have seen the campers, who had a perfect view of Hank Gibson plummeting to his bloody death, screaming as he fell, and of Roy standing on the cliff, watching him. . . .

Triangle became Pete's Bible. He read it cover to cover—to see how Roy had planned the crime and to find out how the police had investigated it.

Tonight, with Mo asleep, Pete read *Triangle* once again. Paying particular attention to the parts he'd underlined. Then he walked back upstairs, packed the book in the bottom of his suitcase and lay on the couch in the office, looking out the window at the hazy summer stars and thinking about his trip to Maryland from every angle.

Because he wanted to make sure he got away with the crime. He didn't want to go to jail for life—like Roy.

Oh, sure there were risks. Pete knew that. But nothing was going to stop him.

Doug had to die.

Pete realized he'd been thinking about the idea, in the back of his mind, for months, not long after Mo met Doug.

She worked for a drug company in Westchester—the same company Doug was a sales manager for, with his office in the company's headquarters in Baltimore. They met when he came to the branch office in New York for a sales conference. Mo had told Pete that she was having dinner with "somebody" from the com-

pany but she didn't say who. Pete didn't think anything of it until he overheard her tell one of her girlfriends on the phone about this really interesting guy she was working for. But then she realized Pete was standing near enough to hear and she changed the subject.

Over the next few months Pete noticed that Mo was getting distracted, paying less and less attention to him. And he heard her mention Doug more and more.

One night Pete asked her about him.

"Oh, Doug?" she said, sounding irritated. "Why, he's my boss. And a friend. That's all. Can't I have friends? Aren't I allowed?"

Pete noticed that Mo was starting to spend a lot of time on the phone and online. He tried to check the phone bills to see if she was calling Baltimore but she hid them or threw them out. He also tried to read her e-mails but found she'd changed her pass code. Pete's specialty was computers, though, and he easily broke into her account. But when he went to read her e-mails he found she'd deleted them all on the main server.

He was so furious he nearly smashed the computer.

Then, to Pete's dismay, Mo started inviting Doug to dinner at their house when he was in Westchester on company business. He was older than Mo and sort of heavy. Slick—slimy, in Pete's opinion. Those dinners were the worst. . . . They'd all three sit at the dinner table and Doug would try to charm Pete and ask him about computers and sports and the things that Mo obviously had told Doug that Pete was into. But it was awkward and you could tell he didn't give a damn about Pete. He kept glancing at Mo when he thought Pete wasn't looking.

By then Pete was checking up on Mo all the time. Sometimes he'd pretend to go to a game with some friends but he'd come home early and find that she was gone too. Then she'd get home at eight or nine and look all flustered, not expecting to find him,

 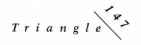

and she'd say she'd been working late even though she was just an office manager and hardly ever worked later than five before she met Doug. Once, when she claimed she was at the office, Pete called Doug's number in Baltimore and the message said he'd be out of town for a couple of days.

Everything was changing. Mo and Pete would have dinner together but it wasn't the same as it used to be. They didn't have picnics and they didn't take walks in the evenings. And they hardly ever sat together on the porch anymore and looked out at the fireflies and made plans for trips they'd wanted to take.

"I don't like him," Pete said. "Doug, I mean."

"Oh, quit being so jealous. He's a good friend, that's all. He likes both of us."

"No, he doesn't like me."

"Of course he does. You don't have to worry."

But Pete did worry and he worried even more when he found a Post-It note in her purse last month. It said, *D.G.—Sunday, motel 2 p.m.*

Doug's last name was Grant.

That Sunday morning Pete tried not to react when Mo said, "I'm going out for a while, honey."

"Where?"

"Shopping. I'll be back by five."

He thought about asking her exactly where she was going but he didn't think that was a good idea. It might make her suspicious. So he said cheerfully, "Okay, see you later."

As soon as her car had pulled out of the driveway he'd started calling motels in the area and asking for Douglas Grant.

The clerk at the Westchester Motor Inn said, "One minute, please. I'll connect you."

Pete hung up fast.

He was at the motel in fifteen minutes and, yep, there was

Mo's car parked in front of one of the doors. Pete snuck up close to the room. The shade was drawn and the lights were out but the window was partly open. Pete could hear bits of the conversation.

"I don't like that."

"That . . . ? " she asked.

"That color. I want you to paint your nails red. It's sexy. I don't like that color you're wearing. What is it?"

"Peach."

"I like bright red," Doug said.

"Well, okay."

There was some laughing. Then a long silence. Pete tried to look inside but he couldn't see anything. Finally, Mo said, "We have to talk. About Pete."

"He knows something," Doug was saying. "I know he does."

"He's been like a damn spy lately," she said, with that edge to her voice that Pete hated. "Sometimes I'd like to strangle him."

Pete closed his eyes when he heard Mo say this. Pressed the lids closed so hard he thought he might never open them again.

He heard the sound of a can opening. Beer, he guessed.

Doug said, "So what if he finds out?"

"So *what?* I told you what having an affair does to alimony in this state? It *eliminates* it. We have to be careful. I've got a lifestyle I'm accustomed to."

"Then what should we do?" Doug asked.

"I've been thinking about it. I think you should do something with him."

"Do something with him?" Doug had an edge to his voice too. "Get him a one-way ticket . . . ."

"Come on."

"Okay, baby, sorry. But what do you mean by do something?"

"Get to know him."

"You're kidding."

 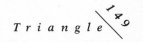

"Prove to him you're just my boss."

Doug laughed and said in a soft, low voice, "Does *that* feel like I'm just a boss?"

She laughed too. "Stop it. I'm trying to have a serious talk here."

"So, what? We go to a ball game together?"

"No, it's got to be more than that. Ask him to come visit you."

"Oh, that'd be fun." With that same snotty tone that Mo sometimes used.

She continued, "No, I like it. Ask us both to come down—maybe the weekend I'm having that shower for my niece. I won't be able to make it. Maybe he'll come by himself. You two hang out, paint the town. Pretend you've got a girlfriend or something."

"He won't believe that."

"Pete's only smart when it comes to computers and sports. He's stupid about everything else."

Pete wrung his hands together. Nearly sprained a thumb—like the time he jammed his finger on the basketball court.

"That means I have to pretend I like him."

"Yeah, that's *exactly* what it means. It's not going to kill you."

"Pick another weekend. You come with him."

"No," she said. "I'd have trouble keeping my hands off you."

A pause. Then Doug said, "Oh, hell, all right. I'll do it."

Pete, crouching on a strip of yellow grass beside three discarded soda cans, shook with fury. It took all his willpower not to scream.

He hurried home, threw himself down on the couch in the office and turned on the game.

When Mo came home—which wasn't at five at all, like she promised, but at six-thirty—he pretended he'd fallen asleep.

That night he decided what he had to do. The next day he went to the bookstore and stole the copy of *Triangle*.

On Saturday Mo drove him to the airport.

"You two're going to have fun together?"

"You bet," Pete said. He sounded cheerful because he *was* cheerful. "We're gonna have a fine time."

On the day of the murder, while his wife and her lover were sipping wine in a room at the Mountain View Lodge, Roy had lunch with a business associate. The man, who wished to remain anonymous, reported that Roy was in unusually good spirits. It seemed his depression had lifted and he was happy once more.

Fine, fine, fine . . .

Mo kissed him and then hugged him hard. He didn't kiss her back, though he did give her a hug, reminding himself that he had to be a good actor.

"You're looking forward to going, aren't you?" she asked.

"I sure am," he answered. This was true.

"I love you," she said.

"I love you too," he responded. This was not true. He hated her. He hoped the plane left on time. He didn't want to wait here with her any longer than he had to.

The flight attendant, a pretty blonde woman, kept stopping at his seat. This wasn't unusual for Pete. Women liked him. He'd heard a million times that he was cute, he was handsome, he was charming. Women were always leaning close and telling him that. Touching his arm, squeezing his shoulder. But today he answered her questions with a simple yes or no. And kept reading *Triangle*. Reading the passages he'd underlined. Memorizing them.

Learning about fingerprints, about interviewing witnesses, about footprints and trace evidence. There was a lot he didn't understand but he did figure out how smart the cops were and that he'd have to be very careful if he was going to kill Doug and get away with it.

"We're about to land," the flight attendant said. "Could you put your seat belt on, please?" She smiled at him.

He clicked the belt on and went back to his book.

Hank Gibson's body had fallen one hundred and twelve feet. He'd landed on his right side and of the more than two hundred bones in the human body, he'd broken seventy-seven of them. His ribs had pierced all his major internal organs and his skull was flattened on one side.

"Welcome to Baltimore, where the local time is twelve twenty-five," the flight attendant said. "Please remain in your seat with the seat belt fastened until the plane has come to a complete stop and the pilot has turned off the *Fasten Seat Belt* sign. Thank you."

The medical examiner estimated that Hank was traveling 80 mph when he struck the ground and that death was virtually instantaneous.

Welcome to Baltimore . . .

■

Doug met him at the airport. Shook his hand.

"How you doing?" Doug asked.

"Okay."

This was so weird. Spending the weekend with a man that Mo knew so well and that Pete hardly knew at all.

Going hiking with somebody he hardly knew at all.

Going to kill somebody he hardly knew at all . . .

He walked along beside Doug.

"I need a beer and some crabs," Doug said as they got into his car. "You hungry?"

"Sure am."

They stopped at the waterfront and went into an old dive. The place stunk. It smelled like the cleanser Mo used on the floor when Randolf, their Labrador retriever puppy, made a mess on the carpet.

Doug whistled at the waitress before they'd even sat down. "Hey, honey, think you can handle two real men?" He gave her the sort of grin he'd seen Doug give Mo a couple of times. Pete looked away, a little embarrassed but plenty disgusted.

When they started to eat, Doug calmed down, though that was probably the beers more than the food. Like Mo got after her third glass of Gallo in the evenings.

Pete wasn't saying much. Doug tried to be cheerful. He talked and talked but it was just garbage. Pete didn't pay any attention.

"Maybe I'll give my girlfriend a call," Doug said suddenly. "See if she wants to join us."

"You have a girlfriend? What's her name?"

"Uhm. Cathy," he said.

The waitress's name tag said, *Hi, I'm Cathleen.*

"That'd be fun," Pete said.

"She might be going out of town this weekend." He avoided Pete's eyes. "But I'll call her later."

Pete's only smart when it comes to computers and sports. He's stupid about everything else. . . .

Finally Doug looked at his watch and said, "So what do you feel like doing now?"

Pete pretended to think for a minute and asked, "Anyplace we can go hiking around here?"

"Hiking?"

"Like any mountain trails?"

Doug finished his beer, shook his head. "Naw, nothing like that I know of."

Pete felt rage again—his hands were shaking, the blood

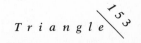

Triangle 153

roaring in his ears—but he covered it up pretty well and tried to think. Now, what was he going to do? He'd counted on Doug agreeing to whatever he wanted. He'd counted on a nice high cliff.

Hank was traveling 80 mph when he struck the ground. . . .

But then Doug continued. "But if you want to be outside, one thing we could do maybe is go hunting."

"Hunting?"

"Nothing good's in season now," Doug said. "But there's always rabbits and squirrels."

"Well—"

"I've got a couple guns we can use."

Pete debated for only a moment and then said, "Okay. Let's go hunting."

■

"You shoot much?" Doug asked him.

"Some."

In fact, Pete was a good shot. His father had taught him how to load and clean guns and how to handle them. ("Never point it at anything unless you're prepared to shoot it.")

But Pete didn't want Doug to know he knew anything about guns so he let the man show him how to load the little twenty-two and how to pull the slide to cock it and where the safety was.

I'm a much better actor than Mo.

They were in Doug's house, which was pretty nice. It was in the woods and it was a big place, full of stone walls and glass. The furniture wasn't like the cheap things Mo and Pete had. It was mostly antiques.

Which depressed Pete even more, made him angrier, because he knew that Mo liked money and she liked *people* who had money even if they were idiots, like Doug. When Pete looked at Doug's beautiful house he knew that if Mo ever saw it then she'd

want Doug even more. Then he wondered if she *had* seen it. Pete had gone to Wisconsin a few months ago, to see his father and cousins. Maybe Mo had come down here to spend the night with Doug.

"So," Doug said. "Ready?"

"Where're we going?" Pete asked.

"There's a good field about a mile from here. It's not posted. Anything we can hit, we can take."

"Sounds good to me," Pete said.

They got into the car and Doug pulled onto the road.

"Better put that seat belt on," Doug warned. "I drive like a crazy man."

■

Pete was looking around the big, empty field.

Not a soul.

"What?" Doug asked, and Pete realized that the man was staring at him.

"I said it's pretty quiet."

And deserted. No witnesses. Like the ones who screwed up Roy's plans in *Triangle.*

"Nobody knows about this place. I found it by my little old lonesome." Doug said this real proud, as if he'd discovered a cure for cancer. "Lessee." He lifted his rifle and squeezed off a round.

Crack . . .

He missed a can sitting about thirty feet away.

"Little rusty," he said. "But, hey, aren't we having fun?"

"Sure are," Pete answered.

Doug fired again, three times, and hit the can on the last shot. It leapt into the air. "There we go!"

Doug reloaded and they started through the tall grass and brush.

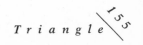

They walked for five minutes.

"There," Doug said. "Can you hit that rock over there?"

He was pointing at a white rock about twenty feet from them. Pete thought he could have hit it but he missed on purpose. He emptied the clip.

"Not bad," Doug said. "Came close the last few shots." Pete knew he was being sarcastic.

Pete reloaded and they continued through the grass.

"So," Doug said. "How's she doing?"

"Fine. She's fine."

Whenever Mo was upset and Pete'd ask her how she was she'd say, "Fine. I'm fine."

Which didn't mean fine at all. It meant, I don't feel like telling you anything. I'm keeping secrets from you.

I don't love you anymore.

They stepped over a few fallen logs and started down a hill. The grass was mixed with blue flowers and daisies. Mo liked to garden and was always driving up to the nursery to buy plants. Sometimes she'd come back without any and Pete began to wonder if, on those trips, she was really seeing Doug instead. He got angry again. Hands sweaty, teeth grinding together.

"She get her car fixed?" Doug asked. "She was saying that there was something wrong with the transmission."

How'd he know that? The car broke down only four days ago. Had Doug been there and Pete didn't know it?

Doug glanced at Pete and repeated the question.

Pete blinked. "Oh, her car? Yeah, it's okay. She took it in and they fixed it."

But then he felt better because that meant they *hadn't* talked yesterday or otherwise she would have told him about getting the car fixed.

On the other hand, maybe Doug was lying to him now. Mak-

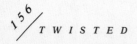

ing it *look* as if she hadn't told him about the car when they really had talked.

Pete looked at Doug's pudgy face and couldn't decide whether to believe him or not. He looked sort of innocent but Pete had learned that people who seemed innocent were sometimes the most guilty. Roy, the husband in *Triangle*, had been a church choir director. From the smiling picture in the book, you'd never guess he'd kill somebody.

Thinking about the book, thinking about murder.

Pete was scanning the field. Yes, there . . . about fifty feet away. A fence. Five feet high. It would work just fine.

Fine . . .

As fine as Mo.

Who wanted Doug more than she wanted Pete.

"What're you looking for?" Doug asked.

"Something to shoot."

And thought: Witnesses. That's what I'm looking for.

"Let's go that way," Pete said and walked toward the fence.

Doug shrugged. "Sure. Why not?"

Pete studied it as they approached. Wood posts about eight feet apart, five strands of rusting wire.

Not too easy to climb over but it wasn't barbed wire like some of the fences they'd passed. Besides, Pete didn't want it *too* easy to climb. He'd been thinking. He had a plan.

Roy had thought about the murder for weeks. It had obsessed his every waking moment. He'd drawn charts and diagrams and planned every detail down to the nth degree. In his mind, at least, it was the perfect crime. . . .

Pete now asked, "So what's your girlfriend do?"

"Uhm, my girlfriend? She works in Baltimore."

"Oh. Doing what?"

"In an office. Big company."

 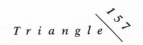

"Oh."

They got closer to the fence. Pete asked, "You're divorced? Mo was saying you're divorced."

"Right. Betty and I split up two years ago."

"You still see her?"

"Who? Betty? Naw. We went our separate ways."

"You have any kids?"

"Nope."

Of course not. When you had kids you had to think about somebody else. You couldn't think about yourself all the time.

Like Doug did.

Like Mo.

Pete was looking around again. For squirrels, for rabbits, for witnesses.

Then Doug stopped and he looked around too. Pete wondered why but then Doug took a bottle of beer from his knapsack and drank the whole bottle down and tossed it on the ground. "You want something to drink?" Doug asked.

"No," Pete answered. It was good that Doug'd be slightly drunk when they found him. They'd check his blood. They did that. That's how they knew Hank'd been drinking when they got what was left of the body (80 mph, after all) to the Colorado Springs hospital—they checked the alcohol in the blood.

The fence was only twenty feet away.

"Oh, hey," Pete said. "Over there. Look."

He pointed to the grass on the other side of the fence.

"What?" Doug asked.

"I saw a couple of rabbits."

"You did? Where?"

"I'll show you. Come on."

"Okay. Let's do it," Doug said.

They walked to the fence. Suddenly Doug reached out and took Pete's rifle. "I'll hold it while you climb over. Safer that way."

Jesus . . . Pete froze with terror. He realized now that Doug was going to do exactly what Pete had in mind. He'd been planning on holding Doug's gun for him. And then when Doug was at the top of the fence he was going to shoot him. Making it look like Doug had tried to carry his gun as he climbed the fence but he'd dropped it and it went off.

Roy bet on the old law enforcement rule that what looks like an accident probably is an accident. . . .

Pete didn't move. He thought he saw something odd in Doug's eyes, something mean and sarcastic. It reminded him of Mo's expression. Pete took one look at those eyes and he could see how much Doug hated him and how much he loved Mo.

"You want me to go first?" Pete asked. Not moving, wondering if he should just run.

"Sure," Doug said. "You go first. Then I'll hand the guns over to you." His eyes said, You're not afraid of climbing over the fence, are you? You're not afraid to turn your back on me, are you?

Then Doug was looking around too.

Looking for witnesses, just like Pete had been.

"Go on," Doug encouraged.

Pete—his hands shaking now from fear—started to climb. Thinking: This is it. He's going to shoot me. Last month I left the motel too early! Doug and Mo had kept talking and planned out how he was going to ask me down here and pretend to be all nice then he'd shoot me.

Remembering it was Doug who'd suggested hunting.

But if I run, Pete thought, he'll chase me down and shoot me. Even if he shoots me in the back he'll just claim it's an accident.

Roy's lawyer argued to the jury that, yes, the men had met on the path and struggled, but that Hank had fallen accidentally. He urged the jury to find that, at worst, Roy was guilty of negligent homicide. . . .

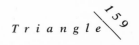

He put his foot on the first rung of wire. Started up.

Second rung of wire . . .

Pete's heart was beating a million times a minute. He had to pause to wipe his palms.

He thought he heard a whisper, as if Doug were talking to himself.

He swung his leg over the top wire.

Then he heard the sound of a gun cocking.

And Doug said in a hoarse whisper, "You're dead."

Pete gasped.

Crack!

The short, snappy sound of the twenty-two filled the field.

Pete choked a cry and looked around, nearly falling off the fence.

"Damn," Doug muttered. He was aiming away from the fence. Nodding toward a tree line. "Squirrel. Missed him by two inches."

"Squirrel," Pete repeated manically. "And you missed him."

"Two goddamn inches."

Hands shaking, Pete continued over the fence and climbed to the ground.

"You okay?" Doug asked. "You look a little funny."

"I'm fine," he said.

Fine, fine, fine . . .

Doug handed Pete the guns and started over the fence. Pete debated. Then he put his rifle on the ground and gripped Doug's gun tight. He walked to the fence so that he was right below Doug.

"Look," Doug said as he got to the top. He was straddling it, his right leg on one side of the fence, his left on the other. "Over there." He pointed nearby.

There was a big gray lop-eared rabbit on his haunches only twenty feet away.

"There you go!" Doug whispered. "You've got a great shot."

Pete shouldered the gun. It was pointing at the ground, halfway between the rabbit and Doug.

"Go ahead. What're you waiting for?"

Roy was convicted of premeditated murder in the first degree and sentenced to life in prison. Yet he came very close to committing the perfect murder. If not for a simple twist of fate he would have gotten away with it. . . .

Pete looked at the rabbit, looked at Doug.

"Aren't you going to shoot?"

Uhm, okay, he thought.

Pete raised the gun and pulled the trigger once.

Doug gasped, pressed at the tiny bullethole in his chest. "But . . . but . . . No!"

He fell backward off the fence and lay on a patch of dried mud, completely still. The rabbit bounded through the grass, panicked by the sound of the shot, and disappeared in a tangle of bushes that Pete recognized as blackberries. Mo had planted tons of them in their backyard.

■

The plane descended from cruising altitude and slowly floated toward the airport.

Pete watched the billowy clouds and his fellow passengers, read the in-flight magazine and the "Sky Mall" catalog. He was bored. He didn't have his book to read. Before he'd talked to the Maryland state troopers about Doug's death he'd thrown *Triangle* into a trash bin.

One of the reasons the jury convicted Roy was that, upon examining his house, the police found several books about disposing of evidence. Roy had no satisfactory explanation for them. . . .

The small plane glided out of the skies and landed at White Plains airport. Pete pulled his knapsack out from underneath the

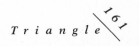

seat in front of him and climbed out of the plane. He walked down the ramp, beside the flight attendant, a tall black woman, talking with her about the flight.

Pete saw Mo at the gate. She looked numb. She wore sunglasses and Pete supposed she'd been crying. She was clutching a Kleenex in her fingers.

Her nails weren't bright red anymore, he noticed.

They weren't peach either.

They were just plain fingernail color.

The flight attendant came up to Mo. "You're Mrs. Jill Anderson?"

Mo nodded.

The woman held up a sheet of paper. "Here. Could you sign this, please?"

Numbly, Mo took the pen the woman offered and signed the paper.

It was an unaccompanied-minor form, which adults had to sign to allow their children to get on planes by themselves. The parent picking up the child also had to sign it. After his parents were divorced Pete flew back and forth between his dad in Wisconsin and his mother, Mo, in White Plains so often he knew all about airlines' procedures for kids who flew alone.

"I have to say," she said to Mo, smiling down at Pete, "he's the best behaved youngster I've ever had on one of my flights. How old are you, Pete?"

"I'm ten," he answered. "But I'm going to be eleven next week."

She squeezed his shoulder. Then looked at Mo. "I'm so sorry about what happened," she said in a soft voice. "The trooper who put Pete on the plane told me your boyfriend was killed in a hunting accident."

"No," Mo said, struggling to say the words, "he wasn't my boyfriend."

Though Pete was thinking: Of course he was your boyfriend. Except you didn't want the court to find that out because then Dad wouldn't have to pay you alimony anymore. Which is why she and Doug had been working so hard to convince Pete that Doug was "just a friend."

Can't I have friends? Aren't I allowed?

No, you're not, Pete thought. You're not going to get away with dumping your son the way you dumped Dad.

"Can we go home, Mo?" he asked, looking as sad as he could. "I feel real funny about what happened."

"Sure, honey."

"Mo?" the flight attendant asked.

Mo, staring out the window, said, "My name's Jill. But when he was five Pete tried to write *mother* on my birthday card. He just wrote *M-O* and didn't know how to spell the rest. It became my nickname."

"What a sweet story," the woman said and looked like *she* was going to cry. "Pete, you come back and fly with us real soon."

"Okay."

"Hey, what're you going to do for your birthday?"

"I don't know," he said. Then he looked up at his mother. "I was thinking about maybe going hiking. In Colorado. Just the two of us."

ALL THE WORLD'S
A STAGE

The couple were returning from the theater to the Thames ferry, through a deserted, unsavory area of South London, at four hours past candle-lighting.

Charles and Margaret Cooper ought, by rights, to have been home now with their small children and Margaret's mother, a plague widow, who lived with them in a small abode in Charing Cross. But they had dallied at the Globe to visit with Will Shakespeare, whom Charles Cooper counted among his friends. Shakespeare's family and Charles's had long ago owned adjoining acreage on the Avon River and their fathers would on occasion hunt together with falcons and enjoy pints at one of the Stratford taverns. The playwright was busy this time of year—unlike many London theaters, which closed when the Court was summering out of the city, the Globe gave performances year round—but he had been able to join the Coopers for a time to sip Jerez sherry and claret and to talk about recent plays.

The husband and wife now made their way quickly through the dark streets—the suburbs south of the river had few dependable candle-lighters—and they concentrated carefully on where they put their feet.

The summer air was cool and Margaret wore a heavy linen gown, loose in the back and with a tight bodice. Being married, she cut her dress high enough to cover her breasts but she eschewed the felt or beaver cap customary among older wives and wore only silk ribbons and a few glass jewels in her hair. Charles wore simple breeches, blouse and leather vest.

"'Twas a delightful night," Margaret said, holding tighter to his arm as they negotiated a crook in the narrow road. "I thank thee, my husband."

The couple greatly enjoyed attending plays but Charles's wine-importing company had only recently begun to show profit and the Coopers had had little money to spend on their own amusements. Until this year, indeed, they had only been able to afford the penny admission to be understanders—those crowded in the central gallery of the theater. But of late Charles's industry was showing some rewards and tonight he had surprised his wife with threepence seats in the gallery, where they had sat upon cushions and shared nuts and an early-season pear.

A shout from behind startled them and Charles turned to see, perhaps fifteen yards away, a man in a black velvet hat and baggy, tattered doublet, dodging a rider. It seemed that the man had been so intent on crossing the street quickly that he had not noticed the horse. Perhaps it was Charles's imagination, or a trick of the light, but it appeared to him that the pedestrian looked up, noted Charles's gaze and turned with haste into an alleyway.

Not wishing to alarm his wife, though, Charles made no mention of the fellow and continued his conversation. "Perhaps next year we shall attend Black Friars."

Margaret laughed. Even some peers shunned paying the six-pence admission at that theater, though the venue was small and luxurious and boasted actors of the highest skill. "Perhaps," she said dubiously.

Charles glanced behind them once more but saw no sign of the hatted man.

As they turned the corner onto the road that would take

them to the ferry, however, the very man appeared from an adjacent alleyway. He had flanked their route at a run, it seemed, and now stepped forward, breathing hard.

"I pray thee, sir, madam, a minute of thy time."

A beggar only, Charles assumed. But they often turned dangerous if you did not come forth with coin. Charles drew a long dagger from his belt and stood between his wife and this man.

"Ah, no need for pig-sticking," the man said, nodding at the dagger. "This pig is not himself armed." He held up empty hands. "Not armed with a bodkin, that is to say. Only with the truth."

He was a strange sack of a creature. Eyes sunken in his skull, jaundiced skin hanging upon his body. It was clear that some years ago a whore or loose woman had bestowed upon him the bone-ache, and the disease was about to work its final misery upon him; the doublet, which Charles had assumed to be stolen from a fatter man, undoubtedly was his own and hung loose because of recent emaciation.

"Who art thou?" Charles demanded.

"I am one of those to whom thou owe this evening's playgoing, to whom thou owe thy profession as a bestower of the grape's nectar, to whom thou owe thy life in this fine city." The man inhaled air that was as sulfurous and foul as always in these industrial suburbs, then spat upon the cobblestones.

"Explain thyself and why thou have been dogging me or, faith, sir, I shall levy a hue and cry for the sheriff."

"No need for that, young Cooper."

"Thou know me?"

"Indeed, sir. I know thee too well." The man's yellow eyes grew troubled. "Let me be forthright and speak no more in riddles. My name is Marr. I have lived a life of a rogue and I would have been content to die a rogue's death. But a fortnight ago the Lord our God did appear to me in a dream and admonish me to make amends for my sins in life, lest I be denied entrance to the glorious court of Heaven. In truth, sir, I warrant that I should need *two* lifetimes to make such amends, when I have merely a fraction of one left, so I have but chosen the most worrisome deed I have committed and have sought out he whom I have wronged the worst."

Charles looked over the puny man and put the dagger away. "And how hast thou wronged me?"

"As I said before, it is I—and several of my comrades, now all gone to the plague and infesting hell, I warrant—who be responsible for ending thy idyllic life in the countryside near Stratford and coming to this mischievous city so many years ago."

"Howbeit that this is so?"

"I pray thee, sir, tell me what great tragedy befell thy life?"

Charles did not need a moment to reflect. "My loving father taken from us and our lands forfeited."

Fifteen years ago, it was claimed by the sheriff near Stratford that Richard Cooper was caught poaching deer on the property of Lord Westcott, Baron of Habershire. When the sheriff's bailiffs tried to arrest him he launched an arrow their way. The bailiffs gave chase and, after a struggle, stabbed and killed him. Richard Cooper was a landed gentleman with no need to poach deer and it was widely believed that the incident was a tragic misunderstanding. Still, a local court—sympathetic to the noble class—decreed that the family's land be forfeited to Westcott, who sold it for considerable profit. The rogue would not give so much as a tuppence to Charles's mother, who died soon after from grief. Eighteen-year-old Charles, the only child, had no choice but to walk to London to seek his fortune. He worked labor for some years, then apprenticed to the vintner's trade, became a member of the guild and over the years turned his thoughts away from the tragedy.

Marr wiped his unpleasant mouth, revealing as few teeth as

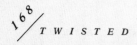

a puking babe, and said, "I knew well that this would be thy answer." He looked about and whispered, "Faith, sir, I have intelligence about what truly happened that sad day."

"Continue," Charles commanded.

"Westcott was as many nobles then and now," Marr said. "His life was lived far beyond his means and he found himself increasingly in debt."

This was well known to anyone who read the Fleet Street pamphlets or listened to gossip in the taverns. Many of the nobles were selling off their goods and portions of their estates to meet the costs of their extravagant lifestyles.

"There came to Westcott an ignoble scoundrel named Robert Murtaugh."

"I know the name," Margaret said. "For reasons I cannot recall, there be an unsavory association accompanying it."

"Faith, good lady, I warrant that is so. Murtaugh is a peer of the realm, but a lowly knight, an office he himself did purchase. He hath made an enterprise of seeking out nobles deep in debt. He then arranges various schemes whereby they come into lands or property through illicit means. He himself takes a generous percentage of their gain."

Charles whispered in horror, "And my father was a victim of such a scheme?"

"Faith, sir, he was. It was I and those other scoundrels I made mention of who waylaid him on his own land and conveyed him, bound, to Lord Westcott's fields. There, by prior arrangement, the sheriff's bailiffs did arrive and kill him. A dead hart and a bow and quiver were set next to his cold body to testify, by appearance, that he had been poaching."

"Thy father, murdered," Margaret whispered.

"O merciful Lord in heaven," Charles said, his eyes burning with hatred. He drew his bodkin once more and pressed the blade against Marr's neck. The rogue moved not an inch.

"No, husband, thou cannot. Please." Margaret took his arm.

The man said, "Verily, sir, I did not know the bailiffs had murder in mind. I thought they be merely intent on extracting a bribe from thy father for his release, as such rustic lawmen are wont to do. No one was more shocked than I by the deadly turn the events that day took. But I am nonetheless as guilty of this heinous crime as they, and I will not beg for mercy. If God moves thy hand to slit my throat in retribution for what I have done, so be it."

The memory of that terrible night flooded through him—the sheriff's ignominiously carting the body to the house, his mother's wailing in grief, then the long days after: his mother's decline, the poverty, the struggle to start a new life in the unforgiving city of London. And yet Charles found his hand unable to harm this pitiful creature. Slowly he lowered the dagger and replaced it in the scabbard on his girdle. He studied Marr closely. He saw such penitence in the man's face that it seemed he had spoken truly. Still, he asked, "If Murtaugh be as thou say, then many would have cause to despise him. How know I that thou art not merely one of those aggrieved by him and have spun this tale to—as thy very name suggests—mar his reputation?"

"By God's body, sir, I speak the truth. Of bitterness against Sir Murtaugh I have none, for it was my choice to corrupt my soul with the foul deed I have revealed to thee. Yet thy jaundiced view of my motives I do comprehend and can offer unto thee a token of proof."

Marr took from his pocket a golden ring and placed it in Charles's hand.

The vintner gasped. "It is my father's signet ring. See, Margaret, see his reversed initials? I remember I would sit with him some evenings and watch him press this ring into hot wax red as a rose to seal his correspondence."

"I took this as part recompense for our efforts; my comrades

partook of the coinage in thy father's purse. I oft thought: Had I taken and spent his money, as did they, thus disposing of the mementos of our deed, perhaps then the guilt would not have burned me like smelter's coals all these years, as hath this tiny piece of gold. But now I am glad I kept it, for I can at least return it to its rightful owner, before I cast away my mortal sheath."

"My father, not I, be the rightful owner," Charles muttered darkly. He closed his hand tightly around the ring. He leaned against the stone wall beside him and shook with rage and sorrow. A moment later he felt his wife's hand upon his. The fierce pressure with which he gripped the ring subsided.

Margaret said to him, "We must to the courts. Westcott and Murtaugh will feel the lash of justice upon them."

"Faith, madam, that cannot be. Lord Westcott is dead these five years. And his brigand son after him hath spent every pence of the inheritance. The land is gone to the Crown for taxes."

"What of Murtaugh?" Charles asked. "He lives still?"

"Oh, yes, sir. But though he is well and keeps quarters in London, he is further from the reach of justice than Lord Westcott in heaven. For Sir Murtaugh is much in favor with the duke and others highly placed at Court. Many have availed themselves of the villain's services to diminish their debt. The judges at Queen's Bench will not even hear thy claim and, in truth, thou will put thy freedom, indeed thy life, in jeopardy to bring these charges into the open. My desire this night was not to set thy course on a reckless journey of revenge, sir. I intend merely to make amends to one I have wronged."

He gazed at Marr for a moment and then said, "Thou art an evil man and though I am a good Christian, I cannot find it in my heart to forgive thee. Still, I will pray for thy soul. Perhaps God will be more lenient than I. Now, get thee gone. I swear that should ever thou cross my path again, my bodkin hand will not be stayed from its visit to thy throat and thou shall find thyself pleading thy case in the holy court of heaven far sooner than thou didst intend."

"Yes, good sir. So shall it be."

Charles's attention turned momentarily to the ring so that he might place it on his finger. When he looked up once more, the alleyway was empty; the ruffian had vanished silently into the night.

■

Near candle-lighting the next day Charles Cooper closed his wares house and repaired to the home of his friend, Hal Pepper, a man near to Charles's age but of better means, having inherited several apartments in a pleasant area of the city, which he let out for good profit.

Joining them was a large man of deliberate movement and speech. His true name was lost in the annals of his own history and everyone knew him only as Stout, the words not referring to his girth—significant though that be—but to his affection for black ale. He and Charles had met some years ago because the vintner bought Stout's wares; the man made and sold barrels and he often joked that he was a cooper by trade while Charles was a Cooper by birth.

The three had become close comrades, held together by common interests—cards and taverns and, particularly, the love of theater; they often ferried south of the Thames to see plays at the Swan, the Rose or the Globe. Pepper also had occasional business dealings with James Burbage, who had built many of the theaters in London. For his part, Charles harbored not-so-secret desires to be a player. Stout had no connection with the theater other than a childlike fascination with plays, which he seemed to believe were his portal to the world outside working-class London. As he would plane the staves of his barrels and pound the red-hot hoops with a smithy's hammer he would recite lines from the latest works of Shakespeare or Jonson or from the classics of the late Kyd and Marlowe, much in vogue of late. These words he had memorized from the performance, not the printed page; he was a poor reader.

Charles now told them the story that Marr had related to him. The friends reeled at the news of the death of Richard Cooper. They began to question Charles but he brought all conversing to a halt by saying, "He who committed this terrible deed shall die by my hand, I am determined."

"But," Stout said, "if thou kill Murtaugh, suspicion will doubtless fall immediately upon thee, as one aggrieved by his foul deeds against thy father."

"I think not," Charles replied. "It was Lord Westcott who stole my father's land. Murtaugh was merely a facilitator. No, I warrant that this brigand hath connived so much from so many that surely to examine all those with reason to kill him would keep the constable busy for a year. I believe I can have my revenge and escape with my life."

Hal Pepper, who being of means and thus knowledgeable in the ways of the Court, said, "Thou know not what thou say. Murtaugh hath highly placed friends who will not enjoy his loss. Corruption is a hydra, a many-headed creature. Thou may cut off one head, but another will poison thee before the first grow back—as it surely will."

"I care not."

Stout said, "But doth thy *wife* care? I warrant thee, friend, she doth very truly. Would thy *children* care if their father be drawn and quartered?"

Charles nodded at a fencing foil above Hal's fireplace. "I could meet Murtaugh in a duel."

Hal replied, "He is an expert swordsman."

"I may still win. I am younger, perchance stronger."

"Even if thou best him, what then? A hobnob with the jury at the Queen's Bench and, after, a visit to the executioner." Hal waved his arm in disgust. "Pox . . . at best thou would end up like Jonson."

Ben Jonson, the actor and playwright, had killed a man in a duel several years ago and barely escaped execution. He saved himself only by reciting the neck verse—Psalm 50, verse 1—and pleading the benefit of clergy. But his punishment was hard: to be branded with a hot iron.

"I will find some way to kill Murtaugh."

Hal persisted in his dissuasion. "But what advantage can his death gain thee?"

"It can gain me justice."

Hal's face curled into an ironic smile. "Justice in London town? That be like the fabled unicorn, of which everyone speaks but no one can find."

Stout took a clay pipe, small in his massive woodworker's hands, and packed it with aromatic weed from the Americas, which was currently very much in style. He touched a burning straw to the bowl and inhaled deeply. Soon smoke wafted to the ceiling. He slowly said to Hal, "Thy mockery is not entirely misplaced, my friend, but my simple mind tells me that justice is not altogether alien to us, even among the denizens of London. What of the plays we see? Ofttimes they abound with justice. The tragedy of Faustus . . . and that which we saw at the Globe a fortnight ago, inked by our friend Will Shakespeare: the story of Richard the Third. The characters therein are awash with evil— but right prevails, as Henry Tudor doth prove by slaying the 'bloody dog.' "

"Exactly," Charles whispered.

"But they be make-believe, my friends," Hal countered.

"They are of no more substance than the ink with which Kit Marlowe and Will penned those entertainments."

Charles would not, however, be diverted. "What know thou of this Murtaugh? Hath he any interests?"

Hal answered, "Other men's wives and other men's money."

"What else know thou?"

"As I said, he is a swordsman or so fancies himself. And he rides with the hounds whenever he quits London for the country. He is intoxicated with pride. One cannot flatter him too much. He strives constantly to impress members of the Court."

"Where lives he?"

Stout and Hal remained silent, clearly troubled by their friend's deadly intent.

"Where?" Charles persisted.

Hal sighed and waved his hand to usher away a cloud of smoke from Stout's pipe. "That weed is most foul."

"Faith, sir, I find it calming."

Finally Hal turned to Charles. "Murtaugh hath but an apartment fit for a man of no station higher than journeyman and far smaller than he boasts. But it is near the Strand and the locale puts him in the regular company of men more powerful and richer than he. Thou will find it in Whitefriars, near the embankment."

"And where doth he spend his days?"

"I know not for certain but I would speculate that, being a dog beneath the table of Court, he goes daily to the palace at Whitehall to pick through whatever sundry scraps of gossip and schemes he might find and doth so even now, when the queen is in Greenwich."

"And therefore what route would he take on the way from his apartment to the palace?" Charles asked Stout, who through his trade knew most of the labyrinthine streets of London.

"Charles," Stout began. "I like not what thou suggest."

"What route?"

Reluctantly the man answered, "On horse he would follow the embankment west then south, when the river turns, to White-hall."

"Of the piers along that route, know thou the most deserted?" Charles inquired.

Stout said, "The one in most disuse would be Temple wharf. As the Inns of Court have grown in number and size, the area hath fewer wares houses than once it did." He added pointedly, "It also be near to the place where prisoners are chained at water level and made to endure the tides. Perchance thou ought shackle thyself there following thy felony, Charles, and, in doing, save the Crown's prosecutor a day's work."

"Dear friend," Hal began, "I pray thee, put whatever foul plans are in thy heart aside. Thou cannot—"

But his words were stopped by the staunch gaze of their friend, who looked from one of his comrades to the other and said, "As when fire in one small house doth leap to the thatch of its neighbors and continue its rampaging journey till all the row be destroyed, so it did happen that many lives were burned to ash with the single death of my father." Charles held his hand up, displaying the signet ring that Marr had given him yesterday. The gold caught the light from Hal's lantern and seemed to burn with all the fury in Charles's heart. "I cannot live without avenging the vile alchemy that converted a fine man into nothing more than this paltry piece of still metal."

A look passed between Hal and Stout, and the larger of the two said to Charles, "Thy mind is set, that much is clear. Faith, dear friend, whatever thy decision be, we shall stand by thee."

Hal added, "And for my part I shall look out for Margaret and thy children—if the matter come to that. They shall want for nothing if it be in my means to so provide."

Charles embraced them then said mirthfully, "Now, gentlemen, we have the night ahead of us."

"Wherefore shall we go?" asked Stout uneasily. "Thou art not bent on murder this evening, I warrant?"

"Nay, good friend—it shall be a week or two before I am prepared to meet the villain." Charles fished in his purse and found coins in sufficient number for that evening's plans. He said, "I am in the mood to take in a play and visit our friend Will Shakespeare after."

"I am all for that, Charles," Hal said as they stepped into the street. Then he added in a whisper, "Though if I were as dearly set on saying heigh-ho to God in person as thou seem to be, then I myself would forego amusement and scurry to a church, that I might find a priest's rump to humbly kiss with my exceedingly penitent lips."

■

The constable, whose post was along the riverbank near the Inns of Court, was much pleased with his life here. Yes, one could find apple-squires offering gaudy women to men upon the street and cutthroats and pick-purses and cheats and ruffians. But unlike bustling Cheapside, with its stores of shoddy merchandise, or the mad suburbs south of the river, his jurisdiction was populated largely with upstanding gentlemen and ladies and he would often go a day or two without hearing an alarum raised.

This morning, at nine of the clock, the squat man was sitting at a table in his office, arguing with his huge bailiff, Red James, regarding the number of heads currently resting on pikes upon London Bridge.

"It be thirty-two if it be one," Red James muttered.

"Then 'tis one, for thou art wrong, you goose. The number be no more than twenty-five."

"I did count them at dawn, I did, and the tally was thirty-two." Red James lit a candle and produced a deck of cards.

"Leave the tallow be," the constable snapped. "It cost money and must needs come out of our allowance. We shall play by the light of day."

"Faith, sir," Red James grumbled, "if I be a goose, as you claim, then I cannot be a cat and hence have not the skill to see in the dark." He lit another wick.

"What good art thou, sir?" The constable bit his thumb at the bailiff and was about to rise and blow the tapers out when a young man dressed in workman's clothing ran to the window.

"Sirs, I seek the constable at once!" he gasped.

"And thou have found him."

"Sir, I am Henry Rawlings and I am come to raise a hue and cry! A most grievous attack is under way."

"What be thy complaint?" The constable looked over the man and found him to be apparently intact. "Thou seem untouched by bodkin or cudgel."

"Nay, it is not I who am hurt but another who is *about* to be. And most grievously, I fear. I was walking to a warehouse on the embankment not far from here. And—"

"Get on, man, important business awaits."

"—and a gentleman pulled me aside and pointed below to Temple wharf, where we did see two men circling with swords. Then I did hear the younger of the two state his intent to kill the other, who cried out for help. Then the dueling did commence."

"An apple-squire fighting with a customer over the price of a woman," Red James said in a tired voice. "Of no interest to us." He began to shuffle the cards.

"Nay, sir, that is not so. One of them—the older, and the man most disadvantaged—was a peer of the realm. Robert Murtaugh."

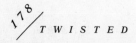

"Sir Murtaugh, friend to the lord mayor and in the duke's favor!" Alarmed, the constable rose to his feet.

"The very same, sir," the lackey said breathlessly. "I come to thee in haste to raise hue and cry."

"Bailiffs!" the constable cried and girded himself with his sword and dagger. "Bailiffs, come forth at once!"

Two men stumbled into the room from quarters next to the den, their senses muddled by the difficult marriage of this morning's sleep and last night's wine.

"Violence is afoot upon Temple wharf. We go forthwith."

Red James picked up a long pike, his weapon of choice.

The men hurried out into the cool morning and turned south toward the Thames, over which smoke and mist hung thick as fleece on a lamb. In five minutes they were at the porch overlooking Temple wharf, where, as the lackey had assured, a dreadful contest was under way.

A young man was fighting vigorously with Sir Murtaugh. The peer fought well but he was dressed in the pompous and cumbersome clothing then fashionable at Court—a Turkish theme, replete with gilt robe and feathered turban—and, because of the restrictive garments, was losing ground to the young cutthroat. Just as the ruffian drew back to strike a blow at the knight, the constable shouted, "Cease all combat at once! Put down thy weapons!"

But what might have ended in peace turned to unexpected sorrow as Sir Murtaugh, startled by the constable's shout, lowered his parrying arm and looked up toward the voice.

The attacker continued his lunge and the blade struck the poor knight in the chest. The blow did not pierce his doublet but Sir Murtaugh was knocked back against the rail. The wood gave way and the man fell to the rocks forty feet below. A multitude of swans fled from the disturbance as his body rolled down the embankment and into the water, where it sank beneath the grim surface.

"Arrest him!" cried the constable, and the three bailiffs proceeded to the startled ruffian, whom Red James struck with a cudgel before he could flee. The murderer fell senseless at their feet.

The bailiffs then climbed down a ladder and proceeded to the water's edge. But of Sir Murtaugh, no trace was visible.

"Murder committed this day! And in my jurisdiction," said the constable with a grim face, though in truth he was already reveling in the promise of the reward and celebrity that his expeditious capture of this villain would bring.

■

The Crown's head prosecutor, Jonathan Bolt, an arthritic, bald man of forty, was given the duty of bringing Charles Cooper to justice for the murder of Robert Murtaugh.

Sitting in his drafty office near Whitehall palace, ten of the clock the day after Murtaugh's body was fished from the Thames, Bolt reflected that the crime of murdering an ass like Murtaugh was hardly worth the trouble to pursue. But the nobility desperately needed villains like Murtaugh to save them from their own foolishness and profligacy, so Bolt had been advised to make an example of the vintner Charles Cooper.

However, the prosecutor had also been warned to make certain that he proceed with the case in such a way that Murtaugh's incriminating business affairs not be aired in public. So it was decided that Cooper be tried not in Sessions Court but in the Star Chamber, the private court of justice dating back to His Highness Henry VIII.

The Star Chamber did not have the authority to sentence a man to die. Still, Bolt reflected, an appropriate punishment

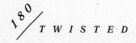

would be meted out. Upon rendering a verdict of guilt against the cutthroat, the members of the Star Chamber bench would surely order that Cooper's ears be hacked off, that he be branded with a hot iron and then transported—banished—probably to the Americas, where he would live as a ruined beggar all his life. His family would forfeit whatever estate he had and be turned out into the street.

The unstated lesson would be clear: Do not trouble those who are the de facto protectors of the nobility.

Having interviewed the constable and the witness in the cases—a lackey named Henry Rawlings—Bolt now left his office and proceeded to Westminster, the halls of government.

In an anteroom hidden away in the gizzard of the building, a half dozen lawyers and their clients awaited their turn to go before the bench, but Cooper's case had been placed top on the docket and Jonathan Bolt walked past the others and entered the Star Chamber itself.

The dim room, near the Privy Council, was much smaller and less decorous than its notorious reputation imputed. Quite plain, it boasted only candles for light, a likeness of Her Majesty and, upon the ceiling, the painted celestial objects that bestowed upon the room its unjudicial name.

Inside, Bolt observed the prisoner in the dock. Charles Cooper was pale and a bandage covered his temple. Two large sergeants at arms stood behind the prisoner. The public was not allowed into Star Chamber proceedings but the lords, in their leniency, had allowed Margaret Cooper, the prisoner's wife, to be in attendance. A handsome woman otherwise, Bolt observed, her face was as white as her husband's and her eyes red from tears.

At the table for the defense was a man Bolt recognized as a clever lawyer from the Inns of Court and another man in his late thirties, about whom there was something slightly familiar. He was lean, with a balding pate and lengthy brown hair, and dressed in shirt and breeches and short buskin boots. A character witness, perhaps. Bolt knew that, based on the facts of this case, Cooper could not avoid guilt altogether; rather, the defense would concentrate on mitigating the sentence. Bolt's chief challenge would be to make sure such a tactic was not successful.

Bolt took his place beside his own witnesses—the constable and the lackey, who sat nervously, hands clasped before them.

A door opened and five men, robed and wigged, entered, the members of the Star Chamber bench, which consisted of several members of the Queen's Privy Council—today, they numbered three—and two judges from the Queen's Bench, a court of law. The men sat and ordered the papers in front of them.

Bolt was pleased. He knew each of these men and, judging from the look in their eyes, believed that they had in all likelihood already found in the Crown's favor. He wondered how many of them had benefitted from Murtaugh's skills in vanquishing debts. All, perhaps.

The high chancellor, a member of the Privy Council, read from a piece of paper. "This special court of equity, being convened under authority of Her Royal Highness Elizabeth Regina, is now in session. All ye with business before this court come forward and state thy cause. God save the queen." He then fixed his eyes on the prisoner in the dock and continued in a grave voice, "The Crown charges thee, Charles Cooper, with murder in the death of Sir Robert Murtaugh, a knight and peer of the realm, whom thou did without provocation or excuse most grievously assault and cause to die on fifteen June in the forty-second year of the reign of our sovereign, Her Majesty the queen. The Crown's inquisitor will set forth the case to the chancellors of equity and judges of law here assembled."

"May it please this noble assemblage," offered Bolt, "we have here a case of most clear delineation, which shall take but little of thy time. The vintner named Charles Cooper did, before wit-

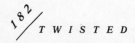

nesses, assault and murder Sir Robert Murtaugh on Temple wharf for reasons of undiscerned enmity. We have witnesses to this violent and unprovoked event."

"Call them forth."

Bolt nodded to the lackey Henry Rawlings, who rose and, his oath being sworn, gave his deposition, "I, sir, was making my way to the Temple wharf when a man did bid me come running. He said, 'Behold, there is mischief before us, for that is Sir Robert Murtaugh.' Faith, sirs, before our eyes the prisoner there in the dock was challenging Sir Murtaugh with a sword. Then he did leap toward the unfortunate peer and utter words most threatening against him."

"And what, pray, were those words?"

"They were somewhat to this order, sirs: 'Villain, thou diest!' Whereupon the dueling commenced. And Sir Murtaugh cried, 'Help! Help! Murder, murder!'

"I then did run to seek the aid of the constable. We did return, with the advantage of bailiffs, and arrived to see the prisoner strike poor Sir Murtaugh. He fell through the railing to his death. It was a most awful and unpleasant sight."

The court then allowed the defense lawyer to cross-examine the lackey Rawlings but the attorney for Cooper chose not to ask any questions of him.

Bolt then had the constable rise and take the witness's dock and tell much the same story. When he had done, Cooper's lawyer declined to examine this man too.

Bolt said, "I have no more to present by way of the Crown's case, my lords." He sat down.

The lawyer for the defense rose and said, "If it please this noble body, I shall let the prisoner report on the incident, and thy most excellent chancellors and most noble judges will behold, beyond doubt, that this is but a most egregious misunderstanding."

The men on the bench regarded one another with some

irony, and the high chancellor administered the oath to Charles Cooper.

One of the judges from the Queen's Bench asked, "What say thou to these charges?"

"That they, my good lord, be erroneous. Sir Murtaugh's death was but a tragic accident."

"Accident?" a privy council member said with a laugh. "How say thou 'accident' when thou attacked a man with thy sword and he fell to his death? Perchance the instrument of his death was the rocks upon the embankment but the instigating force was thy thrust, which sent him headlong to embrace the unyielding stones."

"Aye," offered another, "I warrant to say, had the unfortunate Mr. Murtaugh not fallen, thou would have skewered him like a boar."

"I respectfully submit, lord, that, nay, I would not have harmed him in any way. For we were not fighting; we were practicing."

"Practicing?"

"Yes, my lord. I have aspirations to be a player in the theater. My profession, though, as thou have heard, is that of vintner. I was at Temple wharf to arrange for delivery of some claret from France and, having surplus time, thought I would practice a portion of a theatrical role, which chanced to involve some swordplay. I was so engaged when Sir Murtaugh happened by, on his way to Whitehall palace. He is—sadly, *was*, I should say—quite an accomplished swordsman and he observed me for a moment then reported to me what, alas, is true—that my talent with a blade be quite lacking. We fell into conversation and I said that if he might deign to show me some authentic thrusts and parries I would inquire about getting him a small part on the stage. This intrigued him greatly and he offered me the benefit of his considerable expertise at dueling." The prisoner cast his eyes toward the

constable. "All would have gone well had not that man disturbed us and caused Sir Murtaugh to lose his stride. I merely tapped him on the doublet with my sword, Most High Chancellor, and he stepped back against the rail, which tragically was loose. For my part, I am heartsick at the good man's demise."

There was some logic to this, Prosecutor Bolt thought grimly. He had learned something of Cooper in the hours before the trial and it was true that he frequented the theaters south of the Thames. Nor could he find a true motive for the murder. Cooper was a guildsman, with no need for or inclination toward robbery. Certainly much of London would rejoice at the death of a lout like Murtaugh. But, as the nobles wished the case prosecuted swiftly, Bolt had not had time to make a proper inquiry into any prior relationship between Cooper and Murtaugh.

The knight, for his part, as everyone knew, had been vain as a peacock, and the thought of getting up on a stage and preening before members of the Court would surely have appealed to him.

Yet even if Cooper were telling the truth, the nobles would want Murtaugh's killer punished, whether his death was an accident or not, and indeed the five men on the bench seemed little swayed by the prisoner's words.

Cooper continued. "Those words of anger and threat reported by the lackey there? Sirs, they were not mine."

"And whose be they, then?"

Cooper glanced at his lawyer, who rose and said, "Prithee, sirs, we have a witness whose deposition shall bear on the events. If it please the bench, may we have William Shakespeare step forward."

Ah, yes, Bolt thought, *that* is who the witness is: the famed playwright and director of the Lord Chamberlain's Men troupe. Bolt himself had seen several of the man's plays at the Rose and the Globe. What was transpiring here? The playwright stepped to the front of the courtroom.

"Master Shakespeare, thou will swear oath to our holy Lord that thy deposition here shall be honest and true?"

"I so confirm, my lord."

"What have thou to say that bears on this case?"

"I pray thee, Lord Chancellor, I am here to add to the deposition thou have previous heard. Some weeks ago, Charles Cooper did come to me and say that he had always been a lover of the player's craft and had hoped to try his hand upon the stage. I bid him attempt some recitation for me and observed that he performed several passages, of my own creation, with exceeding grace.

"I told him I had no place for him just then but I gave him portions of a draft of the play I am presently writing and told him to practice it. When Court returns in the fall, I assured him, I might find a part for him."

"How *exactly* doth this bear on the case, Master Shakespeare?"

The playwright withdrew from a leather pouch a large sheaf of parchment with writing upon it. He read: *"Enter Cassio. . . . RODERIGO: 'I know his gait, 'tis he. Villain, thou diest! . . .' Roderigo makes a pass with his blade at Cassio. . . . CASSIO draws his own weapon and wounds Roderigo. . . . RODERIGO: 'O, I am slain! . . .' Iago from behind wounds Cassio in the leg, and exeunt. CASSIO: 'I am maim'd for ever. Help, ho! Murder! murder!'"*

Shakespeare fell silent and bowed his head. "My lords, so fall my humble words."

" 'Villain, thou diest . . . Help, ho! Murder! . . .' Why those," the high chancellor said, "with some alteration, are the very words that the witness heard the prisoner and Sir Murtaugh exchange. They are from a play of thine?"

"Yes, my lord, they are. It is as yet unperformed and I am presently reworking it." Shakespeare paused for a moment then added, "This shall be the play I did promise Her Highness the

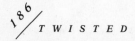

queen for her enjoyment when she and the Court return this fall."

A Privy Council member frowned and then asked, "Thou art, if I am not mistaken, much in the queen's favor."

"Humbly, sir, I am but a journeyman playwright. But I can say with little exaggeration that Her Highness hath from time to time offered expressions of pleasure at my work."

Hell's bells, thought the prosecutor. Shakespeare is *indeed* much in the queen's favor. This fact was well known. It was rumored that Her Highness would name his the sole royal acting company within the next year or two. The course of the case was now clear: To find Cooper guilty would require the judges to disavow Shakespeare's testimony. The queen would hear and there would be consequences. Bolt recalled an expression: "A hundred dukes against a single queen leaves a hundred coffins on the green."

The high chancellor turned to the rest of the Privy Council and they conferred again among themselves. A moment later he pronounced, "In light of the evidence presented, this court of equity rules that the death of Sir Robert Murtaugh was caused by no man's intent and Charles Cooper is herewith free to go forth unfettered, and untainted by any further accusation in this matter." He cast a stern gaze toward the prosecutor. "And, Sir Jonathan, if it be not too taxing in the future, the court would be honored if thou might at least *peruse* the evidence and consult with the prisoner *before* thou deign to waste the time of this court."

"I shall do, my noble lord."

One of the judges leaned forward, nodded at the sheaf that the playwright was replacing in his sack and asked, "May I ask, Mr. Shakespeare, what will this play be titled?"

"I know not for certain, my lord, what the final title shall be. I presently call it 'Othello, the Moor of Venice.' "

"And might I be assured from the testimony we have heard

today that the audience may look forward to some good sword-play in this work?"

"Oh, yes, my lord."

"Good. I far prefer such plays to thy comedies."

"If I may be so bold, sir, I believe thou will then enjoy this piece," William Shakespeare said and joined Cooper and his wife as they left the dark room.

■

Near candle-lighting that night, three men sat in the Unicorn and Bear tavern in Charing Cross, tankards of ale before them: Charles Cooper, Stout and William Shakespeare.

A shadow filled the doorway as a man walked into the tavern.

"Behold, 'tis the mysterious gentleman on the wharf," Charles said.

Hal Pepper joined them and was served up an ale of his own.

Charles lifted his tankard. "Thou did well, my friend."

Hal drank long and nodded proudly to acknowledge the compliment. His role in the daring play, as writ by William Shakespeare and Charles Cooper in collaboration, was critical. After Charles had stopped Murtaugh on the wharf and, as he'd told the Court, piqued the knight's interest with the promise of an appearance onstage, it had been Hal's task to snare a passerby at just the right moment so that he witness the exchange of dialogue between Charles and Murtaugh at the start of their mock duel. Hal had then given the lackey Rawlings a half sovereign to raise the hue and cry with the constable, whom Shakespeare, as master plotter, had decided should perforce be a witness to the duel as well.

Shakespeare now examined Charles gravely and said, "Regarding thy performance in Court, friend, thou need some study

as a player, yet on the whole"—the man from Stratford could not resist a smile—"I would venture to say that thou *acquitted* thyself admirably."

Will Shakespeare often deflected the course of the conversation to allow for the inclusion of puns, which he loved. But neither was Charles Cooper a stranger to wordplay. He riposted, "Ah, but 'tis sadly true, friend, that my talent for *bearing* witness in Court is no match for thy *over*bearing *witti*ness in taverns."

"Touché," cried Shakespeare and the men laughed hard.

"And here is to thee too, my friend." Charles tapped his tankard against Stout's.

It had been the big man's task to wield his barrel-maker's tools with sufficient skill to loosen the railing at Temple wharf just the right degree so that it would not give way under casual hands but would fall apart when Murtaugh stumbled against it.

Stout was not as quick as either Shakespeare or Charles and attempted no cleverness in reply. He merely blushed fiercely with pleasure at the recognition.

Charles then embraced Shakespeare. "But thou, Will, were the linchpin."

Shakespeare said, "Thy father was a good man to me and my family. I will always remember him with pleasure. I am glad to have played a small part in the avenging of his death."

"What might I do to repay thee for the risks thou took and thy efforts on my behalf?" Charles asked.

The playwright said, "Indeed thou have already. Thou have bestowed upon me the most useful gift possible for a dabbler in the writer's craft."

"What might that be, Will?"

"Inspiration. Our plot was the midwife for a sonnet which I completed just an hour ago." He drew a piece of paper from his jacket. He looked over the assembled men and said solemnly, "It seemed a pity that Murtaugh knew not the reason for his death.

In my plays, you see, the truth must ultimately out—it needs be revealed, at the least to the audience, if not the characters. That Murtaugh died in ignorance of our revenge set my pen in motion." The playwright then read the sonnet slowly:

To a Villain

When I do see a falcon in the wild
I think of he, the man who gave me life,
Who loved without restraint his youthful child
And bestow'd affection on his wife.
When I do see a vulture in its flight
I can think of naught but thee, who stole
Our family's joy away that evil night
Thou cut my father's body from his soul.
The golden scissors of a clever Fate
Decide how long a man on earth shall dwell.
But as my father's son I could not wait
To see thy wicked soul entombed in hell.
This justice I have wrought is no less fine,
Being known but in God's heart and in mine.

"Well done, Will," Hal Pepper called out.

Charles clapped the playwright on the back.

"It be about Charles?" Stout asked, staring down at the paper. His lips moved slowly as he attempted to form the words.

"In spirit, yes," Shakespeare said, turning the poem around so that the big man could examine the lines right-way up. He added quietly, "But not, methinks, enough so that the Court of Sessions might find it evidentiary."

"I do think it best, though, that thou not publish it just yet," Charles said cautiously.

Shakespeare laughed. "Nay, friend, not for a time. This verse would find no market now, in any case. Romance, romance, romance . . . that be the only form of poesy that doth sell these days. Which, by the by, is most infuriating. No, I shall secrete it safe away and retrieve it years hence when the world hath forgot about Robert Murtaugh. Now, it is near to candle-lighting, is it not?"

"Very close to," Stout replied.

"Faith, then . . . Now that our real-life tale hath come to its final curtain, let us to a fictional one. My play *Hamlet* hath a showing tonight and I must needs be in attendance. Collect thy charming wife, Charles, then we shall to the ferry and onward to the Globe. Drink up, gentlemen, and let's away!"

GONE FISHING

"Don't go, Daddy."

"Rise and shine, young lady."

"Please?"

"And what's my little Jessie-Bessie worried about?"

"I don't know. Nothing."

Alex sat on the edge of her bed and hugged the girl. He felt the warmth of her body, surrounded by the peculiar, heart-swelling smell of a child waking.

From the kitchen a pan clattered, then another. Water running. The refrigerator door slamming. Sunday-morning sounds. It was early, six-thirty.

She rubbed her eyes. "I was thinking . . . what we could do today is we could go to the penguin room at the zoo. You said we could go there soon. And if you have to go to the lake, I mean really *have* to, we could go to Central Park instead and go rowing like we did that time. Remember?"

Alex shivered in mock disgust. "What sorts of fish do you think I'd catch *there*? Icky fish with three eyes and scales that glow in the dark."

"You don't have to go fishing. We could just row around and feed the ducks."

He looked out the window at the dim, gray horizon of New Jersey across the Hudson River. The whole state seemed asleep. And probably was.

"Please, Daddy? Stay home with us."

"We played all day yesterday," he pointed out, as if this would convince her that she could do without him today. He was, of course, aware that children's logic and adults' bore no resemblance to each other; still, he continued. "We went to FAO Schwarz and Rockefeller Center and I bought you two, count 'em, two hot dogs from Henri's *à côté du* subway. And then Rumplemeyer's."

"But that was *yesterday*!"

Youngsters' logic, Alex decided, was by far the most compelling.

"And what did you eat at Rumpelstiltskin's?"

When logic failed, he was not above diversion.

The eight-year-old tugged at her nightgown. "Banana split."

"You did?" He looked shocked. "No!"

"Did too, and you know it. You were there."

"How big was it?"

"You know!"

"I know nothing, I remember nothing," he said in a thick German accent.

"Thisssss big." She held her hands far apart.

Alex said, "Impossible. You would've blown up like a balloon. Pop!" And she broke into giggles under his tickling fingers.

"Up and at 'em," he announced. "Breakfast together before I leave."

"Daddy," she persisted. But Alex escaped from her room.

He assembled his fishing tackle, stacked it by the door and walked into the kitchen. Kissed Sue on the back of the neck and slipped his arms around her as she flipped pancakes in the skillet.

Pouring orange juice for the three of them, Alex said, "She doesn't want me to go today. She's never complained before."

For the last year he'd taken off a day or two every month to go fishing in the countryside around New York City.

His wife stacked the pancakes on a plate and set them in the

oven to warm. Then she glanced down the hall where their daughter, in her purple Barney slippers, wandered sleepily into the bathroom and shut the door behind her.

"Jessie was watching the tube the other night," Sue said. "I was finishing up some homework and wasn't paying attention. Next thing I knew she ran out of the room crying. I didn't see the program but I looked it up in *TV Guide*. It was some made-for-TV movie about a father who was kidnapped and held hostage. The kidnapper killed him and then came after his wife and daughter. I think there were some pretty graphic scenes. I talked to her about it but she was pretty upset."

Alex nodded slowly. He'd grown up watching horror flicks and shoot-'em-up westerns; in fact he'd found Saturday matinees a sanctuary from his abusive, temperamental father. As an adult he'd never thought twice about violence in films or on TV—until he became a father himself. Then he immediately began censoring what Jessica watched. He didn't mind that she knew death and aggression existed; it was the gratuitous, overtly gruesome carnage lacing popular shows that he wanted to keep from her.

"She's afraid I'm going to get kidnapped while I'm fishing?"

"She's eight. It's a big bad world out there."

It was so difficult with children, he reflected. Teaching them to be cautious of strangers, aware of real threats, but not making them so scared of life they couldn't function. Learning the difference between reality and make-believe could be tough for adults, let alone youngsters.

Five minutes later the family was sitting around the table, Alex and Sue flipping through the Sunday *Times*, reading portions of stories that seemed interesting. Jessica, accompanied by Raoul, a stuffed bear, methodically ate first her bacon, then her pancakes and finally a bowl of cereal.

The girl pretended to feed Raoul a spoonful of cereal and asked thoughtfully, "Why do you like to fish, Daddy?"

"It's relaxing."

"Oh." The bits of cereal were in the shape of some cartoon creatures. Ninja Turtles, Alex thought.

"Your father needs some time off. You know how hard he works."

As the creative director of a Madison Avenue ad agency, Alex regularly clocked sixty- and seventy-hour weeks.

Sue continued, "He's a type-A personality through and through."

"I thought you had a secretary, Daddy. Doesn't she do your typing?"

Her parents laughed. "No, honey," Sue said. "That means somebody who works real hard. Everything he does has to get him closer to his goal or he isn't interested in it." She rubbed Alex's muscular back. "That's why his ads are so good."

"The Cola Koala!" Jessica's face lit up.

As a surprise for the girl, Alex had just brought home some of the original art cells of the animated cartoon figure he'd created to hawk a product its manufacturer hoped would cut large chunks out of Pepsi's and Coke's market shares. The pictures of the cuddly creature hung prominently on her wall next to portraits of Cyclops and Jean Grey, of X-Men fame. Spider-Man too and, of course, the Power Rangers.

"Fishing helps me relax," Alex repeated, looking up from the sports section.

"Oh."

Sue packed his lunch and filled a thermos of coffee.

"Daddy?" Moody again, the girl stared at her spoon then let it sink down into the bowl.

"What, Jessie-Bessie?"

"Were you ever in a fight?"

"A fight? Good grief, no." He laughed. "Well, in high school I was. But not since then."

"Did you beat the guy up?"

"In high school? Whupped the tar out of him. Patrick Briscoe. He stole my lunch money. I let him have it. Left jab and a right hook. Technical knockout in three rounds."

She nodded, swallowed a herd, or school, of Ninja Turtles and set her spoon down again. "Could you beat up somebody now?"

"I don't believe in fighting. Adults don't have to fight. They can talk out their disagreements."

"But what if somebody, like a robber, came after you? Could you knock him out?"

"Look at these muscles. Is this Schwarzenegger, or what?" He pulled up the sleeves of his plaid Abercrombie hunting shirt and flexed. The girl lifted impressed eyebrows.

So did Sue.

Alex paid nearly two thousand dollars a year to belong to a midtown health club.

"Honey . . ." Alex leaned forward and put his hand on the girl's arm. "You know that the things they show on TV, like that movie you saw, they're all made up. You can't think real life is like that. People are basically good."

"I just wish you weren't going today."

"Why today?"

She looked outside. "The sun isn't shining."

"Ah, but that's the best time to go fishing. The fish can't see me coming. Hey, pumpkin, tell you what . . . how 'bout if I bring you something?"

Her face brightened. "Really?"

"Yup. What would you like?"

"I don't know. Wait, yes, I do. Something for our collection. Like last time?"

"You bet, sweetie. You got it."

Last year Alex had seen a counselor. He'd come close to a

breakdown, struggling to juggle his roles as overworked executive, husband of a law school student, father and put-upon son (his own father, often drunk and always unruly, had been placed in an expensive mental hospital Alex could barely afford). The therapist had told him to do something purely for himself—a hobby or sport. At first he'd resisted the idea as a pointless frivolity but the doctor firmly warned that the relentless anxiety he felt would kill him within a few years if he didn't do something to help himself relax.

After considerable thought Alex had taken up freshwater fishing (which would get him away from the city) and then collecting (which he could pursue at home). Jessica, with no interest in the "yucky" sport of fishing, became his coconspirator in the collecting department. Alex would bring home the *items* and the girl would log them into the computer and mount or display the collectibles. Lately they'd been specializing in watches.

This morning he asked his daughter, "Now, young lady, is it okay for me to go off and catch us dinner?"

"I guess," the little girl said, though she wrinkled her nose at the thought of actually eating fish. But Alex could see some relief in her blue eyes.

When she'd wandered off to play on the computer Alex helped Sue with the dishes. "She's fine," he said. "We'll just have to be more careful about what she watches. That's the problem—mixing up make-believe and reality. . . . Hey, what is it?"

For his grim-looking wife continued to dry what was already a very dry plate.

"Oh, nothing. It's just . . . I never really thought about you going off to the wilderness alone before. I mean, you always think about somebody getting mugged in the city but at least there're people around to help. And the cops're just a few minutes away."

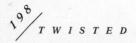

Alex hugged her. "This isn't exactly the Outback we're talking. It's only a few hours north of here."

"I know. But I never thought to worry till Jessie said something."

He stepped back and shook a stern finger at her. "All right, young lady. No more TV for you either."

She laughed and patted his butt. "Hurry home. And clean the fish *before* you get back. Remember that mess last time?"

"Yes'm."

"Hey, hon," she asked, "were you really in a fight in high school?"

He glanced toward Jessica's room and whispered, "Those three rounds? They were more like three seconds. I pushed Pat down, he pushed me, and the principal sent us both home with notes to our parents."

"I didn't think you and John Wayne had anything in common." Her smile faded. "Safe home," she said, her family's traditional valediction. And kissed him once more.

■

Alex turned off the highway, snapped the Pathfinder into four-wheel drive and made his way along a dirt road toward Wolf Lake, a large, deep body of water in the Adirondacks. As he progressed farther into the dense woods, Alex decided that he agreed with his daughter: The monotonous countryside needed sunlight. The March sky was gray and windy and the leafless trees were black from an early-morning rain. Fallen branches and logs filled the scruffy forest like petrified bones.

Alex felt the familiar anxiety twisting in his stomach. Tension and stress—the banes of his life. He breathed slowly, forcing himself to think comforting thoughts of his wife and his daughter.

Come on, boy, he told himself, I'm here to relax. That's the whole point of it. Relax.

He drove another half mile through the thickening woods. Deserted.

The temperature wasn't cold but the threat of rain, he supposed, had scared off the weekend fishermen. The only vehicle he'd seen for miles was a beat-up pickup truck, mud-spattered and dented. Alex drove fifty yards farther on, to the point where the road vanished, and parked.

The airy smell of the water drew him forward, his tackle box and spinning rod in one hand, his lunch and thermos in the other. Through the white pine and juniper and hemlock, over small, moss-covered hummocks. He passed a tree with seven huge black crows sitting in it. They seemed to watch him as he walked beneath their skeletal perch. Then he broke from the trees and climbed down a rocky incline to the lake.

Standing on the shore of a narrow cove, Alex looked over the water. Easily a mile wide, the lake was an iridescent gray, choppy toward the middle but smoothing to a linenlike texture closer to shore. The bleakness didn't make him feel particularly sad but it didn't help his uneasiness either. He closed his eyes and breathed in the clean air. Rather than calming him, though, he felt a surge race through him—a fear of some sort, raw, electric—and he spun about, certain that he was being watched. He couldn't see a soul but he wasn't convinced that he was alone; the woods were too dense, too entangled. Someone could easily have been spying on him from a thousand different nooks.

Re-lax, he told himself, stretching the word out. The city's behind you, the problems of work, the tensions, the stress. Forget them. You're here to calm down.

For an hour he fished with a vengeance, casting spoons, then jigs. He switched to a surface popper and had a couple of jumps but the fish never took the hook. Once, just after he launched the

green, froglike lure through the air, he heard the snap of a branch behind him. A painful chill shot down his back. He turned quickly and studied the forest. No one.

Selecting a different lure, Alex glanced down at his perfectly ordered and cleaned toolbox he used for tackle. He saw his spotless, honed fishing knife. He had a fleeting memory of his father, years ago, pulling off his belt and wrapping the end around his fist, telling young Alex to pull down his jeans and bend over. "You left that screwdriver outside, boy. How many times I gotta tell you to treat your tools with respect? Oil the ones that rust, dry the ones that warp, and keep your knives sharp as razors. Now, I'm giving you five for ruining that screwdriver. Here it comes. One . . ."

He'd never known what screwdriver the man had been talking about. Probably there wasn't one. But afterward, Alex the boy and now Alex the man always oiled, dried and sharpened. Yet he knew that his father's approach was so wrong. He could teach Jessie-Bessie the right way to live without resorting to losing his temper, without beatings, without screaming—all those traumas whose aftermath lasted forever.

He'd calmed for a while but thinking of his father made him anxious again. He recalled the conversation he'd had with his daughter earlier—about fighting, about school-yard bullies—and that made him anxious too. Alex knew he kept everything bottled up. He wondered if he had actually spoken back to his father, face-to-face, then maybe he wouldn't feel the tension and stress as painfully as he did now. Alex tended to take the easy way, avoiding confrontations.

Fist fights . . . a new self-help concept, he laughed to himself.

He halfheartedly cast a few more times then hooked the lure into the bail of his reel and began walking along the shore, heading east. He stepped from rock to rock carefully, looking down the whole time, mindful of the slippery rocks. Once he nearly tumbled into the cold, black water as he stared at the reflections of the fast-moving strips of clouds, gray and grayer, in the oily water near his feet.

Because he was gazing at his footing he didn't see the man until he was only ten or twelve feet from him. Alex stopped. The driver of the pickup truck, he assumed, crouching at the shore.

He was in his mid-forties, dressed in jeans and a workshirt. Gaunt and wiry, his face was foxlike, an impression accentuated because of a two- or three-day growth of beard. His right hand held a galvanized pipe over his head. His left gripped the tail of a walleye pike, holding the thrashing, shimmering fish against a rock. He glanced at Alex, took in his expensive, designer-label outdoor clothing, and then slammed the pipe down on the fish's head, killing it instantly. He pitched it into a bucket and picked up his rod and reel.

"How you doing?" Alex asked.

The man nodded.

"Having any luck?"

"Some." The fellow eyed the clothes again, walked to the shore and began casting.

"Haven't caught a thing."

The man said nothing for a minute. He cast, the lure sailing far into the lake. "What're you using?" he asked finally.

"Poppers. On a twelve-inch leader. Fifteen-pound line."

"Ah." As if this explained why he wasn't catching anything. He said nothing else. Alex felt his anxiety flutter like the crows' wings. Fishermen were usually among the friendliest of sportsmen, willing to share their intelligence about lures and locations. It wasn't as if they were competing for the only fish in the whole damn lake, he thought.

What the hell's so hard about being polite? he wondered. If people behaved the way they ought to, the decent way he'd told Jessie that they behaved, the world would be different—no hate, no anger, no scared little girls. No boys afraid of their fathers, no boys growing up into anxious men.

"What time you got?" Alex asked.

The man looked at the combination compass/watch hanging on his belt. "Half past noon. Thereabouts."

Alex nodded at a nearby picnic bench. "Mind if I have my lunch here?"

"Suit yourself."

He sat down, opened the bag and pulled out his sandwich and apple. His hand touched something else—a piece of drawing paper, folded in quarters. Opening it, Alex felt a rush of emotion. Jessica had drawn him a picture with the colored pencils he'd bought for her birthday last month. It was of him—a square-jawed, clean-shaven man with thick black hair—reeling in a shark about ten times his size. The fish had a terrified expression on its face. Beneath it she'd written:

> *Fish beware . . . my daddy's out there!!!*
> —*Jessica Bessie Mollan*

He thought fondly of his family once more and his anger dissipated. He ate the meat loaf sandwich slowly. Then opened the thermos. He was aware that the other fisherman was glancing his way. "Hey, mister, you like some coffee? My wife made it special. It's French roast."

"Can't drink it. My gut." Not smiling, glancing away. Not even thanking him. The man gathered up his tackle and walked to a tree stump, sawn off smooth about three feet above the ground, like a table, and stained with old blood. He set down the bucket he carried and pulled a fish out. He beheaded it fast, with a long, sharp knife, and slit open the slick belly, scooping out the entrails with his fingers. He pitched the head and the guts ten feet away into a cluster of waiting crows and they began to fight noisily over the wet, sticky flesh. The man tossed the cleaned carcass back into the bloody bucket.

Alex looked around and saw they were completely alone. The only sound was the faint lapping of lake water, the caws of the mad crows. He started to take a bite of sandwich but the sight of the birds ripping apart the slick entrails sickened him and he shoved the food away.

It was then that he noticed a piece of paper on the ground. It had apparently been blown off a message board at the picnic area or been pulled down by the rain. He was curious and walked over, picked it up. Though the sheet was water stained he could still make out the words. The notice wasn't from Fishery and Game, as he'd thought. It was from the county sheriff.

He felt a fast, uneasy twist within him as he read the stark words. The notice offered a reward of $50,000 for information about the killer of four individuals in and around Wolf Lake State Park over the past six months. They'd all been knifed to death, but robbery wasn't the apparent motive—only a few valuables were missing. The deaths were thought to have been caused by the same man who'd killed two hikers in a Connecticut state park last month. No one had gotten a good look at him, though one witness described him as in his mid-forties and slim.

Alex's skin felt hot and he looked up toward the fisherman.

He was gone.

But his tackle wasn't. The man had simply left everything there and vanished into the woods. Almost everything, that is. Alex noted that he'd taken his knife with him.

The notice from the sheriff's department fell from his hand. Alex studied the forest again, a full circle. No sign. No sound.

Alex gulped down the coffee he now had no taste for and took a deep breath. *Calm down,* he instructed himself harshly. Calm, calm, calm . . .

"Don't go, Daddy. . . . Please."

He screwed the thermos back together, watching his hands shake fiercely. Was that a snap in the woods behind him? But he couldn't tell; the sound of anxiety roared in his head. Alex started along the path through rocks that led deeper into the forest.

He got only a few yards.

His $300 L.L. Bean boots slid off a smooth piece of granite and he tumbled into a shallow ravine. His tackle box fell open and the contents scattered onto the damp ground. Alex landed on his feet but pitched forward into a rock and rolled onto his back, cradling his leg. He cried out.

Moaning loudly, he rocked back and forth. "Oh, it hurts. . . . Oh, God . . ."

Then, a shuffle of feet. The scrawny fisherman was looking over the rock at him. His face was flecked with blood from the energetic fish cleaning. Behind him the crows cawed madly.

"My ankle," Alex gasped.

"I'll come help ya," he said slowly. "Don't you move."

But rather than climbing down the short distance Alex had fallen, the man disappeared behind a tall outcropping of rock.

Alex moaned again. He started to call out to the man but he stopped. He listened carefully and heard nothing. But a moment later the man's footsteps began to approach, from behind—he'd circled around and was walking toward Alex through a narrow alley between two huge rocks.

Still clutching his leg with his hands, he felt his heart pounding with the dreaded anxiety. Alex slid around so that he'd be facing the man when he arrived.

The footsteps grew closer.

"Hello?" Alex called in a gasp.

No response.

The sound of boots on sand became boots on rocks as the disheveled man approached. He carried a small metal box in his left hand.

He paused, standing directly above Alex, looking him over. Then he said, "Too bad I went to get my lunch outa my truck just now." He nodded at the metal box. "I coulda told you these rocks're slipperier than eels. There's a safer way round. Now, don't you worry. I was a medic for a time. Lemme take a look at that ankle of yours." He crouched down and added, "Do apologize lookin' at you like you was from outer space, mister. Since them killings started I check out everybody comes here pretty close."

Have you ever been in a fight, Daddy?

"Don't you worry, now," the man muttered, focusing on Alex's leg, "you'll be right as rain in no time."

No, sweetheart, I hate fighting . . . I'd much rather catch 'em by surprise. . . .

Alex leapt to his feet, sweeping up his own knife. He stepped behind the astonished fisherman, caught him in a neck lock. He smelled unclean hair, dirty clothes and the piquant scent of fish entrails. He jammed the staghorn knife into the man's gut. The man's voice wailed in a piercing scream.

As he worked the blade leisurely up to the shuddering man's breastbone, Alex was pleased to find, as with his other victims, here and in Connecticut, that the anxiety that'd been boiling within him vanished immediately—just about the moment they died. He also noted that playing the injured fisherman was still an effective way to put his victims at ease. True, he was still a bit concerned about the sheriff's department notice—somebody must've gotten a glimpse of him around the time of the last murder. Oh, well, he joked to himself, he'd just have to find himself a new fishin' hole. Maybe it was time to try Jersey.

He slowly eased the man to the ground, where he lay on his back, quivering. Alex glanced toward the road but the park was still deserted. He bent low and examined the man carefully, a pleasant smile on Alex's face. No, he wasn't quite dead yet though he soon would be, perhaps before the crows started to work on him.

Perhaps not.

Alex climbed back up to the path and had a second cup of coffee—this one he enjoyed immensely; Sue was truly a master with the espresso maker. Then he cleaned the blood off the knife meticulously. Not only because he didn't want any evidence to connect him to the crime but simply because Alex had learned his lesson well; he always oiled, dried and sharpened.

■

Later that night Alex Mollan returned home to find *60 Minutes* on, Jessica and Sue sitting on the couch in front of the tube, sharing a huge bowl of popcorn. He was pleased that the show was about a government contractor's malfeasance and not murder or rape or anything that might upset the little girl. He hugged them both hard.

"Hey, Jessie-Bessie, how's the world's best daughter?"

"Missed you, Daddy. Mommy and I baked gingerbread boys and girls today and I made a dog."

He winked at Sue and could see in her face that she was pleased to find him in such a good mood. She was more pleased still when he told her that all the fish he'd caught were below size and he'd had to throw them back. She was a sport, but fish, to her, were entrees served by a man in a black jacket who deftly deboned them while you sipped a nice cold white wine.

"Did you bring me something, Daddy?" Jessica asked coyly, tilting her head and letting her long blonde hair hang down over her shoulder.

Alex thought, as he often did: She'll be a heartbreaker someday.

"Sure did."

"Something for our collection?"

"Yep."

He dug into his pocket and handed her the present.

"What is it, Daddy? Oh, this's totally cool!" she said and his heart hummed with contentment to see her take the watch in her hand. "Look, Mommy, it's not just a watch. It's got a compass in it. And it fits on your belt. This's neat!"

"You like it?"

"I'll make a special box just for it," the girl said. "I'm glad you're home, Daddy."

His daughter hugged him hard, and then Sue called to them from the dining room, saying that dinner was ready and could they please come and sit down.

NOCTURNE

L ate night on the West Side of Manhattan.

The young cop walked past Central Park, through the misty spring air, wondering where was the downpour the Channel 9 meteorologist had promised.

Patrol Officer Anthony Vincenzo turned west. He crossed Columbus then Broadway, half listening to the static from the speaker/mike of his Motorola Handi-Talkie pinned to the shoulder of his uniform blouse, under the black rain slicker.

He looked at his watch. Nearly eleven P.M. "Hell," he snapped and walked faster. He was in a bad mood because he'd spent most of his tour at the precinct house, typing up an arrest report and then accompanying the perp—a young chain snatcher—down to Bellevue because he'd OD'ed after he'd been collared. He'd probably swallowed his whole stash before Tony ran him down so the DA wouldn't add a drug count to the larceny. Now, he'd not only go down for the smack or rock but he'd had a tube suck his gut clean. Some people. Man.

Anyway, the collar made the cop miss the best part of his beat.

Every night for the last hour of his tour Tony Vincenzo would coincidentally on purpose find himself circling a block in the West Seventies, which just happened to be the site of the New York Concert Hall, a dark brown auditorium dating from the last century. The building was not well soundproofed. So, if he got close to a window, he could easily hear the performances. Tony considered this a perk of the job. And he felt entitled to it; he'd wanted to be a cop since he was a kid, but not just any cop—a detective. The problem was he was only in his mid-twenties and it was hard as hell for a youngster like that to get a gold shield these days. He'd have another four or five years of boring Patrol to get through before he'd even be considered for Detective Division.

So as long as he was forced to walk a beat, he was going to walk a beat *his* way. With a perk or two. Forget free doughnuts and coffee; he wanted music.

Which he loved almost as much as he loved being a cop.

Any kind of music. He had Squirrel Nut Zippers CDs. He had Tony Bennett LPs from the fifties and Django Reinhardt disks from the forties. He had Diana Ross on 45s and Fats Waller on 78s. He had the Beatles' White Album in every format known to man: CD, LP, eight-track, cassette, reel to reel. If they'd sold it on piano roll he'd have one of those too.

Tony even loved classical music and had since he'd been a kid. Which, if you grew up in Bay Ridge, Brooklyn, was risky business and could get you pounded bad in the parking lot after school if you admitted it to anybody. But listen to it he did, and admit it he did. He came by this love from his parents. His mother had been a funeral parlor organist before she got pregnant with the first of Tony's three older brothers. She'd quit the job but continued to play at home for the family on their old upright piano in the living room of their attached house on Fourth. Tony's dad knew music too. He played the concertina and zither and owned probably a thousand LPs, mostly of opera and classic Italian songs.

Tonight, as he walked up to the fire escape of the concert hall, where he liked to perch to listen to the performance, he heard the finale of a symphony, followed by enthusiastic applause and shouts. The New American Symphony Orchestra had been appearing, he saw from the poster, and they'd been playing an all-

Mozart program. Tony clicked his tongue angrily, sorry he'd missed the show. Tony liked Mozart; his father had played his *Don Giovanni* LP until it wore out. (The old man would pace around the living room, nodding in time to the music, muttering, "Mozart is good, Mozart is good.").

The audience was leaving. Tony took a flyer about an upcoming concert and decided to hang around the stage door. Sometimes he got to talk to the musicians and that could be a big kick.

He ambled up to the corner, turned right and walked right into the middle of a stickup.

Twenty feet away, a young man in a ski mask, sweats and running shoes was holding a gun, protruding from the front pouch of his black sweatshirt, on a tall, immaculate man in a tuxedo—one of the musicians, about fifty-five or so. The mugger was after his violin.

"No," the man cried, "don't take it. You can't!"

Drawing his service Glock, dropping into a crouch, Tony spoke into his mike, "Portable three eight eight four, robbery in progress at Seven Seven and Riverside. Need immediate backup. Suspect is armed."

The perp and the victim both heard and turned toward Tony.

The mugger's eyes went wide with fear as the policeman dropped further into a two-handed firing stance. "Hands in the air!" he screamed. "Now! Do it now!"

But the boy was panicked. He froze for a moment then swung the musician in front of him, a shield. The tall man continued to clutch the violin case desperately.

"Please! Don't take it!"

Hands shaking, Tony tried to sight on the mugger's head. But what little skin was visible was as black as the mask and he blended with the shadows along the street. There was no clear target.

 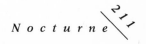

"Don't move," the boy said, voice cracking. "I'll kill him."

Tony stood upright, lifted his left hand, palm outward. "Okay, okay. Look, nobody's hurt," he said. "We can work this out."

Sirens sounded in the distance.

"Gimme it!" the boy snapped to the musician.

"No!" The tall man turned and swung his fist at the boy's head.

"Don't!" Tony cried. Certain he'd hear the pop of a pistol shot and see the man fall. Then Tony'd have to draw a target and pull the trigger of his own gun, making his first kill in the line of duty.

But the boy didn't shoot. Just then the stage door swung open and a half dozen other musicians stepped out. They saw what was happening and scattered in panic—some in between Tony and the mugger. The boy pulled the violin from the musician's grip and turned and fled.

Tony lifted his gun, shouting, "Hold it!"

But the kid kept going. Tony sighted on his back and started to apply pressure to the trigger. Then he stopped and lowered the gun. He sighed and sprinted after the boy but the mugger had vanished. A moment later Tony heard a car engine start and an old gray car—he couldn't see the plate or make—skidded away from the curb and disappeared uptown. He called the getaway in and ran to the musician who'd been robbed, helped him to his feet. "You all right, sir?"

"No, I'm not all right," the man spat out, holding his chest. He was bent in agony. His face was bright red and sweat ran from his forehead.

"Are you shot?" Tony asked, thinking he might not have heard the gun if it was just a twenty-two or twenty-five.

But the musician didn't mean that.

Eyes narrow with fury, he straightened up. "That violin," he said evenly, "was a Stradivarius. It was worth over a half million dollars." He turned his piercing eyes on Tony. "Why the hell didn't you shoot him, Officer? *Why?*"

■

Sergeant Vic Weber, Tony's supervisor, was first on the scene, followed by two detectives from the precinct. Then, because word got out that Edouard Pitkin, conductor, composer and first violinist with the New American Symphony, had been robbed of his priceless instrument, four detectives from headquarters showed up. And the media too, of course. Tons of media.

Pitkin, still immaculate except for a slight tear in his monkey-suit slacks, stood with his arms crossed, anger etched into his face. He seemed to be having trouble breathing but he'd waved off the medics as if spooking irritating flies. He said to Weber, "This is unacceptable. Completely."

Weber, gray-haired and resembling a military rather than police sergeant, was trying to explain. "Mr. Pitkin, I'm sorry for your loss—"

"*Loss?* You make it sound like my MasterCard was stolen."

"—but there wasn't anything more Officer Vincenzo could do."

"That kid was going to kill me, and he"—Pitkin nodded toward Tony—"let him get away. With my violin. There is no other instrument like that in the world."

Not exactly true, thought Tony, a man raised by a father who loved to dish out musical trivia at the dinner table while his mother dished out tortellini. He remembered the man solemnly telling his wife and children there were about six hundred Antonio Stradivari violins in existence—about half the number the Italian craftsman had made. Tony decided not to share this tidbit with the violinist at the moment.

"Everything went by the book," Weber continued, not much interested in the uniqueness of the stolen merch.

"Well, the book ought to be changed," Pitkin snapped.

"I didn't have a clear target," Tony said, angry that he felt he had to defend himself to a civilian. "You can't go shooting suspects in the back."

"He was a criminal," Pitkin said. "And, my God, it wasn't as if . . . I mean, he was black."

Weber's face grew still. He glanced at the lead detective, a round man in his forties, who rolled his eyes.

"I'm sorry," Pitkin said quickly. "It's just that it's terrifying, having someone push a gun in your ribs."

"Hey," a reporter shouted from the crowd. "How 'bout a statement?"

Tony was about to say something but the detective said, "No statements at this time. The chief's going to give a press conference in a half hour."

Another detective walked up to Pitkin. "What can you tell us about the assailant?"

Pitkin thought for a moment. "I guess he was about six feet—"

"Six-two," Tony corrected. "He was taller than you." At five-seven, Tony Vincenzo was a good observer of height.

Pitkin continued, "He was heavyset." A glance at Weber. "He was *African American*. He wore a black ski mask and black sweat clothes."

"And red-and-black Nike Air pumps," Tony said.

"And an expensive watch. A Rolex. Wonder who he killed to get that?" Now Tony got a glance. "Wonder who he's *going* to kill next? Now that he got away."

"Anything else?" the detective asked matter-of-factly.

"Wait. I do remember something. He had powder on his hands. White powder."

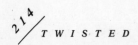

The detectives looked at each other. One said, "Drugs. Coke. Heroin maybe. Probably needed a fix and you happened to be at the wrong time and the wrong place. Okay, sir, that's helpful. It'll give us something to start with. We'll get on it."

They hurried off to their black Ford and sped away.

A young woman in a red dress walked up to Weber, Tony and the violinist. "Mr. Pitkin, I'm from the mayor's office," she announced. "His Honor's asked me to convey his deepest apologies on behalf of the people of New York. We're not going to stop until we get that violin back and put your attacker behind bars."

But Pitkin hadn't calmed one bit. He spat out, "This is what I get for coming to places like this. . . ." He nodded toward the concert hall, though he might have meant the whole city. "From now on I'm only doing studio work. What good is it to perform anyway? The audience sits there like logs, they cough and sneeze, they don't dress up anymore. Do you know what it's like playing Brahms for people wearing blue jeans and T-shirts? . . . And then to have *this* happen!"

"We'll do everything we can, sir," she said. "I promise you."

The violinist hadn't heard her. "That violin. It cost more than my town house."

"Well—" she began.

"It was made in 1722. Paganini played it. Vivaldi owned it for five years. It was in the pit at the first performance of *La Bohème*. It accompanied Caruso and Maria Callas, and when Domingo asked me to play with him at the Albert Hall, *that* was the instrument I played. . . ." His eyes swung to Weber and he asked with genuine curiosity, "Do you understand what I'm saying?"

"Not really, sir," the sergeant said cheerfully. Then he turned to Tony. "Come over here, I wanna talk to you."

■

"You know music. Who the hell is this guy?" Weber asked him, as they stood together under the fire escape. There was still no rain though the mist had coalesced into dense, cold fog.

"Pitkin? He's a conductor and composer. You know. Like Bernstein."

"Who?"

"Leonard Bernstein. *West Side Story.*"

"Oh. You mean he's famous."

"Think of him as the Mick Jagger of the classical circuit."

"Fuck. Eyes of the world on us, huh?"

"I guess."

"Tell me true. No way you could've capped the perp?"

"Nope," Tony said. "When he was facing me I didn't have a clear target and the backdrop wasn't clean. Slug could've gone anywhere. After that all I had was his back."

Weber sighed and his face grew even more disgruntled than it usually was. "Well, we'll just have to take the heat." He looked at his watch. It was nearly midnight. "Your tour's over. Write up the report and get home."

Tony held up a hand. "I gotta favor."

"What?"

"My eleven-eighteen."

The application form for Detective Division. Presently sitting with about three thousand other applications. Or, more likely, *under* three thousand other applications.

The wily old sergeant caught on. He grinned. One thing that could get your app shuffled to the top of the deck was collaring a showcase perp—a serial killer or a shooter who'd killed a cop or a nun, say.

Or the guy who'd stolen a half million bucks' worth of fiddle and embarrassed the mayor.

"You want a piece of the case," Weber said.

"No," Tony answered, not smiling, "I want the whole thing."

"You can't *have* the whole thing. What you can have is four hours. Half tour. But no overtime. And you work with the detectives." The sergeant looked into the young cop's eyes. "You're not going to work with the detectives, are you?"

"No."

Weber debated. "Okay. But listen—for this to work, Vincenzo, we need the perp. Not just the damn violin." He nodded toward the woman from the mayor's office. "They need somebody to crucify."

"Understood."

"Get going. The clock's running."

Tony started east, toward the precinct house. But he stopped and returned to Pitkin and the mayor's aide. He looked up at the musician. "Gotta question. You mentioned Paganini?"

A blink. "I did, yes. What about it?"

"Well, I got a Paganini story. See, one time his friends decided to rag him a little. . . . And what they did was they wrote a piece of violin music that was so complicated it couldn't be played. Like, human hands just wouldn't work that way. They left it on a music stand and invited him over. Paganini walks into the room and glances at the music then goes into the corner and picks up this violin and tunes it. Then, get this, he looks at his friends and he smiles. And he plays the whole thing perfectly. From memory. Blew them away. Is that a great story, or what?"

Pitkin stared at Tony coldly for a moment. "You should've shot that man, Officer." He turned away and climbed into his limousine. "The Sherry-Netherland," he said. The door slammed shut.

■

Tony called Jean Marie from the precinct and told her not to wait up. He was on special assignment.

 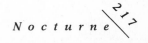

"It's not dangerous, is it, honey?"

"Naw, they just want me to help out on a case with this music bigwig."

"Really? That's great."

"Get some sleep. Love you."

"Love you too, Tony."

Then he changed into street clothes and drove uptown in his own car. The jeans and sneakers were only for comfort; there was no way he could work undercover where he was going—the Johnny B pool hall on 125th Street—since Tony's was the only white face in the place. And nobody had *cop* written on him as clearly as Tony Vincenzo. But that didn't matter. He wasn't here to fool anybody. He'd worked the street long enough to know there was only one way to get information out of people who weren't otherwise inclined to give it to you: buying and selling. Of course, he didn't have any snitch money, being just a patrol officer, but he thought he had some negotiable tender to shop with.

"Hey, Sam," he called, walking up to the bar.

"Yo, Tony. Whatchu doing here?" the white-haired old bartender asked in a raspy voice. "Looking for a game?"

"No, I'm looking for an asshole."

"Heh. Got plenty of them round here."

"Naw, my boy's gone to ground. 'Jacked something tonight and got away from me."

"Personal, huh?"

Tony didn't answer. "So how's your brother?"

"Billy? Whatta you think? How'd *you* like it you spent four years in a ten-by-ten cell and was looking at four more?"

"I wouldn't like it one bit. But I also wouldn't like being the teller he threatened to shoot."

"Yeah, well. He *didn't* shoot her, did he?"

"Tell me, how'd Billy boy like to be looking at maybe *three* to go 'stead of four?"

Sam poured a beer for Tony. He drank down half of it.

"I dunno," Sam said. "Bet he'd like to be looking at *one* year 'stead of four."

Tony thought for a minute. "How's eighteen months sound?"

"You a beat cop. You can do that?"

Tony decided that he'd have the mayor's support on this one. Cultural New York was at stake. "Yeah, I can do it."

"But listen up. I ain't getting my ass capped for snitching on bad boys."

"I saw him in action. Don't worry. No backup. No gang colors. He also picked on the wrong guy and's going away for a long, long time. He'll be old and gray 'fore he get out of Ossining."

"Okay. You got a name?"

"No name."

"What's he look like?" Sam asked.

Tony asked, "I look like I can see through ski masks?"

"Oh."

"He's six-two, give or take. Heavy. Was wearing black sweats and black-and-red Nike Air pumps. Oh, and a fake Rolex."

Because no crook was dumb enough to wear a three-thousand-dollar watch on a job—too easy to get messed up or lost.

"And he's a pool player."

"You know that?"

"I know that."

Because whatever the detectives from downtown thought, Tony knew it'd been cue chalk dust that Pitkin had seen on his hands. No drug dealer or junkie'd be so careless with coke or smack that he'd get visible residue on his hands. And if he did, he'd lick them clean in a second. That's why Tony was here—he knew the perp had to be a serious pool player if he'd got chalk on his hands before a job like this. And while there were a lot of pool parlors in New York City, there weren't many that catered to serious players and there were fewer still that catered to serious black players.

But, after thinking for a long moment, the bartender shook his head, sad. "Man, I wish I could say I seen him. But you know Uptown Billiards?"

"On Lex?"

"Yeah," Sam said. "They had a tournament tonight. Five hunnerd bucks. Know a lotta players was there. Check it out. Talk to Izz. Little dude hangs in the back. Tell him you know me and it's cool."

"Okay, it pans out, I'll talk to D of C. Get your brother knocked down."

"Thanks, man. Hey, you want another beer?"

"You still got Smokey Robinson on the box?" He nodded to the jukebox.

Sam frowned indignantly. "Course I do."

"Good. I'll take a rain check."

■

At Uptown Billiards Tony's reception was a lot cooler but he found Izz, who *was* little and *was* in the back though not just hanging out; he was relieving a cocky young shark of a good wad of bills by sweeping the table at eight ball without even paying much attention. After he pocketed the money and watched the loser slink out of the parlor, Izz turned to Tony and lifted a plucked eyebrow.

Tony introduced himself and mentioned Sam's name.

Izz looked at him like he was a bare wall. Tony continued. "I'm looking for somebody." He described the perp.

Without a word Izz stepped away and made a phone call. Tony heard enough of the conversation to know he'd called Sam and verified the story.

He returned to the table and racked the balls.

"Yeah," Izz said, "guy like that was in here earlier. I remember the Rolex. Took it off and left it on the bar when he played so I knowed it was fake. He was good but he washed out the second round. He was trying too hard, you know what I'm saying? You can't never win, you play that way. Soon as you start trying, you already lost."

"He hangs here?"

"Some. I've seen him around the 'hood. Mostly he keeps to himself."

"What's his name?" Tony said good-bye to five twenties.

Izz walked to the bar and flipped through a soggy, dog-eared stack of papers. Contestants in the tournament, Tony guessed. "Devon Williams. Yeah, gotta be him. I know everybody else in here."

Another $100 changed hands. "Got his address?"

"Here you go."

It was on 131st Street, just four blocks away.

"Thanks, man. Later."

Izz didn't answer. He sank two balls on the break, one striped, one solid. He walked around the table, muttering, "Decisions, fucking decisions."

Outside, Tony stood on Lexington Avenue, debating. If he called for backup they'd know what was going down and the detectives would swoop in like hawks. They'd snatch the case away from him in a minute. Somebody else'd take the collar and his chance for the boost with his detective application would disappear.

Okay, he decided. I'll handle it solo.

And so, armed with his Glock and his backup revolver strapped to his ankle, Tony Vincenzo plunged into residential Harlem. The fog and air were heavy here, absorbing the sounds of the city. It was as if he were in a different time or a different place—maybe a forest or the mountains. Quiet, very quiet, and eerie. A word came to him. A term his father had used once, talking about music: *nocturne*. Tony wasn't sure what it meant but he knew it had to do with night. And he thought it had to do with something peaceful.

Which was pretty damn funny, he decided. Here he was on his way to collar an armed and dangerous perp by himself. And he was thinking about peaceful music.

Nocturne . . .

Five minutes later he was at Devon Williams's tenement.

He turned down the receiver volume of his Motorola speaker/mike and pinned it to the shoulder of his leather jacket, where even if he was shot and down he could still maybe call in a 10–13 officer needs assistance. He clipped his shield to the pocket of the jacket and drew his Glock.

He crept into the lobby, read the directory. Williams lived in one of the first-floor apartments. Tony stepped outside again and climbed the fire escape. The window was open but the curtains were drawn. He couldn't see inside clearly, though he caught a glimpse of Williams, walking into what seemed to be the kitchen. Bingo!

He was carrying the violin case and was still in the sweats. Which meant he'd probably still be armed.

A deep breath.

Okay, whatta we do? Backup or not?

No . . . Once-in-a-lifetime chance. I do it myself, I get the gold shield.

Or get killed.

Don't think about it.

Just go!

Silently Tony climbed through the window into a small parlor. He smelled sour food and dirty clothes. He moved slowly into the hallway and paused just outside the kitchen. Wiped the sweat off his gun hand.

Okay, do it.

One . . .

Two . . .

Tony froze.

From inside the kitchen came music.

Violin music.

A little scratchy, a little squeaky. A rusty-door sound. But then, as the player worked on some scales, the tone became smooth and resonant. Tony, heart pounding, plastered against the wall, cocked his head as he heard the violinist break into some jazzy riffs.

So, there were two people inside, maybe more. Williams's fence probably. Or maybe even the buyer of the Strad. Did that mean more weapons?

Now backup?

No, Tony thought. Too late. Nothing to do but go for the collar.

He spun around the corner, crouching. Gun up at eye level.

He shouted, "Freeze! Everybody!"

But there was no everybody.

There was only tall, chubby Devon Williams, holding the violin under his chin, the bow gripped in his right hand. Gasping in shock at Tony's entrance, mouth open, eyes wide.

"Man, you scared the shit outa me." Slowly his shoulders slumped and he let out a sigh. "Man, it's you. The cop."

"You're Devon Williams?"

"Yeah, that's me."

"Put it down."

He slowly set the violin on a table.

"Empty your pockets."

"Yo, man, keep the noise down. There're kids in th'other room. They're sleeping."

Tony laughed to himself at the boy's stern directive.

"Anybody else?"

"No, just the kids."

"You wouldn't be lying to me now, would you?"

"No, man." He sighed in disgust. "I'm not lying."

"Empty the pockets. I'm not going to tell you again."

He did.

"Where's the piece?" Tony snapped.

"Of what?"

"Don't be cute. Your gun."

"Gun? I don't have one."

"I saw it tonight. At the concert hall."

Williams gestured at the table. "That's what I used." He pointed to a bubble-gum cigar, wrapped in cellophane. "I just held it in my pocket. I saw that in a movie one time."

"Don't bullshit me."

"I'm not." He turned his pockets and the pouch of the sweatshirt inside out. They were empty.

Tony cuffed him then eyed Williams carefully. "How old're you?"

"Seventeen."

"You live here?"

"Yeah."

"Alone?"

"No, man, I told you, the kids."

"They yours?"

He laughed. "They're my brothers and sister."

"Where're your parents?"

Another laugh. "Wherever they be, they ain't here."

Tony read him his *Miranda* rights. Thinking: Got the perp,

got the fiddle and nobody's hurt. I'll be Detective Vincenzo by the next cycle.

"Listen, Devon, you give me the name of your fence and I'll tell the DA you cooperated."

"I don't have a fence."

"Bullshit. How were you going to move the fiddle without a fence?"

"Wasn't gonna sell it, man. I stole it for me."

"You?"

"What I'm saying. To play. Make some money in the subways."

"Bullshit."

"'S'true."

"Why risk hard time? Why didn't you just buy one? It's not like a Beemer. Could've picked one up in a pawnshop for two, three bills."

"Oh, yeah, where'm I gonna get three hundred? My old man, he took off and my mama's off with who the hell knows what boyfriend and I got left with the kids, need food and clothes and day care. So whatta I buy a violin *with*, man? I ain't got no money."

"Where'd you learn to play? In school?"

"Yeah, in school. I was pretty good too." He gave a smile and Tony caught the glitter of a gold tooth.

"And you, what, dropped out to work?"

"When Daddy took off, yeah. Couple years ago."

"And you just decided you'd take up violin again? 'Cause you can make more money at that than pool. Right?"

Williams blinked. Then sighed angrily, figuring out how he'd been made. "What they pay me stacking boxes at A&P—it just ain't enough, man." He closed his eyes and gave a bitter laugh. "So, I'm going into the system. . . . Hell. Never thought it'd happen to me. Man, I tried hard to stay out. I just wanted to make

 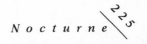

enough to get my aunt here. From North Carolina. To help take care of the kids. She said she'd move but she ain't got the money. Cost a couple thousand."

"You know what they say: Don't do the crime, you can't do the time."

"Shit." Williams was gazing at the violin, a curious look in his eyes, a longing almost.

Tony looked at the young man's dark eyes. He said, "Tell you what I'll do. I'll take those cuffs off for a few minutes, you wanta play a little, one last time."

A faint grin. "Yeah?"

"Sure. But I tell you, you move an inch a way I don't like, I'll park one in your ass."

"No, man. I'm cool."

Tony unhooked the cuffs and stood back, the Glock pointed near his prisoner.

Williams picked up the violin and played another riff. He was getting a feel for it. The sound was much more resonant, fuller, this time. He launched into "Go Tell Aunt Rhody," and played some variations on it. Then a few little classical exercises. Some Bach, Tony thought. A bit of "Ain't Misbehavin'" too. And a few pieces he remembered his mother playing when he was a boy. Finally, Williams finished, sighed and tossed the instrument into the case. He nodded toward it. "Funny, ain't it? You think about stealing something for months and months and you finally get it up to do it, and what happens but you perp some old piece of crap like this, all messed up and everything."

Tony too looked at the nicks in the wood, the scratches, the worn neck.

It cost more than my town house. . . .

"Okay, son, it's time to go." He picked up the handcuffs from the table. "We'll get somebody from social services to take care of the kids."

The smile faded from Williams's face as he looked toward the bedroom. "Man," he said. "Man."

■

The lobby of the Sherry-Netherland hotel seemed pretty stark to Tony Vincenzo, who judged the quality of hotels by the length of the happy hour and the square footage of chrome in the lobby. But this was rich person territory and what did he know about rich people?

It was small too. And it looked even smaller because it was filled with reporters and cops. Along with the woman in the red dress, the one from the mayor's office. Sergeant Weber was here too, as well, looking pissed he'd been called out of bed at two A.M. to appear at a dog-and-pony show for an asshole, however famous he was.

Tony walked into the lobby, carrying the violin under his arm. He stopped in front of Weber, whose perpetual frown deepened slightly as he waved off reporters' questions.

Beaming, a coiffed Edouard Pitkin, wearing a suit and tie, Jesus, at this hour, stepped out of the elevator and into the glare of the lights. He strode forward to take the violin. But Tony didn't offer it to him. Instead, he merely shook the musician's hand.

Pitkin dropped the beat for a moment, then—aware of the press—smiled again and said, "What can I say, Officer? Thank you so much."

"For what?"

Another beat. "Well, for recovering my Stradivarius."

Tony gave a short laugh. Pitkin frowned. Then the cop motioned to the back of the crowd. "Come on, don't be shy."

Devon Williams, wearing his A&P uniform and work shoes, walked awkwardly through the forest of reporters.

Pitkin spun to Weber. "Why isn't he in handcuffs?" he raged.

The sergeant looked at Tony, silently asking the same question.

Tony shook his head. "I mean, why would I cuff the guy recovered your violin?"

"He . . . what?"

"Tell us what happened," a reporter shouted.

Weber nodded and Tony stepped into the crescent of reporters. He cleared his throat. "I spotted the perpetrator on One hundred twenty-fifth Street carrying the instrument in question and gave pursuit. This young man, Devon Williams, at great risk to himself, intervened and tackled the assailant. He was able to rescue the instrument. The perpetrator fled. I pursued him but unfortunately he got away."

He'd worried that this might sound too rehearsed, which it was. But, hell, everybody's used to cop-speak. If you sound too normal nobody believes you.

Pitkin said, "But . . . I just thought he looked like . . . I mean . . ."

Tony said, "I saw the perpetrator without the ski mask. He looked nothing like Mr. Williams." A glance at Pitkin. "Other than the fact they were both African American. I asked Mr. Williams to join us here so he could collect his reward. He said no but I insisted he come. I think good citizenship ought to be, you know, encouraged."

A reporter called, "How much is the reward, Mr. Pitkin?"

"Well, I hadn't . . . it's five thousand dollars."

"What?" Tony whispered, frowning.

"But ten if the instrument's undamaged," Pitkin added quickly.

Tony handed him the case. The musician turned abruptly and walked to a table near the front desk. He opened the case and examined the violin carefully.

Tony called, "It's okay?"

"Yes, yes, it's in fine shape."

Weber crooked his finger toward Tony. They stepped into the corner of the lobby. "So what the hell's is going on?" the sergeant muttered.

Tony shrugged. "Just what I said."

The sergeant sighed. "You don't have a perp?"

"Got away."

"And the kid got the fiddle. Not you. This ain't gonna do shit for your application."

"Figured that."

Weber looked Tony up and down and continued in a coy voice, "But then maybe you wouldn't want this *particular* case to go on the report anyway, would you?"

"Naw, I probably wouldn't."

"Tough break."

"Yeah," Tony said. "Tough."

"Hey, Mr. Williams," a reporter called. "Mr. Williams?"

Williams looked around, not used to a *Mr.* being joined with his last name.

"Oh, what?" he asked, catching on.

"Could you come over here, answer some questions?"

"Uhm, yeah, I guess."

As the young man walked uneasily toward the growing crowd of reporters, Tony leaned forward and, a big smile on his face, caught him by the arm. The boy stopped and lowered his ear to Tony, who whispered, "Devon, I gotta get home but I'm just checking . . . your aunt gets up here, she's making me ham hocks and collards, right?"

"She's the best."

"And the rest of that money's going in an account for the kids?"

Another gold-toothed grin. "You bet, Officer." They shook hands.

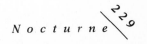

Tony pulled on his rain slicker as Williams stopped in front of the cameras. Tony paused at the revolving doors, looked back.

"Mr. Williams, tell us: You like music?"

"Uh, yeah. I like music."

"You like rap?"

"Naw, I don't like it too much."

"Do you play anything?"

"Little piano, guitar."

"After this incident do you think you might want to take up the violin?"

"Well, sure." He glanced toward Edouard Pitkin. The musician looked back at the young man as if he were from outer space. Holding Pitkin's eye, Williams continued, "I've seen people play 'em and it doesn't seem that hard. I mean, that's just my opinion, you know."

"Mr. Williams, one more question . . ."

Tony Vincenzo pushed outside into the night, where the fog was gone and the rain had finally started to fall—steadily and chill but oddly quiet. The night was still peaceful. Jean Marie would be asleep, but he still wanted to get home. Have a beer, put on a CD. Tony knew what he wanted to listen to. Mozart was good. Smokey Robinson was better.

LESSER-INCLUDED
OFFENSE

"Y ou're gonna lose this one."

"Am I, now?" asked Prosecutor Danny Tribow, rocking back in his desk chair and studying the man who'd just spoken.

Fifteen years older and forty pounds heavier than Tribow, the defendant Raymond Hartman nodded slowly and added, "On all counts. Simple as that."

The man next to Hartman touched his client's arm to restrain him.

"Ah, he doesn't mind a little sparring," Hartman said to his lawyer. "He can take it. Anyway, I'm just telling it like it is." The defendant unbuttoned his navy suit jacket, blue and rich as an ocean at night.

The truth was that Tribow *didn't* mind sparring. Not one bit. The man could say whatever he wanted. Tribow wasn't going to prosecute the case against Hartman any more vigorously because of the man's arrogance than he would've held back if the man had been tearful and contrite.

On the other hand, the thirty-five-year-old career prosecutor wasn't going to get walked on either. He fixed his eye on Hartman's and said in a soft voice, "It's been my experience that what looks pretty clear to one person may turn out to be the opposite. I'm convinced the jury's going to see the facts my way. Which means *you're* going to lose."

Hartman shrugged and looked at his gold Rolex watch. He couldn't've cared less about the time, Tribow suspected. He was simply delivering an aside: that this one piece of jewelry of mine equals your annual salary.

Danny Tribow wore a Casio and the only message a glance at that timepiece would deliver was that this meeting had been a waste of a good half hour.

In addition to the defendant, his lawyer and Tribow, two other people sat in the office, which was as small and shabby as one would expect for a district attorney's. On Tribow's left was his law clerk, a handsome man in his twenties, Chuck Wu, who was a brilliant, meticulous—some said compulsive—worker. He now leaned forward, typing notes and observations about this meeting into the battered laptop computer he was inseparable from. The keyboarding was a habit that drove most defendants nuts but it had no apparent effect on Ray Hartman.

The other one of the fivesome was Adele Viamonte, the assistant DA who'd been assigned to Tribow in the violent felonies division for the past year. She was almost ten years older than Tribow; she'd picked up her interest in law later in life after a successful first career: raising twin boys, now teenagers. Viamonte's mind and tongue were as sharp as her confidence was solid. She now looked over Hartman's tanned skin, taut belly, silvery hair, broad shoulders and thick neck. She then turned to his lawyer and asked, "So can we assume that this meeting with Mr. Hartman and his ego is over with?"

Hartman gave a faint, embarrassed laugh, as if a student had said something awkward in class, the put-down motivated solely because, the prosecutor guessed, Viamonte was a woman.

The defense lawyer repeated what he'd been saying all along. "My client isn't interested in a plea bargain that involves jail time."

Tribow echoed his own litany. "But that's all we're offering."

"Then he wants to go to trial. He's confident he'll be found innocent."

Tribow didn't know how *that* was going to happen. Ray Hartman had shot a man in the head one Sunday afternoon last March. There was physical evidence—ballistics, gunpowder residue on his hand. There were witnesses who placed him at the scene, searching for the victim just before the death. There were reports of earlier threats by Hartman and statements of intent to cause the victim harm. There was a motive. While Danny Tribow was always guarded about the outcomes of the cases he prosecuted, this was as solid as any he'd ever had.

And so he tried one last time. "If you accept murder two I'll recommend fifteen years."

"No way," Hartman responded, laughing at the absurdity of the suggestion. "You didn't hear my shyster here. No jail time. I'll pay a fine. I'll pay a *big* goddamn fine. I'll do community service. But no jail time."

Daniel Tribow was a slight man, unflappable and soft-spoken. He would have looked right at home in a bow tie and suspenders. "Sir," he said now, speaking directly to Hartman, "you understand I'm going to prosecute you for premeditated murder. In this state that's a special circumstances crime—meaning I can seek the death penalty."

"What I understand is that I don't see much point in continuing this little get-together. I've got a lunch date waiting and, if you ask me, you boys and girls better bone up on your law—you sure as hell need to if you think you're getting me convicted."

"If that's what you want, sir." Tribow stood. He shook the lawyer's hand though not the suspect's. Adele Viamonte glanced at both lawyer and client as if they were clerks who'd short-changed her and remained seated, apparently struggling to keep from saying what she really felt.

When they were gone Tribow sat back in his chair. He spun to look out the window at the rolling countryside of suburbia, bright green with early summer colors. Tribow played absently with the only artwork in his office: a baby's mobile of Winnie-the-Pooh characters, stuck to his chipped credenza top with a suction cup. It was his son's—well, *had* been, when the boy, now ten, was an infant. When Danny Junior had lost interest in the mobile, his father didn't have the heart to throw it away and brought it here to the office. His wife thought this was one of those silly things he did sometimes, like his infamous practical jokes or dressing up in costumes for his son's parties. Tribow didn't tell her that he wanted the toy here for one reason only: to remind him of his family during those long weeks preparing for and prosecuting cases, when it seemed that the only family he had were judges, jurors, detectives and colleagues.

He now mused, "I offer him ten years against a possible special-circumstances murder and he says he'll take his chances? I don't get it."

Viamonte shook her head. "Nope. Doesn't add up. He'd be out in seven. If he loses on special circumstances—and that's likely—he could get the needle."

"How 'bout the answer?" a man's voice asked from the doorway.

"Sure." Tribow spun around in the chair and nodded Richard Moyer, a senior county detective, into the room. "Only what's the question?"

Moyer waved greetings to Viamonte and Wu and sat down in a chair, yawning excessively.

"So, Dick, bored with us already?" Wu asked wryly.

"Tired. Too many bad guys out there. Anyway, I overheard

what you were saying—about Hartman. I know why he won't take the plea."

"Why's that?"

"He can't go into Stafford." The main state prison, through which had passed a number of graduates of the Daniel Tribow School of Criminal Prosecution.

"Who wants to go to prison?" Viamonte asked.

"No, no, I mean he *can't*. They're already sharpening spoon handles and grinding down glass shivs, waiting for him."

Moyer continued, explaining that two of the OC—organized crime—bosses that Hartman had snitched on were in Stafford now. "Word's out that Hartman wouldn't last a week inside."

So *that* was why he'd killed the victim in this case, Jose Valdez. The poor man had been the sole witness against Hartman in an extortion case. If Hartman had been convicted of that he'd have gone to Stafford for at least six months—or, apparently, until he was murdered by fellow prisoners. That explained Valdez's cold-blooded killing.

But Hartman's reception in prison wasn't Tribow's problem. The prosecutor believed he had a simple task in life: to keep his county safe. This attitude was considerably different from many other prosecutors.' They took it personally that criminals committed offenses, and went after them vindictively, full of rage. But to Danny Tribow, prosecuting wasn't about being a gunslinger; it was simply making sure his county was safe and secure. He was far more involved in the community than a typical DA. He'd worked with congressmen and the courts, for instance, to support laws that made it easier to get restraining orders against abusive spouses and that established mandatory felony sentences for three-strikes offenders, anyone carrying a gun near a school or church, and drivers whose drinking resulted in someone's death.

Getting Ray Hartman off the streets was nothing more than

yet another brick in the wall of law and order, to which Tribow was so devoted.

This particular man's conviction, however, was a very important brick. At various stages in his life Hartman had been through court-ordered therapy and though he'd always escaped with a diagnosis of sanity, the doctors had observed that he was close to being a sociopath, someone for whom human life meant little.

This was certainly reflected in his MO. He was a bully and petty thug who sold protection to and extorted recent immigrants like Jose Valdez. And Hartman would intimidate or murder anyone who threatened to testify against him. No one was safe.

"Hartman's got money in Europe," Tribow said to the cop. "Who's watching him—to make sure he doesn't head for the beach?" The suspect had been released on a $2 million bond, which he'd easily posted, and he'd had his passport lifted. But Tribow remembered the killer's assured look not long before as he'd said, "You're going to lose," and wondered if Hartman conveyed a subconscious message that he was planning to jump bond.

But Detective Moyer—helping himself to the cookies that Tribow's wife had once again sent her husband to work with—said, "We don't have to worry. He's got baby-sitters like you wouldn't believe. Two, full-time. He steps over the county line or into an airport and, bang, he's wearing bracelets. These oatmeal ones're my favorite. Can I get the recipe?" He yawned again.

"You don't cook," Tribow told him. "How 'bout if Connie just makes you a box?"

"That'd work too." The cop wandered back out of the office to find some criminals to arrest—or to get some sleep—and Chuck Wu accompanied Viamonte to her office, where they'd spend the evening preparing questions for voir dire—jury selection.

Tribow himself turned to the indictment and continued to plan out the trial.

He'd carefully studied the facts of the Valdez killing and decided to bring Hartman up on three charges. The backbone of the case—the conviction that Tribow wanted most badly—was first-degree murder. This was premeditated homicide, and if convicted of it Hartman could be sentenced to death, a punishment that Tribow intended to recommend to the court. But this was a difficult case to prove. The state had to establish beyond a reasonable doubt that Hartman had planned out Valdez's murder ahead of time, went looking for him, and killed him under circumstances that showed no heat of passion or emotional turmoil.

But there were several other charges included in the indictment too: murder two and manslaughter. These were backups—what were called "lesser-included offenses." They were easier to prove than murder one. If the jury decided, for instance, that Hartman hadn't planned the murder ahead of time but decided impulsively to kill Valdez, they could still convict for second-degree murder. He could go to prison for life for this type of murder but he couldn't be sentenced to death.

Finally Tribow included the manslaughter charge as a last-ditch backup. He'd have to prove only that Hartman had killed Valdez either under conditions of extreme recklessness or in the heat of passion. This would be the easiest of the crimes to prove and on these facts the jury would undoubtedly convict.

That weekend the three prosecutors prepared questions to ask the jury, and over the course of the next week they battled Hartman's impressive legal team during the voir dire process. Finally, on Friday, the jury was empaneled and Tribow, Wu and Viamonte returned to the office to spend the weekend coaching witnesses and preparing evidence and exhibits.

Every time he got tired, every time he wanted to stop and return home to play with Danny Junior or just sit and have a cup of coffee with his wife, he pictured Jose Valdez's wife and thought that she'd never spend *any* time with her husband again.

And when he thought that, he pictured Ray Hartman's arrogant eyes.

You're going to lose this one. . . .

Danny Tribow would then stop daydreaming and return to the case.

■

When he'd been in law school Tribow had hoped for the chance to practice law in a Gothic courthouse filled with portraits of stern old judges and dark-wood paneling and the scent of somber justice.

Where he plied his trade, however, was a brightly lit, low-ceilinged county courtroom filled with blond wood and beige drapes and ugly green linoleum. It looked like a high school classroom.

On the morning of trial, nine A.M. sharp, he sat down at the counsel table, flanked by Adele Viamonte—in her darkest suit, whitest blouse and most assertive visage—and Chuck Wu, who was manning his battered laptop. Hundreds of papers and exhibits and law books surrounded them.

Across the aisle Ray Hartman sat at the other table. He was surrounded by three high-ticket partners in the law firm he'd hired, two associates, and *four* laptops.

The uneven teams didn't bother Tribow one bit, however. He believed he was put on earth to bring people who did illegal things to justice. Some of them would always be richer than you and have better resources. That was how the game worked and Tribow, like every successful prosecutor throughout history, accepted it. Only weak or incompetent DAs whined about the unfairness of the system.

He noticed Ray Hartman staring at him, mouthing something. The DA couldn't tell what it was.

Viamonte translated. "He said, 'You're going to lose.' "

Tribow gave a brief laugh.

He looked behind him. The room was filled. He nodded at Detective Dick Moyer, who'd been after Hartman for years. A nod too and a faint smile for Carmen Valdez, the widow of the victim. She returned his gaze with a silent, desperate plea that he bring this terrible man to justice.

I'll do my best, he answered, also silently.

Then the clerk entered and called out, "Oyez, oyez, this court is now in session. All those with business before this court come forward and be heard." As he always did, Tribow felt a chill at these words, as if they were an incantation that shut out reality and ushered everyone here into the solemn and mysterious world of the criminal courtroom.

A few preliminaries were disposed of and the bearded judge nodded for Tribow to start.

The prosecutor rose and gave his opening statement, which was very short; Danny Tribow believed the divining rod that most effectively pointed toward justice in a criminal case wasn't rhetoric but the truth as revealed by the facts you presented to the jury.

And so for the next two days he produced witness after witness, exhibits, charts and graphs.

"I've been a professional ballistics expert for twenty-two years. . . . I conducted three tests of the bullets taken from the defendant's weapon and I can state without a doubt that the bullet that killed the victim came from the defendant's gun. . . ."

"I sold that weapon to the man sitting there—the defendant, Ray Hartman. . . ."

"The victim, Mr. Valdez, had gone to the police complaining that the defendant had extorted him. . . . Yes, that's a copy of the complaint. . . ."

"I've been a police officer for seven years. I was one of the first on the scene and I took that particular weapon off the person of the defendant, Ray Hartman. . . ."

"We found gunshot residue on the hand of the defendant, Ray Hartman. The amount and nature of this residue is consistent with what we would've found on the hands of someone who fired a pistol about the time the victim was shot. . . ."

"The victim was shot once in the temple. . . ."

"Yes, I saw the defendant on the day of the shooting. He was walking down the street next to Mr. Valdez's shop and I heard him stop and ask several people where the defendant was. . . ."

"That's correct, sir. I saw the defendant the day Mr. Valdez was killed. Mr. Hartman was asking where he could find Mr. Valdez. His coat was open and I saw that he had a pistol. . . ."

"About a month ago I was at a bar. I was sitting next to the defendant and I heard him say he was going to 'get' Mr. Valdez and that'd take care of all his problems. . . ."

By introducing all this testimony, Tribow established that Hartman had a motive to kill Valdez; he'd intended to do it for some time; he went looking for the victim the day he was shot, armed with a gun; he'd behaved with reckless disregard by attacking the man with a pistol and firing a shot that could have injured innocent people; and that he in fact was the proximate cause of Valdez's death.

"Your Honor, the prosecution rests."

He returned to the table.

"Open and shut," said Chuck Wu.

"Shhhh," whispered Adele Viamonte. "Bad luck."

Danny Tribow didn't believe in luck. But he did believe in not prematurely counting chickens. He sat back and listened to the defense begin its case.

The slickest of Hartman's lawyers—the one who'd been in Tribow's office during the ill-fated plea bargain session—first in-

troduced into evidence a pistol permit, which showed that Hartman was licensed to carry a weapon for his own personal safety.

No problem here, Tribow thought. He'd known about the permit.

But Hartman's lawyer had no sooner begun to question his first witness—the doorman in Hartman's building—than Tribow began to feel uneasy.

"Did you happen to see the defendant on the morning of Sunday, March thirteenth?"

"Yessir."

"Did you happen to notice if he was carrying a weapon?"

"He was."

Why was he asking this? Tribow asked himself. It'd support the *state's* case. He glanced at Viamonte, who shook her head.

"And did you notice him the day before?"

"Yessir."

Uh-oh. Tribow had an idea where this was headed.

"And did he have his gun with him then?"

"Yes, he did. He'd run into some trouble with the gangs in the inner city—he was trying to get a youth center started and the gangs didn't want it. He'd been threatened a lot."

Youth center? Tribow and Wu exchanged sour glances. The only interest Hartman would have in a youth center was as a venue to sell drugs.

"How often did he have a gun with him?"

"Every day, sir. For the past three years I've been working there."

Nobody would notice something every day for three years. He was lying. Hartman had gotten to the doorman.

"We got a problem, boss," Wu whispered.

He meant this: If the jury believed that Hartman *always* carried the gun, that fact would undermine Tribow's assertion that he'd taken it with him only that one time—on the day of the murder—for the purpose of killing Valdez. The jury could therefore conclude that he hadn't planned the murder, which would eliminate the premeditation element of the case and, with it, the murder-one count.

But if the doorman's testimony endangered the first-degree murder case, the next witness—a man in an expensive business suit—risked destroying it completely.

"Sir, you don't know the defendant, do you?"

"No. I've never had anything to do with him. Never met him."

"He's never given you anything or offered you any money or anything of value?"

"No, sir."

He's lying, Tribow thought instinctively. The witness delivered his lines like a bad actor in a dinner-theater play.

"Now you heard the prosecution witness say that Mr. Hartman was going to quote 'get' the victim and that would take care of all his problems."

"Yessir, I did."

"You were near the defendant and that witness when this conversation supposedly took place, is that right?"

"Yessir."

"Where was that?"

"Cibella's restaurant on Washington Boulevard, sir."

"And was the conversation the same as the witness described?"

"No, it wasn't," the man answered the defense lawyer. "The prosecution witness, he misunderstood. See, I was sitting at the next table and I heard Mr. Hartman say, 'I'm going to get Valdez to take care of some problems I've been having in the Latino community.' I guess that witness didn't hear right or something."

"I see," the lawyer summarized in a slick voice. "He was going to *get* Valdez to *take care of* some problems?"

"Yessir. Then Mr. Hartman said, 'That Jose Valdez is a good man and I respect him. I'd like him to explain to the community that I'm concerned for their welfare.'"

Chuck Wu mouthed a silent obscenity.

The lawyer pushed his point home. "So Mr. Hartman was concerned for the welfare of the Latino community?"

"Yes, very much so. Mr. Hartman was really patient with him. Even though Valdez started all those rumors, you know."

"What rumors?" the lawyer asked.

"About Mr. Hartman and Valdez's wife."

Behind him Tribow heard the man's widow inhale in shock.

"What were those rumors?"

"Valdez got it into his head that Mr. Hartman'd been seeing his wife. I know he wasn't, but Valdez was convinced of it. The guy was a little, you know, nuts in the head. He thought a lot of guys were, you know, seeing his wife."

"Objection," Tribow snapped.

"Let me rephrase. What did Mr. Valdez ever say to you about Mr. Hartman and his wife?"

"He said he was going to get even with Hartman because of the affair—I mean, the supposed affair."

"Objection," Tribow called again.

"Hearsay exception," the judge called. "I'll let it stand."

Tribow glanced at the face of Valdez's widow, shaking her head slowly, tears running down her cheeks.

The defense lawyer said to Tribow, "Your witness."

The prosecutor did his best to punch holes in the man's story. He thought he did a pretty good job. But much of the testimony had been speculation and opinion—the rumors of the affair, for instance—and there was little he could do to discredit him. He returned to his chair.

Relax, Tribow told himself and set down the pen he'd been playing with compulsively. The murder-two charge was still alive and well. All they'd have to find was that Hartman had in fact killed Valdez—as Tribow had already proven—and that he'd decided at the last minute to murder him.

The defense lawyer called another witness.

He was a Latino—a grandfatherly sort of man, balding, round. A friendly face. His name was Cristos Abrego and he described himself as a good friend of the defendant's.

Tribow considered this and concluded that the jury's concerns about Abrego's potential bias were outweighed by the fact that the suspect, it seemed, had "good friends" in the minority community (a complete lie, of course; Hartman, Anglo, saw minorities not as friends but only as golden opportunities for his extortion and loan-sharking operations).

"Now you heard the prosecution witness say that Mr. Hartman went looking for Mr. Valdez the day of the tragic shooting?"

"Tragic?" Wu whispered. "He's making it sound like an accident."

"Yessir," the witness answered the lawyer's question.

"Can you confirm that Mr. Hartman went looking for Mr. Valdez on the day of the shooting?"

"Yessir, it is true. Mr. Hartman did go looking for him."

Tribow leaned forward. Where was this going?

"Could you explain what happened and what you observed?"

"Yessir. I'd been in church with Mr. Hartman—"

"Excuse me," the lawyer said. "Church?"

"Yeah, him and me, we went to the same church. Well, he went more than me. He went at least twice a week. Sometimes three."

"Brother," an exasperated Adele Viamonte said.

Tribow counted four crucifixes hanging from the necks of the jury, and not a single eyebrow among these men and women rose in irony at this gratuitous mention of the defendant's piety.

"Please go on, Mr. Abrego."

"And I stopped in the Starbucks with Mr. Hartman and we got some coffee and sat outside. Then he asked a couple of people if they'd seen Valdez, 'cause he hangs out in Starbucks a lot."

"Do you know why the defendant wanted to see Valdez?"

"He wanted to give him this game he bought for Valdez's kid."

"*What?*" the widow, behind Tribow, whispered in shock. "No, no, no . . ."

"A present, you know. Mr. Hartman loves kids. And he wanted to give it to Valdez for his boy."

"Why did he want to give Mr. Valdez a present?"

Abrego said, "He said he wanted to patch things up with Valdez. He felt bad the man had those crazy ideas about him and his wife and was worried that the boy would hear and think they were true. So he thought a present for the kid'd break the ice. Then he was going to talk to Valdez and try to convince him that he was wrong."

"Keep going, sir. What happened next?"

"Then Mr. Hartman sees Valdez outside his store and he gets up from the table and goes over to him."

"And then?"

"Ray waves to Valdez and says, 'Hi,' or something like that. 'How you doing?' I don't know. Something friendly. And he starts to hand him the bag but Valdez just pushes it away and starts yelling at him."

"Do you know what they were yelling about?"

"Valdez was saying all kinds of weird stuff. Like: 'I know you've been seeing my wife for five years.' Which was crazy 'cause Valdez just moved here last year."

"No!" the widow cried. "It's all a lie!"

The judge banged his gavel down, though it was with a lethargy that suggested his sympathies were with the woman.

Tribow sighed in disgust. Here the defense had introduced a

motive suggesting that Valdez, not Hartman, might have been the aggressor in the fight that day.

"I *know* it wasn't true," the witness said to the defense lawyer. "Mr. Hartman'd never do anything like that. He was really religious."

Two references to the archangel Raymond C. Hartman.

The lawyer then asked, "Did you see what happened next?"

"It was all kind of a blur but I saw Valdez grab something—a metal pipe or a piece of wood—and swing it at Mr. Hartman. He tried to back away but there was no place for him to go—they were in this alley. Finally—it looked like he was going to get his head cracked open—Mr. Hartman pulled out his gun. He was just going to threaten Valdez—"

"Objection. The witness couldn't know what the defendant's intentions were."

The lawyer asked the witness, "What, Mr. Abrego, was your *impression* of Mr. Hartman's intention?"

"It *looked* like he was just going to threaten Valdez. Valdez swung at him a few more times with the pipe but Mr. Hartman still didn't shoot. Then Valdez grabbed his arm and they were struggling for the gun. Mr. Hartman was yelling for people to get down and shouting to Valdez, 'Let go! Let go! Somebody'll get hurt.' "

Which was hardly the reckless behavior or heat of passion that Tribow had to show in proving the manslaughter count.

"Mr. Hartman was pretty brave. I mean, he coulda run and saved himself but he was worried about bystanders. He was like that, always worrying about other people—especially kids."

Tribow wondered who'd written the script. Hartman himself, he guessed, it was so bad.

"Then I ducked 'cause I thought if Valdez got the gun away he'd just start shooting like a madman and I got scared. I heard a gunshot and when I got up off the ground I saw that Valdez was dead."

"What was the defendant doing?"

"He was on his knees, trying to help Valdez. Stopping the bleeding, it looked like, calling for help. He was very shaken up."

"No further questions."

On cross, Tribow tried to puncture Abrego's testimony too but because it was cleverly hedged (*"It was all kind of a blur. . . ."* *"I'm not sure. . . ."* *"There was this rumor. . . ."*) he had nothing specific with which to discredit the witness. The prosecutor planted the seeds of doubt in the minds of the jury by asking again, several times, if Hartman had paid the witness anything or threatened him or his family. But, of course, the man denied that.

The defense then called a doctor, whose testimony was short and to the point.

"Doctor, the coroner's report shows the victim was shot once in the side of the head. Yet you heard the testimony of the prior witness that the two men were struggling face-to-face. How could the victim have been shot in that way?"

"Very simple. A shot in the side of the head would be consistent with Mr. Valdez turning his head away from the weapon while he was exerting pressure on the trigger, hoping to hit Mr. Hartman."

"So, in effect, you're saying that Mr. Valdez shot himself."

"Objection!"

"Sustained."

The lawyer said, "You're saying that it's *possible* Mr. Valdez was turning away while he himself pulled the trigger of the weapon, resulting in his own death?"

"That's correct."

"No further questions."

Tribow asked the doctor how it was that the coroner didn't

find any gunshot residue on Valdez's hands, which would have been present if he'd fired the gun himself, while Mr. Hartman's had residue on them. The doctor replied, "Simple. Mr. Hartman's hands were covering Mr. Valdez's and so they got all the residue on them."

The judge dismissed the witness and Tribow returned to the table with a glance at the stony face of the defendant, who was staring back at him.

You're going to lose. . . .

Well, Tribow hadn't thought that was possible a short while before, but now there was a real chance that Hartman would walk.

Then the defense lawyer called his final witness: Raymond Hartman himself.

His testimony gave a story identical to that of the other witnesses and supported his case: that he always carried his gun, that Valdez had this weird idea about Hartman and Valdez's wife, that he'd never extorted anyone in his life, that he bought a present for the Valdez boy, that he wanted to enlist Valdez's help in putting money into the Latino community, that the struggle occurred just as the witness said. Though he added a coda: his giving mouth-to-mouth resuscitation to Valdez.

He continued, with a glance at the four Latino and three black jurors. "I get a lot of hassles because I want to help minority businesses. For some reason the police and the city and state— they don't like that. And here I ended up accidentally hurting one of the very people I'm trying to help." He looked sorrowfully at the floor.

Adele Viamonte's sigh could be heard throughout the courtroom and drew a glare from the judge.

The lawyer thanked Hartman and said to Tribow, "Your witness."

"What're we going to do, boss?" Wu whispered.

Tribow glanced at the two people on his team, who'd worked so tirelessly, for endless hours, on this case. Then he looked behind him into the eyes of Carmen Valdez, whose life had been so terribly altered by the man sitting on the witness stand, gazing placidly at the prosecutors and the people in the gallery.

Tribow pulled Chuck Wu's laptop computer closer to him and scrolled through the notes that the young man had taken over the course of the trial. He read for a moment then stood slowly and walked toward Hartman.

In his trademark polite voice he asked, "Mr. Hartman, I'm curious about one thing."

"Yessir?" the killer asked, just as polite. He'd been coached well by his attorneys, who'd undoubtedly urged him never to get flustered or angry on the stand.

"The game you got for Mr. Valdez's son."

The eyes flickered. "Yes? What about it?"

"What was it?"

"One of those little video games. A GameBoy."

"Was it expensive?"

A smile of curiosity. "Yeah, pretty expensive. But I wanted to do something nice for Jose and his kid. I felt bad because his father was pretty crazy—"

"Just answer the question," Tribow interrupted.

"It cost about fifty or sixty bucks."

"Where did you get it?"

"A toy store in the mall. I don't remember the name."

Tribow considered himself a pretty good lie detector and he could see that Hartman was making all this up. He'd probably seen an ad for GameBoys that morning. He doubted, however, that the jury could tell. To them he was simply cooperating and politely answering the prosecutor's somewhat curious questions.

"What did this video game do?"

"Objection," the lawyer called. "What's the point?"

"Your Honor," Tribow said. "I'm just trying to establish a relationship between the defendant and the victim."

"Go ahead, Mr. Tribow, but I don't think we need to know what kind of box this toy came in."

"Actually, sir, I was going to ask that."

"Well, don't."

"I won't. Now, Mr. Hartman, what did this game do?"

"I don't know—you shot spaceships or something."

"Did you play with it before giving it to Mr. Valdez?"

From the corner of his eye he saw Viamonte and Wu exchange troubled glances, wondering what on earth their boss was up to.

"No," Hartman answered. For the first time on the stand he seemed testy. "I don't like games. Anyway, it was a present. I wasn't gonna open it up before I gave it to the boy."

Tribow nodded, raising an eyebrow, and continued his questioning. "Now the morning of the day Jose Valdez was shot did you have this game with you when you left your house?"

"Yessir."

"Was it in a bag?"

He thought for a moment. "It was, yeah, but I put it in my pocket. It wasn't that big."

"So your hands would be free?"

"I guess. Probably."

"And you left your house when?"

"Ten-forty or so. Mass was at eleven."

Tribow then asked, "Which church?"

"St. Anthony's."

"And you went straight there? With the game in your pocket?"

"Yes, that's right."

"And the game was with you in the church?"

"Correct."

"But no one would have seen it because it was in your pocket."

"I guess that'd be right." Still polite, still unflustered.

"And when you left the church you walked along Maple Street to the Starbucks in the company of the earlier witness, Mr. Cristos Abrego?"

"Yes, that's right."

"And the game was still in your pocket?"

"No."

"It wasn't?"

"No. At that point I took it out and was carrying it in the bag."

Tribow whirled to face him and asked in a piercing voice, "Isn't it true that you *didn't* have the game with you in church?"

"No," Hartman said, blinking in surprise but keeping his voice even and low, "that's not true at all. I had the game with me all day. Until I was attacked by Valdez."

"Isn't it true that you left church, returned home, got the game and then *drove* to Starbucks?"

"No, I wouldn't've had time to go home after church and get the game. Mass was over at noon. I got to Starbucks about ten minutes later. I told you, my house is a good twenty minutes away from the church. You can check a map. I went straight from St. Anthony's to Starbucks."

Tribow looked away from Hartman to the faces of the jury. He then glanced at the widow in the front row of the gallery, crying softly. He saw the perplexed faces of his prosecution team. He saw spectators glancing at one another. Everyone was waiting for him to drop some brilliant bombshell that would pull the rug out from underneath Hartman's testimony and expose him as the liar and killer that he was.

Tribow took a deep breath. He said, "No further questions, Your Honor."

There was a moment of silence. Even the judge frowned and seemed to want to ask if the prosecutor was sure he wanted to do this. But he settled for asking the defense lawyer, "Any more witnesses?"

"No, sir. The defense rests."

■

The sole reason for a jury's existence is that people lie.

If everyone told the truth a judge could simply ask Raymond C. Hartman if he planned and carried out the murder of Jose Valdez and the man would say yes or no and that would be that.

But people don't tell the truth, of course, and so the judicial system relies on a jury to look at the eyes and mouths and hands and postures of witnesses and listen to their words and decide what's the truth and what isn't.

The jury in the case of the *State* v. *Hartman* had been out for two hours. Tribow and his assistants were holed up in the cafeteria in the building across from the courthouse. Nobody was saying a word. Some of this silence had to be attributed to their uneasiness—if not outright embarrassment—at Tribow's unfathomable line of questioning about the game Hartman had allegedly bought for the victim's son. They would probably be thinking that even experienced prosecutors get flustered and fumble the ball from time to time and it was just as well it happened during a case like this, which was, apparently, unwinnable.

Danny Tribow's eyes were closed as he lounged back in an ugly orange fiberglass chair. He was replaying Hartman's cool demeanor and the witnesses' claims that they hadn't been threatened or bribed by Hartman. They'd *all* been paid off or threatened, he knew, but he had to admit they looked and sounded fairly credible to him; presumably they'd seemed that way to the jury as well. But Tribow had great respect for the jury system and for jurors on the whole and, as they sat in the small deliberation room behind the courthouse, they might easily be concluding at this moment that Hartman had lied and coerced the witnesses into lying as well.

And that he was guilty of murder one.

But when he opened his eyes and glanced over at Adele Viamonte and Chuck Wu, their discouraged faces told him that there was also a pretty good chance that justice might not get done at this trial.

"Okay," Viamonte said, "so we don't win on premeditated murder. We've still got the two lesser-includeds. And they'll *have* to convict on manslaughter."

Have to? thought Tribow. He didn't think that was a word that ever applied to a jury's decision. The defense had pitched a great case for a purely accidental death.

"Miracles happen," said Wu with youthful enthusiasm.

And that was when Tribow's cell phone rang. It was the clerk with the news that the jury was returning.

"Them coming back this fast—is that good or bad?" Wu asked.

Tribow finished his coffee. "Let's go find out."

∎

"Ladies and gentlemen of the jury, have you reached a verdict?"

"We have, Your Honor."

The foreman, a middle-aged man in a plaid shirt and dark slacks, handed a piece of paper to the bailiff, who carried it to the judge.

Tribow kept his eyes on Hartman's but the killer was sitting back in the swivel chair with a placid expression. He cleaned a fingernail with a paper clip. If he was worried about the outcome of the trial he didn't show it.

The judge read the slip of paper silently and glanced over at the jury.

Tribow tried to read the jurist's expression but couldn't.

"The defendant will rise."

Hartman and his lawyer stood.

The judge handed the paper to the clerk, who read, "In the case of the People versus Raymond C. Hartman, on the first count, murder in the first degree, the jury finds the defendant not guilty. On the second count, murder in the second degree, the jury finds the defendant not guilty. On the third count, manslaughter, the jury finds the defendant not guilty."

Complete silence in the courtroom for a moment, broken by Hartman's whispered, "Yes!" as he raised a fist of victory in the air.

The judge, clearly disgusted at the verdict, banged his gavel down and said, "No more of that, Mr. Hartman." He added gruffly, "See the clerk for the return of your passport and bail deposit. I only hope that if you're brought up on charges again, you appear in *my* courtroom." Another angry slap of the gavel. "This court stands adjourned."

The courtroom broke into a hundred simultaneous conversations, all laced with disapproval and anger.

Hartman ignored all the comments and glares. He shook his lawyers' hands. Several of his confederates came up to him and gave him hugs. Tribow saw a smile pass between Hartman and his choirboy buddy, Abrego.

Tribow formally shook Viamonte's and Wu's hands—as was his tradition when a verdict, good or bad, came down. Then he went over to Carmen Valdez. She was crying softly. The DA hugged her. "I'm sorry," he said.

"You did your best," the woman said and nodded at Hartman. "I guess people like that, really bad people, they don't play by the rules. And there's nothing you can do about it. Sometimes they're just going to win."

"Next time," Tribow said.

"Next time," she whispered cynically.

Tribow turned away and whispered a few words to Detective Moyer. The prosecutor noticed Hartman walking toward the front door of the courtroom. He stepped forward quickly, intercepting him. "Just a second, Hartman," Tribow said.

"Nice try, Counselor," the larger-than-life man said, pausing, "but you should've listened to me. I told you you were going to lose."

One of his lawyers handed Hartman an envelope. He opened it and took out his passport.

"Must've cost you a lot to bribe those witnesses," Tribow said amiably.

"Oh, I wouldn't do that," Hartman frowned. "That'd be a crime. As you, of all people, ought to know."

Viamonte leveled a finger at him and said, "You're going to stumble and we're going to be there when it happens."

Hartman replied calmly, "Not unless you're moving to the south of France. Which is what I'm doing next week. Come visit."

"To help the minority community in Saint-Tropez?" Chuck Wu asked.

Hartman offered a smile then turned toward the door.

"Mr. Hartman," Tribow said. "One more thing?"

The killer turned. "What?"

Tribow nodded to Detective Dick Moyer. He stepped forward, paused and gazed coldly into Hartman's eyes.

"Something you want, Officer?" the killer asked.

Moyer gripped Hartman roughly and handcuffed him.

"Hey, what the hell're you doing?"

Abrego and two of Hartman's bodyguards stepped forward but by now a number of other police officers were next to Tribow and Moyer. The thugs backed off immediately.

Hartman's lawyer pushed his way to the front of the crowd. "What's going on here?"

Moyer ignored him and said, "Raymond Hartman, you're under arrest for violation of state penal code section eighteen point three-one dash B. You have the right to remain silent, you have the right to an attorney." He continued the litany of the *Miranda* warning in a rather monotonous voice, considering the frenzy around him.

Hartman snapped to his lawyer, "Why the hell're you letting him do this? I'm paying you—do something!"

This attitude didn't sit well with the lawyer but he said, "He's been acquitted of all charges."

"Actually not all charges," Tribow said. "There was one lesser-included offense I didn't bring him up on. Section eighteen point three one."

"What the hell is that?" Hartman snapped.

His lawyer shook his head. "I don't know."

"You're a goddamn lawyer. What do you mean, you don't know?"

Tribow said, "It's a law that makes it a felony to have a loaded firearm within one hundred yards of a school—Sunday schools included." He added with a modest smile, "I worked with the state legislature myself to get that one passed."

"Oh, no . . ." the defense lawyer muttered.

Hartman frowned and said ominously, "You can't do that. It's too late. The trial's over."

The lawyer said, "He can, Ray. It's a different charge."

"Well, he can't prove it," Hartman snapped. "Nobody saw any guns. There were no witnesses."

"As a matter of fact there *is* a witness. And he happens to be one you can't bribe or threaten."

"Who?"

"You."

Tribow walked to the computer on which Chuck Wu had transcribed much of the testimony.

He read, "Hartman: 'No, I wouldn't've had time to go home after church and get the game. Mass was over at noon. I got to Starbucks about ten minutes later. I told you, my house is a good twenty minutes away from the church. You can check a map. I went straight from St. Anthony's to Starbucks.' "

"What's this all about? What's with this goddamn game?"

"The game's irrelevant," Tribow explained. "What's important is that you said you didn't have time to go home between leaving the church and arriving at Starbucks. That means you *had* to have the gun with you in church. And that's right next to the Sunday school." The prosecutor summarized, "You admitted under oath that you broke section eighteen thirty-one. This transcript's admissible at your next trial. That means it's virtually an automatic conviction."

Hartman said, "All right, all right. Let me pay the fine and get the hell out of here. I'll do it now."

Tribow looked at his lawyer. "You want to tell him the other part of eighteen point thirty-one?"

His lawyer shook his head. "It's a do-time felony, Ray."

"What the hell's that?"

"It carries mandatory prison time. Minimum six months, maximum five years."

"What?" Terror blossomed in the killer's eyes. "But I can't go to prison." He turned to his lawyer, grabbing his arm. "I *told* you that. They'll kill me there. I can't! Do something, earn your goddamn fee for a change, you lazy bastard!"

But the lawyer pulled the man's hand off. "You know what, Ray? Why don't you tell your story to your new lawyer. I'm in the market for a better grade of client." The man turned and walked out through the swinging doors.

"Wait!"

The detective and two other officers escorted Hartman away, shouting his protests.

After some congratulations from the police officers and spectators, Tribow and his team returned to the prosecution table and began organizing books and papers and laptops. There was a huge amount of material to pack up; the law, after all, is nothing more or less than words.

"Hey, boss, sleight of hand," Chuck Wu said. "You got him focusing on that game and he didn't think about the gun."

"Yeah, we thought you'd gone off the deep end," Viamonte offered.

"But we weren't going to say anything," Wu said.

Viamonte said, "Hey, let's go celebrate."

Tribow declined. He hadn't spent much time with his wife and son lately and he was desperate to get home to them. He finished packing up the big litigation bags.

"Thank you," a woman's voice said. Tribow turned to see Jose Valdez's widow standing in front of him. He nodded. She seemed to be casting about for something else to say but then she just shook the prosecutor's hand and she and an older woman walked out of the nearly empty courtroom.

Tribow watched her leave.

I guess people like that, really bad people, they don't play by the rules. And there's nothing you can do about it. Sometimes they're just going to win. . . .

But that means sometimes they're not.

Danny Tribow hefted the largest of the litigation bags and together the three prosecutors left the courtroom.

THE BLANK CARD

The little things.

Like the way she'd leave the office at five but sometimes not get home until six-twenty.

He knew his wife was a fast driver and could make the trip in maybe forty minutes that time of day. So where did she spend the remaining minutes?

And little things like the phone calls.

He'd come home and find Mary on the phone and, sure, she'd smile at him and blow him a little kiss-across-the-room. But it seemed that the tone of her voice would change as soon as she saw him and she'd hang up soon after. So Dennis would go to take a shower and pretend to forget a clean towel and call for Mary to get one for him, please, honey, and when she disappeared into the laundry room he'd go into the kitchen and debate a minute or so but then he'd go ahead and hit redial on the phone. And sometimes it turned out to be a neighbor or Mary's mother. But sometimes nobody picked up. He remembered seeing in a movie once, about spies or something, one guy would call this other one and they'd let it ring twice then call back exactly one minute later and he knew it was safe to pick up. Dennis tried to figure out the numbers from the sound of the dialing but they went too fast.

He'd be embarrassed because he was acting so paranoid. But then there'd be another little thing, and he'd get suspicious again. Like the wine. Sometimes he'd meet his wife at the door of their spacious Colonial in Westchester County, after she'd been out; he'd walk up to her fast and kiss her hard. She'd act surprised, all the passion and everything. But occasionally he'd smelled wine on her breath. She'd claim she'd been at a church fund-raising meeting at Patty's or Kit's. But do you drink wine at church meetings? Dennis Linden didn't think so.

Dennis's suspicions of his wife smacked of midlife crisis. But they also made some sense. He was too generous—that was his problem—and the women he'd ended up with in his life had taken advantage of him. He never thought it would be that way with Mary, a sharp, ambitious businesswoman in her own right, but not long after they'd been married, five years ago, he'd started to wonder about her. Nothing big, just being cautious. Sometimes in life you have to be smart.

But he hadn't really found any proof until about three months ago, in late September—after Dennis had met his best buddy, Sid Farnsworth, for drinks in White Plains.

"I don't know, I have this feeling she's seeing somebody," Dennis had muttered, hunched over his V&T.

"Who? Mary?" Sid had shook his head. "You're nuts. She loves you." The men had known each other since college and Sid was one of the few people who'd be completely straight with Dennis.

"She made this big deal out of going on a business trip to San Francisco last week."

"Whatta you mean, made a big deal? She didn't want to go?"

"No, she *did* want to go. But I wasn't sure it was a good idea."

"*You* thought it wasn't a good idea?" Sid hadn't understood. "Whatta you mean?"

"I was worried she'd get into trouble."

"Why you think that?"

" 'Cause she's a beautiful woman, why else? Everybody's always flirting with her and coming on to her."

"Mary?" Sid had laughed. "Gimme a break. Guys flirt with

women. If they don't they're gay or dead. But she doesn't flirt back or anything. She's just . . . nice. She smiles at everybody."

"Men take it the wrong way and then, bang, it could be a problem. I told her I didn't want her to go."

Sid had sipped his beer, cautiously eyeing his friend. "Listen, Denny, you just can't tell your wife you're not going to *let* her do something. That's bad form, man."

"I know, I know. I didn't go that far. Just kind of said I didn't want her to. And she got all upset. Why'd she have to go? Why was it so important?"

"Duh . . . 'cause she's a senior marketing manager and she needed to go on the trip?" Sid asked sarcastically.

"Except she doesn't cover the West Coast."

"My company has its conferences all over the country, Den. So does yours. Has nothing to do with territory . . . You thought she was going to meet somebody? A lover or something?"

"I guess. Yeah, that's what I was worried about."

"Get real."

"I called the hotel every night. Couple times she was out until eleven or so."

Sid had rolled his eyes. "What, she's got a curfew? It was a *business* trip, for Christ's sake. When you're away, how late do *you* stay out?"

"That's different."

"Oh, yeah, right. Different. So why do you think she's cheating on you?"

Dennis had said, "Just a feeling, I guess. I mean, I don't know why she would. Look at me. I'm only forty-five. I'm in great shape—check out this gut. Solid as a board. Not a single gray hair. I bring home a good paycheck. I take her out to dinner, movies. . . ."

"Look, all I know is, I cut Doris some slack. She's my wife and I trust her. Do the same with Mary."

"You don't understand," Dennis had responded sullenly. "I can't explain it."

"What I understand," Sid had laughed, "is that Mary volunteers for the Homeless Coalition, she's on the church board, she puts together parties like Martha Stewart and she still works a full-time job. She's a saint."

"Saints can sin too," Dennis had snapped.

Sid had whispered, "Look, you're so worried about it, check up on her. Keep track of where she's going, how long she's away. Go through her receipts. Look for the little things."

"The little things," Dennis repeated. He smiled. He liked that.

"I tell you, buddy, you're going to feel like an idiot. She's *not* cheating on you."

■

But the irony was that Sid's advice didn't clear Mary at all—not in her husband's mind. No, he *found* some little things: the trips home from work that took longer than they should have, the funny tone during phone calls, the wine on her breath. . . . All of which fueled his obsession to find out the truth.

And now, tonight, a snowy evening two weeks before Christmas, Dennis found a *big* thing.

It was five-thirty. Mary was still at work and would be late tonight because, she claimed, she had some Christmas shopping to do. Which was fine with him, honey, take all the time you want, because Dennis was ransacking their bedroom. He was searching for something that had been gnawing at him all day.

That morning just before he'd left for work, Dennis had slipped off his shoes and walked quietly past the bedroom where Mary was getting dressed. Dennis peered into the room and saw her take a small red object out of her briefcase and quickly hide it in the bottom drawer of her dresser. He'd waited a moment then stepped into the bedroom. "How's my tie?" he asked loudly. She'd jumped and spun around. "You scared me," she said. But she'd recovered fast. She'd smiled and didn't glance at either the open briefcase or the dresser.

"Looks fine to me," she'd said, adjusting the knot, and turned back to the closet to finish dressing.

Dennis had left for his office. He did a little work but spent most of the day brooding, thinking about the red object in the bottom of the dresser. It didn't help that his boss told him there was a client meeting in Boston next week, would Dennis be able to attend it? It reminded him of Mary's trip to San Francisco and left him thinking that maybe her trip had been optional too. She probably hadn't had to go at all. Dennis left the office early and returned home, ran upstairs and ripped open the dresser drawer.

Whatever she'd hidden was gone.

Had she taken it with her? Had she given it to a lover as a Christmas present?

But, no, she hadn't taken it; after a half hour of prowling through every conceivable hiding place in the room he found what he'd seen. It was a red Christmas card envelope, sealed. After he'd left she'd taken it out of the drawer and put it in the pocket of her black silk robe. There was no name or address on the front.

He cradled the envelope and it seemed to him that the card was a burning ingot. His fingers stung and he could barely lift it, the cardboard square felt so heavy. He went into the bathroom and locked the door, just in case Mary came home early. He turned the envelope over and over in his hands. A dozen times. Two dozen. He studied it carefully. She hadn't licked the flap completely; he could pry up most of it but one part was firmly fixed and he couldn't get it open without tearing the paper.

He dug under the wash basin and he found an old razor blade then spent a half hour carefully scraping away at the glue on the flap.

At six-thirty, with another quarter inch of flap to go, the phone rang and for once he was actually glad to hear Mary's voice telling him that she'd be late. She said she'd met a friend at the mall and they were going to stop for a drink on the way home. Did Dennis want to join them?

He told her he was too tired, hung up, and hurried back to the bathroom. Twenty minutes later, he scraped off the last bit of glue and with shaking hands he opened the flap.

He pulled the card out.

On the front was a picture of a Victorian couple, holding hands and looking out over a snowy backyard as candles glowed around them.

He took a deep breath and opened the card.

It was blank.

And Dennis Linden understood that all his fears were true. There was only one reason to give someone a blank card. She and her lover were too afraid of being caught to write anything—even a harmless note. Hell, now that he thought about it, a blank card was far worse than an inscribed one—the understood message was of such deep love and passion that words wouldn't convey what they felt.

The little things . . .

Something within his mind clicked and he knew without a doubt that Mary *was* seeing someone and probably had been for months.

Who?

Somebody at the company, he bet. How could he find out who'd gone with her to San Francisco in September? Maybe he could call the company and pretend to be somebody with an air-

line, asking about travel records. Or an accountant? Or he could call the men in her company phone directory. . . .

Rage consumed him.

Dennis tore the card into a dozen pieces, flung them across the room, then fell back on the bed and stared at the ceiling for a half hour. Trying to calm himself.

But couldn't. He kept replaying all the opportunities Mary'd had to cheat on him. Her church bake sales, her drives to and from work, her lunch hours, the nights she and Patty (well, she *claimed* it was Patty) would stay in the city after shopping and a play . . .

The phone rang. Was it her? he wondered. He grabbed the receiver. "Yeah?"

There was a pause. Sid Farnsworth said, "Den? You okay?"

"Not really, no." He explained what he'd found.

"Just a . . . You said it was blank?"

"Oh, you bet it was."

"And it wasn't addressed to anybody?"

"Nope. That's the point. That's what makes it so bad."

Silence. Then his friend said, "Tell you what, Den . . . I'm thinking maybe you shouldn't be alone right now. How 'bout you meet Doris and me for a drink?"

"I don't want a goddamn drink. I want the truth!"

"Okay, okay," Sid said fast. "But you're sounding a little freaked out, man. Let me come over, we'll watch the game or something. Or go up the road to Joey's."

How could she do this to him? After everything he'd done for her! He'd put food in her mouth, a roof over her, he'd given her a Lexus. He satisfied her in bed. He struggled to keep his temper in check. And the one time he hit her . . . hell, he apologized right after and bought her the car to make up for it. He did all of this for her and she didn't appreciate it one bit.

Lying whore . . .

Where the hell was she? Where?

"What'd you say, Den? I couldn't hear you. Listen, I'm on my way—"

He looked at the phone then dropped it into the cradle.

Sid lived only ten minutes away. Dennis had to leave now. He didn't want to see the man. He didn't want his friend to talk him out of what he had to do.

Dennis stood up. He went to his dresser and took something that *he'd* hidden not long ago. A Smith & Wesson .38 revolver.

He pulled on his down jacket—a birthday present from Mary last October, one that she'd probably bought on her way to a hotel to meet her lover—and dropped the gun into his pocket. Outside he climbed into his Bronco and sped down the driveway.

■

Dennis Linden was nobody's fool.

He knew the location of all the watering holes between Mary's office and the house—places she'd be inclined to stop at with a lover. But he also knew where she'd be likely to go on the way home from the mall. (He regularly made stops at many of them just to see if he could catch her.) He hadn't snared her yet but tonight he felt that luck was on his side.

And he was right.

Mary's black Lexus was parked outside of the Hudson Inn.

He skidded to a stop in the middle of the driveway and leapt out of the truck. A couple driving toward the exit had to swerve out of his way and they honked at him. He slammed his fist against their hood, shouting, "Go to hell!" They stared in terror. He pulled the gun from his pocket, walked up to the window and peered inside.

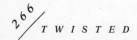

Yes, there was his wife: blonde, trim, a heart-shaped face. And she was sitting next to her lover.

The man must have been ten years younger than Mary. He wasn't handsome and he had a belly. How could she be seeing someone like him? How on earth? He didn't look rich either—he was wearing a cheap, unstylish suit. No, there was only one reason to see him. . . . He must be good in bed.

Dennis could taste the familiar metallic flavor of his rage.

And then he realized that Mary was wearing the navy blue dress that he'd bought for her last Christmas! He'd purposely picked a high-necked one so she couldn't go flaunting her breasts at every man she passed. And he realized that she'd picked it today as a private joke—an insult to him. Dennis pictured this fat slob slowly undoing the buttons, slipping his pudgy fingers under the cloth while Mary whispered words that this fat asshole would hear every time he looked at the blank Christmas card.

Dennis Linden wanted to scream.

He spun away from the window and strode to the front door of the inn. He pushed it open and stepped inside, shoving a waiter out of the way. The man fell to the floor.

The maître d' saw the gun and gasped, backing away. Other patrons too.

Mary glanced at him, still smiling from her conversation with fat boy, then her face went white. "Dennis, honey, what—?"

"Am I doing here?" he raged sarcastically.

"My God, a gun!" The boyfriend lifted his hands. He stumbled backward and his bar stool fell over.

"I'm here, *honey*," he shouted to Mary, "to do what I should've done a long time ago."

"Dennis, what're you talking about?"

"Who's he?" the chubby man asked, his eyes huge with fear.

"My husband," Mary whispered. "Dennis, please, put the gun down!"

"What's your name?" Dennis shouted at the man.

"I— It's Frank Chilton. I—"

Chilton? Dennis remembered him. He was married to Patty, Mary's good friend from the church committee. She was betraying her friend too.

Dennis lifted the gun.

"No, please!" Frank pleaded. "Don't hurt us!"

Mary stepped in front of her lover. "Dennis, Christ! Please put the gun away. Please!"

He muttered, "You cheat on somebody, there's going to be payback. Oh, you bet there is."

"Cheat? What do you mean?" The actress within Mary was looking innocent as a child.

A scream from nearby, a woman's voice. "Frank! Mary!"

Dennis glanced toward the bar and saw a young woman freeze as she stepped out of the rest room, a horrified look on her face. She ran to Frank and put her arm around him.

What was going on?

Dennis was confused. It was Patty.

Eyes wide, breathless, Mary gasped, "Dennis, did you think I was seeing Frank?"

He said nothing.

"I ran into Patty at the mall," she explained. "I told you that. We decided to have a drink and she called Frank. I invited you too. But you didn't want to come. How could you think—?" She was crying. "How could you—"

"Oh, nice try. I know what you've been up to. Maybe it's not him. But it *is* somebody." He aimed the gun at his wife. "Too many discrepancies, *honey.* Too many things don't quite add up, *honey.*"

"Oh, Dennis, I don't have a clue what you're talking about.

I'm not seeing anyone. I love you! I was just out buying you a Christmas present tonight." She held up a shopping bag.

"Did you get me a card too?"

"A—"

"Did you buy me a Christmas card?" he screamed.

"Yes!" More tears. "Of course I did."

"You buy cards for anyone else?"

She looked completely confused. "Just the ones we're sending together. To our friends. To my family . . ."

"What about the card you hid in the closet?"

She blinked. "You mean, in my bathrobe?"

"Yes! Who's that one for?"

"It's for *you!* It's your card."

"Then how come it was sealed up and blank?" he asked, smiling triumphantly.

The tears had stopped and now anger blossomed in her face. It was an expression he'd seen only twice before. When he'd told her he wouldn't let her go back to work and then when he'd asked her not to take that business trip to San Francisco.

"I didn't seal it up," she snapped. "It was snowing yesterday when I came out of the Hallmark store. The flap got wet and it stuck. I was going to work it open when I got a chance. I hid it so you wouldn't find it."

He lowered the gun. Debating. Then he smiled coldly. "Oh, you're good. But you're not fooling me." He aimed the pistol at her chest and started to pull the trigger.

"No, Dennis, please!" she cried, lifting her hands helplessly.

"Hold it right there!" a man's voice barked.

"Drop the weapon! Now!"

Dennis spun around and found himself facing two New York State troopers, who were pointing their own guns at him.

"No, you don't understand," he began, but as he spoke the Smith & Wesson strayed toward the cops.

Both officers hesitated for a fraction of a second then fired their guns.

■

Dennis spent three weeks recuperating in the detention center hospital, during which time several psychiatrists gave him a thorough evaluation. They recommended a sanity hearing prior to trial.

At the hearing, held on a cold, bright day in February, Dennis's long history of depression, uncontrolled temper and paranoid behavior came to light. Even the prosecutor gave up on the idea of finding him fit to stand trial and conceded that he was incompetent. There was, however, some disagreement about the type of hospital to place him in. The DA wanted him committed indefinitely in a high-security facility while Dennis's lawyer urged that he go to an unsecured hospital for six months or so of observation.

The gist of the defense argument was that no one had actually been endangered by Dennis because, it turned out, the firing pin of his gun had been removed and the weapon couldn't be fired. Dennis had known this, the lawyer explained, and had merely wanted to scare people.

But no sooner had he made that point then Dennis leapt up and shouted that, no, he *had* thought the gun was working properly.

"See, the firing pin is the key to the whole case!"

His lawyer sighed and, when he couldn't get Dennis to shut up, sat down in disgust.

"Can you swear me in as a witness?" Dennis asked the judge.

"This isn't a trial, Mr. Linden."

"But can I talk?"

"All right, go ahead."

"I've been thinking about it for a long time, Your Honor."

"Have you, now?" the bored judge asked.

"Yessir. And I've finally figured it out." Dennis went on to explain: Mary, he told the judge, had been having an affair with somebody, maybe not her boss, but *somebody*. And had arranged the business trip to San Francisco to meet him.

"I know this 'cause I looked for the little things. My friend told me to look for the little things and I did."

"The little things?" the judge inquired.

"Yes!" Dennis said emphatically. "And that's just what I started doing. See, she wanted me to find evidence."

He explained: Mary knew he'd try to kill her, which would get Dennis arrested or shot. "So she took the firing pin out of the gun. It was all a setup."

"You have any proof of this, Mr. Linden?" the judge asked.

Dennis sure did. He read from weather reports showing that it hadn't rained or snowed the day before the assault.

"And why's that relevant?" the judge asked, glancing at Dennis's lawyer, who lifted his eyebrows hopelessly.

His client laughed. "The wet flap, Your Honor."

"How's that?"

"She really *did* lick the flap of the envelope. It wasn't the snow at all, like she claimed."

"Envelope?"

"She sealed it to make me think she was going to give it to her lover. To push me over the edge. Then she hid it, knowing I was watching her."

"Uh-huh, I see." The judge began reading files for the next case.

Dennis then gave a long speech, rambling on about the significance of blank messages—about how what is unsaid can often be a lot worse than what's said. "A message like that, or a *nonmessage*, I should say, would definitely justify killing your wife and her lover. Don't you agree, Your Honor?"

It was at that point that the judge had Dennis escorted out of the courtroom and ruled from the bench that he be indefinitely committed to the Westchester County Maximum Security Facility for the Criminally Insane.

"You're not fooling anyone!" Dennis screamed to his tearful wife as she sat in the back of the courthouse. The two bailiffs muscled him through the door and his frantic shouts echoed through the courthouse for what seemed like an eternity.

■

It was eight months later that the orderly supervising the game room at the mental hospital happened to see in the local newspaper a short notice that Dennis's ex-wife was remarrying—an investment banker named Sid Farnsworth.

The article mentioned that the couple were going to honeymoon in San Francisco, which was "my favorite city," Mary was quoted as saying. "Sid and I had our first real date here."

The orderly thought about mentioning the story to Dennis but then decided it might upset him. Besides, the patient was, as usual, completely lost in one of his projects and wouldn't want to be disturbed. Dennis spent most of his time these days sitting at a crafts table, making greeting cards out of red construction paper. He'd give them to the orderly and ask him to mail them. The man never did, of course; patients weren't allowed to send mail from the facility. But the orderly couldn't have posted them anyway— the cards were always blank. Dennis never wrote any messages inside, and there was never a name or address on the front of the envelope.

THE CHRISTMAS PRESENT

"How long has she been missing?"

Stout Lon Sellitto—his diet shot because of the holiday season—shrugged. "That's sort of the problem."

"Go on."

"It's sort of—"

"You said that already," Lincoln Rhyme felt obliged to point out to the NYPD detective.

"About four hours. Close to it."

Rhyme didn't even bother to comment. An adult was not even considered missing until at least twenty-four hours had passed.

"But there're circumstances, " Sellitto added. "You have to know who we're talking about."

They were in an impromptu crime scene laboratory—the living room of Rhyme's Central Park West town house in Manhattan—but it had been impromptu for years and had more equipment and supplies than most small-town police departments.

A tasteful evergreen garland had been draped around the windows, and tinsel hung from the scanning electron microscope. Benjamin Britten's *Ceremony of Carols* played brightly on the stereo. It was Christmas Eve.

"It's just, she's a sweet kid. Carly is, I mean. And here her mother knows she's coming over but doesn't call her and tell her she's leaving or leave a note or anything. Which she always does.

273

Her mom—Susan Thompson's her name—is totally buttoned up. Very weird for her just to vanish."

"She's getting the girl a Christmas present," Rhyme said. "Didn't want to give away the surprise."

"But her car's still in the garage." Sellitto nodded out the window at the fat confetti of snow that had been falling for several hours. "She's not going to be walking anywhere in this weather, Linc. And she's not at any of the neighbors'. Carly checked."

Had Rhyme had the use of his body—other than his left ring finger, shoulders and head—he would have given Detective Sellitto an impatient gesture, perhaps a circling of the hand, or two palms skyward. As it was, he relied solely on words. "And how did this not-so-missing-person case all come about, Lon? I detect you've been playing Samaritan. You know what they say about good deeds, don't you? They never go unpunished. . . . Not to mention, it seems to *sort of* be falling on my shoulders, now, doesn't it?"

Sellitto helped himself to another homemade Christmas cookie. It was in the shape of Santa, but the icing face was grotesque. "These're pretty good. You want one?"

"No," Rhyme grumbled. Then his eye strayed to a shelf. "But I'd be more inclined to listen agreeably to your sales pitch with a bit of Christmas cheer."

"Of . . . ? Oh. Sure." He walked across the lab, found the bottle of Macallan and poured a heathy dose into a tumbler. The detective inserted a straw and mounted the cup in the holder on Rhyme's chair.

Rhyme sipped the liquor. Ah, heaven . . . His aide, Thom, and the criminalist's partner, Amelia Sachs, were out shopping; if they'd been here Rhyme's beverage might have been tasty but, given the hour, would undoubtedly have been nonalcoholic.

"All right. Here's the story. Rachel's a friend of Susan and her daughter."

So it was a friend-of-the-family good deed. Rachel was Sellitto's girlfriend. Rhyme said, "The daughter being Carly. See, I *was* listening, Lon. Go on."

"Carly—"

"Who's how old?"

"Nineteen. Student at NYU. Business major. She's going with this guy from Garden City—"

"Is any of this relevant, other than her age? Which I'm not even sure *is* relevant."

"Tell me, Linc: You always in this good a mood during the holidays?"

Another sip of the liquor. "Keep going."

"Susan's divorced, works for a PR firm downtown. Lives in the burbs, Nassau County—"

"Nassau? Nassau? Hmm, would they *sort of* be the right constabulary to handle the matter? You understand how that works, right? That course on jurisdiction at the Academy?"

Sellitto had worked with Lincoln Rhyme for years and was quite talented at deflecting the criminalist's feistiness. He ignored the comment and continued. "She takes a couple days off to get the house ready for the holidays. Rachel tells me she and her daughter have a teenage thing—you know, going through a rough time, the two of them. But Susan's *trying*. She wants to make everything nice for the girl, throw a big party on Christmas Day. Anyway, Carly's living in an apartment in the Village near her school. Last night she tells her mom she'll come by this morning, drop off some things and then's going to her boyfriend's. Susan says good, they'll have coffee, yadda yadda . . . Only when Carly gets there, Susan's gone. And her—"

"Car's still in the garage."

"Exactly. So Carly waits for a while. Susan doesn't come back. She calls the local boys but they're not going to do anything for twenty-four hours, at least. So, Carly thinks of me—I'm the only cop she knows—and calls Rachel."

"We can't do good deeds for everybody. Just because 'tis the season."

"Let's give the kid a Christmas present, Linc. Ask a few questions, look around the house."

Rhyme's expression was scowly but in fact he was intrigued. How he hated boredom. . . . And, yes, he was often in a bad mood during the holidays—because there was invariably a lull in the stimulating cases that the NYPD or the FBI would hire him to consult on as a forensic scientist, or "criminalist" as the jargon termed it.

"So . . . Carly's upset. You understand."

Rhyme shrugged, one of the few gestures allowed to him after the accident at a crime scene some years ago had left him a quadriplegic. Rhyme moved his one working finger on the touch pad and maneuvered the chair to face Sellitto. "Her mother's probably home by now. But, if you really want, let's call the girl. I'll get a few facts, see what I think. What can it hurt?"

"That's great, Linc. Hold on." The large detective walked to the door and opened it.

What was this?

In walked a teenage girl, looking around shyly.

"Oh, Mr. Rhyme, hi. I'm Carly Thompson. Thanks so much for seeing me."

"Ah, you've been waiting outside," Rhyme said and offered the detective an acerbic glance. "If my friend Lon here had shared that fact with me, I'd've invited you in for a cup of tea."

"Oh, that's okay. Nothing for me."

Sellitto lifted a cheerful eyebrow and found a chair for the girl.

She had long, blonde hair and an athletic figure and her round face bore little makeup. She was dressed in MTV chic—flared jeans and a black jacket, chunky boots. To Rhyme the most remarkable thing about her, though, was her expression: Carly gave no reaction whatsoever to his disability. Some people grew tongue-tied, some chatted mindlessly, some locked their eyes on to his and grew frantic—as if a glance at his body would be the faux pas of the century. Each of those reactions pissed him off in its own way.

She smiled. "I like the decoration."

"I'm sorry?" Rhyme asked.

"The garland on the back of your chair."

The criminalist swiveled but couldn't see anything.

"There's a garland there?" he asked Sellitto.

"Yeah, you didn't know? And a red ribbon."

"That must have been courtesy of my aide," Rhyme grumbled. "Soon to be ex, he tries that again."

Carly said, "I wouldn't've bothered Mr. Sellitto or you. . . . I wouldn't have bothered *anyone* but it's just so weird, Mom disappearing like this. She's never done that before."

Rhyme said, "Ninety-nine percent of the time there's just been a mix-up of some kind. No crime at all . . . And only four hours?" Another glance at Sellitto. "That's nothing."

"Except, with Mom, whatever else, she's dependable."

"When did you talk to her last?"

"It was about eight last night, I guess. She's having this party tomorrow and we were making plans for it. I was going to come over this morning and she was going to give me a shopping list and some money and Jake—that's my boyfriend—and I were going to go shopping and hang out."

"Maybe she couldn't get through on your cell," Rhyme suggested. "Where was your friend? Could she have left a message at his place?"

"Jake's? No, I just talked to him on my way here." Carly gave a rueful smile. "She likes Jake okay, you know." She played nervously with her long hair, twining it around her fingers. "But they're not the best of friends. He's . . ." The girl decided not to go into the details of the disapproval. "Anyway, she wouldn't call his house. His dad's . . . difficult."

"And she took today off from work?"

"That's right."

The door opened and Rhyme heard Amelia Sachs and Thom enter, the crinkle of paper from the shopping bags.

The tall woman, dressed in jeans and a bomber jacket, stepped into the doorway. Her red hair and shoulders were dusted with snow. She smiled at Rhyme and Sellitto. "Merry Christmas and all that."

Thom headed down the hall with the bags.

"Ah, Sachs, come on in here. It seems Detective Sellitto has volunteered our services. Amelia Sachs, Carly Thompson."

The women shook hands.

Sellitto asked, "You want a cookie?"

Carly demurred. Sachs too shook her head. "I decorated 'em, Lon—yeah, Santa looks like Boris Karloff, I know. If I never see another cookie again it'll be too soon."

Thom appeared in the door, introduced himself to Carly and then walked toward the kitchen, from which Rhyme knew refreshments were about to appear. Unlike Rhyme, his aide loved the holidays, largely because they gave him the chance to play host nearly every day.

As Sachs pulled off her jacket and hung it up, Rhyme explained the situation and what the girl had told them so far.

The policewoman nodded, taking it in. She reiterated that a person's missing for such a short time was no cause for alarm. But they'd be happy to help a friend of Lon's and Rachel's.

"Indeed we will," Rhyme said with an irony that everyone except Sachs missed.

No good deed goes unpunished. . . .

Carly continued. "I got there about eight-thirty this morning. She wasn't home. The car was in the garage. I checked all the neighbors'. She wasn't there and nobody's seen her."

"Could she have left the night before?" Sellitto asked.

"No. She'd made coffee this morning. The pot was still warm."

Rhyme said, "Maybe something came up at work and she didn't want to drive to the station, so she took a cab."

Carly shrugged. "Could be. I didn't think about that. She's in public relations and's been working real hard lately. For one of those big Internet companies that went bankrupt. It's been totally tense. . . . But I don't know. We didn't talk very much about her job."

Sellitto had a young detective downtown call all the cab companies in and around Glen Hollow; no taxis had been dispatched to the house that morning. They also called Susan's company to see if she'd come in, but no one had seen her and her office was locked.

Just then, as Rhyme had predicted, his slim aide, wearing a white shirt and a Jerry Garcia Christmas tie, carted in a large tray of coffee and tea and a huge plate of pastries and cookies. He poured drinks for everyone.

"No figgy pudding?" Rhyme asked acerbically.

Sachs asked Carly, "Has your mom been sad or moody?"

Thinking for a minute, she said, "Well, my grandfather—her dad—died last February. Grandpa was a great guy and she was totally bummed for a while. But by the summer, she'd come out of it. She bought this really cool house and had a lot of fun fixing it up."

"How about other people in her life, friends, boyfriends?"

"She's got some good friends, sure."

"Names, phone numbers?"

Again the girl fell quiet. "I know some of their names. Not exactly where they live. I don't have any numbers."

"Anybody she was seeing romantically?"

"She broke up with somebody about a month ago."

Sellitto asked, "Was this guy a problem, you think? A stalker? Upset about the breakup?"

The girl replied, "No, I think it was his idea. Anyway, he lived in L.A. or Seattle or some place out west. So it wasn't, you know, real serious. She just started seeing this new guy. About two weeks ago." Carly looked from Sachs to the floor. "The thing is, I love Mom and everything. But we're not real close. My folks were divorced seven, eight years ago, and that kind of changed a lot of things. . . . Sorry I don't know more about her."

Ah, the wonderful family unit, thought Rhyme cynically. It was what made Park Avenue shrinks millionaires and kept police departments around the world busy answering calls at all hours of the day and night.

"You're doing fine," Sachs encouraged. "Where's your father?"

"He lives in the city. Downtown."

"Do he and your mother see each other much?"

"Not anymore. He wanted to get back together but Mom was lukewarm and I think he gave up."

"Do *you* see him much?"

"I do, yeah. But he travels a lot. His company imports stuff, and he goes overseas to meet his suppliers."

"Is he in town now?"

"Yep. I'm going to see him on Christmas, after Mom's party."

"We should call him. See if he's heard from her," Sachs said.

Rhyme nodded and Carly gave them the man's number. Rhyme said, "I'll get in touch with him. . . . Okay, get going, Sachs. Over to Susan's house. Carly, you go with her. Move fast."

"Sure, Rhyme. But what's the hurry?"

He glanced out the window, as if the answer were hovering there in plain view.

Sachs shook her head, perplexed. Rhyme was often piqued that people didn't tumble to things as quickly as he did. "Because the snow might tell us something about what happened there this morning." And, as he often liked to do, he added a dramatic coda: "But if it keeps coming down like this, there won't be any story left to read."

■

A half hour later Amelia Sachs pulled up on a quiet, tree-lined street in Glen Hollow, Long Island, parking the bright red Camaro three doors from Susan Thompson's house.

"No, it's up there," Carly pointed out.

"Here's better," Sachs said. Rhyme had drummed into her that access routes to and from the site of the crime could be crime scenes in their own right and could yield valuable information. She was ever-mindful about contaminating scenes.

Carly grimaced when she noticed that the car was still in the garage.

"I'd hoped . . ."

Sachs looked at the girl's face and saw raw concern. The policewoman understood: Mother and daughter had a tough relationship, that was obvious. But you never cut parental ties altogether—can't be done—and there's nothing like a missing mother to set off primal alarms.

"We'll find her," Sachs whispered.

Carly gave a faint smile and pulled her jacket tighter around her. It was stylish and obviously expensive but useless against the cold. Sachs had been a fashion model for a time but when not on the runway or at a shoot she'd dressed like a real person, to hell with what was in vogue.

Sachs looked over the house, a new, rambling two-story Colonial on a small but well-groomed lot, and called Rhyme. On a real case she'd be patched through to him on her Motorola. Since this wasn't official business, though, she simply used her hands-free cord and cell phone, which was clipped to her belt a few inches away from her Glock automatic pistol.

"I'm at the house," she told him. "What's that music?"

After a moment "Hark, the Herald Angels Sing" went silent.

"Sorry. Thom insists on being in the *spirit*. What do you see, Sachs?"

She explained where she was and the layout of the place. "The snow's not too bad here but you're right: in another hour it'll cover up any prints."

"Stay off the walks and check out if there's been any surveillance."

"Got it."

Sachs asked Carly what prints were hers. The girl explained that she had parked in front of the garage—Sachs could see the tread marks in the snow—and then had gone through the kitchen door.

Carly behind her, Sachs made a circuit of the property.

"Nothing in the back or side yard, except for Carly's footprints," she told Rhyme.

"There are no visible prints, you mean," he corrected. "That's not necessarily 'nothing.'"

"Okay, Rhyme. That's what I meant. Damn, it's cold."

They circled to the front of the house. Sachs found footsteps in the snow on the path between the street and the house. A car had stopped at the curb. There was one set of prints walking toward the house and two walking back, suggesting the driver had picked Susan up. She told Rhyme this. He asked, "Can you tell anything from the shoes? Size, sole prints, weight distribution?"

"Nothing's clear." She winced as she bent down; her arthritic joints ached in the cold and damp. "But one thing's odd—they're real close together."

"As if one of them had an arm around the other person."

"Right."

"Could be affection. Could be coercion. We'll assume—hope—the second set is Susan's, and that, whatever happened, at least she's alive. Or was a few hours ago."

Then Sachs noticed a curious indentation in the snow, next to one of the front windows. It was as if somebody had stepped off the sidewalk and knelt on the ground. In this spot you could see clearly into the living room and kitchen beyond. She sent Carly to open the front door and then whispered into the microphone, "May have a problem, Rhyme . . . It looks like somebody was kneeling down, looking through the window."

"Any other evidence there, Sachs? Discernible prints, cigarette butts, other impressions, trace?"

"Nothing."

"Check the house, Sachs. And, just for the fun of it, pretend it's hot."

"But how could a perp be inside?"

"Humor me."

The policewoman stepped to the front door, unzipping her leather jacket to give her fast access to her weapon. She found the girl in the entryway, looking around the house. It was still, except for the tapping and whirs of household machinery. The lights were on—though Sachs found this more troubling than if it'd been dark; it suggested that Susan had left in a hurry. You don't shut out the lights when you're being abducted.

Sachs told the girl to stay close and she started through the place, praying she wouldn't find a body. But, no; they looked everywhere the woman might be. Nothing. And no signs of a struggle.

"The scene's clear, Rhyme."

"Well, that's something."

"I'm going to do a fast grid here, see if we can find any clue where she went. I'll call you back if I find anything."

On the main floor Sachs paused at the mantel and looked over a number of framed photographs. Susan Thompson was a tall, solidly built woman with short blonde hair, feathered back. She had an agreeable smile. Most of the pictures were of her with Carly or with an older couple, probably her parents. Many had been taken out-of-doors, apparently on hiking or camping trips.

They looked for any clue that might indicate where the woman was. Sachs studied the calendar next to the phone in the kitchen. The only note in today's square said *C here.*

The girl gave a sad laugh. Were the single letter and terse notation an emblem of how Carly believed the woman saw her? Sachs wondered what exactly the problems were between daughter and mother. She herself had always had a complex relationship with her own mother. "Challenging" was how she'd described it to Rhyme.

"Day-Timer? Palm Pilot?"

Carly looked around. "Her purse is gone. She keeps them in there. . . . I'll try her cell again." The girl did and the frustrated, troubled look told Sachs that there was no answer. "Goes right to voice mail."

Sachs tried all three phones in the house, hitting "redial." Two got her directory assistance. The other was the number for a local branch of North Shore Bank. Sachs asked to speak to the manager and told her they were trying to locate Susan Thompson. The woman said she'd been in about two hours ago.

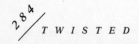

Sachs told this to Carly, who closed her eyes in relief. "Where did she go after that?"

The policewoman asked the manager the question and the woman responded that she had no idea. Then she asked hesitantly, "Are you calling because she wasn't feeling well?"

"What do you mean?" Sachs asked.

"It's just that she didn't look very good when she was in. That man she was with . . . well, he had his arm around her the whole time. I was thinking maybe she was sick."

Sachs asked if they could come in and speak with her.

"Of course. If I can help."

Sachs told Carly what the woman had said.

"Not feeling well? And some man?" The girl frowned. "Who?"

"Let's go find out."

As they approached the door, though, Sachs stopped. "Do me a favor," she said to the girl.

"Sure. What?"

"Borrow one of your mother's jackets. You're making me cold just looking at you."

■

The branch manager of the bank explained to Sachs and Carly, "She went into her safety deposit box downstairs and then cashed a check."

"You don't know what she did down there, I assume?" the policewoman asked.

"No, no, employees are never around when customers go into their boxes."

"And that man? Any idea who he was?"

"No."

"What did he look like?" Sachs asked.

"He was big. Six-two, six-three. Balding. Didn't smile much."

The police detective glanced at Carly, who shook her head. "I've never seen her with anybody like that."

They found the teller who'd cashed the check but Susan hadn't said anything to her either, except how she'd like the money.

"How much was the check for?" Sachs asked.

The manager hesitated—probably some confidentiality issue—but Carly said, "Please. We're worried about her." The woman nodded to the teller, who said, "A thousand."

Sachs stepped aside and called Rhyme on her cell. She explained what had happened at the bank.

"Getting troubling now, Sachs. A thousand doesn't seem like much for a robbery or kidnapping, but wealth's relative. Maybe that's a lot of money to this guy."

"I'm more curious about the safe deposit box."

Rhyme said, "Good point. Maybe she had something he wanted. But what? She's just a businesswoman and mother. It's not like she's an investigative reporter or cop. And the bad news is, if that's the case, he's got what he was after. He might not need her anymore. I think it's time to get Nassau County involved. Maybe . . . Wait, you're at the bank?"

"Right."

"The video! Get the video."

"Oh, at the teller cage, sure. But—"

"No, no, no," Rhyme snapped. "Of the *parking* lot. All banks have video surveillance of the lots. If they parked there it'll have his car on tape. Maybe the tag number too."

Sachs returned to the manager and she called the security chief, who disappeared into a back office. A moment later he gestured them inside and ran the tape.

"There!" Carly cried. "That's her. And that guy? Look, he's still holding on to her. He's not letting her go."

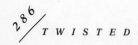

"Looks pretty fishy, Rhyme."

"Can you see the car?" the criminalist asked.

Sachs had the guard freeze the tape. "What kind of—"

"Chevy Malibu," the guard said. "This year's model."

Sachs told this to Rhyme and, examining the screen, added, "It's burgundy. And the last two numbers on the tag are seventy-eight. The one before it could be three or eight, maybe six. Hard to tell. It's a New York plate."

"Good, Sachs. Okay. It's up to the uniforms now. Lon'll have them put out a locator. Nassau, Suffolk, Westchester and the five boroughs. Jersey too. We'll prioritize it. Oh, hold on a minute. . . ." Sachs heard him speaking to someone. Rhyme came back on the line. "Susan's ex is on his way over here. He's worried about his daughter. He'd like to see her."

Sachs told Carly this. Her face brightened. The detective added, "There's nothing more we can do here. Let's go back to the city."

■

Amelia Sachs and Carly Thompson had just returned to the lab in Rhyme's town house when Anthony Dalton arrived. Thom led him inside and he stopped abruptly, looking at his daughter. "Hello, honey."

"Dad! I'm so glad you came!"

With both affection and concern in his eyes, he stepped toward the girl and hugged her hard.

Dalton was a fit man in his late forties with a boyish flop of salt-and-pepper hair. He wore a complicated ski jacket, straps and flaps going every which way. He reminded Rhyme of the college professors he sometimes shared the podium with when he was lecturing on forensics at criminal justice colleges.

"Do they know anything?" he asked, apparently only now realizing that Rhyme was in a wheelchair—and finding the fact un-remarkable. Like his daughter, Anthony Dalton earned serious points with Rhyme for this.

The criminalist explained exactly what had happened and what they knew.

Dalton shook his head. "But it doesn't necessarily mean she's been kidnapped," he said quickly.

"No, no, not at all," Sellitto said. "We're just not taking any chances."

Rhyme asked, "Do you know anyone who'd want to hurt her?"

He shook his head. "I have no idea. I haven't seen Susan in a year. But when we were together? No, everybody liked her. Even when some of her PR clients had done some pretty shady things, nobody had a problem with her personally. And she always seemed to have the particularly nasty clients."

Rhyme was troubled—for reasons beyond the danger to Susan Thompson. The problem was that this wasn't a real case. They'd backed into it, doing a favor for someone; it was a Christmas present, as Sellitto had said. He needed more facts; he needed serious forensics. He'd always felt you run a case 110 percent or you don't run it at all.

Thom brought more coffee in and replenished the plate of ugly cookies. Dalton nodded at the aide and thanked him. Then the businessman poured coffee from the pot for himself. "You want some?" he asked Carly.

"Sure, I guess."

He poured it and asked, "Anyone else?"

No one else wanted anything. But Rhyme's eyes flipped to the Macallan on the shelf and, lo and behold, without a syllable of protest, Thom took the bottle and walked to Rhyme's Storm Arrow. He opened the tumbler, then frowned. He sniffed it. "Odd, I thought I washed this out last night. I guess I forgot," he added wryly.

"We can't all be perfect, now," Rhyme said.

Thom poured a few fingers into the tumbler and replaced it in the holder.

"Thank you, Balthazar. You can keep your job for now—despite the weeds on the back of my chair."

"You don't like them? I told you I was going to decorate for the holidays."

"The house. Not me."

"What do we do now?" Dalton asked.

"We wait," Sellitto said. "DMV's running all the Malibus with that fragment of a tag number. Or, if we're real lucky, some officer on the street'll notice it." He pulled his coat off a chair. "I gotta go down to the Big Building for a while. Call me if anything happens."

Dalton thanked him, then he looked at his watch, took out his mobile phone and called his office to say he'd have to miss his office Christmas party. He explained that the police were looking into his ex-wife's disappearance and he was with his daughter at the moment. He wasn't going to leave the girl alone.

Carly hugged him. "Thanks, Dad." Her eyes lifted to the window, staring at the swirling snow. A long moment passed. Carly glanced at the others in the room and turned toward her father. In a soft voice she said, "I always wondered what would have happened if you and Mom hadn't broken up."

Dalton laughed, ran his hand through his hair, mussing it further. "I've thought about that too."

Sachs glanced at Rhyme and they turned away, letting the father and daughter continue talking in relative privacy.

"The guys Mom's dated? They were okay. But nobody special. None of them lasted very long."

"It's tough to meet the right person," Dalton said.

"I guess . . ."

"What?"

"I guess I've always wished you'd get back together."

Dalton seemed at a loss for words. "I tried. You know that. But your mom was in a different place."

"But you stopped trying a couple of years ago."

"I could read the writing on the wall. People have to move on."

"But she misses you. I know she does."

Dalton laughed, "Oh, I don't know about that."

"No, no, really. When I ask her about you, she tells me what a cool guy you were. You were funny. She said you made her laugh."

"We had some good times."

Carly said, "When I asked Mom what happened between you, she said it wasn't anything totally terrible."

"True," Dalton said, sipping his coffee. "We just didn't know how to be husband and wife back then. We got married too young."

"Well, you're not young anymore. . . ." Carly blushed. "Oh, I didn't mean it like that."

But Dalton said, "No, you're right. I've grown up a lot since then."

"And Mom's really changed. She used to be so quiet, you know. Just no fun. But she's into all kinds of things now. Camping and hiking, rafting, all that out-of-doors stuff."

"Really?" Dalton asked. "I never pictured her going in for that kind of thing."

Carly looked off for a moment. "Remember those business trips you'd take when I was a kid? You'd go to Hong Kong or Japan?"

"Setting up our overseas offices, sure."

"I wanted all of us to go. You, Mom and me . . ." She played with her coffee cup. "But she was always like, 'Oh, there's too much to do at home.' Or, 'Oh, we'll get sick if we drink the water,' or whatever. We never did take a family vacation. Not a real one."

"I always wanted that too." Dalton shook his head sadly.

"And I'd get mad when she didn't want to come along and bring you. But she's your mother; it's her job to look out for you. All she wanted was for you to be safe." He smiled. "I remember once when I was in Tokyo and calling home. And—"

His words were interrupted when Rhyme's phone rang. He spoke into the microphone on his chair, "Command, answer phone."

"Detective Rhyme?" the voice clattered through the speaker.

The rank was out of date—a "Ret." belonged with it—but he said, "Go ahead."

"This's Trooper Bronson, New York State Police."

"Go ahead."

"We had an emergency vehicle locator request regarding a burgundy Malibu and understand you're involved in the case."

"That's right."

"We've found the vehicle, sir."

Rhyme heard Carly gasp. Dalton stepped beside the girl and put his arm around her shoulder. What would they hear? That Sue Thompson was dead?

"Go ahead."

"The car's moving west, looks like it's headed for the George Washington Bridge."

"Occupants?"

"Two. Man and a woman. Can't tell anything more."

"Thank God. She's alive." Dalton sighed.

Heading toward Jersey, Rhyme reflected. The flats were among the most popular places for dumping bodies in the metro area.

"Registered to a Richard Musgrave, Queens. No warrants."

Rhyme glanced at Carly, who shook her head, meaning she had no clue who he was.

Sachs leaned forward toward the speaker and identified herself. "Are you near the car?"

"About two hundred feet behind."

"You in a marked vehicle?"

"That's right."

"How far from the bridge?"

"A mile or two east."

Rhyme glanced at Sachs. "You want to join the party? You can stay right on their tail in the Camaro."

"You bet." She ran for the door.

"Sachs," Rhyme called.

She glanced back.

"You have chains on your Chevy?"

Sachs laughed. "Chains on a muscle car, Rhyme? No."

"Well, try not to skid into the Hudson, okay? It's probably pretty cold."

"I'll do my best."

■

True, a rear-wheel-drive sports car, with more than four hundred eager horses under the hood, was not the best vehicle to drive on snow. But Amelia Sachs had spent much of her youth skidding cars on hot asphalt in illegal races around Brooklyn (and sometimes just because, why not, it's always a blast to do one-eighties); this little bit of snow meant nothing to her.

She now slipped her Camaro SS onto the expressway and pushed the accelerator down. The wheels spun for only five seconds before they gripped and sped her up to eighty.

"I'm on the bridge, Rhyme," she called into her headset. "Where are they?"

"About a mile west. Are you—"

The car started to swerve. "Hold on, Rhyme, I'm going sideways."

She brought the skid under control. "A VW doing fifty in the fast lane. Man, doesn't that just frost you?"

In another mile she'd caught up to the trooper, keeping back, just out of sight of the Malibu. She looked past him and saw the car ease into the right lane and signal for an exit.

"Rhyme, can you get me a patch through to the trooper?" she asked.

"Hold on . . ." A long pause. Rhyme's frustrated voice. "I can never figure out—" He was cut off and she heard two clicks. Then the trooper said, "Detective Sachs?"

"I'm here. Go ahead."

"Is that you behind me, in that fine red set of wheels?"

"Yep."

"How do you want to handle this?"

"Who's driving? The man or the woman?"

"The man."

She thought for a moment. "Make it seem like a routine traffic stop. Taillight him or something. After he's on the shoulder I'll get in front and sandwich him in. You take the passenger side and I'll get the driver out. We don't know that he's armed and we don't know that he's not. But the odds are it's an abduction, so assume he's got a weapon."

"Roger that, Detective."

"Okay, let's do it."

The Malibu exited. Sachs tried to look through the rear window. She couldn't see anything through the snow. The burgundy car rolled down the ramp and braked slowly to a stop at a red light. When it turned green the car eased forward through the slush and snow.

The trooper's voice crackled into her ear. "Detective Sachs, are you ready?"

"Yep. Let's nail him."

The light bar on his Police Interceptor Crown Victoria started flashing and he hit the squeal once. The driver of the Malibu looked up into the rearview mirror and the car swerved momentarily. Then it pulled to a stop on the side of road, bleak town houses on the left and reedy marshes on the right.

Sachs punched the accelerator and skidded to a stop in front of the Malibu, blocking it. She was out the door in an instant, pulling her Glock from her holster and jogging fast toward the car.

■

Forty minutes later a grim Amelia Sachs walked into Rhyme's town house.

"How bad was it?" Rhyme asked.

"Pretty bad." She poured herself a double scotch and drank down half the liquor fast. Unusual for her; Amelia Sachs was a sipper.

"Pretty bad," she repeated.

Sachs was not, however, referring to any bloody shootout in Jersey, but to the embarrassment of what they'd done.

"Tell me."

Sachs had radioed in from the roadside to tell Rhyme, Carly and Anthony Dalton that Susan was fine. Sachs hadn't been able to go into the details then, though. Now she explained, "The guy in the car was that man she's been seeing for the past couple of weeks." A glance at Carly. "Rich Musgrave, the one you mentioned. It's his car. He called this morning and they'd made plans to go shopping at the Jersey outlet malls. Only what happened was, when she went out to get the newspaper this morning she slipped on the ice."

Dalton nodded. "The front path—it's like a ski slope."

Carly winced. "Mom always said that she was a born klutz."

Sachs continued, "She hurt her knee and didn't want to drive. So she called Rich back and asked him to pick her up. Oh, the spot in the snow where I thought somebody was looking in the window? It was where she fell."

"That's why he was so close to her," Rhyme mused. "He was helping her walk."

Sachs nodded. "And at the bank, there was no mystery—she really did need something out of the safe deposit box. And the thousand bucks was for Christmas shopping."

Carly frowned. "But she knew I was coming by. Why didn't she call me?"

"Oh, she wrote you a note."

"Note?"

"It said she'd be out for the day but she'd be back home by six."

"No! . . . But I never saw it."

"Because," Sachs explained, "after she fell she was pretty shaken up and forgot to leave it on the entryway table like she'd planned. She found it in her purse when I told her it wasn't there. And she didn't have her cell phone turned on."

Dalton laughed. "All a misunderstanding." He put his arm around his daughter's shoulders.

Carly, blushing again, said, "I'm really, really sorry I panicked. I should've known there was an explanation."

"That's what we're here for," Sachs said.

Which wasn't exactly true, Rhyme reflected sourly. No good deed . . .

As she pulled on her coat, Carly invited Rhyme, Sachs and Thom to the Christmas party tomorrow afternoon at her mother's. "It's the least we can do."

"I'm sure Thom and Amelia would be *delighted* to go," Rhyme said quickly. "Unfortunately, I think I have plans." Cocktail parties bored him.

"No," Thom said. "You don't have any plans."

Sachs added, "Nope, no plans."

A scowl from Rhyme. "I think I know my calendar better than anyone else."

Which wasn't exactly true either.

After the father and daughter had gone, Rhyme said to Thom, "Since you blew the whistle on my unencumbered social schedule tomorrow, you can do penance."

"What?" the aide asked cautiously.

"Take the goddamn decorations off my chair. I feel like Santa Claus."

"Humbug," Thom said and did as asked. He turned the radio on. A carol streamed into the room.

Rhyme nodded toward the speaker. "Aren't we lucky there are only *twelve* days of Christmas? Can you imagine how interminable that song would be if there were twenty?" He sang, "Twenty muggers mugging, nineteen burglars burgling . . ."

Thom sighed and said to Sachs, "All I want for Christmas is a nice, complicated jewelry heist right about now—something to pacify him."

"Eighteen aides complaining," Rhyme continued the song. He added, "See, Thom, I *am* in the holiday spirit. Despite what you think."

■

Susan Thompson climbed out of Rich Musgrave's Malibu. The large, handsome man was holding the door for her. She took his hand and he eased her to her feet; her shoulder and knee still ached fiercely from the spill she'd taken on the ice that morning.

"What a day," she said, sighing.

"I don't mind getting pulled over by the cops," Rich said, laughing. "I could've done without the guns, though."

Carrying all her shopping bags in one hand, he helped her to the front door. They walked carefully over the three-inch blanket of fine snow.

"You want to come in? Carly's here—that's her car. You can watch me prostrate myself in front of her and apologize for being such a bozo. I could've sworn I left that note on the table."

"I think I'll let you run the gauntlet on your own." Rich was divorced too and was spending Christmas eve with his two sons at his place in Armonk. He needed to pick them up soon. She thanked him again for everything and apologized once more for the scare with the police. He'd been a nice guy about the whole thing. But, as she fished her keys out of her purse and watched him walk back to the car, she reflected that there was no doubt the relationship wasn't going anywhere. What was the problem? Susan wondered. Rough edges, she supposed. She wanted a gentleman. She wanted somebody who was kind, who had a sense of humor. Somebody who could make her laugh.

She waved good-bye and stepped into the house, pulled the door shut behind her.

Carly had already started on the decorations, bless her, and Susan smelled something cooking in the kitchen. Had the girl made dinner? This was a first. She looked into the den and blinked in surprise. Carly'd decked out the room beautifully, garlands, ribbons, candles. And on the coffee table was a big plate of cheese and crackers, a bowl of nuts, fruit, two glasses sitting beside a bottle of California sparkling wine. The girl was nineteen, but Susan let her have some wine when they were home alone.

"Honey, how wonderful!"

"Mom," Carly called, walking to the doorway. "I didn't hear you come in."

The girl was carrying a baking dish. Inside were some hot canapés. She set it on the table and hugged her mother.

Susan threw her arms around the girl, ignoring the pain from the fall that morning. She apologized for the mistake about the note and for making her daughter worry so much. The girl, though, just laughed it off.

"Is it true that policeman's in a wheelchair?" Susan asked. "He can't move?"

"He's not a policeman anymore. He's kind of a consultant. But, yeah, he's paralyzed."

Carly went on to explain about Lincoln Rhyme and how they'd found her and Rich Musgrave. Then she wiped her hands on her apron and took it off. "Mom, I want to give you one of your presents tonight."

"Tonight? Are we starting a new tradition?"

"Maybe we are."

"Well, okay . . ." Then Susan took the girl's arm. "In that case, let me give you mine first." She got her purse from the table and dug inside. She found the small velvet box. "This is what I got out of the safe deposit box this morning."

She handed it to the girl, who opened it. Her eyes went wide. "Oh, Mom . . ."

It was an antique diamond and emerald ring.

"This was—"

"Grandma's. Her engagement ring." Susan nodded. "I wanted you to have something special. I know you've had a rough time lately, honey. I've been too busy at work. I haven't been as nice to Jake as I should. And some of the men I've dated . . . well, I know you didn't like them that much." A laughing whisper. "Of course, *I* didn't like them that much either. I'm resolving not to date losers anymore."

Carly frowned. "Mom, you've never dated losers. . . . More like semi-losers."

"That's even worse! I couldn't even find a red-blooded, full-fledged loser to date!"

Carly hugged her mother again and put the ring on. "It's so beautiful."

"Merry Christmas, honey."

"Now, time for your present."

"I think I like our new tradition."

Her daughter instructed, "Sit down. Close your eyes. I'm going outside to get it."

"All right."

"Sit on the couch right there."

She sat and closed her eyes tight.

"Don't peek."

"I won't." Susan heard the front door open and close. A moment later she frowned, hearing the sound of a car engine starting. Was it Carly's? Was she leaving?

But then she heard footsteps behind her. The girl must have come back in through the kitchen door.

"Well, can I look now?"

"Sure," said a man's voice.

Susan jumped in surprise. She turned and found herself staring at her ex-husband. He carried a large box with a ribbon on it.

"Anthony . . ." she began.

Dalton sat on the chair across from her. "Been a long time, hasn't it?"

"What are you doing here?"

"When Carly thought you were missing, I went over to that cop's place to be with her. We were worried about you. We got to talking and, well, that's her Christmas present to you and me: getting us together tonight and just seeing what happens."

"Where is she?"

"She went to her boyfriend's to spend the night with him." He smiled. "We've got the whole evening ahead of us. All alone. Just like the old days."

Susan started to rise. But Anthony stood up fast and swung his palm into her face with a jarring slap. She fell back on the couch. "You get up when I tell you to," he said cheerfully, smiling down at her. "Merry Christmas, Susan. It's good to see you again."

■

She looked toward the door.

"Don't even think about it." He opened the sparkling wine and poured two glasses. He offered her one. She shook her head. "Take it."

"Please, Anthony, just—"

"Take the goddamn glass," he hissed.

Susan did, her hand shaking violently. As they touched flutes, memories from when they were married flooded back to her: His sarcasm, his rage. And, of course, the beatings.

Oh, but he'd been clever. He never hurt her in front of people. He was especially careful around Carly. Like the psychopath that he was, Anthony Dalton was the model father to the girl. And the model husband to the world.

Nobody knew the source of her bruises, cuts, broken fingers . . .

"Mommy's such a klutz," Susan would tell young Carly, fighting back the tears. "I fell down the stairs again."

She'd long ago given up trying to understand what made Anthony tick. A troubled childhood, a glitch in the brain? She didn't know and after a year of marriage she didn't care. Her only goal was to get out. But she'd been too terrified to go to the police. Finally, in desperation, she'd turned to her father for help. The burly man owned several construction companies in New York and he had "connections." She'd confessed to him what had happened and her father took charge of the problem. He had two associates from Brooklyn, armed with baseball bats and a gun, pay

Anthony a visit. The threats, and a lot of money, had bought her freedom from the man, who reluctantly agreed to a divorce, to give up custody of Carly and not to hurt Susan again,

But, with terror flooding through her now, she realized why he was here tonight. Her father had passed away last spring.

Her protector was gone.

"I love Christmas, don't you?" Anthony Dalton mused, drinking more wine.

"What do you want?" she asked in a quivering voice.

"I can never get too much of the music." He walked to the stereo and turned it on. "Silent Night" was playing. "Did you know that it was first played on guitar? Because the church organ was broken."

"Please, just leave."

"The music . . . I like the decorations too."

She started to stand but he rose fast, slapping her again. "Sit down," he whispered, the soft sound more frightening than if he'd screamed.

Tears filled her eyes and she held her hand to her stinging cheek.

A boyish laugh. "And presents! We all love presents. . . . Don't you want to see what I got you?"

"We are not getting back together, Anthony. I do not want you in my life again."

"Why would I want someone like *you* in my life? What an ego . . ." He looked her over, smiling faintly, with his placid blue eyes. She remembered this too—how calm he could be. Sometimes even when he was beating her.

"Anthony, there's no harm so far, nobody's been hurt."

"Shhhh."

Without his seeing, her hand slipped to her jacket pocket where she'd put her cell phone. She'd turned it back on after the mix-up with Carly earlier. She didn't, however, think she could hit

911 without looking. But her finger found the "send" button. By pressing it twice the phone would call the last number dialed. Rich Musgrave's. She hoped his phone was still on and that he'd hear what was happening. He'd call the police. Or possibly even return to the house. Anthony wouldn't dare hurt her in front of a witness—and Rich was a large man and looked very strong. He outweighed her ex by fifty pounds.

She pressed the button now. After a moment she said, "You're scaring me, Anthony. Please leave."

"Scaring you?"

"I'll call the police."

"If you stand up I'll break your arm. Are we clear on that?"

She nodded, terrified but thankful, at least, that if Rich was listening, he would have heard this exchange and probably be calling the police now.

Dalton looked under the tree. "Is *my* present there?" He browsed through the packages, seeming disappointed that there was none with his name on it.

She recalled this too: One minute he'd be fine. The next, completely out of touch with reality. He'd been hospitalized three times when they were married. Susan remembered telling Carly that her father had to go to Asia on monthlong business trips.

"Nothing for poor me," he said, standing back from the tree.

Susan's jaw trembled. "I'm sorry. If I'd known—"

"It's a joke, Susan," he said. "Why would you get me anything? You didn't love me when we were married; you don't love me now. The important thing is that I got *you* something. After the scare about what'd happened to you this afternoon I went shopping. I wanted to find just the right present."

Dalton drank down more wine and refilled his glass. He eyed her carefully. "Probably better if you stay snuggled in right where you are. I'll open it for you."

Her eyes glanced at the box. It had been carelessly wrapped—by him, of course—and he ripped the paper off roughly. He lifted out something cylindrical, made of metal.

"It's a camping heater. Carly said you'd taken that up. Hiking, out-of-doors . . . Interesting that you never liked to do anything fun when we were married."

"I never liked to do anything with *you*," she said angrily. "You'd beat me up if I said the wrong thing or didn't do what you'd told me."

Ignoring her words, he handed her the heater. Then he took out something else. A red can. On the side: *Kerosene*. "Of course," Anthony continued, frowning, "that's one *bad* thing about Christmas . . . lot of accidents this time of year. You read that article in *USA Today*? Fires, particularly. Lot of people die in fires."

He glanced at the warning label and took a cigarette lighter from his pocket.

"Oh, God, no! . . . Please. Anthony."

It was then that Susan heard a car's brakes squeal outside. The police? Or was it Rich?

Or was it her imagination?

Anthony was busying himself taking the lid off the kerosene.

Yes, there were definitely footsteps on the walk. Susan prayed it wasn't Carly.

Then the doorbell rang. Anthony looked toward the front door, startled.

And as he did, Susan flung the champagne glass into his face with all her strength and leapt to her feet, sprinting for the door. She glanced behind her to see Anthony stumbling backward. The glass had broken and cut his chin. "Goddamn bitch!" he roared, starting for her.

But she had a good head start and flung the door open.

Rich Musgrave stood there, eyes wide in shock. "What?"

"It's my ex!" she gasped. "He's trying to kill me!"

"Jesus," Rich said. He put his arm around her. "Don't worry, Susan."

"We have to get away! Call the police."

She took his hand and started to flee into the front yard.

But Rich didn't move. What the hell was he doing? Did he want to *fight*? This was no time for any chivalry crap. "Please, Rich. We have to run!"

Then she felt his hand tighten on hers. The grip became excruciating. His other hand took her by the waist and he turned her around. He shoved her back inside. "Yo, Anthony," Rich called, laughing. "Lose something?"

■

In despair, Susan sat on the couch and sobbed.

They'd tied her hands and feet with Christmas ribbon, which would burn away, leaving no evidence that she'd been bound after the fire, Rich had explained, sounding like a carpenter imparting a construction tip to a homeowner.

It had all been planned for months, her ex-husband was smugly pleased to tell her. As soon as he'd learned that Susan's father had died, he started making plans to get even with her—for her "disobedience" when they were married and then for divorcing him. So he'd hired Rich Musgrave to work his way into her life and wait for an opportunity to kill her.

Rich had picked her up at a shopping mall a few weeks ago and they'd hit it off at once. They'd had a lot in common, it seemed—though Susan realized now that he'd merely been fed information about her from Anthony to make it seem like they were soul mates. Planning the killing itself was tough; Susan led a very busy life and she was rarely alone. But Rich learned that she was taking today off. He suggested they meet in Jersey and go to the malls. Then he'd suggest driving to an inn for lunch. But they'd never make it that far. He'd kill her and dump her body in the flats.

But she'd called Rich this morning, asking him if he'd drive; she'd fallen and hurt her knee. He'd be happy to. . . . Then he'd called Anthony and they'd decided that they could still go ahead with the plan. This worked out even better, in fact, because it turned out that Susan *had* left the note and shopping list for her daughter on the entryway table after all. When he picked her up that morning he'd pocketed the note and list and slipped them into her purse—to be buried with her—so there'd be no trace of him. Rich had also made sure her cell phone was off so she couldn't call for help if she saw what he was up to.

Then they'd run a few errands and headed toward Jersey.

But it hadn't worked out as planned. Carly had gone to the police and, to Anthony's shock, they'd tracked down Rich's car. Her ex had called Rich from Lincoln Rhyme's apartment, pretending to be talking to a business associate about missing an office party; in fact, he was alerting Rich that the police were after him. Susan remembered him taking a call in the car and seeming uneasy with whatever news he was receiving. "What? You're shitting me!" (Rough edges, yep, she'd thought at the time.) Ten minutes later that red-haired cop, Amelia, and the state trooper had pulled them over.

After that incident Rich had been reluctant to proceed with the murder. But Anthony had coldly insisted they go ahead. Rich finally agreed when Anthony said they'd make the death look like an accident—and when he promised that after Susan died and Carly'd inherited a couple of million dollars, Anthony would make certain Rich got some of that.

"You son of a bitch! You leave her alone!"

Anthony ignored his ex-wife. He was amused. "So she just called you now?"

"Yeah," Rich said. "Hit 'redial,' I guess. Pretty fucking smart."

"Damn," Anthony said, shaking his head.

"Good thing I was the last person she called. Not Pizza Hut."

Anthony said to Susan, "Nice thought. But Rich was coming back anyway. He was parked up the street, waiting for Carly to leave."

"Please . . . don't do this."

Anthony poured the kerosene on the couch.

"No, no, no . . ."

He stood back and watched her, enjoying her terror.

But through her tears of panic Susan saw that Rich Musgrave was frowning. He shook his head. "Can't do it, man," he said to Anthony as he stared at Susan's tearful face.

Anthony looked up, frowning. Was his friend having pangs of guilt?

Help me, please, she begged Rich silently.

"Whatta you mean?" Anthony asked.

"You can't burn somebody to death. That's way harsh. . . . We have to kill her first."

Susan gasped.

"But the police'll know it's not an accident."

"No, no, I'll just—" He held his hand to his own throat. "You know. After the fire they won't have a clue she was strangled."

Anthony shrugged. "Okay." He nodded to Rich, who stepped up behind her, as Anthony poured the rest of the liquid around Susan.

"Oh, no, Anthony, don't! Please . . . God, no . . ."

Her words were choked off as she felt Rich's huge hands close around her neck, felt them tightening.

As she began to die, a roaring filled her ears, then blackness. Finally huge bursts of light speckled her vision. Brighter and brighter.

What were the flashes? she wondered, growing calm as the air was cut off from her lungs.

Were they from her dying brain cells?

Were they the flames from the kerosene?

Or was this, she thought manically, the brilliance of heaven? She'd never really believed in it before. . . . Maybe . . .

But then the lights faded. The roaring too. And suddenly she was breathing again, the air flowing into her lungs. She felt a huge weight on her shoulders and neck. Something dug into her face, stinging.

Gasping, she squinted as her vision returned. A dozen police officers, men and women, in those black outfits you saw on TV shows, gripping heavy guns, were filling the room. The guns had flashlights on them; their beams had been the bright lights she'd seen. They'd kicked the door in and grabbed Rich Musgrave. He'd fallen, trying to escape; it had been his belt buckle that'd cut her cheek. They cuffed him roughly and dragged him out the door.

One of the officers in black and that woman detective, Amelia Sachs, wearing a bulletproof vest, pointed their guns toward Anthony Dalton. "On the floor, now, face down!" she growled.

The shock of the ex-husband's face gave way to righteous indignation. Then the madman gave a faint smile. "Put your guns down." He held out the cigarette lighter near the fuel-soaked couch, a few feet away from Susan. One flick and the couch would burst into a sea of fire.

One officer started for her.

"No!" Dalton raged. "Leave her." He moved the lighter closer to the liquid, put his thumb on the tab.

The cop froze.

"You're going to back out of here. I want everybody out of this room, except . . . you," he said to Sachs. "You're going to give me your gun and we're walking out of here together. Or I'll burn us all to death. I'll do it. I goddamn will do it!"

The redhead ignored his words. "I want that lighter on the ground now. And you face down right after it. Now! I *will* fire."

"No, you won't. The flash from your gun'll set off the fumes. This whole place'll go up."

The policewoman lowered her black gun, frowning as she considered his words. She looked at the cop beside her and nodded. "He's right."

She glanced around her, picked up a pillow from an old rocking chair and held it over the muzzle of her gun.

Dalton frowned and dropped to the couch, started to click the lighter. But the policewoman's idea was a good one. There was no flash at all when she fired through the pillow, three times, sending Susan's ex-husband sprawling back against the fireplace.

■

The Rollx van was parked at the curb. The Storm Arrow wheelchair, which was devoid of ribbons and spruce, was on the van's elevator platform, lowered to the ground, resting on the snow. Lincoln Rhyme was in the thick parka that Thom had insisted he wear, despite the criminalist's protests that it wasn't necessary since he was going to remain in the van.

But, when they'd arrived at Susan Thompson's house, Thom had thought it would be good for Rhyme to have a little fresh air.

He grumbled at first but then acquiesced to being lowered to the ground outside. He rarely got out in cold weather—even places that were disabled-accessible were often hard to negotiate on snow and ice—and he was never one for the out-of-doors anyway, even before the accident. But he was now surprised to find how much he enjoyed feeling the crisp chill on his face, watching the ghost of his breath roll from his mouth and vanish in the crystalline air, smelling the smoke from fireplaces.

The incident was mostly concluded. Richard Musgrave was

in a holding cell in Garden City. Firemen had rendered the den in Susan's house safe, removing the sofa and cleaning up or neutralizing the kerosene Dalton had tried to kill her with, and she'd been given an okay from the medics. Nassau County had run the crime scene, and Sachs was now huddled with two county detectives. There was no question she'd acted properly in shooting Anthony Dalton but there'd still be a formal shooting-incident inquiry. The officers finished their interview, wished her a merry Christmas and crunched through the snow to the van, where they spent a few minutes speaking to Rhyme with a sliver of awe in their voices; they knew the criminalist's reputation and could hardly believe that he was here in their own backyard.

After the detectives left, Susan Thompson and her daughter walked down to the van, the woman moving stiffly, wincing occasionally.

"You're Mr. Rhyme."

"Lincoln, please."

Susan introduced herself and thanked him effusively. Then she asked, "How on earth did you know what Anthony was going to do?"

"He told me himself." A glance at the walkway to the house.

"The path?" she asked.

"I could have figured it out from the evidence," Rhyme muttered, "if we'd had all our resources available. It would have been more *efficient*." A scientist, Rhyme was fundamentally suspicious of words and witnesses. He nodded to Sachs, who tempered Rhyme's deification of physical evidence with what he called "people cop" skills, and she explained, "Lincoln remembered that you'd moved into the house last summer. Carly mentioned it this morning."

The girl nodded.

"And when your ex was at the town house this afternoon he said that he hadn't seen you since last Christmas."

Susan frowned and said, "That's right. He told me last year that he was going away on business for six months so he brought two checks for Carly's tuition to my office. I haven't seen him since. Well, until tonight."

"But he also said that the path from this house to the street was steep."

Rhyme took up the narrative. "He said it was like a ski slope. Which meant he *had* been here, and since he described the walk that way, it was probably recently, sometime after the first snow. Maybe the discrepancy was nothing—he might've just dropped something off or picked up Carly when you weren't here. But there was also a chance he'd lied and had been stalking you."

"No, he never came here that I knew about. He must have been watching me."

Rhyme said, "I thought it was worth looking into. I checked him out and found out about his times in the mental hospitals, the jail sentences, assaults on two recent girlfriends."

"Hospital?" Carly gasped. "Assaults?"

The girl knew nothing about this? Rhyme lifted an eyebrow at Sachs, who shrugged. The criminalist continued. "And last Christmas, when he told you he was going away on business? Well, that 'business' was a six-month sentence in a Jersey prison for road rage and assault. He nearly killed another man over a fender bender."

Susan frowned. "I didn't know about that one. Or that he'd hurt anybody else."

"So we kept speculating, Sachs and Lon and I. We got a down-and-dirty warrant to check his phone calls and it turned out he'd called Musgrave a dozen times in the last couple of weeks. Lon checked on him and the word on the street is that he's for-hire muscle. I figured that Dalton met somebody in jail who hooked him up with Musgrave."

"He wouldn't do anything to me while my father was alive,"

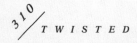

Susan said and explained how it had been her dad who'd gotten the abusive man away from her.

The woman's words were spoken to all of them, clustered in the snow around the van, but it was Carly's eyes she gazed at. This was, in effect, a stark confession that her mother had been lying to her about her father for years and years.

"When the plan with Musgrave didn't work out this afternoon, Dalton figured he'd do it himself."

"But . . . no, no, no, not Dad!" Carly whispered. She stepped away from her mother, shivering, tears running down her red cheeks. "He . . . It can't be true! He was so nice! He . . ."

Susan shook her head. "Honey, I'm sorry, but your father was a very sick man. He knew how to put on a perfect facade, he was a real charmer—until he decided he didn't trust you or you did something he didn't like." She put her arm around her daughter. "Those trips he took to Asia? No, those were the times in the hospitals and jails. Remember I always said I was banging into things?"

"You were a klutz," the girl said in a small voice. "You don't mean—"

Susan nodded. "It was your father. He'd knock me down the stairs, he'd hit me with a rolling pin, extension cords, tennis rackets."

Carly turned away and stared at the house. "You kept saying what a good man he was. And all I could think of was, well, if he was so damn good, why didn't you want to get back together?"

"I wanted to protect you from the truth. I wanted you to have a loving father. But I couldn't give you one—he hated me so much."

But the girl was unmoved. Years of lies, even those offered for the best of motives, would take a long time to digest, let alone forgive.

If they could ever be forgiven.

There were voices from the doorway. The Nassau County coroner's men were wheeling Anthony Dalton's body out of the house.

"Honey," Susan began. "I'm sorry. I—"

But the girl held up a hand to silence her mother. They watched as the body was loaded into the coroner's van.

Susan wiped the tears from her face. She said, "Honey, I know this is too much for you. . . . I know you're mad. I don't have any right to ask . . . but can you just do one thing to help me? I have to tell everybody coming to the party tomorrow that we're canceling. It'll get too late if I have to call them all myself."

The girl stared as the van disappeared down the snowy street.

"Carly," her mother whispered.

"No," she answered her mother.

Her face flooding with resignation and pain, Susan nodded knowingly. "Sure, sweetheart, I understand. I'm sorry. I shouldn't've asked. You go see Jake. You don't have to—"

"That's not what I mean," the girl said bluntly. "I mean, we're not canceling the party."

"We can't, not after—"

"Why not?" the girl asked. There was flint in her voice.

"But—"

"We're going to have our party," Carly said firmly. "We'll find a room in a restaurant or hotel somewhere. It's late but let's start making some calls."

"You think we could?" Susan asked.

"Yes," the girl said, "we can."

Susan too invited the three of them to the party.

"I may have other commitments," Rhyme said quickly. "I'll have to check my schedule."

"We'll see," Sachs told her coyly.

Eyes wet with tears, mouth unsmiling, Carly thanked Rhyme, Sachs and Thom.

The two women returned to the house, daughter helping mother up the steep path. They moved in silence. The girl was angry, Rhyme could see. And numb. But she hadn't walked away from her mother. A lot of people would have.

The door to the house closed with a loud snap, carried through the compact, cold air.

"Hey, anybody want to drive around and look at the decorations on the houses?" Thom asked.

Sachs and Rhyme looked at each other. The criminalist said, "I think we'll pass. How 'bout we get back to the city? Look at the hour. It's late. Forty-five minutes till Christmas. Doesn't the time fly when you're doing good deeds?"

Thom repeated, "Humbug." But he said it cheerfully.

Sachs kissed Rhyme. "I'll see you back home," she said and walked toward the Camaro as Thom swung the door of the van shut. In tandem, the two vehicles started down the snowy street.

"A few people, a very few people're lucky enough to find a special kind of love. A love that's . . . more. That goes beyond anything that ever was."

"I suppose so."

"I *know* so. Allison and me, we're in that category." Manko's voice then dropped to a discreet whisper as he looked at me with his barracks-buddy's grin. "I've had a barrelful of women. You know me, Frankie boy. You know I've been around."

Manko was in the mood to perform and all I could do was play both straight man and audience. "So you've said, Mr. M."

"Those other girls, looking back, some of 'em were lovers. And some were just, you know, for the night. Wham, bam. That sort of thing. But till I met Allison, I didn't understand what love was all about."

"It's a transcendent love."

"Transcendent." He tasted the word, nodding slowly. "What's that mean?"

Just after I'd met Manko I'd learned that while he was poorly read and generally uninformed, he never hesitated to own up to his ignorance, which a lot of smart people never do. That had been my first clue as to the kind of man he was.

"It's exactly what you're describing," I explained. "A love that rises above what you normally see and experience."

"Yeah. I like that, Frankie boy. Transcendent. That says it. That's what we've got. You ever love anyone that way?"

"Sort of. A long time ago." This was partially true. But I said nothing more. Although I considered Manko a friend in some ways, our souls were worlds apart and I wasn't going to share my deepest personal life with him. Not that it mattered, for at the moment he was more interested in speaking about the woman who was the center of his own solar system.

"Allison Morgan. Allison *Kimberly* Morgan. Her father gave her a nickname. Kimmie. But that's crap. It's a kid's name. And one thing she isn't is a kid."

"Has a Southern sound to it." I'm a native of North Carolina and went to school with a bevy of Sally Mays and Cheryl Annes.

"It does, yeah. But she's not. She's from Ohio. Born and bred." Manko glanced at his watch and stretched. "It's late. Almost time to meet her."

"Allison?"

He nodded and smiled the trademarked, toothy Manko smile. "I mean, you're cute in your own way, Frank, but if I gotta choose between the two of you . . ."

I laughed and repressed a yawn. It *was* late—eleven-twenty P.M. An unusual hour for me to be finishing dinner but not to be engaged in conversation over coffee. Not having an Allison of my own to hurry home to, or anyone other than a cat, I often watched the clock slip past midnight or one A.M. in the company of friends.

Manko pushed aside the dinner dishes and poured more coffee.

"I'll be awake all night," I protested mildly.

He laughed this aside and asked if I wanted more pie.

When I declined he raised his coffee cup. "My Allison. Let's drink to her."

We touched the rims of the cups with a ringing clink.

I said, "Hey, Mr. M, you were going to tell me all 'bout the trouble. You know, with her father."

He scoffed. "That son of a bitch? You know what happened."

"Not the whole thing."

"Don'tcha?" He dramatically reared his head back and gave a wail of mock horror. "Manko's falling down on the job." He leaned forward, the smile gone, and gripped my arm hard. "It's not a pretty story, Frankie boy. It's not outta *Family Ties* or *Roseanne*. Can you stomach it?"

I leaned forward too, just as dramatically, and growled. "Try me."

Manko laughed and settled into his chair. As he lifted his cup the table rocked. It had done so throughout dinner but he only now seemed to notice it. He took a moment to fold and slip a piece of newspaper under the short leg to steady it. He was meticulous in this task. I watched his concentration, his strong hands. Manko was someone who actually enjoyed working out—lifting weights, in his case—and I was astonished at his musculature. He was about five-six, and, though it's hard for men—for me at least—to appraise male looks, I'd call him handsome.

The only aspect of his appearance I thought off-kilter was his haircut. When his stint with the Marines was over he kept the unstylish crew cut. From this, I deduced his experience in the service was a high point in his life—he'd worked factory and mediocre sales jobs since—and the shorn hair was a reminder of a better, if not an easier, time.

Of course, that was my pop-magazine-therapy take on the situation. Maybe he just liked short hair.

He now finished with the table and eased his strong, compact legs out in front of him. Manko the storyteller was on duty. This was another clue to the nature of Manko's spirit: Though I don't think he'd ever been on a stage in his life he was a born actor.

"So. You know Hillborne? The town?"

I said I didn't.

"Southern part of Ohio. Piss-water river town. Champion

used to have a mill there. Still a couple factories making, I don't know, radiators and things. And a big printing plant, does work for Cleveland and Chicago. Kroeger Brothers. When I was in Seattle I learned printing. Miehle offsets. The four- and five-color jobs, you know. Big as a house. I learned 'em cold. Could print a whole saddle-stitched magazine myself, inserts included, yessir, perfect register and not one goddamn staple in the centerfold's boobs . . . Yessir, Manko's a hell of a printer. So there I was, thumbing 'cross country. I ended up in Hillborne and got a job at Kroeger's. I had to start as a feeder, which was crap, but it paid thirteen an hour and I figured I could work my way up.

"One day I had an accident. Frankie boy, you ever seen coated stock whipping through a press? Zip, zip, zip. Like a razor. Sliced my arm. Here." He pointed out the scar, a wicked-looking one. "Bad enough they took me to the hospital. Gave me a tetanus shot and stitched me up. No big deal. No whining from Manko. Then the doctor left and a nurse's aide came in to tell me how to wash it and gave me some bandages." His voice dwindled.

"It was Allison?"

"Yessir." He paused and gazed out the window at the overcast sky. "You believe in fate?"

"In a way I do."

"Does that mean yes or no?" He frowned. Manko always spoke plainly and expected the same from others.

"Yes, with qualifiers."

Love tamed his irascibility and he grinned, chiding goodnaturedly, "Well, you better. Because there *is* such a thing. Allison and me, we were fated to be together. See, if I hadn't been running that sixty-pound stock, if I hadn't slipped just when I did, if she hadn't been working an extra shift to cover for a sick friend, if, if, if . . . See what I'm saying? Am I right?"

He sat back in the creaky chair. "Oh, Frankie, she was fantastic. I mean, here I am, this, like, four-inch slash in my arm,

twenty stitches, I could've bled to death, and all I'm thinking is she's the most beautiful woman I ever saw."

"I've seen her picture." But that didn't stop him from continuing to describe her. The words alone gave him pleasure.

"Her hair's blonde. Gold blonde. Natural, not out of a bottle. And curly but not teased, like some high-hair slut. And her face, it's heart-shaped. Her body . . . Well, she has a nice figure. Let's leave it at that." His glance at me contained a warning. I was about to assure him that I had no impure thoughts about Allison Morgan when he continued. He said, "Twenty-one years old." Echoing my exact thought he added sheepishly, "Kind of an age difference, huh?"

Manko was thirty-seven—three years younger than I—but I learned this after I'd met him and had guessed he was in his late twenties. It was impossible for me to revise that assessment upward.

"I asked her out. There. On the spot. In the emergency room, you can believe it. She was probably thinking, How d'I get rid of this bozo? But she was interested, yessir. A man can tell. Words and looks, they're two different things, and I was getting the capital *M* message. She said she had this rule she never dated patients. So I go, 'How 'bout if you married somebody and he cuts his hand in an accident and goes to the emergency room and there you are? Then you'd be *married* to a patient.' She laughed and said, no, that was somehow backwards. Then this emergency call came in, some car wreck, and she had to go off.

"The next day I came back with a dozen roses. She pretended she didn't remember me and acted like I was a florist delivery boy. 'Oh, what room are those for?'

"I said, 'They're for you . . . if you have *room* in your heart for me.' Okay, okay, it was a bullshit line." The rugged ex-Marine fiddled awkwardly with his coffee cup. "But, hey, if it works, it works."

I couldn't argue with him there.

"The first date was magic. We had dinner at the fanciest restaurant in town. A French place. It cost me two days' pay. It was embarrassing 'cause I wore my leather jacket and you were suppose to have a suit coat. One of *those* places. They made me wear one they had in the coat room and it didn't fit too good. But Allison didn't care. We laughed about it. She was all dressed up in a white dress, with a red, white and blue scarf around her neck. Oh, God, she was beautiful. We spent, I don't know, three, four hours easy there. She was pretty shy. Didn't say much. Mostly she stared like she was kind of hypnotized. Me, I talked and talked, and sometimes she'd look at me all funny and then laugh. And I'd realize I wasn't making any sense 'cause I was looking at her and not paying any attention to what I was saying. We drank a whole bottle of wine. Cost fifty bucks."

Manko had always seemed both impressed by and contemptuous of money. Myself, I've never come close to being rich so wealth simply perplexes me.

"It was the best," he said dreamily, replaying the memory.

"Ambrosia," I offered.

He laughed as he sometimes did—in a way that was both amused and mocking—and continued his story. "I told her all about the Philippines, where I was stationed for a while, and about hitching around the country. She was interested in everything I'd done. Even—well, I should say *especially*—some of the stuff I wasn't too proud of. Grifting, perping cars. You know, when I was a kid, going at it. Stuff we all did."

I held back a smile. Speak for yourself, Manko.

"Then all of a sudden, the sky lit up outside. Fireworks! Talk about signs from God. You know what it was? It was the Fourth of July! I'd forgotten about it 'cause all I'd been thinking about was going out with her. *That's* why she was wearing the red, white and blue. We watched the fireworks from the window."

His eyes gleamed. "I took her home and we stood on the steps of her parents' house—she was still living with them. We talked for a while more then she said she had to get to bed. You catch that? Like she could've said, 'I have to be going.' Or just 'Good night.' But she worked the word *bed* into it. I know, you're in love, you look for messages like that. Only in this case, it wasn't Manko's imagination working overtime, no sir."

Outside, a light rain had started falling and the wind had come up. I rose and shut the window.

"The next day I kept getting distracted at work. I'd think about her face, her voice. No woman's ever affected me like that. On break I called her and asked her out for the next weekend. She said sure and said she was glad to hear from me. That set up my day. Hell, it set up my *week*. After work I went to the library and looked some things up. I found out about her last name. Morgan—if you spell it a little different—it means 'morning' in German. And I dug up some articles about the family. Like, they're rich. Filthy. The house in Hillborne wasn't their only place. There was one in Aspen, too, and one in Vermont. Oh, and an apartment in New York."

"A pied-à-terre."

His brief laugh again. The smile faded. "And then there was her father. Thomas Morgan." He peered into his coffee cup like a fortune-teller looking at tea leaves. "He's one of those guys a hundred years ago you'd call him a tycoon."

"What would you call him now?"

Manko laughed grimly, as if I'd made a clever but cruel joke. He lifted his cup toward me—a toast, it seemed—then continued. "He inherited this company that makes gaskets and nozzles and stuff. He's about fifty-five and is he *tough*. A big guy, but not fat. A droopy black mustache, and his eyes look you over like he couldn't care less about you but at the same time he's sizing you up, like every fault, every dirty thought you ever had, he knows it.

"We caught sight of each other when I dropped Allison off, and I knew, I just somehow *knew* that we were going to go head to head some day. I didn't really think about it then but deep inside, the thought was there."

"What about her mother?"

"Allison's mom? She's a socialite. She flits around, Allison told me. Man, what a great word. *Flit.* I can picture the old broad going to bridge games and tea parties. Allison's their only child." His face suddenly grew dark. "That, I figured out later, explains a lot."

"What?" I asked.

"Why her father got on my case in a big way. I'll get to that. Don't rush the Manko Man, Frankie."

I smiled in deference.

"Our second date went even better than the first. We saw some movie, I forget what, then I drove her home. . . ." His voice trailed off. Then he said, "I asked her out for a few days after that but she couldn't make it. Ditto the next day and the next too. I was pissed at first. Then I got paranoid. Was she trying to, you know, dump me?

"But then she explained it. She was working two shifts whenever she could. I thought, This's pretty funny. I mean, her father's loaded. But, see, there was a *reason.* She's just like me. Independent. She dropped out of college to work in the hospital. She was saving her own money to travel. She didn't want to owe the old man anything. *That's* why she loved listening to me talk, telling her 'bout leaving Kansas when I was seventeen and thumbing around the country and overseas, getting into scrapes. Allison had it in her to do the same thing. Man, that was great. I love having a woman with a mind of her own."

"Do you, now?" I asked, but Manko was immune to irony.

"In the back of my mind I was thinking about all the places I'd like to go with her. I'd send her clippings from travel maga-

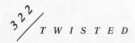

zines. *National Geographic*s. On our first date she'd told me that she loved poetry so I wrote her poems about traveling. It's funny. I never wrote anything before in my life—a few letters maybe, some shit in school—but those poems, man, they just poured out of me. A hundred of 'em.

"Well, next thing I knew, bang, we were in love. See, that's the thing about . . . *transcendent* love. It happens right away or it doesn't happen at all. Two weeks, and we were totally in love. I was ready to propose. . . . Ah, I see that look on your face, Frankie boy. Didn't know the Manko man had it in him? What can I say? He's the marryin' kind after all.

"I went to the credit union and borrowed five hundred bucks and bought this diamond ring. Then I asked her out to dinner on Friday. I was going to give the ring to the waitress and tell her to put it on a plate and bring it to the table when we asked for dessert. Cute, huh?

"So, Friday, I was working the P.M. shift, three to eleven, for the bonus, but I ducked out early, at five, and showed up at her house at six-twenty. There were cars all over the place. Allison came outside, looking all nervous. My stomach twisted. Something funny was going on. She told me her mother was having a party and there was a problem. Two maids had got sick or something. Allison had to stay and help her mother. I thought that was weird. *Both* of them getting sick at the same time? She said she'd see me in a day or two."

I saw the exact moment that the thought came into his mind; his eyes went dead as rocks.

"But there was more to it than that," Manko whispered. "A hell of a lot more."

"Allison's father, you mean?"

But he didn't explain what he meant just then and returned to his story of the aborted proposal. He muttered, "That was one of the worst nights of my life. Here, I'd ditched work, I was in hock because of the ring, and I couldn't even get five minutes alone with her. Man, it was torture. I drove around all night. Woke up at dawn, in my car, down by the railroad tracks. And when I got home there was no message from her. Jesus, was I depressed.

"That morning I called her at the hospital. She was sorry about the party. I asked her out that night. She said she really shouldn't, she was so tired—the party'd gone to two in the morning. But how 'bout tomorrow?"

A gleam returned to Manko's eyes. I thought his expression reflected a pleasant memory about their date.

But I was wrong.

His voice was bitter. "Oh, what a lesson we learned. It's a mistake to underestimate your enemy, Frankie. You listen to Manko. Never do it. That's what they taught us in the Corps. *Semper Fi*. But Allison and me, we got blindsided.

"That next night I came over to pick her up. I was going to take her to this river bluff, like a lover's lane, you know, to propose. I had my speech down cold. I'd rehearsed all night. I pulled up to the house but she just stood on the porch and waved for me to come up to her. Oh, she was beautiful as ever. I just wanted to hold her. Put my arms around her and hold her forever.

"But she was real distant. She stepped away from me and kept glancing into the house. Her face was pale and her hair was tied back in a ponytail. I didn't like it that way. I'd told her I liked it when she wore it down. So when I saw the ponytail it was like a signal of some kind. An SOS.

"'What is it?' I asked her. She started to cry and said she couldn't see me anymore. 'What?' I whispered. God, I couldn't believe it. You know what it felt like? On Parris Island, basic training, you know? They fire live rounds over your head on the obstacle course. One time I got hit by a ricochet. I had a flak vest

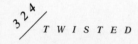

on but the slug was a full metal jacket and it knocked me clean on my ass. That's what it was like.

"I asked her why. She just said she thought it was best and wouldn't go into any details. But then I started to catch on. She kept looking around and I realized that there was somebody just inside the door, listening. She was scared to death—*that's* what it was. She begged me please not to call her or come by and I figured out she wasn't talking to *me* so much as saying it for whoever was spying on us. I played along. I said okay, if that's what she wanted, blah, blah, blah . . . Then I pulled her close and told her not to worry. I'd look out for her. I whispered it, like a secret message.

"I went home. I waited as long as I could then called, hoping that I'd get her alone. I had to talk to her. I had to hear her voice, like I needed air or water. But nobody picked up the phone. They had an answering machine but I didn't leave a message. I didn't get any sleep that weekend—not a single hour. I had a lot to think about. See, I knew what'd happened. I knew exactly.

"Monday morning I got to her hospital at six and waited just outside the entrance. I caught up with her just before she went inside. She was still scared, looking around like somebody was following her, just like on the porch.

"I asked her point-blank, 'It's your father, isn't it?' She didn't say anything for a minute then nodded and said that, yeah, he'd forbidden her to see me. Doesn't that sound funny? Old fashioned? 'Forbidden.' 'He wants you to marry some preppy, is that it? Somebody from his club?' She said she didn't know about that, only that he'd told her not to see me anymore. The son of a bitch!"

Manko sipped his coffee and pointed a blunt finger at me. "See, Frankie, love means zip to somebody like Thomas Morgan. Business, society, image, money—that's what counts to bastards like that. Man, I was so goddamn desperate. . . . It was too much. I threw my arms around her and said, 'Let's get away. Now.'

" 'Please,' she said, 'you have to leave.'

"Then I saw what she'd been looking out for. Her father'd sent one of his security men to spy on her. He saw us and came running. If he touched her I was going to break his neck, I swear I would've. But Allison grabbed my arm and begged me to run. 'He has a gun,' she said.

" 'I don't care,' I told her." Manko lifted an eyebrow. "Not exactly true, Frankie boy, I gotta say. I was scared shitless. But Allison said she didn't want me to get hurt. And if I left, the guy wouldn't hurt her. That made sense but I wasn't going just yet. I turned back and held her hard. 'Do you love me? Tell me! I have to know. Say it!'

"And she did. She whispered, 'I love you.' I could hardly hear it but it was enough for me. I knew everything would be fine. Whatever else, we had each other.

"I got back into the routine of life. Working, playing softball on the plant team. But all the time I kept writing her poetry, sending her articles and letters, you know. I'd put fake return addresses on the envelopes so her father wouldn't guess it was me writing. I even hid letters in Publishers Clearing House envelopes addressed to her! How's that for thinking?

"Once in a while I'd see her in person. I found her in a drugstore by herself and snuck up to her. I bought her a cup of coffee. She said how happy she was to see me but also was nervous as hell and I could see why. The goons were outside. We talked for about two minutes is all then one of 'em saw us and I had to vanish. I kicked my way out the back door. After that I began to notice these dark cars driving past my apartment or following me down the street. They said 'MCP' on the side. Morgan Chemical Products. They were keeping an eye on me.

"One day this guy came up to me in the hallway of my apartment and said Morgan'd pay me five thousand to leave town. I laughed at him. Then he said if I didn't stay away from Allison there'd be trouble.

"Suddenly I just snapped. I grabbed him and pulled his gun out of his holster and threw it on the floor then I shoved him against the wall and said, 'You go back and tell Morgan to leave us alone or *he's* the one's gonna be in trouble. You got me?'

"Then I kicked him down the stairs and threw his gun after him. I gotta say I was pretty shook up. I was seeing just how powerful this guy was."

"Money is power," I offered.

"Yeah, you're right there. Money's power. And Thomas Morgan was going to use all of his to keep us apart. You know why? 'Cause I was a threat. Fathers are jealous. Turn on any talk show. Oprah. Sally Jesse. Fathers *hate* their daughters' boyfriends. It's like an Oedipus thing. Especially—what I was saying before—with Allison being an only child. Here I was, a rebel, a drifter, making thirteen bucks an hour. It was like a slap in his face, Allison loving me so completely. She was rejecting him and everything he stood for." Manko's face shone with pride for Allison's courage.

Then the smile vanished. "But Morgan was always one step ahead of us. One day I ditched work and snuck into the hospital. I waited for an hour but Allison never showed up. I asked where she was. They told me she wasn't working there anymore. Nobody'd give me a straight answer but finally I found this young nurse who told me her father'd called and told 'em that Allison was taking a leave of absence. Period. No explanation. She didn't even clean out her locker. Jesus. All her plans to travel, all her plans with me—gone, just like that. I called the house to get a message to her but he'd changed the number and had it, you know, unlisted. I mean, this guy was in-*credible*.

"And he didn't stop there. Next, he comes after me. I go in to

work and the foreman tells me I'm fired. Too many unexcused absences. That was bullshit—I didn't have more than most of the guys. But Morgan must've been a friend of the Kroegers. I was still new so the union wouldn't go to bat for me. I was out. Just like that.

"Well, I couldn't beat him at his game so I decided to play by my rules." Manko grinned and scooted forward. Our knees touched and I felt all the energy that was in him pulse against my skin. "Oh, I wasn't worried for me. But Allison, she's so . . ." As he searched for a word his hands made a curious gesture, as if stretching thread between them, a miniature cat's cradle.

I suggested, "Fragile."

The snap of his fingers startled me. He sat up. "Ex-*actly*. Fragile. She didn't have any defense against her father. I had to do something fast. I went to the police. I wanted 'em to go to the house and see if she was okay. But also it'd be a sign to her father that I wasn't going to take any crap from him." Manko whistled. "Mistake, Frankie. Bad mistake. Morgan was one step ahead of me. This sergeant, some big guy, pushed me into a corner and said if I didn't stay away from Morgan's daughter, the family'd get a restraining order. I'd end up in a cell. Then he looked me over and said something about did I know all sorts of accidents could happen to prisoners. It was a risky place, jail. Man, was I stupid. I should've known the cops'd be on Morgan's payroll too.

"By then I was going crazy. I hadn't seen Allison for weeks. Jesus, had he sent her off to a convent or something?"

Serenity returned to his face. "Then she gave me a signal. I was hiding in the bushes in a little park across the street, watching the house with binoculars. I just wanted to *see* her is all. I wanted to know she was all right. She must've seen me because she lifted the shade all the way up. Oh, man, there she was! The light was behind her and it made her hair glow. Like those things, you know, gurus see."

"Auras."

"Right, right. She was in a nightgown, and I could just see the outline of her body beneath it. She looked like an angel. I was like I was gonna have a heart attack, it was such an incredible thing. There she was, telling me she was all right and she missed me. Then the shade went down and she shut the light out.

"I spent the next week planning. I was running out of money. Thanks again to Thomas Morgan. He'd put out the word to all the factories in town and nobody'd hire me. I added up what I had and it wasn't much. Maybe twelve hundred bucks. I figured it'd get us to Florida. Give me a chance to find work with a printer and Allison could get a job in a hospital."

Then Manko laughed. He studied me critically. "I can be honest with you, Frank. I feel I'm close to you."

So I was no longer Frankie boy. I'd graduated. My pulse quickened and I was moved.

"Fact is, I look tough. Am I right? But I get scared. Real scared. I never saw any action. Grenada, Panama, Desert Storm. I missed 'em all, you know what I'm saying? I was never *tested*. I always wondered what I'd do under fire. Well, this was my chance. I was going to rescue Allison. I was going up against the old man himself.

"I called his company and told his secretary I was a reporter from *Ohio Business* magazine. I wanted to do an interview with Mr. Morgan. We tried to find a time he could see me. I couldn't believe it—she bought the whole story. She told me he'd be in Mexico on business from the twentieth through the twenty-second of July. I made an appointment for August 1, then hung up fast. I was worried somebody was tracing the call.

"On July twentieth I staked out the house all day. Sure enough, Morgan left with his suitcase at ten in the morning and didn't come back that night. There was a security car parked in the driveway and I figured one of the goons was inside the house. But

I'd planned on that. At ten it started to rain. Just like now." He nodded toward the window. "I remember hiding in the bushes, real glad about the overcast. I had about a hundred feet of exposed yard to cover and the security boys would've spotted me for sure in the moonlight. I managed to get to the house without anybody seeing me and hide beneath this holly tree while I caught my breath.

"Then it was dues time, Frank. I leaned against the side of the house, listening to the rain and wondering if I'd have the guts to go through with it."

"But you did."

Manko grinned boyishly and did a decent Pacino gangster impersonation. "I broke in through the basement, snuck up to her room and busted her out of the joint.

"We didn't take a suitcase or anything. We just got out of there fast as we could. Nobody heard us. The security guy was in the living room but he'd fallen asleep watching the *Tonight Show*. Allison and I, we got into my car and we hit the highway. Man, *Easy Rider*. We were free! On the road, just her and me. We'd escaped. We were on that adventure Allison'd always wanted. At last, we were both happy.

"I headed for the interstate, driving sixty-two, right on the button, because they don't arrest you if you're doing just seven miles over the limit. It's a state police rule, I heard somewhere. I stayed in the right lane and pointed that old Dodge east-southeast. Didn't stop for anything. Ohio, West Virginia, Virginia, North Carolina. Once we started crossing borders, I felt better. Her father was sure to come home from his trip right away and call the local cops but whether they'd get the highway patrol in, I had my doubts. I mean, he'd have some explaining to do—about how he kept his daughter a prisoner and everything." Manko shook his head. "But you know what I did?"

From the rueful look on his face I could guess. "You underestimated the enemy."

Manko shook his head. "Thomas Morgan," he mused. "I think he must've been a godfather or something."

"I suppose they have them in Ohio too."

"He had friends everywhere. Virginia troopers, Carolina, everywhere! Money is power, we were saying. We were heading south on Route Twenty-one, making for Charlotte, when I ran into 'em. I went into a 7-Eleven to buy some food and beer and what happens but there're some good ole boys right there, Smoky hats and everything, asking the clerk about a couple on the run from Ohio. I mean, *us!* I managed to get out without them seeing us and we peeled rubber outta there, I'll tell you. We drove for a while but by then it was almost dawn and I figured we better lay low for the day.

"I pulled into a big forest preserve. We spent the whole day together, lying there, my arms around her, her head on my chest. We just lay in the grass beside the car and I told her stories about places we'd travel to. The Philippines, Thailand, California. And I told her what life'd be like in Florida too."

He looked at me with a grave expression on his taut face. "I could've had her, Frank. You know what I'm saying? Right there. On the grass. The insects buzzing around us. You could hear this river, a waterfall, nearby." Manko's voice fell to a murmur. "But it wouldn't've been right. I wanted everything to be perfect. I wanted us to be in our own place, in Florida, in our bedroom, married. That sounds old-fashioned, I know. You think that was stupid of me? You don't think so, do you?"

"No, Manko, it's not stupid at all." Awkwardly I looked for something to add. "It was good of you."

He looked forlorn for a minute, perhaps regretting, stupid or wise, his choosing to keep their relationship chaste.

"Then," he said, smiling devilishly, "things got hairy. At midnight we headed south again. This car passed us then hit the brakes and did a U-ie. Came right after us. Morgan's men. I

turned off the highway and headed east over back roads. Man, what a drive! One-lane bridges, dirt roads. Zipping through small towns. Whoa, Frankie boy, I had four wheels treading air! It was fan-*tastic*. You should've seen it. There must've been twenty cars after us. I managed to lose 'em but I knew we couldn't get very far, the two of us. I figured we better split up.

"I knew that part of the state pretty good. Had a couple buddies in the service from Winston-Salem. We'd go hunting and stayed in this old, abandoned lodge near China Grove. Took some doing but I finally found the place.

"I pulled up and made sure it was empty. We sat in the car and I put my arm around her. I pulled her close and told her what I decided—that she should stay here. If her father got his hands on her, it'd be all over. He'd send her away for sure. Maybe even brainwash her. Don't laugh. Morgan'd do it. Even his own flesh and blood. She'd hide out here and I'd lead 'em off for a ways. Then . . ."

"Yes?"

"I'd wait for him."

"For Morgan? What were you going to do?"

"Have it out with him once and for all. One-on-one, him and me. Oh, I don't mean kill him. Just show him he wasn't king of the universe. Allison begged me not to. She knew how dangerous he was. But I didn't care. I knew he'd never leave us alone. He was the devil. He'd follow us forever if I didn't stop him. She begged me to take her with me but I knew I couldn't. She had to stay. It was so clear to me. See, Frank, that's what love is, I think. Not being afraid to make a decision for someone else."

Manko, the rough-hewn philosopher.

"I held her tight and told her not to worry. I told her how there wasn't enough room in my heart for all the love I felt for her. We'd be together again soon."

"Was it safe there, you think?"

"The cabin? Sure. Morgan'd never find it."

"It was in China Grove?"

"Half hour away. On Badin Lake."

I laughed. "You're kidding me?"

"You know it?"

"Sure I do. I used to go skinny-dipping there eons ago." I nodded that it was a good choice. "Hard to spot those cabins on the western shore."

"It's a damn pretty place too. You know, I was driving off and I looked back and I remember thinking how nice it'd be if that was our house and there Allison'd be in the doorway waiting for me to come home from work."

Manko rose and walked to the window. He gazed through his reflection into the wet night.

"After I left I drove to a state road. I pulled right in front of them and made like I was heading back to her, but really leading the hounds off, you know. But they caught me . . . man, everybody. Cops, the security boys . . . and Morgan himself.

"He stormed up to me, all pissed off, red in the face. He threatened me. And then he begged me to tell him where she was hiding. But I just looked back at him. I didn't say a word. And all his bucks, all his thugs . . . nothing. Money's power, sure, but so is love. I didn't even *have* to fight him. He looked me in the eyes and he knew that I'd won. His daughter loved me, not him. Allison was safe. We'd be together, the two of us. We'd beat Thomas Morgan—tycoon, rich son of a bitch, and father of the most beautiful woman on earth. He just turned around and walked back to his limo. End of story."

Silence fell between us. It was nearly midnight and I'd been here for over three hours. I stretched. Manko paced slowly, his face aglow with anticipation. "You know, Frank, a lot of my life hasn't gone the way I wanted it to. Allison's either. But one thing we've got is our love. That makes everything okay."

"A transcendent love."

A ping sounded and I realized that Manko'd touched his cup to mine once again. We emptied them. He looked out the window into the black night. The rain had stopped and a faint moon was evident through the clouds. A distant clock started striking twelve. He smiled. "Time to go meet her, Frank."

A solid rap struck the door, which swung open suddenly. I was startled and stood.

Manko turned calmly, the smile still on his face.

"Evening, Tim," said a man of about sixty. He wore a rumpled brown suit. From behind him several sets of eyes peered at Manko and me.

It rankled me slightly to hear the given name. Manko'd always made it clear that he preferred his nickname and considered the use of Tim or Timothy an insult. But tonight he didn't even notice; he smiled. There was silence for a moment as another man, wearing a pale blue uniform, stepped into the room with a tray, loaded it up with the dirty dishes.

"Enjoy it, Manko?" he asked, nodding at the tray.

"Ambrosia," he said, lifting a wry eyebrow toward me.

The older man nodded then took a blue-backed document from his suit jacket and opened it. There was a long pause. Then in a solemn Southern baritone he read, "Timothy Albert Mankowitz, in accordance with the sentence pronounced against you pursuant to your conviction for the kidnapping and murder of Allison Kimberly Morgan, I hereby serve upon you this death warrant issued by the governor of the State of North Carolina, to be effected at midnight this day."

The warden handed Manko the paper. He and his lawyer had already seen the faxed version from the court and tonight he merely glanced with boredom at the document. In his face I noted none of the stark befuddlement you almost always see in the faces of condemned prisoners as they read the last correspondence they'll ever receive.

"We got the line open to the governor, Tim," the warden drawled, "and he's at his desk. I just talked to him. But I don't think . . . I mean, he probably won't intervene."

"I told you all along." Manko said softly, "I didn't even want those appeals."

The execution operations officer, a thin, businesslike man who looked like a feed-and-grain clerk, cuffed Manko's wrists and removed his shoes.

The warden motioned me outside and I stepped into the corridor. Unlike the popular conception of a dismal, Gothic death row, this wing of the prison resembled an overly lit Sunday school hallway. His head leaned close. "Any luck, Father?"

I lifted my eyes from the shiny linoleum. "I think so. He told me about a cabin on Badin Lake. Western shore. You know it?"

The warden shook his head. "But we'll have the troopers get some dogs over there. Hope it pans out," he added, whispering, "Lord, I hope that."

So ended my grim task on this grim evening.

Prison chaplains always walk the last hundred feet with the condemned but rarely are they enlisted as a last-ditch means to wheedle information out of the prisoners. I'd consulted my bishop and this mission didn't seem to violate my vows. Still, it was clearly a deceit and one that would trouble me, I suspected, for a long time. Yet it would trouble me less than the thought of Allison Morgan's body lying in an unconsecrated grave, whose location Manko adamantly refused to reveal—his ultimate way, he said, of protecting her from her father.

Allison Kimberly Morgan—stalked relentlessly for months after she dumped Manko following their second date. Kidnapped from her bed then driven through four states with the FBI and a hundred troopers in pursuit. And finally . . . finally, when it was clear that Manko's precious plans for a life together in Florida would never happen, knifed to death while—apparently—he held her close and told her how there wasn't enough room in his heart for all the love he felt for her.

Until tonight her parents' only consolation was in knowing that she'd died quickly—her abundant blood in the front seat of his Dodge testified to that. Now there was at least the hope they could give her a proper burial and in doing so offer her a bit of the love that they may—or may not—have denied her in life.

Manko appeared in the hallway, wearing disposable paper slippers the condemned wear to the execution chamber. The warden looked at his watch and motioned him down the corridor. "You'll go peaceful, won't you, son?"

Manko laughed. He was the only one here with serenity in his eyes.

And why not?

He was about to join his own true love. They'd be together once again.

"You like my story, Frank?"

I told him I did. Then he smiled at me in a curious way, an expression that seemed to contain a hint both of forgiveness and of something I can only call the irrepressible Manko challenge. Perhaps, I reflected, it would not be this evening's deceit that would weigh on me so heavily but rather the simple fact that I would never know whether or not Manko was on to me.

But who could tell? He was, as I've said, a born actor.

The warden looked at me. "Father?"

I shook my head. "I'm afraid Manko's going to forgo absolution," I said. "But he'd like me to read him a few psalms."

"Allison," Manko said earnestly, "loves poetry."

I slipped the Bible from my suit pocket and began to read as we started down the corridor, walking side by side.

THE WIDOW
OF PINE CREEK

"Sometimes help just appears from the sky."

This was an expression of her mother's and it didn't mean angels or spirits or any of that New Age stuff but meant "from thin air"—when you were least expecting it.

Okay, Mama, let's hope. 'Cause I can use some help now. Can use it bad.

Sandra May DuMont leaned back in a black-leather office chair and let the papers in her hand drop onto the old desk that dominated her late husband's office. As she looked out the window she wondered if she was looking at that help right now.

Not exactly appearing from the sky—but walking up the cement path to the factory, in the form of a man with an easy smile and sharp eyes.

She turned away and caught sight of herself in the antique mirror she'd bought for her husband ten years ago, on their fifth anniversary. Today, she had only a brief memory of that happier day; what she concentrated on now was her image; a large woman, though not fat. Quick green eyes. She was wearing an off-white dress imprinted with blue cornflowers. Sleeveless—this *was* Georgia in mid May—revealing sturdy upper arms. Her long hair was dark blond and was pulled back and fixed with a matter-of-fact tortoiseshell barrette. Just a touch of makeup. No perfume. She was thirty-eight but, funny thing, she'd come to realize, her weight made her look younger.

By rights she should be feeling calm and self-assured. But she wasn't. Her eyes went to the papers in front of her again.

No, she wasn't feeling that way at all.

She needed help.

From the sky.

Or from anywhere.

The intercom buzzed, startling her, though she was expecting the sound. It was an old-fashioned unit, brown plastic, with a dozen buttons. It had taken her some time to figure out how it worked. She pushed a button. "Yes?"

"Mrs. DuMont, there's a Mr. Ralston here."

"Good. Send him in, Loretta."

The door opened and a man stepped inside. He said. "Hi, there."

"Hey," Sandra May responded as she stood automatically, recalling that in the rural South women rarely stood to greet men. And thinking too: How my life has changed in the last six months.

She noticed, as she had when she'd met him last weekend, that Bill Ralston wasn't really a handsome man. His face was angular, his black hair unruly, and though he was thin he didn't seem to be in particularly good shape.

And that accent! Last Sunday, as they'd stood on the deck of what passed for a country club in Pine Creek, he'd grinned and said, "How's it going? I'm Bill Ralston. I'm from New York."

As if the nasal tone in his voice hadn't told her already.

And "how's it going?" Well, that was hardly the sort of greeting you heard from the locals (the "Pine Creakers," Sandra May called them—though only to herself).

"Come on in," she said to him now. She walked over to the couch, gestured with an upturned palm for him to sit across from her. As she walked, Sandra May kept her eyes in the mirror, fo-

cused on his, and she observed that he never once glanced at her body. That was good, she thought. He passed the first test. He sat down and examined the office and the pictures on the wall, most of them of Jim on hunting and fishing trips.

She thought again of that day just before Halloween, the state trooper's voice on the other end of the phone, echoing with a sorrowful hollowness.

"Mrs. DuMont . . . I'm very sorry to tell you this. It's about your husband. . . ."

No, don't think about that now. Concentrate. You're in bad trouble, girl, and this might be the only person in the world who can help you.

Sandra May's first impulse was to get Ralston coffee or tea. But then she stopped herself. She was now president of the company and she had employees for that sort of thing. Old traditions die hard—more words from Sandra May's mother, who was proof incarnate of the adage.

"Would you like something? Sweet tea?"

He laughed. "You folks sure drink a lot of iced tea down here."

"That's the South for you."

"Sure. Love some."

She called Loretta, Jim's longtime secretary and the office manager.

The pretty woman—who must have spent two hours putting on her makeup every morning—stuck her head in the door. "Yes, Mrs. DuMont?"

"Could you bring us some iced tea, please?"

"Be happy to." The woman disappeared, leaving a cloud of flowery perfume behind. Ralston nodded after her. "Everybody's sure polite in Pine Creek. Takes a while for a New Yorker to get used to it."

"I'll tell you, Mr. Ralston—"

"Bill, please."

"Bill . . . It's second nature down here. Being polite. My mother said a person should put on their manners every morning the way they put on their clothes."

He smiled at the homily.

And speaking of clothes . . . Sandra May didn't know what to think of his. Bill Ralston was dressed . . . well, *Northern*. That was the only way to describe it. Black suit and a dark shirt. No tie. Just the opposite of Jim—who wore brown slacks, a powder-blue shirt and a tan sports coat as if the outfit were a mandatory uniform.

"That's your husband?" he asked, looking at the pictures on the wall.

"That's Jim, yes," she said softly.

"Nice-looking man. Can I ask what happened?"

She hesitated for a minute and Ralston picked up on it immediately.

"I'm sorry," he said, "I shouldn't've asked. It's—"

But she interrupted. "No, it's all right. I don't mind talking about it. A fishing accident last fall. At Billings Lake. He fell in, hit his head and drowned."

"Man, that's terrible. Were you on the trip when it happened?"

Laughing hollowly, she said, "I wish I had been, I could've saved him. But, no, I only went with him once or twice. Fishing's so . . . messy. You hook the poor thing, you hit it over the head with a club, you cut it up. . . . Besides, I guess you don't know the Southern protocol. Wives don't fish." She gazed up at some of the pictures. Said reflectively, "Jim was only forty-seven. I guess when you're married to someone and you think about them dying you think it'll happen when they're old. My mother died when she was eighty. And my father passed away when he was eighty-one. They were together for fifty-eight years."

"That's wonderful."

"Happy, faithful, devoted," she said wistfully.

Loretta brought the tea and vanished again with the demure exit of a discreet servant.

"So," he said. "I'm delighted the attractive woman I picked up so suavely actually gave me a call."

"You Northern boys are pretty straightforward, aren't you?"

"You betcha," he said.

"Well, I hope it's not going to be a blow to your ego when I tell you that I asked you here for a purpose."

"Depends on what that purpose is."

"Business," Sandra May said.

"Business is a good start," he said. Then he nodded for her to continue.

"I inherited all the stock in the company when Jim died and I became president. I've been trying to run the show best I can but the way I see it"—she nodded to where the accountant's reports sat on the desk—"unless things improve pretty damn fast we'll be bankrupt within the year. I got a bit of insurance money when Jim died so I'm not going to starve, but I refuse to let something my husband built up from scratch go under."

"Why do you think I can help you?" The smile was still there but it had less flirt than it had a few minutes ago—and a lot less than last Sunday.

"My mother had this saying. 'A Southern woman has to be a notch stronger than her man.' Well, I am *that*, I promise you."

"I can see," Ralston said.

"She also said, 'She has to be a notch more resourceful too.' And part of being resourceful is knowing your limitations. Now, before I married Jim I had three and a half years of college. But I'm in over my head here. I need somebody to help me. Somebody who knows about business. After what you were telling me on Sunday, at the club, I think you'd be just the man for that."

When they'd met—he'd explained that he was a banker and broker. He'd buy small, troubled businesses, turn them around and sell them for a profit. He'd been in Atlanta on business and somebody had recommended he look into real estate in northeast Georgia, here in the mountains, where you could still get good bargains on investment and vacation property.

"Tell me about the company," he said to her now.

She explained that DuMont Products Inc., with sixteen full-time employees and a gaggle of high school boys in the summer, bought crude turpentine from local foresters who tapped longleaf and slash pine trees for the substance.

"Turpentine . . . That's what I smelled driving up here."

After Jim had started the company some years ago Sandra May would lie in bed next to his sleeping form, smelling the oily resin—even if he'd showered. The scent had never seemed to leave him. Finally she'd gotten used to it. She sometimes wondered exactly when she'd stopped noticing the piquant aroma.

She continued, telling Ralston, "Then we distill the raw turpentine into a couple different products. Mostly for the medical market."

"Medical?" he asked, surprised. He took his jacket off and draped it carefully on the chair next to him. Drank more iced tea. He really seemed to enjoy it. She thought New Yorkers only drank wine and bottled water.

"People think it's just a paint thinner. But doctors use it a lot. It's a stimulant and antispasmodic."

"Didn't realize that," he said. She noticed that he'd started to take notes. And that the flirtatious smile was gone completely.

"Jim sells . . ." Her voice faded. "The company sells the refined turpentine to a couple of jobbers. They handle all the distribution. We don't get into that. Our sales seem to be the same as ever. Our costs haven't gone up. But we don't have as much money as we ought to. I don't know where it's gone and I have payroll taxes and unemployment insurance due next month."

She walked to the desk and handed him several accounting

statements. Even though they were a mystery to her he pored over them knowingly, nodding. Once or twice he lifted his eyebrow in surprise. She suppressed an urge to ask a troubled What?

Sandra May found herself studying him closely. Without the smile—and with this businesslike concentration on his face—he was much more attractive. Involuntarily she glanced at her wedding picture on the credenza. Then her eyes fled back to the documents in front of them.

Finally he sat back, finished his iced tea. "There's something funny," he said. "I don't understand it. There've been some transfers of cash out of the main accounts but there's no record of where the money went. Did your husband mention anything to you about it?"

"He didn't tell me very much about the company. Jim didn't mix business and his home life."

"How about your accountant?"

"Jim did most of the books himself. . . . This money? Can you track it down? Find out what happened? I'll pay whatever your standard fee is."

"I might be able to."

She heard a hesitancy in his voice. She glanced up.

He said, "Let me ask you a question first."

"Go ahead."

"Are you sure you *want* me to go digging?"

"How do you mean?" she asked.

His sharp eyes scanned the accounting sheets as if they were battlefield maps. "You know you could hire somebody to run the company. A professional businessman or woman. It'd be a hell of a lot less hassle for you. Let him or her turn the company around."

She kept her eyes on him. "But you're not asking me about hassles, are you?"

After a moment he said, "No, I'm not. I'm asking if you're sure you want to know anything more about your husband and his company than you do right now."

"But it's *my* company now," she said firmly. "And I want to know everything. Now, all the company's books are over there." She pointed to a large, walnut credenza. It was the piece of furniture atop which sat their wedding picture.

Do you promise to love, honor, cherish and obey . . .

As he turned to see where she was pointing, Ralston's knee brushed hers. Sandra May felt a brief electrical jolt. He seemed to freeze for a moment. Then he turned back.

"I'll start tomorrow," he said.

■

Three days later, with the evening orchestra of crickets and cicadas around her, Sandra May sat on the porch of their house. . . . No, *her* house. It was so strange to think of it that way. No longer *their* cars, *their* furniture, *their* china. Hers alone now.

Her desk, her company.

She rocked back and forth in the swing, which she'd installed a year ago, screwing the heavy hooks into the ceiling joists herself. She looked out over the acres of trim grass, boarded by loblolly and hemlock. Pine Creek, population sixteen hundred, had trailers and bungalows, shotgun apartment buildings and a couple of modest subdivisions but only a dozen or so houses like this—modern, glassy, huge. If the Georgia-Pacific had run through town, then the pristine development where Jim and Sandra May DuMont had settled would have defined which was the right side of the tracks.

She sipped her iced tea and smoothed her denim jumper. Watched the yellow flares from a half dozen early fireflies.

I think he's the one can help us, Mama, she thought.

Appearing from the sky . . .

Bill Ralston had been coming to the company every day since she'd met with him. He'd thrown himself into the job of saving DuMont Products Inc. When she'd left the office tonight at six he was still there, had been working since early morning, reading through the company's records and Jim's correspondence and diary. He'd called her at home a half hour ago, telling her he'd found some things she ought to know.

"Come on over," she'd told him.

"Be right there," he said. She gave him directions.

Now, as he parked in front of the house, she noticed shadows appear in the bay windows of houses across the street. Her neighbors, Beth and Sally, checking out the activity.

So, the widow's got a man friend come a-calling . . .

She heard the crunching on the gravel before she could see Ralston approach through the dusk.

"Hey," she said.

"You all really *do* say that down here," he said. " 'Hey.' "

"You bet. Only it's 'y'all.' Not 'you all.' "

"Stand corrected, ma'am."

"You Yankees."

Ralston sat down on the swing. He'd Southernized himself. Tonight he wore jeans and a work shirt. And, my Lord, boots. He looked like one of the boys at a roadside tap, escaping from the wife for the night to drink beer with his buddies and to flirt with girls pretty and playful as Loretta.

"Brought some wine," he said.

"Well. How 'bout that."

"I love your accent," he said.

"Hold on—*you're* the one with an accent."

In a thick mafioso drawl: "Yo, forgeddaboutit. I don't got no accent." They laughed. He pointed to the horizon. "Look at that moon."

"No cities around here, no lights. You can see the stars clear as your conscience."

He poured some wine. He'd brought paper cups and a corkscrew.

"Oh, hey, slow up there." Sandra May held up a hand. "I haven't had much to drink since . . . Well, after the accident I decided it'd be better if I kept a pretty tight rein on things."

"Just drink what you want," he assured her. "We'll water the geranium with the rest."

"That's a bougainvillea."

"Oh, I'm a city boy, remember." He tapped her cup with his. Drank some wine. In a soft voice he said, "It must've been really rough. About Jim, I mean."

She nodded, said nothing.

"Here's to better times."

"Better times," she said. They toasted and drank some more.

"Okay, I better tell you what I've found."

Sandra May took a deep breath then another sip of wine. "Go ahead."

"Your husband . . . well, to be honest with you? He was hiding money."

"Hiding?"

"Well, maybe that's too strong a word. Let's say putting it in places that'd be damn hard to trace. It looks like he was taking some of the profits from the company for the last couple of years and bought shares in some foreign corporations. . . . He never mentioned it to you?"

"No. I wouldn't have approved. Foreign companies? I don't even hold much with the U.S. stock market. I think people ought to keep their money in the bank. Or better yet under the bed. That was my mother's philosophy. She called it the First National Bank of Posturepedic."

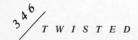

He laughed. Sandra May finished her wine. Ralston poured her some more.

"How much money was there?" she asked him.

"Two hundred thousand and some change."

She blinked. "Lord, I sure could use it. And soon. Is there any way to get it?"

"I think so. But he was real cagey, your husband."

"Cagey?" she drew the word out.

"He wanted to hide those assets bad. It'd be a lot easier to find if I knew why he did it."

"I don't have a clue." She lifted her hand and let it fall onto her solid thigh. "Maybe it's retirement money."

But Ralston was smiling.

"I say something silly?"

"A four-oh-one K is where you put retirement money. The Cayman Islands isn't."

"Is it illegal, what Jim did?"

"Not necessarily. But it might be." He emptied his cup. "You want me to keep going?"

"Yes," Sandra May said firmly. "Whatever it takes, whatever you find. I have to get that cash."

"Then I'll do it. But it's going to be complicated, real complicated. We'll have to file suits in Delaware, New York and the Cayman Islands. Can you be away from here for months at a time?"

A pause. "I could be. But I don't want to. This's my home."

"Well, you could give me power of attorney to handle it. But you don't know me that well."

"Let me think on that." Sandra May took the barrette out of her hair, let the blond strands fall free. She leaned her head back, looking up at the sky, the stars, the captivating moon, which was nearly full. She realized that she wasn't resting against the back of the porch swing at all but against Ralston's shoulder. She didn't move away.

Then the stars and the moon were gone, replaced by the darkness of his silhouette, and he was kissing her, his hand cradling the back of her head, then her neck, then sliding around to the front of her jumper and undoing the buttons that held the shoulder straps. She kissed him back, hard. His hand moved up to her throat and undid the top button of her blouse, which she wore fastened—the way, her mother told her, proper ladies should always do.

■

She lay in bed that night alone—Bill Ralston had left some hours before—and stared up at the ceiling.

The anxiety was back. The fear of losing everything.

Oh, Jim, what's going to happen? she thought to her husband, lying deep in the red clay of Pine Creek Memorial Gardens.

She thought back on her life—how it just hadn't turned out the way she'd planned. How she'd dropped out of Georgia State six months before she graduated to be with him. Thinking about how she gave up her own hopes of working in sales. About how they fell into a routine: Jim running the company while she entertained clients and volunteered at the hospital and the Women's Club and ran the household. Which was supposed to be a household full of children—that was what she'd hoped for anyway. But it never happened.

And now Sandra May DuMont was just a childless widow. . . .

That was how the people in Pine Creek looked at her. The town widow. They knew that the company would fail, that she'd move into one of those dreadful apartments on Sullivan Street and would just melt away, become part of the wallpaper of small-town Southern life. They thought no better of her than that.

But that wasn't going to happen to her.

No, ma'am . . . She could still meet someone and have a family. She was young. She could go to a different place, a big city, maybe—Atlanta, Charleston . . . hell, why not New York itself?

A Southern woman's got to be a notch stronger than her man. And a notch more resourceful too. . . .

She *would* get out of this mess.

Ralston could help her get out of it. She knew she'd done the right thing, picking him.

When she woke up the next morning Sandra May found her wrists were cramping; she'd fallen asleep with her hands clenched into fists.

It was two hours later, when she arrived in the office, that Loretta pulled her aside, gazed at her boss with frantic, black-mascaraed eyes and whispered, "I don't know how to tell you this, Mrs. DuMont, but I think he's going to rob you. Mr. Ralston, I mean."

■

"Tell me."

Frowning, Sandra May sat slowly in the high-backed leather chair. Looked again out the window.

"All right, see, what happened . . . what happened . . ."

"Calm down, Loretta. Tell me."

"See, after you left last night I started to bring some papers into your office and I heard him on the phone."

"Who was he talking to?"

"I don't know. But I looked inside and saw that he was using his cell phone, not the office phone, like he usually does. I figured he used that phone so we wouldn't have a record of who he called."

"Let's not jump to conclusions. What did he say?" Sandra May asked.

"He said he was pretty close to finding everything. But it was going to be a problem to get away with it."

" 'Get away with it.' He said that?"

"Yes, ma'am. Right, right, right. Then he said some stock or something was all held by the company, not by 'her personally.' And that could be a problem. Those were his words."

"Then what?"

"Oh, then I kind of bumped into the door and he heard and hung up real quick. Seemed to me, at any rate."

"That doesn't mean he's going to rob us," Sandra May said. " 'Get away with it.' Maybe that just means get the money out of the foreign companies. Or maybe he's talking about something else altogether."

"Sure, maybe it does, Mrs. DuMont. But he was acting like a spooked squirrel when I came into the room." Then Loretta brushed one of her long, purple nails across her chin. "How well do you know him?"

"Not well. . . . Are you thinking that he somehow arranged this whole thing?" Sandra May shook her head. "Couldn't be. I called *him* to help us out."

"But how did you find him?"

Sandra May grew quiet. Then she said, "He met me . . . Well, he picked me up. Sort of. At the Pine Creek Club."

"And he told you he was in business."

She nodded.

"So," Loretta pointed out, "he might've heard that you'd inherited the company and went there on purpose to meet you. Or maybe he was one of the people Mr. DuMont was in business with—doing something that wasn't quite right. What you were telling me?—about those foreign companies."

"I don't believe it," Sandra May protested. "No, I can't believe it."

She looked into her assistant's face, which was pretty and demure, yes, but also savvy. Loretta said, "Maybe he looks for people who're having trouble running businesses and moves in and, bang, cleans 'em out."

Sandra May shook her head.

"I'm not saying for sure, Mrs. DuMont. I just worry about you. I don't want anybody to take advantage of you. And we all here . . . well, we can't hardly afford to lose our jobs."

"I'm not going to be some timid widow who's afraid of the dark."

"This might not be just a shadow," Loretta said.

"I've talked to the man, I've looked into his eyes, honey," Sandra May said. "I reckon I'm as good a judge of character as my mama was."

"I hope you are, ma'am. For all our sakes. I hope you are."

Sandra May's eyes scanned the office again, the pictures of her husband with the fish and game he'd bagged, the pictures of the company in the early days, the groundbreaking for the new factory, Jim at the Rotary Club, Jim and Sandra May on the company float at the county fair.

Their wedding picture . . .

Honey, don't you worry your pretty little head about anything I'll take care of it everything'll be fine don't worry don't worry don't worry . . .

The words her husband had said to her a thousand times echoed in her head. Sandra May sat down in the office chair once more.

■

The next day Sandra May found Bill Ralston in the office, hunched over an accounting book.

She set a piece of paper in front of him.

He lifted it, frowning.

"What's this?"

"The power of attorney you were talking about. It gives you the authority to find our money, file suit, vote the company's shares—everything. . . ." She laughed. "I must say I was having some doubts about you for a bit."

"Because I'm from New York?" He smiled.

"That War of Northern Aggression, why, it *does* rear its ugly head sometimes. . . . But, no, I'll tell you why I'm giving it to you. Because a widow can't afford to be afraid of her own shadow. People see that and they sense blood in the water and next thing you know, it's good-bye. No, no, I looked you in the eye and I said to myself, I trust him. So now I'm putting my money where my mouth is. Or, should I say, my *husband's* money. The hidden variety." She looked at the document. "Before Jim's accident I would've run to him with a problem. And before Jim I would've run to my mother. I wouldn't've made any decisions. But I'm on my own now and I have to make my own choices. One of those choices was hiring you and trusting you. This is something I'm doing for *me*. Now, use that and find the money and get it back."

He read the power of attorney carefully once more, noted the signature. "It's irrevocable. You can't withdraw it."

"The lawyer said a revocable one is useless for tracing money and filing suits if you need to."

"Good." He gave her another smile . . . but it was different from earlier. There was a coldness to his expression. And even a hint of triumph—like you'd see on the face of a redneck Pine Creek High tackle. "Ah, Sandy, Sandy, Sandy—I'll tell you, I thought it'd take months."

She frowned. "Months?"

"Yes'm. To get control of the company, I'm talking about."

"Get control?" She stared at him. Her breathing was fast. "What're you . . . what're you saying?"

"It could've been a nightmare—and the worst part was I'd have to stay in this hellhole of a town for who knew how long. . . . Pine Creek . . ." He put on a hillbilly accent as he said sarcastically, "Lord above, how do *y'all* keep from going stark, raving mad here?"

"What are you talking about," she whispered.

"Sandy, the whole point of this was to get your company." He tapped the power of attorney. "I'll vote myself in as president, pay myself a nice, big salary and bonus, then sell the place. You'll make some money—don't worry. You're still the owner of the stock. Oh, and don't worry about that hidden money. It wasn't hidden at all. Your husband put some company money into overseas investments, like a million other businessmen last year. He got hurt a little when the market dipped. No big deal. It'll come back. You were never even close to bankruptcy."

"Why . . ." She gasped. "You goddamn bastard! This's fraud!" She reached for the power of attorney but he pushed her hand away.

Ralston shook his head sadly then he paused, frowning. He noticed that the rage on Sandra May's face had turned to amusement. Then she started laughing.

"What?" he asked uncertainly.

She stepped toward him. Ralston grabbed the power of attorney and eased back warily.

"Oh, relax, I'm not going to slap you upside the head—even though I ought to." Sandra May leaned past him and pushed the intercom button.

"Yes?" came the woman's voice.

"Loretta, could you come in here, please?"

"Sure, Mrs. DuMont."

Loretta appeared in the doorway. Sandra May's eyes were still on Ralston's. She said, "That power of attorney gives you the right to vote all my shares. Right?"

He glanced at his jacket pocket, where the document now rested. He nodded.

Sandra May continued, speaking to Loretta. "How many shares in the company do I own?"

"None, Mrs. DuMont."

"*What?*" Ralston asked.

Sandra May said, "We thought you were trying to pull something. So we had to test you. I talked to my lawyer. He said I could transfer my shares to somebody I trusted so that I didn't hold any of them. Then I'd sign the power of attorney, give it to you and see what you did. And I sure learned that fast enough—you planned to rob me blind. It was a test—and you failed, sir."

"Goddamn it. You transferred the shares?"

She laughed and nodded to Loretta. "Yep. To somebody I could trust. I don't own a bit. That power of attorney is useless. She owns a hundred percent of DuMont Products Inc."

But Ralston's shock vanished. He began to smile.

The explanation for his good mood came not from him but from Loretta. She said, "Now you listen here. You'll never guess. Bill *and* I own a hundred percent of the company. Sorry, honey." And she walked forward and put her arm around Ralston. "I don't think we mentioned it but Bill's my brother."

■

"You were in it together!" Sandra May whispered. "The two of you."

"Jim died and didn't leave me a penny!" Loretta snapped. "You *owe* me that money."

"Why would Jim leave *you* anything?" Sandra May asked uncertainly. "Why would . . ." But her voice faded as she looked at the knowing smile on the thin woman's face.

"You and my husband?" Sandra May gasped. "You were *seeing* each other?"

"For the last three years, honey. You never noticed that we were out of town at the same time? That we'd both work late the same nights? Jim was putting money away for *me*!" Loretta spat out. "He just never had a chance to give it to me before he died."

Sandra May stumbled backward, collapsed onto the couch. "The stock . . . Why, I trusted you," she muttered. "The lawyer asked who could I trust and you were the first person I thought of!"

"Just like I trusted Jim," Loretta snapped back. "He kept saying he'd give it to me, he'd open an account for me, I could travel, he'd get me a nice house. . . . But then he died and didn't leave me a penny. I waited a few months then called Bill up in New York. I told him all about you and the company. I knew you were going to Pine Creek Club on Sunday. We figured he should come on down and introduce himself to the poor widow."

"But your last name, it's different," she said to Ralston, picking up one of his business cards and glancing at Loretta.

"Hey, not that hard to figure out," he said, lifting his palms. "It's fake." He laughed. As if this were too obvious to even mention.

"When we sell the company, honey, you'll get *something*," Loretta said. "Don't you fret 'bout that. In recognition of your last six months as president. Now, why don't you just head on home? Oh, hey, you don't mind if I don't call you Mrs. DuMont anymore, do you, Sandy? I really hated—"

The office door swung open

"Sandra May . . . you all right?" A large man stood in the

doorway. Beau Ogden, the county sheriff. His hand was on his pistol.

"I'm fine," she told him.

He eyed Ralston and Loretta, who stared at him uneasily. "These them?"

"That's right."

"I come as soon as I got your call."

Ralston was frowning. "What call?"

Ogden warned, "Just keep your hands where I can see them."

"What the hell're you talking about?" Ralston asked.

"I'd ask you to keep a respectful voice, sir. You don't want to go making your problems any worse than they already are."

"Officer," Loretta said, sounding completely calm, "we've been doing some business dealings here and that's all. Everything's on the up-and-up. We got contracts and papers and everything. Mrs. DuMont sold me the company for ten dollars 'cause it's in debt and she thought me and my brother here could turn it around. Me knowing the company as good as I do since I worked for her husband for so many years. Her own lawyer did the deal. We're going to pay her a settlement as a former employee."

"Yeah, whatever," Ogden said absently; his attention was on a young, crew-cut deputy entering the office. "It matches," he told the sheriff.

Ogden nodded toward Loretta and Ralston. "Cuff 'em both."

"You bet, Beau."

"Cuff us! We haven't done anything!"

Ogden sat on the chair beside Sandra May. He said solemnly, "We found it. Wasn't in the woods, though. Was under Loretta's back porch."

Sandra May shook her head sadly. Snagged a Kleenex and wiped her eyes.

"Found what?" Ralston snapped.

"May as well 'fess up, both of you. We know the whole story."

"What story?" Loretta barked at Sandra May.

She took a deep breath. Finally she struggled to answer, "I knew something wasn't right. I figured out you two were trying to cheat me—"

"And her a poor widow," Ogden muttered. "Shameful."

"So I called Beau before I got to work this morning. Told him what I suspected."

"Sheriff," Loretta continued patiently, "you're making a big mistake. She voluntarily transferred the stock to me. There was no fraud, there was no—"

The sheriff held up an impatient hand. "Loretta, you're being arrested for what you did to Jim, not for fraud or some such."

"Did to Jim?" Ralston looked at his sister, who shook her head and asked, "What's going on here?"

"You're under arrest for the murder of Jim DuMont."

"I didn't murder anybody!" Ralston spat out.

"No, but she did." Ogden nodded at Loretta. "And that makes you an accomplice and probably guilty of conspiracy too."

"No!" Loretta screamed. "I didn't."

"A fella owns a cabin on Lake Billings come forward a couple weeks ago and says he saw a woman with Mr. DuMont on that fishing trip of his back around Halloween. He couldn't see too clear but he said it looked like she was holding this club or branch. This fella didn't think nothing of it and left town for a spell. Soon's he comes back—last month—he hears about Jim dying and gives me a call. I checked with the coroner and he said that Mr. DuMont might not've hit his head when he fell. Maybe he was hit by somebody and shoved in the water. So I reopened the case as a murder investigation. We've been checking witnesses and forensics for the past month and decided it definitely looks like murder but we can't find the weapon. Then Mrs. DuMont calls me this morning about you two and this scam and everything. Seemed like a good motive to murder somebody. I got the magistrate to issue a search warrant. That's what we found under your porch, Loretta: the billy club Mr. DuMont used to kill fish with. It had his blood and hairs on it. Oh, and I found the gloves you worn when you hit him. Ladies' gloves. Right stylish too."

"No! I didn't do it! I swear."

"Read 'em their rights, Mike. Do a good job of it too. Don't want no loopholes. And get 'em outa here."

Ralston shouted, "I didn't do it!"

As the deputy did as instructed and, one by one, led them out, Sheriff Ogden said to Sandra May, "Funny how they all say that. Broken record. 'Didn't do it, didn't do it.' Now I'm truly sorry about all this, Sandra May. Tough enough being newly widowed but to have to go through all this nonsense too."

"That's okay, Beau," Sandra May said, demurely wiping her eyes with a Kleenex.

"We'll be wanting to take a statement but there's no hurry on that."

"Anytime you say, Sheriff," she said firmly. "I want those people to go away for a long, long time."

"We'll make sure that happens. Good day to you now."

When the sheriff had left, Sandra May stood by herself for a long moment, looking at the photo of her husband taken a few years earlier. He was holding up a large bass he'd caught—probably in Billings Lake. Then she walked into the outer office, opened the mini refrigerator and poured herself a glass of sweet tea.

Returning to Jim's, no, *her* office, she sat down in the leather chair and spun slowly, listening to the now-familiar squeak of the mechanism.

Thinking: Well, Sheriff, you were almost right.

There was only one little variation in the story.

Which was that Sandra May had known all along about Jim's affair with Loretta. She'd gotten used to the smell of turpentine on her husband's skin but never used to the stink of the woman's trailer-trash perfume, which hung like a cloud of bug spray around him as he climbed into bed too tired even to kiss her. ("A man doesn't want you three times a week, Sandra, you better start wondering why." Thanks, Mama.)

And so when Jim DuMont drove off to Billings Lake last October, Sandra May followed and confronted him about Loretta. And when he admitted it she said, "Thank you for not lying," took the billy club and crushed his skull with a single blow then kicked him into the frigid water.

She'd thought that would be the end of it. The death was ruled accidental and everybody forgot about the case—until that man at Billings Lake had come forward and reported seeing a woman with Jim just before he'd died. Sandra May knew it was only a matter of time until they tracked her down for the murder.

The threat of a life sentence—not the condition of the company—was the terrible predicament she'd found herself in, the predicament for which she was praying for help "from the sky." (As for the company? Who cared? The "bit of insurance money" totaled nearly a million dollars. To get away with that, she would've gladly watched DuMont Products Inc. go bankrupt and given up the money Jim had socked away for his scrawny slut.) How could she save herself from prison? But then Ralston gave her the answer when he'd picked her up. He was too slick. She'd sensed a scam and it didn't take much digging to find the connection to Loretta. She figured they were planning to get the company away from her.

And so she'd come up with a plan of her own.

Sandra May now opened the bottom drawer of the desk and

took out a bottle of small-batch Kentucky bourbon and poured a good three fingers' worth into the iced tea. She sat back in her husband's former chair, now hers exclusively, and gazed out the window at a stand of tall, dark pine trees bending in the wind as a spring storm moved in.

Thinking to Ralston and Loretta: Never did tell you the rest of Mama's expression, did I?

"Honey," the old woman had told her daughter, "a Southern woman has to be a notch stronger than her man. And she's got to be a notch more resourceful too. And, just between you and me, a notch more conniving. Whatever you do, don't forget that part."

Sandra May DuMont took a long drink of iced tea and picked up the phone to call a travel agent.

THE KNEELING SOLDIER

"**H**e's out there? Again?"

A dish fell to the tile kitchen floor and shattered.

"Gwen, go down to the rec room. Now."

"But, Daddy," she whispered, "how can he be? They said six months. They *promised* six months. At least!"

He peered through the curtains, squinting, and his heart sank. "It's him." He sighed. "It's him. Gwen, do what I told you. The rec room. Now." Then he shouted into the dining room, "Doris!"

His wife hurried into the kitchen. "What is it?"

"He's back. Call the police."

"He's *back*?" the woman muttered in a grim voice.

"Just do it. And Gwen, I don't want him to see you. Go downstairs. I'm not going to tell you again."

Doris lifted the phone and called the sheriff's office. She only had to hit one button; they'd put the number on the speed dialer ages ago.

Ron stepped to the back porch and looked outside.

The hours after dinner, on a cool springtime evening like this, were the most peaceful moments of the year in Locust Grove. The suburb was a comforting thirty-two miles from New York City, on the North Shore of Long Island. Some truly wealthy folk lived here—new money as well as some Rockefeller and Morgan hand-me-downs. Then there were the aspiring rich and a few popular artists, some ad agency CEOs. Mostly, though, the village was made up of people like the Ashberrys. Living comfortably in their six-hundred-thousand-dollar houses, commuting on the LIRR or driving to their management jobs at publishing or computer companies on Long Island.

This April evening found the dogwoods in bloom and the fragrance of mulch and the first-cut grass of the year filling the misty air. And it found the brooding form of young Harle Ebbers crouching in the bushes across the street from Ron Ashberry's house, staring into the bedroom window of sixteen-year-old Gwen.

Oh, dear Lord, Ron thought hopelessly. Not again. It's not starting again. . . .

Doris handed the cordless phone to her husband and he asked for Sheriff Hanlon. As he waited to be connected, he inhaled the stale, metallic scent of the porch screen he rested his head against. He looked across his yard, forty yards, to the bush that had become a fixture in his daydreams and the focus of his nightmares.

It was a juniper, about six feet long and three high, gracing a small municipal park. It was beside this languorous bush that twenty-year-old Harle Ebbers had spent much of the last eight months, in his peculiar crouch, stalking Gwen.

"How d'he get out?" Doris wondered.

"I don't see what good it'll do," Gwen said from the kitchen, panic in her voice, "to call the police. He'll be gone before they get here. He always is."

"Go downstairs!" Ron called. "Don't let him see you."

The thin blonde girl, her face as beautiful as Lladro porcelain, backed away. "I'm scared."

Doris, a tall, muscular woman exuding the confidence of the competitive athlete she'd been in her twenties, put her arm around her daughter. "Don't worry, honey. Your father and I are here. He's not going to hurt you. You hear me?"

The girl nodded uncertainly and vanished down the stairs.

Ron Ashberry kept his gaze coldly fixed on the figure next to the bush.

It was a cruel irony that this tragedy had happened to Gwen.

Conservative by nature, Ron had always been horrified by the neglect he saw on the part of families in the city to which he commuted every day. Absent fathers, crack-addict mothers, guns and gangs, little girls turning to prostitution. He vowed that nothing bad would ever happen to his daughter. His plan was simple: he'd protect Gwen, raise her the right way, teach her good moral values, family values—which, thank God, people had started talking about again. He'd keep her close to home, insist that she get good grades, learn sports, music and social skills.

Then, when she turned eighteen, he'd give her freedom. She'd be old enough then to make the correct decisions—about boys, about careers, about money. She'd go to an Ivy League college and then return to the North Shore for marriage or a career. This was serious work, hard work, this child rearing. But Ron was seeing the results of his efforts. Gwen had scored in the ninety-ninth percentile on the PSATs. She never talked back to adults; her coaches reported she was one of the best athletes they'd ever worked with; she never snuck cigarettes or liquor, never whined when Ron told her no driver's license until she was eighteen. She understood how much he loved her and why he wouldn't let her go into Manhattan with her girlfriends or spend the weekend on Fire Island unchaperoned.

And so he felt it was utterly unfair that Harle Ebbers picked his daughter to stalk.

It had begun last fall. One evening Gwen had been particularly quiet throughout the evening meal. When Ron had asked her to go pick a book out of his library so he could read it aloud, Gwen just stood at the kitchen window, staring outside.

"Gwen, are you listening to me? I asked you to get me a book."

She'd turned and to his shock he saw she was crying.

"Honey, I'm sorry," Ron'd said automatically and stepped forward to put his arm around her. He knew the problem. Several days ago she'd asked if she could take a trip to Washington, D.C., with two teachers and six of the girls and boys from her social studies class. Ron had considered letting her go. But then he'd checked out the group and found that two of the girls had discipline problems—they'd been found drinking in a park near the school last summer. He'd told Gwen she couldn't go and she'd seemed disappointed. He'd assumed this was what troubled her today. "I wish I could let you go, Gwen—" he'd said.

"Oh, no. Daddy, it's not that stupid trip. I don't care about that. It's something else. . . ."

She'd fallen into his arms, sobbing. He was filled with overwhelming parental love. And an unbearable agony for her pain. "What is it, honey? Tell me. You can tell me anything."

She'd glanced out the window.

Following her gaze, he'd seen, in the park across the street, a figure crouching in the bushes.

"Oh, Daddy, he's following me."

Horrified, Ron had led her to the living room, calling out, "Doris, we're having a family conference! Come in here! Now!" He'd gestured his wife into the room then sat next to Gwen. "What is it, baby? Tell us."

Ron preferred that Doris pick up Gwen at school. But occasionally, if his wife was busy, he let Gwen walk home. There were no bad neighborhoods in Locust Grove, certainly not along the trim, manicured route to the high school—the greatest threats were usually aesthetic: a cheap bungalow or a flock of plastic flamingos, herds of plaster Bambis.

Or so Ron had believed.

That autumn night Gwen had sat with her hands in her lap, staring at the floor, and explained in a meek voice, "I was walking home today, okay? And there was this guy."

Ron's heart had gone cold, hands shaking, anger growing within him.

"Tell us," Doris had said. "What happened?"

"Nothing happened. Not like that. He just like started to talk to me. He's going, 'You're so pretty. I'll bet you're smart. Where do you live?' "

"Did he know you?"

"I don't think so. He acted all funny. Like he was sort of retarded, you know. Kind of saying things that didn't make sense. I told him you didn't want me to talk to strangers and I ran home."

"Oh, you poor thing." Her mother embraced her.

"I didn't think he followed me. But . . ." She bit her lip. "But that's him."

Ron had jogged toward the bush where he'd seen the young man. He was in a curious pose. It reminded Ron of one of those green plastic soldiers he'd buy when he was a kid. The kneeling soldier, aiming his rifle.

The boy saw Ron coming and fled.

The sheriff's office knew all about the boy. Harle's parents had moved to Locust Grove a few months before, virtually driven out of Ridgeford, Connecticut, because their son had targeted a young blonde, about Gwen's age, and had begun following her. The boy was of average intelligence but had suffered psychotic episodes when younger. The police hadn't been able to stop him because he'd only hurt one person in all his months of stalking—the girl's brother had attacked him. Harle had nearly beaten the boy to death but all charges were dropped on the grounds of self-defense.

The Ebbers family had at last fled the state, hoping to start over fresh.

But the only change was that Harle had found himself a new victim: Gwen.

The boy had fallen into his obsessive vigil: staring into Gwen's classrooms at school and kneeling beside the juniper bush, keeping his eyes glued to the girl's bedroom.

Ron had tried to get a restraining order but, without any illegal conduct on Harle's part, the magistrate couldn't issue one.

Finally, after Harle had stationed himself beside the juniper bush for six nights straight, Ron stormed into the state mental health department and demanded that something be done. The department had implored the boy's parents to send him to a private-care hospital for six months. The county would pay ninety percent of the fee. The Ebbers agreed and, under an involuntary commitment order, the boy was taken off to Garden City.

But now he was back, kneeling like a soldier beside the infamous juniper bush, only one week after the ambulance had carted him off.

Finally Sheriff Hanlon came on the line.

"Ron, I was going to call you."

"You knew about him?" Ron shouted. "Why the hell didn't you tell us? He's out there right now."

"I just found out about it myself. The boy talked to a shrink at the hospital. Apparently he gave the right answers and they decided to release him. Keeping him any longer on a dicey order like that, there was a risk of liability for the county."

"What about liability for my daughter?" Ron spat out.

"There'll be a hearing in a few weeks but they can't keep him in the hospital till then. Probably not after the hearing either, the way it's shaking out."

Tonight as mist settled on the town of Locust Grove, this

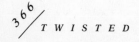

beautiful spring night, crickets chirped like greaseless gears, and Harle Ebbers was frozen in his familiar pose, dark eyes searching for a delicate young girl whose father happened to be deciding at that moment that this couldn't go on any longer.

"Look, Ron," the sheriff said sympathetically, "I know it's tough. But—"

Ron slammed the phone into the cradle, nearly tearing it from the wall.

"Honey," Doris began. He ignored her and as he started for the door she took his arm. She was a strong woman. But Ron was stronger and he pulled away brusquely. Pushed open the screen door and started across the dewy lawn to the park.

To his surprise, and pleasure, Harle didn't flee. He stood up out of his crouching position and crossed his arms, waiting for Ron to approach.

Ron was athletic. He played tennis and golf and he swam like a dolphin. One hundred laps a day when the country club pool was open. He was slightly shorter than Harle but, as he gazed at the boy's prominent eyebrows and disturbingly deep-set eyes, he knew in his heart that he could kill the young man. With his bare hands if he had to. All he needed was the slightest provocation.

"Daddy, no!" Gwen screamed from the porch, her voice like a high violin note, resonating through the mist. "Don't get hurt. It's not worth it!"

Ron turned back, hissed to his girl, "Get back inside!"

Harle was waving toward the house, "Gwennie, Gweenie, Gwennie . . ." a frightening grin on his face.

Neighbors' lights came on, faces appeared in windows and doorways.

Perfect, Ron thought. He makes the least gesture toward me and I'll kill him. A dozen witnesses'll back me up. He stopped two feet from Harle, on whose face the grin had fallen away. "I got sprung. They couldn't make it stick, could they? Make it stick, make it stick, couldn't make it stick. So I. Got. Sprung."

"You listen to me," Ron muttered, fists balling at his side. "You're real close. You know what I mean? I don't care if they arrest me, I don't care if they execute me. You don't leave her alone, I'm going to kill you. Understand?"

"I love my Gwennie, I love her, love her, loveher, loveher, lover, loverloverlover. She loves me, I love her she loves me I love she loves I love she loves she loves sheloves shelovessheloves-shelovessssss . . ."

"Come on. Take a swing at me. Come on. Coward! Haven't got the guts to mix it up like a grown-up, right? You make me sick."

Harle uncrossed his arms.

Okay, here it comes . . .

Ron's heart flexed and an ocean crashed in his ears. He could feel the chill adrenaline race through his body like an electric current.

The boy turned and ran.

Son of a bitch . . .

"Come back here!"

He was racing down the street on his lanky legs, disappearing into the misty dusk, Ron close behind him.

For a few blocks.

Athletic, yes, but a forty-three-year-old's body doesn't have the stamina of someone's half that age and after a quarter mile the boy pulled ahead and disappeared.

Winded, his side cramping fiercely from the run, Ron trotted back to the house, climbed into his Lexus. Gasping, he shouted, "Doris! You and Gwen stay here, lock the doors. I'm going to find him."

She protested but he ignored her and sped out of the drive.

A half hour later, having cruised through the entire neighborhood and finding no sign of the boy, he returned home.

To find his daughter in tears.

Doris and Gwen sat in the living room, the shades down and curtains drawn. Doris held a long kitchen knife in her strong fingers.

"What?" Ron demanded. "What's going on?"

Doris said, "Tell your father."

"Oh, Daddy, I'm sorry. I thought it was best."

"What?" Ron strode forward, dropping onto the couch, gripping his daughter by her shoulders. "Tell me!" he cried.

"He came back," Gwen said. "He was by the bush. And I went out to talk to him."

"You did what? Are you crazy?" Ron shouted, shaking with rage and fear at what might have happened.

Doris said, "I couldn't stop her. I tried, but—"

"I was afraid for you. I was afraid he'd hurt you. I thought maybe I could be nice to him and ask him please just to go away."

Despite his horror, a burst of pride at her courage popped inside of Ron Ashberry.

"What happened?" he asked.

"Oh, Daddy, it was terrible."

The feeling of pride faded and he sat back, staring at his daughter's white face. Ron whispered, "Did he touch you?"

"No . . . not yet."

"What do you mean, 'yet'?" Ron barked.

"He said . . ." Her tearful face looked from her father's furious eyes to her mother's determined ones. "He said that when it's the next full moon, that's when women get a certain way because of their, you know, monthly thing. The next full moon, he's going to find me wherever I am . . ." Her face grew red in shame. She swallowed. "I can't say it, Daddy. I can't tell you what he said he'd do."

"My God."

"I got so scared, I ran back to the house."

Doris, her strong-jawed face turned toward the window, added, "And he just stood there, staring at us, kind of singing in this sick voice. We locked the doors right away." She nodded at the knife, setting it on the table. "I got that from the kitchen just in case."

She loves me, I love her she loves me I love she loves I love she loves she loves . . .

His wife continued. "Then you came back and when he saw the car lights he ran off. It looked like he was headed toward his folks' house."

Ron grabbed the phone, hit the speed dial.

"This is Ron Ashberry," he said to the police dispatcher.

"Yessir, is it the boy again?" she asked.

"Hanlon. Now."

A pause. "Hold, please."

The sheriff came on the line. "Ron, what the hell's going on tonight? I've had four calls from your neighbors about this thing, shouting, people running around."

Ron explained about the threats.

"It's still just words, Ron."

"Goddamn it, I don't care about the law! He said the night of the full moon he's going to rape my little girl. What the hell do you people want?"

"When's the full moon?"

"I don't know, how would I know?"

"Hold on a second. I've got an almanac. . . . Here we go. It's next week. We'll have somebody at your house all day. If he makes a move, we'll get him."

"For what? Trespass? And he'll be out in, what, a week?"

"I'm sorry, Ron. It's the law."

"You know what you and your law can do? You can go straight to hell."

"Ron, I've told you before, if you take things into your own hands, you're going to be in serious trouble. Now good night to you."

Ron jammed the phone into the cradle hard again and this time it flew from the wall fixture.

He shouted to Doris, "Stay here. Keep the doors locked."

"Ron, what are you going to do?"

"Daddy, no . . ."

The door slammed so hard a pane cracked and the fissure lines made a perfect spiderweb.

■

Ron parked on the lawn, narrowly missing a rusting Camaro and a station wagon, lime green except for the front fender, which was the matte color of dried-blood-brown primer.

Pounding on the scabby door, he shouted, "I want to see him. Open up!"

Finally the door swung open and Ron stepped inside. The bungalow was small and it was a mess. Food, dirty plastic plates, beer cans, piles of clothes, magazines, newspapers. A strong animal pee smell too.

He pushed past the diminutive, chubby couple, both wearing jeans and T-shirts. In their late thirties.

"Mr. Ashberry," the man said uneasily, looking at his wife.

"Is your son here?"

"We don't know. Listen, sir, we had nothing to do with him getting out of that hospital. We was all for keeping him there, as I think you know."

"What do you mean you don't know where he is?"

"He comes and goes," his wife said. "Through his bedroom window. Sometimes we don't see him for days."

"Ever try discipline? Ever try a belt? What is it, you think children should walk all over you?"

The father gave a mournful laugh.

His wife said, "Has he done something else?"

As if what the boy had done wasn't enough. "Oh, he's just threatening to rape her, that's all."

"Oh, no, no." She clutched her hands together, fingers dirty and bedecked with cheap rings. "But it's just talk," the woman blurted. "It's always just talk, with him."

Ron whirled to face her. Her short black hair was badly in need of a wash and she smelled of sour onions. He muttered, "It's gone past the talk stage and I'm not going to put up with it. I want to see him."

They glanced at each other and the father led him down a dark corridor toward one of two bedrooms. Something—old food, it seemed—crunched under Ron's feet. The man looked over his shoulder, saw his wife standing in the living room and said, "I'm so sorry for all this, sir. I truly am. I wish I had it in my heart to, you know, make him go away."

"We tried that," Ron said cynically.

"I don't mean a hospital or jail." His voice fell to a whisper. "To go away forever. You know what I mean. I've thought about it some. She has too but she doesn't say it. Being his mother and all. One night I almost done it. When he was asleep." He paused and caressed a crater in the Sheetrock, made by a fist, it seemed. "I wasn't strong enough. I wished I was. But I couldn't do it."

His wife joined them and he fell silent. The father knocked timidly on the door and when there was no response he shrugged. "Ain't much we can do. He keeps it locked and won't give us a key."

"Oh, for God's sake." Ron stepped back and slammed his foot into the door.

"No!" the mother cried. "He'll be mad. Don't—"

The door crashed open and Ron stepped inside, flicking on the light. He stopped, astonished.

In contrast to the rest of the house, Harle's room was immaculate.

The bed was made and the blankets were taut as a buck private's. The desktop ordered and polished. The rug vacuumed. Bookshelves neat, and all the books were alphabetized.

"He does it himself," Harle's mother said with a splinter of pride. "Cleans up. See, he's not really so bad—"

"Not really so bad? Are you out of your mind? Look at that! Just look!"

On the walls were posters from World War Two movies, Nazi paraphernalia, swastikas, bones. A bayonet dangled from one wall. A miniature samurai sword sat on a footlocker. One poster was a comic book scene of a man with knives for feet, ripping apart an opponent he was fighting. Blood sprayed in the air.

Three pairs of spit-polished combat boots sat by the bedside. A tape, *The Faces of Death,* sat on the VCR, attached to a spotless television.

Ron reached for the door to the closet.

"No," his mother said firmly. "Not there. He don't let us go in there. We're never supposed to do that!"

The double door too was locked but with one yank Ron ripped the panels open, nearly wrenching them off the hinges.

Gruesome toys, monsters and vampires, characters from horror films, fell out. Rubber mock-ups of severed limbs, taxidermied animals, a snake's skeleton, Freddy Krueger posters.

And in the center of the closet floor was the main attraction: an altar dedicated to Gwen Ashberry.

Ron cried out in horror as he dropped to his knees, staring at the frightening tableau. Several photographs of Gwen were pinned to the wall. Harle must have taken them on the days when she walked home from school by herself. In two of the snapshots she was strolling obliviously along the sidewalk. In the third she was turning and smiling off into the distance. And in the fourth— the one that struck him like a fist—she was bending down to tie her shoe, her short skirt hiked high on her trim legs. This was the photo in the center of the shrine.

She loves me, I love her she loves me I love she loves I love she loves she loves she loves shelovesshelovessshelovesssss . . .

On the floor, between two candles, what looked like a white flower, sprouting from a dime store coffee mug, printed with the name Gwen on it. Ron touched the flower. It was cloth . . . but what exactly? When he pulled the girl's underpants from the mug all he could do was give a deep moan and clutch the frail garment to his chest. He remembered Doris commenting several months ago that she'd found the outer door to the laundry room open. So, he'd been in the house!

In his fury Ron ripped down the picture of Gwen bending over. Then the others. Shredded them beneath his strong fingers.

"Please, don't do that! No, no!" his mother cried.

"Really, mister!"

"Harle'll be mad. I can't stand it when he gets mad at us."

Ron rose to his feet, flung the cup into a Nazi flag, where it shattered. He pushed past the cowering couple, flung open the front door and strode out into the street.

"Where are you?" he cried. "Where? You son of a bitch!"

The peaceful dusk in Locust Grove had tipped into peaceful night. Ron saw nothing but faint houselights, he heard nothing but his own voice, dulled by the mist, returning to him from a dozen distant places.

Ron leapt into his car and left long black worms of skid marks as he knocked over garbage cans, streaking into the street.

■

Three hours later, he returned home.

The bright security lights were on, one of them trained directly at the juniper bush.

"Where've you been?" Doris demanded. "I've called everybody I could think of, trying to find you."

"Driving around, looking for him. Is everything okay?" he asked.

"I thought I heard somebody in the work shed about an hour ago, rummaging around."

"And?"

"I called the police and they came by. Didn't find anything. Might've been a raccoon. The window was open. But the door was locked."

"Gwen?"

"She's upstairs asleep. Did you find him?"

"No, no trace. At least I hope I put the fear of God into him so we'll have a few days' peace." He looked around the house. "Let's make sure everything's locked up."

Ron walked to the front door and opened it, stepping back in shock at the sight of the huge dark form filling the doorway. Gasping, he instinctively drew back his fist.

"Whoa, there, buddy, take it easy." Sheriff Hanlon stepped forward into the hallway light.

Ron closed his eyes in relief. "You scared me."

"I'll ditto that. Mind if I come in?"

"Yeah, yeah, sure," Ron snapped. The sheriff entered, nodding to Doris, who ushered him into the living room. He declined coffee.

Husband and wife looked at the sheriff, a big man in a tan uniform. He sat on the couch and said simply, "Harle Ebbers was found dead about a half hour ago. He was hit by a train on the LIRR tracks."

Doris gasped. The sheriff nodded grimly. Ron didn't even try to keep the smile off his face. "Praise Him from whom all blessings flow."

The sheriff kept his face emotionless. He looked back to his notebook. "Where've you been for the past three hours, Ron? Since you left the Ebbers' house?"

"You went there?" Doris asked.

Ron knitted his fingers together then decided it made him look guilty and he unlinked them. "Driving around," he answered. "Looking for Harle. Somebody had to. You weren't."

"And you found him," the sheriff said.

"No, I didn't find him."

"Yessir. Well, somebody sure did. Ron, we've got reports of you threatening that boy tonight. The Clarkes and the Phillips heard screaming and looked out. They heard you saying that you didn't care if you got caught, or even executed, you wanted to kill him. And then you took off chasing him down Maple."

"Well, I—"

"And then we got reports that you caused a disturbance at the Ebbers' place and fled." He read from his notebook. " 'In a very agitated frame of mind.' "

" 'Agitated frame of mind.' Of course I was agitated. He had a pair of my daughter's underwear in this goddamn altar in his closet."

Doris's hand rose to her mouth.

"And I found some pictures of her he'd taken on the way home from school."

"And then?"

"I drove around looking for him. I didn't find him. I came home. Look, Sheriff, I said I'd kill him. Sure. I'll admit it. And if he was running from me and got hit when he was crossing the tracks, I'm sorry. If that's, I don't know, negligent homicide or something, then arrest me for it."

The sheriff's broad face cracked a faint smile. " 'Negligent homicide.' Let me ask you, you read about that somewhere? Hear it on Court TV?"

"What do you mean?"

"Just that it sounded a little rehearsed. Like maybe you'd thought it up before. You threw it at me pretty quick just then."

"Look, don't blame me if he got hit by a train. What the hell're you smiling at?"

"You're good is what I'm smiling at. I think you know that boy was dead before the train came along."

Doris was frowning. Her head swiveled toward her husband.

The sheriff continued. "Somebody crushed his skull with a blunt object—that was the cause of death—and dragged him a few feet to the roadbed. Left him on the tracks. The killer was hoping his getting hit by a train'd cover up the evidence of the blows. But the train wheel only hit his neck. The head was intact enough so the medical examiner could be sure about the cause of death."

"Well," Ron said.

"Do you own an Arnold Palmer model forty-seven golf club? A driving wood?"

A long pause.

"I don't know."

"Do you golf?"

"Yes."

"Do you own golf clubs?"

"I've been buying golf clubs all my life."

"I ask 'cause that was the murder weapon. I'm thinking you beat him to death, left him on the tracks and threw the club in Hammond Lake. Only you missed and it ended up in the marsh beside the lake, sticking straight up. Took the county troopers all of five minutes to find it."

Doris turned to the sheriff. "No, it wasn't him! Somebody broke into our shed tonight and must've stolen a club. Ron keeps a lot of his old ones there. He must've stolen one. I can prove it—I called you about it."

"I know that, Mrs. Ashberry. But you said nothing was missing."

"I didn't check the clubs. I didn't think to."

Ron swallowed. "You think I'd be stupid enough to kill that boy after I called the police and after I threatened him in front of witnesses?"

The sheriff said, "People do stupid things when they're upset. And they sometimes do some pretty smart things when they're *pretending* they're upset."

"Oh, come on, Sheriff. With my *own* golf club?"

"Which you were planning to send to the bottom of fifty feet of water and another five of mud. By the way, whether it's yours or not, that club's got your fingerprints all over it."

"How did you get my prints?" Ron demanded.

"The Ebbers'. The boy's closet door and some coffee cup you smashed up. Now, Ron, I want to ask you a few more questions."

He looked out the kitchen window. He happened to catch sight of the juniper bush. He said, "I don't think I want to say anything more."

"That's your right."

"And I want to see a lawyer."

"That's your right too, sir. If you could hold out your hands for me, please. We're gonna slip these cuffs on and then take a little ride."

■

Ron Ashberry entered the Montauk Men's Correctional Facility as an instant hero, having made such a great sacrifice to save his little girl.

And the day that Gwen gave that interview on Channel 9, the whole wing was in the TV room, watching. Ron sat glumly in the back row and listened to her talk with the anchorwoman.

"Here was this creep who'd stolen my underwear and'd taken pictures of me on my way home from school and in my swimsuit and everything. I mean, he was like a real stalker . . . and the police didn't do anything about it. It was my father who saved me. I'm, like, totally proud of him."

Ron Ashberry heard this and thought just what he'd thought a thousand times since that night in April: I'm glad you're proud of me, baby. Except, except, except . . . I *didn't* do it. I didn't kill Harle Ebbers.

Just after he'd been arrested, the defense lawyer had suggested that maybe Doris was the killer though Ron knew she wouldn't have let him take the blame. Besides, friends and neighbors confirmed that she'd been on the phone with them, asking about Ron's whereabouts, at the time of the boy's death. Phone records bore this out too.

Then there was Harle's father. Ron remembered what the man had told him earlier that evening. But Ron's tearing out of the driveway caused such a stir in the Ebbers' neighborhood that several snooping neighbors kept an eye on the house for the rest of the evening and could testify that neither husband nor wife had left the bungalow all night.

Ron had even proposed the theory that the boy had killed himself. He knew Ron was out to get him and, in his psychotic frame of mind, Harle wanted to retaliate, get back at the Ashberry family. He'd stolen the golf club and wandered to the train track, where he'd beat himself silly, flung the club toward the lake and crawled onto the tracks to die. His defense lawyer gave it a shot but the DA and police laughed at that one.

And then in a flash, Ron had figured it out.

The brother of the girl in Connecticut! The girl who'd been the previous victim. Ron envisioned the scenario: the young man had come to Locust Grove and had stalked the stalker, seeking revenge both for his sister and for the beating he himself had taken. The brother—afraid that Harle was about to be sent back to the safety of the hospital—decided to act fast and had broken into the work shed to get a weapon.

The DA hadn't liked that theory either and went forward with the case.

Everyone recommended that Ron take a plea, which he finally did, exhausted with protesting his innocence. There was no trial; the judge accepted the plea and sentenced him to twenty years. He'd be eligible for parole in seven. His secret hope was that the boy in Connecticut would have a change of heart and confess. But until that day Ron Ashberry would be a guest of the people of the State of New York.

Sitting in the TV room, staring at Gwen on the screen, absently playing with the zipper of his orange jumpsuit, Ron was vaguely aware of a nagging thought. What was it?

Something that Gwen had said to the interviewer a moment earlier.

Wait . . .

What pictures of her in her swimsuit?

He sat up.

Ron hadn't found any photos of her in a bathing suit in Harle's closet. And there hadn't been any introduced at trial, since there'd been no trial. He'd never heard about any swimsuit pictures. If there were any, how had Gwen known about them?

A terrible thought came to him, so terrible that it was laughable. Though he didn't laugh; he was compelled to consider it—and the other thoughts that sprang up like ugly crabgrass around it: that the only person who'd ever heard Harle threaten Gwen with the full-moon story was Gwen herself. That nobody'd ever heard Harle's side of the situation—no one except the psychiatrist in Garden City and, come to think of it, he'd let the boy out of the hospital. That all the young man had ever said to Ron was that he loved Gwen and she loved him—nothing worse than what any young man with a crush might say, even if his demeanor was pretty scary.

Ron's thoughts, racing: They'd just been accepting Gwen's story about Harle's approaching her on the way home from school eight months ago. And had been assuming all along that *he'd* pursued Gwen, that she hadn't encouraged him.

And her underpants? . . .

Could *she* have given him the panties herself?

Suddenly enraged, Ron leapt to his feet; his chair flew backward with a loud slam. A guard ambled over and motioned for Ron to pick it up.

As he did, Ron's thoughts raged. Could it actually have happened—what he was now thinking? Was it possible?

Had she been . . . flirting with that psycho all along?

Had she actually posed for him, given him a pair of the underwear?

Why, that little slut!

He'd take her over his knee! He'd ground her so fast. . . . She always behaved when he spanked her, and the harder he whipped her the quicker she toed the line. He'd call Doris, insist she take the Ping-Pong paddle to the girl. He'd—

"Yo, Ashberry," the guard grumbled, looking at Ron's purple face, as it glared up at the screen. "You can't cool it off, git it on outa here."

Ron slowly turned to him.

And he did cool off. Inhaling deep breaths, he realized he was just being paranoid. Gwen was pure. She was innocence itself. Besides, he told himself, be logical. What possible reason would she have to flirt with someone like Harle Ebbers, to encourage him? Ron had raised her properly. Taught her the right values. Family values. She was exactly his vision of what a young woman ought to be.

But thinking of his daughter left him feeling empty, without the heart to continue watching the interview. Ron turned away from the TV and shuffled to the rec room to be by himself.

And so he didn't hear the end of the interview, the part where the reporter asked Gwen what she was going to do now. She answered, with a girlish giggle, that she was about to leave for a week in Washington with her teacher and some classmates, a trip she'd been looking forward to for months. Was she going with her boyfriend? the reporter asked. She didn't have one, the girl said coyly. Not yet. But she sure was in the market.

Then the reporter asked about plans after high school. Was she going to college?

No, Gwen didn't believe college was for her. She wanted to do something fun, something that involved travel. She thought she might try her hand at a sport. Golf probably. Over the past several years her father had spent countless hours forcing her to practice her strokes.

"He always said I should learn a proper sport," she explained. "He was quite a taskmaster. But one thing I'll say—I've got a great swing."

"I know it's been hard for you but I'm sure you're relieved to have that monster out of your life," the reporter offered.

Gwen gave a sudden, curious laugh and turned to the camera as she said, "You have no idea."

Former journalist, folksinger and attorney Jeffery Deaver's novels have appeared on a number of bestseller lists around the world, including *The New York Times*, the *Times* of London and the *Los Angeles Times*. The author of nineteen novels, he's been nominated for five Edgar Awards from the Mystery Writers of America and an Anthony Award, is a three-time recipient of the Ellery Queen Reader's Award for Best Short Story of the Year, and a winner of the British Thumping Good Read Award. His book *A Maiden's Grave* was made into an HBO movie starring James Garner and Marlee Matlin, and his novel *The Bone Collector* was a feature release from Universal Pictures, starring Denzel Washington and Angelina Jolie. His most recent novels are *The Vanished Man*, *The Stone Monkey* and *The Blue Nowhere*. He lives in Virginia and California. Readers can visit his website at www.jeffery deaver.com.